THE PHARAOH'S TOMB

LYNDEE WALKER

BRUCE ROBERT COFFIN

SEVERN RIVER
PUBLISHING

Severn River Publishing
www.SevernRiverBooks.com

This is a work of fiction. Names, characters, businesses, places, events and incidents are either the products of the author's imagination or used in a fictitious manner. Any resemblance to actual persons, living or dead, or actual events is purely coincidental.

ISBN: 978-1-64875-641-2 (Paperback)

ALSO BY THE AUTHORS

The Turner and Mosley Files

The General's Gold

The Cardinal's Curse

The Pirate's Secret

The Pharaoh's Tomb

The Emperor's Palace

BY LYNDEE WALKER

The Faith McClellan Series

The Nichelle Clarke Series

BY BRUCE ROBERT COFFIN

The Detective Justice Series

Never miss a new release!

To find out more about the authors and their books, visit

severnriverbooks.com

For all the first responders who run toward burning buildings and armed criminals to keep the rest of us safe: thank you—and your families—for your sacrifices and service.

"The purpose of life is to live it, to taste experience to the utmost, to reach out eagerly and without fear for newer and richer experience."
—Eleanor Roosevelt

PROLOGUE

Ancient Egypt, 1500 BC

Amunet carefully placed the sealed jar in the nook next to the others. She understood the importance of this ancient ritual, for it was with great reverence that each of the women performed her part. Atop a nearby stone altar lay the earthly remains of Heba, their fallen queen. Amunet turned from the nook to witness the ceremony playing out before her. Standing directly above Her Majesty's head, the High Priestess Zefret prayed aloud, while five other women wrapped Heba's limbs in linen and recited blessings in low, murmured tones.

Dim light and the aroma of burning fat and cloth filtered from the torches in each corner, the smell mixing with the scent of spices. Smoke from the torches glided across the ceiling like mist, reminding Amunet of the spirit world. This small gathering of Heba's most loyal servants and friends knew it was their responsibility to prepare the queen for her journey into the afterlife. Amunet reached out and gently stroked the queen's hand one last time before moving to the other side of the underground chamber.

Hastily prepared by the strongest among them after the coup that claimed Heba's life, the space was nonetheless in acceptable order: Possessions precious to the queen, meant to bring good luck, littered every nook and cranny. Flickering light reflected off golden statues and small trinkets, creating a dazzling kaleidoscope of fire. Their preparations had been rushed, but Amunet knew they had done well. She was confident Heba would enjoy an afterlife befitting her brilliance and station.

Heba's time on earth had been difficult, fraught with peril and the constant battle to retain the throne that was hers—not only by birthright but by the will of the subjects who adored her and thrived in her kingdom. Her undoing came at the hands of her enemies during a sneak attack overnight. Though Heba's army was formidable, the swift, calculated deaths of her top generals had snuffed out any will within their ranks to fight back and the kingdom had fallen. But Amunet knew that there was a mission much greater awaiting them. Today's ceremony was only the beginning.

"We are ready, Madam Vizier," Zefret said softly.

Amunet nodded as she grasped the golden pin nestled inside a bronze cup. She turned and moved back to the altar.

"Let the power of Ammit, who protected our pharaoh in life, continue to guide her on her next journey," Amunet said to a chorus of agreement.

The high priestess and the others knelt, lowering their foreheads to the edge of the altar. As Amunet began to pray, the sound of footfalls echoed from the tunnel. Amunet froze, raising one hand to signal the others to stay still as well. Yes—many footfalls. Had Abasi and his men managed to locate them? Amunet and the others had done their best to prepare the tomb in secret, deep beneath the valley—which meant there was only one way out. If Abasi and his horde had found them, they would need to stand and fight to protect their queen. Keeping Heba safe in the afterlife was their most sacred duty.

Looking around the faces of her friends as the running steps drew near, Amunet's thoughts whirled. She had prayed for peace during the ritual. Without weapons, their number was too few to protect the secret and keep the tomb from desecration. Still, they would fight, to the death if need be.

Amunet clutched the pin, feeling it warm in her hand, and prayed for guidance and strength.

"Get ready," Amunet cried out as the women assumed their positions.

As the intruders approached, Amunet hurried to clip the pin inside of her robe. If the tomb raiders were victorious, they would not make a prize of the queen's most powerful talisman.

As torchlight spilled into the chamber from the tunnel, the royal vizier positioned herself between the invaders and her queen. With one last prayer and a screech, Amunet led them into battle.

1

"Hey, Ave, check this out," Harrison said. "I can see the Capitol dome from this window. How cool is that?"

Avery Turner, who was busy practicing the speech she was due to give to the Senate Appropriations Committee the following day, stopped mid-sentence to shoot him her fiercest scowl.

"Harry, how am I ever going to finish this speech if you keep doing that?" Avery said. "Are you even listening?"

"Sorry, Ave. Of course I am. It's just that I've never stayed in such a cool hotel. I mean, look at that view."

"I thought the Eiffel Tower was a slightly better view," Carter Mosley said from a plush cream velvet armchair opposite the window.

Despite the interruptions from her overly exuberant right-hand man, even Avery had to admit the DC suite was as lavish as anything she had ever seen. "I'd call them equally impressive for different reasons," Avery said. "Now can I please get back to my speech?"

"I for one can't wait to hear the rest of it, Avery." Carter grinned.

"Teacher's pet," Harrison growled as he plopped down like a scolded child on the silk settee beside the window.

"May I?" Avery said.

"By all means," Harrison said. "Please continue."

As the chief technical officer of TreasureTech designs, a venture she and Carter created, Avery was scheduled to pitch the company's signature DiveNav device and proprietary software for use by the US Coast Guard and Navy in human rescue missions. Following months of rigorous field-testing courtesy of some of Harrison's old law enforcement colleagues that culminated in the discovery of an intentionally scuttled yacht, Avery had discovered that the DiveNav could find lost people as well as lost objects.

The missing vessel, named the *Moneymaker*, had been part of an ongoing but stalled New York City homicide investigation. The recovery, and subsequent prosecution of the son of a prominent Wall Street financier with mob ties for murder, had made headlines around the globe, garnering attention—some of it from powerful people. One of those people turned out to be a lobbyist and close friend of Mark Hawkins, Avery's mentor and former boss. That lobbyist had stoked the curiosity of a handful of influential politicians and military brass who now wanted to learn more about the device and what it could do. A government contract was exactly the kind of market Avery and Carter had envisioned when they started TreasureTech. The DiveNav, now essentially bug-free, was on deck to get its first big close-up in the public eye.

"You guys really think I'm ready for this?" Avery said, overcome by a moment of panic. "I mean...this is the big time, right?"

"Of course you're ready," Carter said.

"This is just nerves talking," Harrison said. "I've never seen anyone more ready than you are. Remember, these people put their pants on one leg at a time just like everyone else."

"Yeah, but they're Senate Appropriations Committee pants," Avery said.

"My point exactly, Ave, because you're smarter than all of them combined. Now, let's hear the rest of your pitch."

As Avery continued through her talking points, Carter advanced the PowerPoint slides, highlighting the DiveNav's features, storage capabilities, water resistance depth, and accomplishments to date.

"Thank you all for the invitation to speak here before you today. I'm happy to answer any questions you might have," Avery said in conclusion.

Harrison and Carter both applauded.

"I'm proud of you, Ave," Harrison said, his face stretching into the widest grin Avery had ever seen. "And Val would be proud of you too."

"Thank you, Harry," Avery said as her eyes welled up with tears of longing for her mom, a celebrated NYPD detective and Harrison's former partner, who'd died far too young.

"Hey, I've still got a couple of questions before we go getting all emotional," Carter said, sticking to the script in his hand.

"Oh, yeah," Harrison said, waving his papers. "Me too."

Avery wiped away the tears and cleared her throat. "Yes, Senators. What would you like to know?"

They fired questions at her in no-nonsense tones, running the gamut from production time to data security and encryption to use of artificial intelligence. Avery nailed each and every one of her responses, as calmly and succinctly as any seasoned professional.

"You've got this, Avery," Carter said, putting his script on a side table.

"You're gonna do great, Ave," Harrison said. "Now, who's hungry?"

Avery shook her head, realizing she'd been so caught up in preparations for her address to Congress that she never made reservations for dinner.

"I completely forgot," she admitted.

"No worries." Harrison winked. "I know how focused you are when you're busy. I took the liberty of reserving a table at the Capital Grille."

"Look at you, Harry," Carter said. "You're becoming a full-on travel agent."

"Whatever, Aquaman."

Avery laughed and grabbed her sweater. "Come on. You two can bicker on the way."

As they exited the elevator and headed through the lobby past the hotel bar, Avery caught a glimpse of a familiar face staring in their direction.

"You sure you don't want to catch a cab to the restaurant?" Carter said.

"Why?" Harry said. "It's a beautiful night. Besides, I need the walk after being cooped up inside all day."

"Harry," Avery murmured.

"Yeah, Ave?"

"Don't be obvious about it but I think the guy sitting at the end of the bar is watching us."

"Which one?" Carter leaned in.

"The slightly built man with the shock of thick dark hair," Avery said. "He's sitting by himself, and I caught him looking right at me."

"Like it or not, you are becoming quite famous," Harrison said.

"Maybe he was checking you out because you're hot," Carter suggested.

"I'm serious." Avery swatted at Carter as she rolled her eyes. "I'm almost positive he's the guy who drove us here from the airport."

"Well, he's looking at a menu now," Harrison said. "Maybe he just likes the happy hour specials at this place."

"Then why was he looking at me?"

"Probably because he recognized us from earlier," Harrison said as they passed through the front doors out onto the sidewalk.

"We've been followed before, Harry."

"Yeah, but it's been several months since that's happened. Besides, it's not like you and Junior G-man here are hunting for lost treasure at the moment. I think we're pretty safe, Ave."

"And I'd like it to stay that way."

"He's not following us, Avery," Carter said. "Maybe Harry's actually right."

"Since when have you two ever agreed on anything? And why is it always when you're teaming up on me?"

"I'll keep an eye peeled," Harrison said.

"Thanks, Harry," Avery said as she moved closer and put an arm through his.

"Now relax and enjoy yourself tonight. You've got a big day tomorrow."

Avery took one last look over her shoulder. Happy Hour was gone.

2

As soon as they arrived at the front door to the Capital Grille, flanked on both sides by carved stone lions and gas lamps, Avery knew that their jeans and sweaters weren't nearly dressy enough for them to fit in with the other clientele.

"Jeez, I'm sorry, Ave." Harrison raised both hands. "It's a steakhouse. I never thought to check for a dress code."

"Maybe we should try somewhere else, Avery?" Carter peered in the window at the fashion parade of power suits and silk dresses.

"Avery?" the maître d' said upon hearing her name. "Are you Avery Turner?"

Avery blushed. "I am."

"Oh my God," she said. "I thought you looked familiar."

"See, kid," Harrison said to Carter. "You're not the only celebrity around here."

"And you must be Carter Mosley." The woman waved both hands in front of her face like she was trying to calm down. "I adore your diving videos."

"Thank you for watching." Carter flashed a grin before turning his attention to Harrison. "What's that you were saying?"

"Please, don't worry about the dress code. It's not a strict rule anyway."

The woman winked. "We are so honored that you chose to dine at our restaurant. Right this way."

They were seated at a corner table overlooking the dining room. The grand open space featured warm wood tones and arched cream-colored ceiling accents with matching marble columns and linen table coverings, all of which gave the room a distinctive Tuscan feel.

"This is pretty nice," Carter said.

"I feel completely underdressed," Avery said as she glanced around the room. Silk, sequins, and satin abounded, and every other man was wearing a jacket.

"The hunger is making the embarrassment easy to ignore," Harrison said, smiling at the server who came to take their order and drop off a silver basket of rolls.

They dined on lobster bisque, jumbo crab cocktails, and dry-aged New York strip au poivre with Courvoisier cream sauce. Carter and Harrison each had the Capital Grille cheesecake, while Avery marveled at how either of them found room for it.

As they strolled back to the hotel, a breeze kicked up, giving the night-time DC air a chill. Avery was glad she had worn a sweater.

"Man, I don't think I've ever had a better meal," Harrison said.

"You said it," Carter echoed.

Avery's thoughts were oscillating between tomorrow's speech and the unshakeable feeling they were being followed. Harrison caught her looking over her shoulder again.

"Aw, come on, Ave," Harrison said. "I told you I'd keep an eye out."

"And?" Avery said.

"And I haven't seen hide nor hair of Mr. Happy Hour."

"Or anyone else?"

"No one."

"You sure you're not just nervous about tomorrow's address?" Carter said.

"I wasn't," Avery said. "Thanks."

"Nice going, Ace," Harrison said as they reached their hotel.

Inside they stopped to chat with the concierge, who recognized Avery and Carter instantly.

"I thought that was you two," he said. "I saw you heading out earlier. Man, it's so great to meet you both."

Still a bit uncomfortable with her newfound celebrity status, Avery blushed for the second time in as many hours.

"Would you mind if I took a selfie with you guys?" the concierge asked.

"Why don't we make it a Harry?" Harrison said taking the man's phone.

The concierge fixed Avery with a look of confusion.

"It's a joke," she said. "This is Mr. Harrison. He's getting used to taking photos for us."

"Oh, I get it. Pleased to meet you, Mr. Harrison."

"Likewise," Harrison said as he snapped several photos of Avery and Carter standing on either side of the man.

Harrison returned the camera to the concierge.

"Thanks so much."

"Happy to be of service."

"Wait until I tell my girlfriend about bumping into you guys. If you don't mind me asking, what brings you to DC? Are you here hunting treasure?"

"Avery's speaking in front of Congress tomorrow," Harrison said proudly.

"No kidding?" The concierge's eyebrows went up as Harrison nodded.

"Well, it's not the whole of Congress," Avery said. "Just the Senate Appropriations Committee."

"That is too cool. Are you speaking too?" he asked Carter.

Carter's turn to blush.

"No, just Avery," he said.

They returned to their suite intending to crash, before Harrison noticed the message light flashing on the house phone.

"Looks like you got a message, Ave."

Avery's brow furrowed. "That's odd. Aside from the man who arranged the presentation, nobody knows where we're staying."

"Maybe it's him," Carter said as Harrison pressed play.

The message was garbled, the word fragments interspersed with static blasts nearly impossible to discern.

"What the heck is that?" Harrison asked after twenty seconds with no improvement.

"I have no idea," Avery said, biting her lip. "But I don't like it."

"Sounds like someone talking on a cell phone with a bad signal," Carter said.

"Yeah, with a can over their head," Harrison said.

The message was nearly two minutes in length. When it ended, Avery asked Harry to play it again, but the second playback wasn't any more helpful than the first.

"What do you think, Harry?" Avery asked following the third listen.

"I've no idea, Ave. Seems too long to be a wrong number."

"Could be a sales bot," Carter offered. "Those things don't seem to know if they're playing for a real live person or an answering machine. I get that crap at home all the time."

"Want me to delete it?"

"No," Avery said a little too forcefully. "No, I want to record it on my phone."

"Okay," Harrison said. "Well, I'm hitting the hay."

"Me too," Carter said. "Got to get my beauty rest."

Harrison paused in the doorway to his bedroom. "You should've started hours ago."

After the men retired to their respective rooms, Avery called the front desk.

"How may I help you, Ms. Turner?" the clerk asked.

"I received a strange message on the voicemail in my room. I'm wondering if there is any way you can tell me where it originated from?"

"I'm afraid not, Ms. Turner. The hotel doesn't keep records on guest room calls, out of respect for the privacy of our more notable guests."

Avery blinked when she realized the woman was referring to politicians and power players from around the globe.

"Wait," the clerk said. "What time did the call come in?"

"Sometime between seven and nine, while we were at dinner. Why?"

"I've been working the desk since three and nobody called here asking to be transferred to your room," the clerk said. "The caller must have phoned you directly."

"How can that be?" Avery said. "No one but the people I'm traveling with knows what room I'm in."

The clerk laughed. "Ma'am, this is Washington, DC. You can find out anything you want if you know the right people."

Avery thanked her and hung up, recording the message with her phone before retiring to her own room. As she went through the ritual of laying out tomorrow's clothing, she popped in her earbuds and continued to play back the message through the recording on her cell phone. As she listened to the pops and clicks and unintelligible voice speaking in the background, Avery kept thinking about the desk clerk's comment. Who were the right people, in this case? And who wanted to know where she and Carter were staying? Could be anyone from a rich politician's teenage daughter who was obsessed with Carter to someone they'd outsmarted on a treasure hunt who wanted to hurt them—which was the problem.

She crawled into bed and stopped the playback mid-message. Switching to the phone screen, she called MaryAnn in Florida—MaryAnn was the only person not sleeping in the suite who knew exactly where they were.

The former director of the Florida Museum of Nautical History, MaryAnn had been the research director at TreasureTech from the jump— Avery admired the woman's research skills and had wanted her as an employee as soon as she figured out how smart and thorough MaryAnn was. In addition to vast technical expertise and research capabilities, she also had museum connections around the globe.

MI5 had Q, at least in Ian Fleming's novels.

Avery and Carter had MaryAnn.

"Good evening, boss lady," MaryAnn said after several rings. "How is DC? Are you ready for tomorrow?"

"I'm gonna give it my best," Avery said. She wasn't sure one was ever completely ready to address a congressional subcommittee.

"You'll dazzle them." Confidence dripped from MaryAnn's words.

"I sure hope so," Avery said. "But I didn't call for a pep talk. I got a strange phone message on the hotel voicemail tonight. You didn't call here earlier, did you?"

"No, ma'am. What was the message?"

"That's just the thing. It was undecipherable."

"Were you expecting a call from someone?"

"No. And aside from you, nobody even knows what room we're in. And the call didn't come through the switchboard. According to the desk clerk, someone dialed direct."

"Do you still have the message?" MaryAnn said.

"I made a recording of it on my phone."

"Email it to me as an attachment and I'll see if I can do anything with it."

"It's probably a wrong number, but—"

"Given your history, it's worth checking out," MaryAnn finished the sentence for Avery.

"Thanks, MaryAnn."

"You're welcome. And good luck tomorrow."

Avery ended the call, laid her head back on the pillow, and prayed for sleep.

3

"And exactly how many missing soldiers has your device—with its hefty price tag—located, Ms. Turner?" asked a particularly pinch-faced senator in a rumpled but expensive-looking suit and a red silk tie as he stared down at Avery over the top of his glasses from the dais.

All eyes, including Carter's, from where he sat in the gallery, turned to Avery, waiting to see how she would respond to the antagonistically worded question.

"None yet, Senator." Avery refused to rise to the bait, her voice strong and clear, her face expressionless. "But I respect that the military doesn't usually bring in outside search teams to assist. We did recently discover a—"

"Thank you, Ms. Turner, but you've already answered my question," the senator said, cutting her off in mid-sentence.

"Point of order, Mr. Chairman." A senator from Nebraska with a perfect, no-nonsense updo and a smart hunter-green Donna Karan pantsuit put her hand up.

"Go ahead, Senator," the chairman said.

"With all due respect to my esteemed colleague from New York, he asked Ms. Turner a question, then cut her off when she went to reply. Since we've been empaneled to hear what this device can offer, I for one would very much like to hear the rest of Ms. Turner's response."

"By all means, Ms. Turner." The chairman nodded, his attention turning to Avery. "Please, finish your answer."

It took every ounce of willpower Carter possessed not to stand and cheer, as he figured they might frown on that sort of thing, but his smile was a mile wide.

"I was just going to say that the DiveNav was recently instrumental in recovering a corpse for the New York City police department. That discovery will be indispensable in an important trial slated for this coming winter. The DiveNav's—"

"Thank you," Senator Pinch Face said, cutting Avery off yet again.

"Dean," the chairman cautioned, frowning at his colleague. "Please, Ms. Turner, continue."

"Thank you, Mr. Chairman," Avery said. "The location accuracy record is included in the packet we've provided to each of you. Our DiveNav device is unequalled by any other products currently on the market when it comes to successfully locating items that have been lost for centuries. Our new software makes it relatively easy for the user to input search parameters when working with current maps without the added burden of analyzing historical maps and data."

Pinch Face waited to see if Avery had concluded her comments. When she moved to take a drink of water, he pounced.

"As impressive as your little device's record looks, Ms. Turner, it's still a game of chance, isn't it?"

"I'm not sure I understand the question, Senator," Avery said.

"Then let me clarify: Your dive thingy utilizes artificial intelligence, does it not?"

Carter felt himself growing hot under the collar. It was clear that Senator Pinch Face had an agenda. And did he have to make it sound like Avery was being grilled by Yoda, inverting his sentences seemingly for the sole purpose of convolution?

"Yes, Senator, it does use AI. And it's called the DiveNav."

Carter couldn't help noticing a smile playing around the Nebraska senator's lips at Avery's jab.

"As for its use of artificial intelligence, I can assure you that AI will not turn the DiveNav into the Terminator, or any other wild stories you may have heard. It is simply a super-program that will calculate the best way to respond to or solve a problem. But like any computerized system, our AI is only as good as the information we feed into it. My DiveNav has access to literally millions of digital modern and historical maps through Treasure-Tech's proprietary database, making the answers it provides the best chance in almost any scenario, but it would still be up to the user how they choose to use the information obtained."

Carter couldn't help noticing that the committee chairman was grinning at Pinch Face.

Several of the other lawmakers raised folders in front of their faces like NFL coaches attempting to hide their conversations. Carter wished he could tell what they were saying. When it came to politics, Carter knew that the bluster meant nothing. At the end of the day, it was only the vote that mattered.

Carter looked back at Avery. She was standing at the lectern, hands folded behind her back, looking as cool as a cucumber.

"She's something else, isn't she?" Harrison whispered.

"You can say that again." Carter shook his head.

"Anyone else have questions for Ms. Turner?" the chairman asked.

A forty-something woman in a purple St. John suit and matching square-framed glasses signaled to him as the dais settled down. "I'd like to say something."

"The floor is yours, Senator," the chairman said with a nod.

"Uh-oh," Harrison said. "Friend or foe?"

"I can't tell," Carter said with a shrug, his stomach turning a slow flip as he watched Avery and the purple-suited senator, who'd been quiet until then.

"Ms. Turner, can I just tell you how much I admire you and your accomplishments? And, after listening to you today, your tenacity."

"Thank you, Senator." Avery nodded.

"I don't know if any of you know this," the senator said as she looked around at her colleagues, "but Avery's mother was a first responder who gave her life in the line of duty for the NYPD. It's fair to say that you've taken what she taught you to an entirely different level, Ms. Turner. You are the personification of the American dream. Now I don't know about the rest of you all, but I believe this technology is invaluable, both in practical use and in a larger sense. Not to mention that it was created right here in America by a young woman who exemplifies the very best of what her generation has to offer. Why in the world would anyone on this panel object to purchasing such a useful tool for our military?"

"Because it's damn expensive," Pinch Face said.

"You've had your say already, Senator Everett," said Purple Suit, whose nameplate read *Senator Byers*. "Plus, I've seen your annual budget requisitions. You had no problem spending the cost of two DiveNavs on a decorator for your office last summer."

Everyone on the dais laughed—except Everett.

Harrison raised his hands as if he were about to clap, but Carter stopped him by tugging on his wrist. "You'll embarrass Avery," he whispered. "Not to mention probably get us kicked out of here."

"Spoilsport."

Another senator asked to speak.

"My research assistant mentioned that this device was tested alongside some high-tech diver safety software in the Antarctic. Can you expound on that, Ms. Turner?"

"I can, but I think my partner, Carter Mosley, would be far better suited to speak to that."

To Carter's horror, Avery turned around and pointed him out for the committee.

"Mr. Mosley, would you approach the podium please?" the chairman said.

Carter's stomach tried to give back his breakfast.

Harrison chuckled and clapped Carter on the shoulder. "Looks like you're up, Sport." Leaning down and catching his eye, Harrison softened his tone. "You've got this, Carter. If you can fight off sharks and dive shipwrecks that are actively trying to kill you, you can certainly address these eggheads."

Carter stood, regulating his breathing with each step as he went to the chamber floor. Stopping at the podium, his legs felt like they might give out. "I can't do this, Avery," he whispered.

"Sure you can. They're just the audience on the other side of your mic, Carter. You know how the DiveNav works, and you know diving—it's like taking a pop quiz in your favorite class. Don't look at them, they don't matter. Look directly at the seal on the dais and just answer the questions."

Carter nodded.

"Can you tell us how this device was helpful in your field-testing in Antarctica, Mr. Mosley?" asked the green-suited senator who'd been so kind to Avery.

He pulled in a deep breath. "Our DiveNav helped us locate a sunken ship lost in the world's most inhospitable conditions. Not only was it able to pinpoint the ship's location, in an area completely written off by so-called experts, but our device continued to function while most of the British research station's other high-tech equipment succumbed to the elements."

"So, it was a complete success in a harsh environment, and it beat out the technology used by another government?" the senator asked.

"I'd say so," Carter glanced at Avery and she flashed a thumbs-up.

He chanced a look up at the dais just in time to see Senator Everett's hand go up.

Damn. Panic rose in his chest as he swallowed hard.

"That's all well and good that your DiveNavigator thing found a ship in cold water, but you're asking us to commit to something that we don't know much about, for a great deal of money. Perhaps you'd be willing to enlighten us on exactly how this thing works, Mr. Mosley."

Carter glanced at Avery, then turned back to the dais.

"Talk to me. Forget them," Avery whispered in his ear, making the hair on the back of his neck stand up.

Carter gripped the edges of the podium, trying not to think about Avery's breath on his ear, and stared at the senatorial seal.

"The truth is I wouldn't be here talking to you today if it wasn't for Avery. She is the most brilliant person I have ever met. And that brilliance saved my life in Antarctica. Avery's calm demeanor under pressure and her intellect literally saved me from drowning in four hundred feet of icy black water. While I may not understand all of the technology behind the Dive-Nav, I do understand how important it has been in locating artifacts of historical importance. But more than that, it has saved my butt more than once, as I am confident it will be able to do for the soldiers in our military. I don't know a heck of a lot about your budget—hell, I have a hard enough time managing my own—but I do know that you spend heavily on weapons and armor to protect our troops. You should have as much confidence in Avery's DiveNav as you do that armor. She is the real deal—as smart as she is beautiful and kind. The DiveNav will save lives. And that's something you can't put a price on."

Still nervous, and barely remembering what he just said, Carter turned to look at Avery. She stared at him, her lips parted and her eyes wide, not paying a bit of attention to the discussion happening on the dais.

The senator in the purple suit beamed at Carter, her voice drawing his eyes back to the committee. "Well said, Mr. Mosley."

"You've got yourself a good salesman there, Ms. Turner," the chairman added.

Avery tore her eyes away from Carter and smiled. "Thank you, sir. Carter has many talents."

"Additional questions or discussion?" the chairman asked.

"I'd like more time to review the information presented today." A balding senator from Tennessee in a gray suit that exactly matched his tie looked up from his notepad, speaking for the first time. Peering over his glasses at Avery, he smiled. "You are a very impressive young woman, Miss Turner. I just dislike the idea of impulse buying toys with taxpayer money."

Senator Everett raised his hand. "I agree with my colleague from Tennessee. I move to table this discussion until the committee has had time to thoroughly review the information we heard here today. We can bring it back for a vote at such time that everyone is comfortable with their knowledge of Miss Turner's product."

Avery looked at Harrison, who held up one hand unobtrusively. *Calm,* he mouthed.

Five minutes later, a motion to table the proposed purchase of 275 DiveNav units and 150 software licenses for the dive parameter program was seconded and put to a vote, passing the committee by a vote of 28 to 1. The senator in the purple suit voted no.

"Miss Turner," she said when the results of the vote had been read into the record, "I want you to know I'm impressed with you and your intelligence and drive. While this may not be the exact result you wanted today, this is not a bad thing. We dismiss a whole lot more salespeople around here than we do business with. Tabled is not no." Other heads on the dais bobbed in agreement, but Carter didn't count them fast enough to see if it was a majority of heads.

Avery nodded once. "Thank you, Senator."

"I'm looking forward to seeing more of you and your work, Miss Turner."

Carter pulled Avery into a hug, picking her up and spinning her around. Avery laughed, telling him to put her down. Catching and holding her gaze with a smile, he set her on her feet, keeping one hand on her waist until he was sure she had her balance.

"Nice work." He put his hand out. "Partner."

Avery ducked her head and grasped his hand in hers. "Nothing is decided yet, but if this goes our way, *we* did it. Thank you, Carter. For everything."

"Thank you both for taking the time to be with us here today, Ms. Turner and Mr. Mosley," the chairman said, coming down from the dais and walking toward them. "We greatly appreciate your speaking with us and your expertise. I look forward to talking more with you in the future."

"Thank you for having us," Avery said, releasing Carter's hand to greet the senator.

"Thank you," Carter said, still feeling like he'd had an out-of-body experience.

"What happens now?" Harrison asked, appearing next to Avery.

"Mr. Chairman," Avery said. "This is Harrison."

"Pleased to meet you, Mr. Harrison," the senator said, giving him a firm handshake.

"So, what happens now?" Harrison repeated.

"Once the Appropriations Committee has time to review the material and testimony, we'll call a vote. If it passes here, it moves to the floor of the Senate for a full vote."

"How long will that take?" Harrison said.

"It's difficult to say. Sometimes a few weeks, sometimes longer." He leaned in. "Between us, it may go faster if Senator Everett gets distracted by something else he wants to complain about."

"We'll cross our fingers." Carter grinned, clapping Harrison on the back.

"Easy there, Junior Mint. You try hugging me and see what happens." Harrison turned to Avery and cocked a thumb over his shoulder.

"Your aftershave keeps you safe, my man." Carter laughed.

Harry frowned at Avery. "What's wrong with my aftershave?"

She laughed. "Even you two can't get under my skin today." It wasn't a yes, but maybe was indeed better than no.

They gathered up Avery's briefcase and folders and headed out of the chambers. They didn't make it through the Capitol rotunda before a man in a gray suit stopped them with a raised hand and a flat expression.

"Avery Turner?" the man said.

"Yes," Avery said.

"I need you to come with me."

Avery took a reflexive step backward when the man reached for her arm.

"She's not going anywhere she doesn't want to," Carter said, stepping in front of her slightly.

"You must be Mr. Mosley," the man said.

"And who are you?" Harrison said.

"And Mr. Harrison," the man said. "It's wonderful to meet you all."

"We still didn't catch your name," Harrison said.

"Smith," the man said with a polite grin. "Mr. Smith."

"Mr. Smith, huh?" Harrison said. "Like the old Jimmy Stewart movie?"

"Who?" Carter said.

Avery waved a "big picture" signal in his direction.

"Now that we've done our introductions, would you please follow me?" Smith said. "I promise, you're in no danger here, and everything will be explained shortly."

Carter exchanged a glance with Avery and Harrison. Harrison shrugged. Avery had The Look: lips set, eyes slightly narrowed, one eyebrow just a bit raised, that Carter had learned meant she was more curious than afraid. He'd deciphered most of her facial expressions in the past year, and for the first time in his life, knowing a woman that well didn't make him feel trapped. And he couldn't figure out why.

"Okay," Avery said. "After you, Mr. Smith."

4

Smith escorted them into a private office on the main floor of the building to wait. The room reminded Avery of every TV and movie version of the Oval Office she had seen, only smaller and without a fireplace. Richly appointed furniture filled the space, making it feel homey—like a large, lavishly trimmed den. The walls consisted of dark hardwood paneling and accent trim. The deep-set windows had cushioned seats and were flanked on either side by heavy drapes. Bookcases lined the wall behind a massive antique desk. It was clear to Avery that this office was a seat of real power— and the handiwork of a very good interior designer. She thought about the comment during the hearing about expensive furniture. Surely they weren't about to be ambushed by Senator Everett. Avery swallowed hard, glancing at Smith, who exited the room without another word, closing the door behind him.

"Not sure I like this whole cloak-and-dagger routine, Ave," Harrison said.

"I'm sure it's nothing like that, Harry." Avery smiled and took a seat on the plush white sofa, hoping she was right. The celebratory mood she'd felt immediately following the committee vote had been replaced by one of apprehension.

"Well, whatever this is, I imagine we'll find out soon enough," Carter said.

"Thank you, Nostradamus," Harrison said as he paced the room like a caged lion.

Several minutes later the door opened, and Senator Byers of the fabulous purple suit strolled in. "Thank you for meeting with me in private."

"Didn't seem like we had much choice," Harrison said.

The senator dismissed his concern with a wave of her hand. "Don't mind my assistant. Gregory's heart is in the right place. He just doesn't—play well with others. I suppose we should get the introductions out of the way. I already know two of you, but I don't believe I've had the pleasure of meeting you, Mister...?"

"Harrison."

"Nice to meet you, Mr. Harrison," she said, extending her hand in greeting. "My name is Penelope Byers. I'm the vice chair of the Appropriations Committee."

"Well, in that case, Senator, call me Harry," Harrison said as he accepted the offering.

"My friends call me Penny." She smiled.

"Penny it is," Harrison said.

"Thank you for your help back there," Avery said. "I thought Senator Everett was hell-bent on derailing the DiveNav, but then he moved to table the discussion," Avery said.

Byers waved her hand again as she moved toward a wingback chair across from where Avery sat. "Senator Everett is just an old windbag. Pay him no mind. He puts up a fuss about everything. Makes him feel important. They do what I say because of my other committee."

"And what committee is that?" Avery said.

"I chair the Defense Appropriations Committee, which controls the purse strings for the Army, Navy, and Air Force. Basically, the entire Department of Defense."

"Don't forget the Marines," Carter said.

"Actually, the US Marines are funded by several different appropriations."

"Why wouldn't they be funded the same as the other armed forces?" Avery said.

"It's hard to explain, but basically the Marine Corps is a hybrid force. A specialized jack-of-all-trades if you will."

"That's quite a lot of power you wield," Harrison said.

"You're telling me." Byers winked. "We fund the Central Intelligence Agency too."

Avery exchanged a knowing glance with Harrison.

"CIA, huh?" Harrison said. "Guess that explains Gregory Gray Suit Smith."

Byers gave Harrison a look Avery couldn't quite decode, before she turned back to Avery.

"It is in my DOD capacity that I want to talk to you about something that doesn't concern the DiveNav."

As if on cue, a knock came from the closed office door.

"Come," Byers said. The door opened and Smith entered. "Perfect timing, Gregory."

With that, Smith closed the door and slid the drapes across the windows. As soon as the room was dark, a screen appeared on the wall across from Byers's desk.

The image that appeared was an overhead shot taken of a desert or maybe a beach, but Avery couldn't tell if it was a satellite photo or something else.

Harrison leaned over the couch and pointed. "That's a city. But it doesn't look like anything in the United States. Egypt?"

"Very good, Harry," Byers said.

"What does Egypt have to do with us?" Avery asked.

"It has everything to do with you, Ms. Turner. As my committee colleagues pointed out after you departed from chambers, you could be the perfect weapon."

"I'm sorry?" Avery said, slightly taken aback.

"Don't be so modest. It goes without saying that you're brilliant and cunning. I even hear tell that you possess a mean right hook."

"That's true, Ave," Harrison said, cradling his jaw in one hand.

"And I know you are proficient with a weapon or two," the senator continued.

"So, you've checked up on me," Avery said. "What does any of that have to do with Egypt?"

The on-screen image dissolved into a detailed drawing of a gold bird with a bejeweled alligator head.

"What is that?" Avery said, her curiosity piqued.

"An important cultural artifact has been stolen and we need to recover it."

"Seriously?" Carter blurted.

"I didn't realize that Congress was into recovering lost treasure," Avery said, cutting him a "cool it" glance.

"We aren't. But this artifact has the potential to destabilize the entire Middle Eastern region."

"How so?" Avery said.

Byers nodded at Smith.

"How much do you know about the history of the Middle East?" Smith said.

"Enough to know they're in constant conflict," Harrison said.

"Quite true," Smith said. "And there are more than a few shaky alliances between countries, some of whom share common interests with the United States. And those countries need to maintain the appearance of power."

"The appearance of power?" Carter said.

"Power is an illusion, Mr. Mosley," Smith continued. "It often has more to do with what you believe your enemy is capable of versus actual capability. Do you understand?"

"Not a word of it," Harrison said, earning a dirty look from Avery.

"I think I understand what you're saying," Avery said. "Possessing this artifact is important but not as important as your enemies knowing you lost it."

"Correct," Byers said. "It is about projecting strength, not weakness. And there are people who would stop at nothing to get their hands on it now that they know it has been stolen. When I say nothing, I mean loss of life and economic instability that could spread throughout the world—even here."

Avery crossed the room to study the photo more closely.

"What kind of artifact could disrupt an economy as big as ours halfway around the world?" Carter said.

"All in due time, Mr. Mosley. That is assuming Avery is interested."

"Oh, I'm interested all right."

"Ave," Harrison said, a warning clearly implied in his tone.

Avery turned and faced the senator. "How would recovery of this artifact benefit the US?"

Byers and Smith exchanged a glance.

"Like most everything in government, information is contained," Smith said. "Shared only when there is a need to know."

"In other words, you're planning to use the recovery as leverage for something," Avery said, tapping her chin. "Something to do with preventing conflict and stabilizing world economies, including ours. That means pacifying someone who controls either money or resources."

"I told you she was brilliant," Byers said.

Smith looked slightly alarmed but said nothing.

"Assuming we agree to help recover this artifact, how much time would we have to prepare for this adventure?" Avery asked.

"You would prepare en route."

"En route to where?" Harrison asked. "The Middle East?"

"Of course," Byers said. "As a former homicide detective, you of all people should know that solving a mystery requires starting at the scene of the crime. The artifact in question was stolen from Egypt. That is where you'll need to begin."

"I don't understand," Harrison said. "Why do you even need our help? Why not send the military in to recover this lost trinket?"

"Our aim is to maintain stability, Harry," Byers said. "Nothing would destabilize the region faster than US military involvement."

"Why us?" Avery said.

"Because you have the perfect cover," Byers said. "You have become very well known both for your jaunts around the globe looking for lost things and for your technical prowess and the invention you were here to pitch today. Your official reason for this trip is to meet with the head of the archaeology department and then the board at the university in Cairo—the accomplishments and size of the department makes them a good fit for a pitch for your device. After that meeting, our contact in the department will set up a rendezvous with you to discuss more about the pin. To the entire world, you'll be behaving perfectly normally and, acting purely in your own interests, recovering a stolen artifact that you were asked to find to prove the effectiveness of your invention. No one would ever suspect that you were acting on behalf of the US or any other government."

"You three are a perfect fit for an operation such as this," Smith agreed.

"Operation?" Harrison said.

"A poor choice of words," Byers said smoothly. "But he's right. You are the perfect fit."

Avery turned back to study the image. "Assuming that we were inclined to help, when would you need our answer?"

"Immediately, Ms. Turner," Byers said.

"And if we decline?" Harrison said.

"Then I'd be very disappointed, but I'd understand. Of course, it would also require us to come up with an entirely different strategy for recovery and I'm not sure any of our other options would prove as effective. And with my time and attention focused on this, I would have little remaining to persuade my colleagues to approve the DiveNav purchase."

"That sounds an awful lot like bl—"

"We'll do it," Avery said, cutting Harrison off before he could accuse a United States senator of blackmail.

"We will?" Carter blinked, turning to Avery.

"Splendid, Ms. Turner," Byers said. "I have a car outside waiting to transport all of you to a jet."

"I have my own jet," Avery countered. "And I'd feel more comfortable using my own transportation and pilot."

"Would this be a deal breaker?" Byers said after a quick glance at Smith, causing Avery to wonder exactly who was calling the shots here.

"I'm afraid our method of travel is non-negotiable," Avery said, crossing her arms to emphasize the point.

"There are a great many things about this you do not yet know," Byers said.

"But all will be revealed, right?" Harrison said.

"You'll be given as much information as is required to successfully complete this mission and recover the artifact."

"I trust my pilot with my life," Avery said. "If you need to run some kind of security check on Marco, then do it."

"We already have." Byers sighed. "All right, your jet and your pilot. Anything else?"

"Yeah," Harrison said. "How about a tax write-off on the fuel and mileage?"

Byers grinned. "I'm afraid the IRS is outside my purview, Harry."

"What about our equipment?" Carter said. "We came to DC to address your committee, not go hunting for treasure. We don't have much of anything with us."

"We will supply everything you'll need, Mr. Mosley."

"I've got a bad feeling about this, Ave," Harrison cautioned.

"While I certainly understand your apprehension, Harry," Byers said, "you must think of this as an opportunity to serve your government."

"I already served my government, remember? The government of New York."

"When will we be briefed further?" Avery said.

"Briefing packets will be provided to you as soon as you board the jet, Ms. Turner. And not a moment before."

"I'm assuming there will be a point of contact in Egypt?" Avery said.

"Yes," Byers said. "The identity of your contact is included in your packets."

Avery looked to Carter. "You in?"

"I'm in if you are."

Avery turned her attention to Harrison. "Harry?"

"You did promise to show me the world if I retired. Guess I'm in too."

"Great," Byers said. "Welcome to the team. Gregory will show you the way to your car. Best of luck to all of you."

5

Avery sat in the back of the limo with Carter and Harrison, while Smith rode up front with their driver. She sent a quick text to Marco. He replied almost immediately, asking why she wanted to go to Cairo. Avery furrowed her brow—Marco didn't usually ask questions, and she didn't want to text him that answer. She replied that she had a meeting at the museum and he asked if she'd ever been to Jordan. Avery typed quickly that she hadn't, and she wouldn't be going there today either as the car rolled to a stop outside their hotel. Hurrying inside, they packed up their bags and checked out. Smith stayed with the limo.

"Will you be needing transportation to the airport, Ms. Turner?" the concierge said as Avery handed the room cards to the desk clerk.

"Thank you, but we've already got that covered."

As they were headed for the door, Avery caught another glimpse of the man who had driven them to the hotel the day before.

"Harry," Avery said. "Don't look now but there's our driver from the other day."

"Looks like he's picking up another customer, Ave," Harrison said as they watched him pass through the exit with a male customer.

"This is a pretty swanky hotel," Carter said. "He's probably in an out of here all the time."

"I'd say seeing him at the hotel bar last night was probably just a coincidence," Harrison said.

"So, who's going to provide us with this secret briefing, Ave?" Harrison said after they were rolling again toward the airport.

"That's a good question, Harry."

"I hope it's not Gregory the Spook," Harrison said.

Avery was glad the soundproof privacy panel was up. She didn't think Smith would appreciate the comment.

"Yeah, that guy's got CIA agent written all over him," Carter said.

"Officer," Avery said.

"What?" Carter said.

"They're called case officers, not agents," Harrison said. "They get kind of put off by that."

"Whatever," Carter said. "He still gives me the creeps."

"You sure about all this, Ave?" Harrison said. "I mean, it's not too late to back out."

"Come on, Harry. This will be fun. Sun, sand, searching for lost treasure...What's not to love? It will be just like Florida. But serving our country instead of just going home."

"Only without all the water," Carter said.

"Great," Harrison said. "And she didn't say it was lost, Ave. It was stolen."

"Think of this as our next great adventure. Maybe you'll even get to ride a camel," Avery said. "Won't that be cool?"

"We're going to Egypt, Ave. There are like six different deserts there. Trust me, there won't be anything cool about it."

They arrived at the airport and pulled up in front of a remote access gate. The limo driver showed something to the TSA guard, the gate opened, and they drove through.

"That's a first for me," Carter said. "Special access to the tarmac."

"First class all the way." Harrison waggled his eyebrows.

As the driver pulled up next to the sleek blue-and-white Gulfstream

G800, Avery noticed Marco standing outside talking to a man dressed in a charcoal-colored suit. Dark hair, average height, average build, clean-shaven—the man could have been Gregory Smith's twin. As the limo stopped, Smith got out and opened the rear door on Avery's side.

"Ms. Turner," he said as he helped her out. Harrison and Carter followed without the offer of assistance.

"Thank you," Avery said as she glanced at Marco. "All set, are we?"

"You're really sure there's nowhere else you'd rather spend the next few days?" He flashed a smile, but it didn't reach his eyes.

"I'm sure," she said. "What in the world is going on with you? Do you know something we need to know?"

Marco stared at the sky for a moment and then shook his head, meeting her gaze.

"No, Ms. Avery. We are fueled—just let me file the flight plan and we'll be ready to go."

Avery turned her attention to Smith and the other man. Smith's twin said nothing, but his presence unnerved her just the same. She was wondering what Marco had been discussing with the other man when Smith stepped forward.

"As promised," he said, handing a large, sealed envelope to each of them.

"Great," Harrison said. "I always enjoy a bit of light reading when I fly."

Smith showed zero emotion, continuing with his speech as if Harrison wasn't there.

"Everything you need to know has been included."

"What about travel documents?" Harrison said. "Don't we need a visa or something?"

"They're included in your packets. One multiple-entry visa for each of you."

"Thanks," Harrison said.

"You have a long trip ahead of you, which should give you plenty of time to familiarize yourselves with the material. My understanding is you have an onboard vault, Ms. Turner."

"Yes," Avery said. "We do."

"Please see that this material is secured inside the safe before you land. It is highly sensitive."

"What about the equipment you promised?" Carter said.

"The equipment you requested has already been loaded aboard your jet."

Avery looked at Marco, and he confirmed it with a nod.

"And our point of contact?" Avery said.

"Your contact will be awaiting your arrival. As far as anyone else is concerned, you are merely tourists there for a bit of sightseeing."

"I've heard better cover stories," Harrison said, earning a look of displeasure from Smith.

"Any other questions?"

Avery looked at the others. "No, I guess we're all set. Thanks for the ride."

"Very good. Safe travels to all of you."

"Let's hope," Harrison said.

Smith and his twin were halfway to the limo when he stopped and turned around. "I almost forgot, Mr. Mosley," Smith said. "Mr. Harrison is absolutely correct."

"What about?" Carter asked.

"Case officer is the correct terminology."

6

Avery had only recently upgraded the Gulfstream from the G650ER she'd owned previously. After their trip to Antarctica, Marco had planted the seed about acquiring the larger model, as it was better equipped for travel on a global scale. Besides, Avery thought, what good were nearly unlimited funds if you didn't occasionally splurge on something sporty? The fact that their trip to Egypt was just over four thousand miles meant her purchase was paying off already. On top of the G800's increased comfort and cargo space, its tech sheet listed a range of up to eight thousand nautical miles without the need to refuel. *Time to put the new toy through its paces*, she thought.

As soon as they reached cruising altitude, Avery unbuckled and headed to the cockpit to grill Marco about his conversation with the CIA guys.

"I don't know, Ms. Avery," Marco said. "The other man said his name was Jones and he wasn't very forthcoming with information."

"Smith and Jones?" Avery wasn't the least bit surprised, nor impressed.

"He had some men load your gear. He handed me our flight itinerary. But that was about it."

Avery made a mental note to sweep whatever gear they had loaded for tracking devices as soon as they landed.

"Did I do something wrong, Ms. Avery?"

"No, Marco. You were aces as usual. Can I get you anything to eat or drink?"

"I'm fine." He gestured to the state-of-the-art control panel. "The weather looks lovely all the way to Cairo. Just gonna sit back and enjoy this sweet ride."

"You do that, Marco."

Avery returned to the cabin, where Carter and Harrison were already buried in reading.

"Anything interesting?" she asked.

"A lot of this has been redacted, Ave," Harrison said. "I keep waiting for these sheets to self-destruct like something from *Mission Impossible*."

"Or *Inspector Gadget*," Carter quipped.

Avery flipped through her file, stopping at a photo of the artifact from the university archives. "I know there's something she isn't telling us. This thing is too small to be this important."

"And you know what small means?" Harrison asked. "Easy to hide. That should make it super easy to find."

"Have a little faith, Harry," Carter said.

"Oh, I have plenty of faith. Faith that whatever this is will be anything but simple."

Avery shook her head as she began to read. She was disappointed to find the historical contents a little sparse. According to ancient writings, the pin was highly sought after by the Pharaoh Abasi—some thought he killed people in his search—but nothing said where it came from, why he wanted it, or if he ever found it. It was thought to be more legend than actual object for three thousand years until it turned up in 1802 in a mastaba in the Western Cemetery in Gaza. According to articles included in Avery's packet, the pin was studied by both scientists and historians at the university before it was eventually gifted to a longtime, generous supporter of the university's archaeology program. The pin was passed down to his great-grandchildren, who then sold it at auction to a private collector in 1984. The next page was a military report that was more redacted than not, detailing a 1994 US Navy SEAL raid on a terrorist cell—a dozen terrorists and one American were killed, but in their intel sweep after the shooting stopped, the soldiers recorded a pin matching the description of the one from the senator's photo, in a glass case on a desk. By the time the compound was cleared of valuables, the case and pin were gone—or at least, they weren't on the manifest of what was seized. Next was a photograph of a man standing beside a larger display case, the pin inside. Turning the page, Avery found the blank back of the folder.

"Wait a minute," said Carter, who had been reading his own packet. "We're supposed to find something that was stolen from a guy with connections to terrorists? I thought she meant it was stolen from the government or a museum or something. Why are we helping this guy? And who is he?"

"I gotta agree with Boy Wonder on this one, Ave," Harrison said. "Why are we helping to recover some dusty old trinket if some terrorist guy owned it?"

"That's a good question, Harry," Avery said as she picked up the phone to call Senator Byers. "That's too important a detail to be forgotten. She left that out on purpose."

Although Avery knew well that countries in some parts of the world were controlled by groups Americans referred to as terror cells, none of the reasons she thought of immediately for the senator to withhold that information were good.

"Who're you calling?" Carter said.

"Senator Byers."

"You'll never get through," Harrison said. "I guarantee it."

Avery waved one hand at him when the line connected. "This is Avery Turner calling for Senator Byers," she said.

"I'm sorry, Ms. Turner," the senator's aide said. "But they've recessed for the week. She's gone already."

"Well, this is urgent," Avery said. "Can you get a message to her and have her call me back?"

"I can't make any promises, but I'll do my best."

Avery hung up and looked at Harrison. "Don't say it, Harry."

Harrison held up his hands in mock surrender. "Not me."

"So, what do you think, Avery?" Carter said. "It's not too late to turn around and head home."

Avery picked up the phone again.

"Who are you calling now, Ave?" Harrison said.

"MaryAnn."

"Guess that means we're not going home," Carter said.

Avery put MaryAnn on speaker and explained everything that had happened so far.

"Jeez, Avery," MaryAnn said. "Congressional hearings, clandestine meetings, secret packets, and stolen artifacts, sounds like you guys got thrown into a spy novel."

"Under false pretenses," Harrison added.

"I don't understand how something so small as a gold pin can have as much significance as Senator Byers implied," Avery said. "It is very old, and the ancient history that's here is...*sparse* is a generous word...but it seems to indicate that an ancient king really wanted this bauble and never found it, at least that we know of."

"Interesting," MaryAnn said. "A small piece shouldn't be such a big deal no matter how old it is, unless it has a history far beyond what was disclosed to you. I'll start researching it and let you know what I find. Good luck and keep your pretty heads down."

"Thanks, MaryAnn," Avery said, ending the call.

"I still don't understand why the senator wouldn't have told us about the terrorist connection," Carter said.

"Because neither of you would have agreed to help," Harrison said matter-of-factly. "Most governments are very bad at sharing information and very good at protecting their own interests."

"If you think Byers has some ulterior motive, we can still turn around, Avery," Carter said.

"I'm not sure she had an ulterior motive so much as a general reluctance to share facts until she absolutely had to." Avery flipped back to the last photo in the file and studied it. "Like Harry said."

"Make you wonder if the committee was ever going to seriously consider approving that purchase today," Harrison said, echoing Avery's very thought.

"But it was Everett who moved to table it," Carter reminded them. "Byers voted against that."

"Byers also flat told us that her colleagues do what she tells them to," Avery said.

"She sure got on our good side easily," Harry agreed.

Avery nodded. "She rescued me from Everett, which could've been a calculated move to get me to trust her." Avery checked her watch. They'd been in the air for two hours already. "I don't know, guys. Our track record with trouble is just as strong as our treasure hunting mojo. Maybe stronger, since we're never actually looking for the trouble. Do we go, or not? We are nearly halfway there," she said. "And we've got MaryAnn on the case."

"MaryAnn, who we trust one hell of a lot more than some government flunky," Carter said, looking back at his folder. "So this dude on the last page. It doesn't even say who he is. Is this the guy that had the pin before the SEAL raid in '94?"

"I don't think so," Avery said. "The description in their report seems to indicate that the case was much smaller then." She peered at the photo, then pointed. "And here—is that..." She fished around in her bag and came up with a magnifying glass, waving off laughter from Carter as she held it to the photo. "That is a photo of this same dude with President Bush. Forty-three, not forty-one. So this was most likely taken in this century."

"Okay, Mary Poppins," Carter said, still shaking his head over the magnifier.

"I feel like you shouldn't have to play Nancy Drew with a file when the government asks you to go look for something," Harrison said, ignoring Carter. "I don't like this, Avery."

"I don't know that I do, either. But I keep thinking about what Byers said. We can't just turn away from whatever this is and let an unstable corner of the planet get shakier without even trying to help, right?" Avery asked. "Y'all heard her say loss of life, not to mention the economic issues that could even impact Americans."

"We certainly can," Harrison said. "But I'm getting the feeling you don't want to tell her to find someone else."

"I didn't get the impression she had a list of people she could send. She said 'uniquely qualified' when she was talking about us. And her point about the cover story is a good one." She looked at her other two musketeers.

"I agree with you there," Carter said. "It didn't seem like she had anything else in mind."

"That does not make this our problem," Harrison said.

"It is a chance to explore ancient Egypt," Avery said.

"We could just go on vacation for that, Ave," Harrison groaned.

"She as good as promised to fast-track the DiveNav purchase, too," Avery said. "Not that that should be the deciding factor, but I'd be lying if I said it wasn't a consideration."

"I know you don't need the money, but the accomplishment matters to you," Harrison said. "But you really need to ask yourself how much it matters. If whoever is after this bauble has the power to wreak havoc on economies or cause political instability, it means they're not the kind of people you want to have mad at you."

Carter turned the file folder over in his hands. "Point well made. But if we bail now we risk having our own government pissed at us. Not much scares me, but that Smith guy was unsettling."

"Nobody wants powerful enemies," Avery said.

"But from which side?" Harrison sighed.

"When you put it that way it sounds like we're flying into a canyon between a rock and a hard place," Avery said.

"What if that's exactly what we're doing?"

Avery bobbed her head from side to side. "Well, then, I guess I'd have to say Byers will already be mad, and the Egyptian university officials know we're coming already. So how about this: We'll go to Egypt, talk to the folks at the university, and try to figure out a little more about exactly what we're getting into. If we're talking real terrorists, and not just shady political operatives, or if any one of us decides to bail, we'll all go home and hope the CIA doesn't, like, nuke our houses or something."

"Call me curious the cat, but I'm in," Carter said.

"Harry?" Avery said. "Are you with us?"

"Well, I can't very well let you two tenderfoots go off and get into trouble on your own, can I?" He shook his head. "We're already in the air, I don't see what it hurts to go check it out."

Avery grinned. "On the bright side, we might get to experience things that aren't on the regular tour."

"That is exactly what I'm afraid of," Harrison groaned.

7

Ancient Egypt, 1500 BC

Zefret stood over the motionless body of the royal vizier, grieving for her lifelong friend and leader. Amunet's eyes were closed, her breath stilled, as her blood seeped slowly into the sand.

Thanks to a rain of miracles, perhaps even the queen's lingering spirit, they had triumphed over Abasi's band of heretics, but to what end? As Zefret eyed the fallen bodies scattered throughout the chamber, she could see the cost had been great. Maybe too great. Among the casualties was the lifeless body of Heba, their true, forever pharaoh, just barely prepared for her passage, and thankfully undisturbed by the attack.

Even as the stars winked above them, Heba's stepson Abasi, a small, weak man, threatened by any woman who possessed power and intellect, was preparing to assume power over all of them. Zefret knew if they wanted to retain the lives they had made for themselves and restore order to the land, there would be much more work to do. Many more battles to fight. She prayed silently that Abasi's reign would be brief and wrought with troubles.

Several warriors, cut and bruised but still standing, approached Zefret.

"What do we do now?" one of them asked.

"This tomb must be sealed," Zefret said. "The traitors must not find it again. We will record its location along with the story of Heba's life, to be shared with future generations, but it must all be kept safe from Abasi and his court."

The warriors nodded in understanding.

Zefret looked over to the pharaoh's freshly wrapped body and to Amunet's lifeless form.

"They were in love in this life," Zefret said. "Let them enter the next together."

The remaining women murmured a prayer in unison as they slid the queen's body to one side of the altar, making room for Amunet to lie beside her.

Zefret had seen Amunet bless then clip the pin to the inside of her robe before the invaders came. She knew how special the item was to the pharaoh and how Amunet's intent had been to bestow it a place of honor inside the tomb. Zefret felt her pulse quicken when she realized that the pin was missing. She willed herself to remain calm as she checked the opposite side of the robe, to no avail. She turned and walked among the fallen men, counting. Two of Abasi's minions were missing. Cowards who escaped during battle. They must have taken it with them.

Amunet's powers were legend, the pin and its blessing coveted. Zefret kneeled at the feet of the pharaoh and her vizier, bowing her head and making a quiet vow. She would find the pin. She would become the instrument of her friends' rage. Abasi would not benefit from Amunet's power.

Zefret would trade the life of the thief and, if necessary, of Abasi himself, in order to retrieve the stolen pin. She would not rest until they had paid the ultimate price for their treachery. Then, and only then, would Zefret send her friend off to her next life.

8

Present Day

Avery gazed out the window at Cairo's peaceful night sky as Marco set the wheels of the G800 smoothly down on the runway. The slight jolt brought Harrison out of his semi-dozed state. Carter was already awake and champing at the bit to find adventure.

"I can't believe we're already in Egypt," Harrison said as he sat up and rubbed his eyes.

"That's because you slept through half the flight, Harry," Avery said.

"Hey, gotta get my beauty sleep, right?"

"Come on," Avery said as she unbuckled and rose from her seat. "The meeting at the university is in about two hours. Let's find the hotel and freshen up."

Marco taxied toward the terminal buildings as directed by the tower. Avery and the others grabbed their bags and descended the stairs to the tarmac.

"I'm assuming you're just reusing the presentation you gave in Washington on the DiveNav for these university guys?" Harrison asked. "I mean, are they even looking to buy anything? No one really said."

Before Avery could say that she was going to do her best to convince them they needed something called a DiveNav here in the middle of the desert, a loud pop came from above them, and a bullet whizzed past and punched a neat little hole in the stairs attached to the plane.

"Take cover!" Avery shouted as she dove behind a baggage trolley.

Carter ducked under the belly of the Gulfstream and dug a pistol out of his duffel bag, scanning the tarmac and pointing to a man on the roof of the squatty airport building. "There!" He fired a round that sank into the stone side of the building.

Harrison hunched behind a parked truck and returned fire with his handgun, striking a gunman at the corner of a nearby hangar. Avery watched the man crumple to the ground. Pounding steps behind her drew her attention back to her plane as Marco appeared on the top step of the Gulfstream, armed with the gun he now always kept in the cockpit, just as another man began firing at Avery from the roof of the airport. She heard the rounds ricochet off the tarmac, striking the trolley.

"Little help," Avery yelled.

"I got this one," Marco called as he returned fire.

A guard shouting something in Arabic ran out of the building and began shooting in no specific direction.

"What the hell is he shooting at?" Harrison said.

"Maybe he doesn't know whose side he's on," Carter yelled, moving out from under the plane to provide cover fire for Marco to come down the steps.

"I certainly can't tell whose side he's on," Harrison grumbled.

Avery raised her head when the bullets stopped thwacking off the tarmac around her, just in time to hear a sharp cry from behind her. She turned just as Carter pitched face-first onto the blacktop, landing in a heap with blood seeping through his starched white shirt entirely too fast.

"No!" Avery screamed. "Harry, Carter's hit!"

"Damn it," Harrison said as he trained his gun on the rooftop shooter and pulled the trigger repeatedly until the man dropped from view. "I think I got him."

"Take cover under the steps, Carter." Marco hurried to help when Carter didn't move, pulling his friend to a slightly safer location.

Avery ran to them, bullets striking the pavement in her wake and sending chips of concrete flying like tiny missiles as Harry cursed the shooters and Avery's reckless streak in equal measure.

"How bad is it?" Avery said as she knelt next to Carter.

"Hurts like heck, Avery," Carter said as he opened his eyes.

"I think it's a through and through," Marco said. "But there's so much blood I can't tell for sure."

Avery didn't like the sound of that at all.

"We've got to get to better cover," Avery said. "We're sitting ducks out here. He needs a doctor, but we have to be able to get out of here in one piece to get to one."

"Any ideas on how we're going to do that?" Marco asked.

"Just one. Can you run?" she asked Carter. He nodded. Avery took his hand and turned toward Harrison, raising her voice. "Harry, you and Marco give us some cover fire."

"You got it," they yelled in unison.

As soon as the rapid fire began, Avery grabbed Carter's arm and half dragged him to a small metal equipment shed.

"You guys okay?" Marco called as she slammed the door.

"For now," Avery said. "Thanks."

"Don't mention it," Harrison said.

"Um, Harry," Marco said.

"What?"

"I think you missed the guy on the roof."

"How can you tell?"

"'Cause he's shooting at me!"

Avery cracked open the door and peeked out. The shooter's attention was on Marco and she had a clear shot. "Carter, give me your weapon."

"Here."

Avery triple-checked her sight alignment before squeezing the trigger as she'd been trained. The rooftop gunman fired one more round before he staggered backward and collapsed.

"I got him," Avery yelled.

"Nice work." Carter's voice got weaker every time he spoke.

"Thanks, Ms. Avery," Marco said from right behind her, putting a steadying hand on her shoulder.

"Jesus, you scared the heck out of me. I thought you were still pinned down."

"I'm too fast to pin down." He tried to flash a smile.

"Got another shooter," Harrison shouted.

"Where is he, Harry?" Avery replied.

"He's trying to make a run for it."

Avery watched as the man broke for the far corner of the airport building while shouting something she couldn't understand. The man turned his upper body without breaking stride and capped off several more rounds in Avery's direction.

"Maybe y'all should have taken the senator's plane," Marco mused as he tracked the guy with his weapon like Harry had taught him.

"Not helpful," Avery said. "Here, stay with Carter."

"Where are you going?" Carter asked.

Avery, without bothering to answer, sprinted across the tarmac toward the airport. As she rounded the corner, she heard the sound of a motorbike revving, and a headlight swung around in her direction. The man fired another shot at Avery as she dove behind a garbage can. The bullet sailed wide but not far enough that she couldn't hear its whine as it passed by her. The motorcycle revved again and sped off in the opposite direction. Avery regained her feet but it was too late. The shooter was too far out of range to risk taking the shot.

Avery whirled around to the sound of rapidly approaching footfalls, raising her gun as she did.

"It's me, Ave," Harrison yelled.

"Harry!" Avery said. "What are you doing? I nearly shot you."

"You're about the only person who hasn't yet."

"Come on," she said, moving back toward the shed. "We gotta get some help for Carter."

"Help's already on the way," Harrison said as he followed her.

"How did you manage that?" Avery said.

"Not me," Harrison said as he cocked a thumb over his shoulder at the airport guard. "My new best friend here speaks English."

The wounded guard nodded. "I called an ambulance."

"Thank you," Avery said.

9

"How are you doing?" Avery said as she watched the paramedics prep Carter for transport to the local hospital.

"I'm doing okay. Though I might have sat this one out had I known what we were in for."

"That makes two of us, amigo." Harrison fixed Avery with a disapproving stare as the medics loaded Carter into the ambulance and shut the doors.

Before Avery could turn around fully, police cars roared through the open gates, four officers bolting out and disarming everyone while demanding an explanation. Avery did most of the talking, telling one of the bilingual officers that she was just as in the dark about who the shooters were as everyone, though she wasn't entirely sure what she was saying translated well.

After she had finished her account, the officer who seemed to be the one in charge barked at the translator for Avery and her friends to stay put, then walked a distance away and pulled out a cell phone.

"Who's he talking to?" Marco asked.

"Either one of his bosses or the detectives who are undoubtedly en route," Harrison said.

"This is all so crazy," Avery said. "Why were those men shooting at us?"

"We're not in Kansas anymore, Ave," Harrison said. "I don't want to say I told you so, so I'll just say I believe I communicated my bad feelings about this."

"That's just a fancy 'I told you so,'" Avery said. "And nobody even knew we were coming here."

"Obviously, someone knew." Marco waved his hand in the general direction of the destruction around them.

Harrison looked back at their jet and pointed. "Anyone who had the tail number could have tracked us from the United States to Cairo."

Avery shook her head. "I hadn't thought of that. I'm sorry for getting you involved again, Harry. Maybe we should just cut our losses."

"I think that's the wisest thing," Harrison said. "The senator will just have to understand. You charmed that committee chairman enough that I don't think it will kill your sale."

Avery nodded. "No point in getting the luggage off the plane. Let's get Carter patched up and we'll just go straight home to Florida."

"I'm afraid we're going to have to ask you to delay that, Miss Turner."

Avery turned to see a tall, dour man dressed in a suit and tie. "I'm sorry?"

"Ms. Turner, you and your friends are under arrest. You'll be coming with us to answer some questions at the central police station."

"You do understand that we landed in the middle of an ambush here, don't you?" Avery stepped forward when another officer moved to handcuff Marco, and Harrison put a hand on her arm.

"I understand that your pilot, Mr. Lopez, is a wanted criminal."

"On what charges?" Avery demanded.

"Smuggling stolen artifacts." The man looked down his nose at Avery. "If you don't want me to find another set of handcuffs, I suggest you do as you've been asked."

10

The detective in charge separated them before transport to police headquarters. Avery's assigned officer didn't speak a word to her during the twenty-minute drive—she wasn't sure if it was because he didn't speak English or if he had been ordered not to, but she guessed it was likely a combination of the two.

Police headquarters looked nothing like what Avery had pictured. In fact, other than the Arabic lettering on the front of the painted concrete building, and the palm trees bookending the lot, it looked almost like any stateside police station, right down to the communication towers jutting above the roofline.

The officer drove around to the rear of the station, parking next to several other marked units. The officer spoke into the base radio and received a reply from someone Avery guessed must have been the equivalent of a dispatcher. He led her from the car into the building, maintaining both his stoic expression and his silence. Despite the fact that they had only been defending themselves because they were ambushed while exiting the jet, Avery couldn't help feeling a little nervous at the prospect of what might lie ahead. Harrison's "We're not in Kansas anymore, Ave" kept rolling through her thoughts, and not in a charming fashion.

As the officer led her through a maze of hallways, Avery was struck by the strangely contrasting mix of dated décor and high tech. The journey ended at an uninviting interrogation room that reminded Avery of the rooms inside her mother's station house. Without a word the officer gestured for her to enter, promptly closing the door behind her.

After an hour-long wait, the detective they met at the airport entered the room and sat down.

"My apologies for keeping you waiting, Ms. Turner," the man said. "We've been busy trying to figure out what happened to you tonight."

"I'd like to know that myself," Avery said. "Is there any word on Carter Mosley?"

"No word yet, I'm afraid. But we have some of the best surgeons in the world right here in Cairo."

Avery smiled politely as she thought about how many times that same disingenuous line had been delivered around the globe. She wondered if there were any cities where they admitted to only having the second-best surgeons.

"My name is Detective Gamil and I'd like you to take me through what happened today. Beginning with your reason for flying to Cairo and then what transpired after you landed at the airport."

"I already told the officers at the scene."

He smiled. "If you would be so kind as to now tell me. Leave nothing out."

Avery let out a long sigh, then began her story, starting in Washington, DC, where a senator had "made a call to the university here and set up a meeting with the board to discuss my company's flagship device." She managed the lie without so much as a blink.

"And you just decided to come here, right then?"

"I keep a bag packed and on my plane at all times," Avery said—every word of that was true. "What good is having a jet if you can't just get on it and go? The university board was available this afternoon, or not until next month. So we came today."

Gamil bobbed his head side to side, considering that. "I never thought about the opportunities owning a plane would provide. Continue."

It took her what could have been ten minutes or five hours to tell the story—there was no clock, and her phone had been seized, so she had no idea how long she'd been in the room.

As she said, "And now I'm here talking to you," someone knocked on the interrogation room door.

"Come," the detective said.

The door opened and a younger man, also dressed in a suit and tie, entered carrying a stack of notebooks. The man set the books on the table beside the detective, pausing for a moment to look at Avery.

"Thank you, Husani," the detective said. "That will be all."

With a nod and one final glance at Avery, the man departed, leaving her alone with the detective again.

"What are these?"

"These are what you would call mugshots. I would like you to go through them and see if anyone looks familiar to you."

Avery pulled the top notebook from the pile and opened it.

"There must be hundreds of these," Avery said. "This could take all night. Can't we do this later? I might still be able to make the university board meeting. And I'd really like to see my friends."

"I sympathize with your plight, Ms. Turner. I, too, am exhausted, and would very much like to be at home with my wife, where I was when I was disturbed by a phone call concerning four Americans shooting up my airport."

Avery engaged in a short stare down with the detective, though she knew he had a point. While they hadn't started the incident, their presence here had caused the damage.

"Now if you please, Ms. Turner," he said, gesturing to the books. "I would like you to see if you can identify this third shooter you referenced in your statement."

"Fine."

"While you go through those, I'm going to go prepare myself some tea. Would you like me to bring you a cup?"

"Thank you," Avery said curtly. Though she knew what he was really going to do was talk to his investigators and compare notes to see if Marco and Harrison were telling the same story. Lucky for Avery, Harry had come up with it and murmured it to Avery and Marco before the police separated them back at the airport, and it was simple and easy to remember.

"Knock if you spot him," Gamil said as he left the room.

Begrudgingly, Avery flipped through the pages and scanned each image. After a while all of the arrest photos began to look the same to her and she wondered if she could really recognize the man she had chased, the man who fled on a motorcycle, the man she had barely managed a glimpse of as they exchanged gunfire on a darkened tarmac. She was halfway through the third book of mugshots when she stopped and leaned in close to study a familiar-looking face. Not the shooter from a couple of hours ago—it was the man who had driven them from the airport to the hotel in Washington, DC. The same man she had later spotted at the hotel bar.

Avery had assumed she was being monitored the entire time she was in the interrogation room. Her suspicions were confirmed as only a minute after recognizing the mugshot photo, the door to the room swung open and Gamil stepped back inside carrying two cups of tea.

"Find anything interesting, Ms. Turner?"

"As a matter of fact, I have."

Avery spun the notebook around until it faced the detective, then placed her finger on the photograph.

"I know this man," she said. "Who is he and what was he arrested for?"

"Is that the man you called the third shooter?"

"No. He was our driver in DC."

Gamil furrowed his brow as he studied the image. "And when was this?"

"Yesterday," Avery said.

"You must be mistaken, Ms. Turner. This man was a thief who was convicted of treason five years ago."

"Apparently, after he got out he got a job driving a limousine in Washington, DC," Avery said. "Maybe he has family in America."

"I'm afraid that is impossible."

Avery pointed emphatically at the picture. "I am positive this man drove us to the hotel yesterday."

"The man you are pointing to was executed last year for his crimes. I'm sorry, but you are mistaken. Maybe there is a similarity between that man and the man who drove you."

Avery sat back, stunned. She turned the book around until it faced her and stared at the image. She was positive it was him right down to his dark unibrow. She wanted to share the fact that she was pretty sure that the man followed them too but decided to keep that to herself. Whatever else this detective was, he wasn't there to investigate anything other than the shooting at the airport and her part in it.

"You say this man was tried for treason. Can you tell me what he was involved with that gave rise to his execution?"

"Certainly. It was major news at the time. That man, along with several others, stole a ceremonial gold statue from a tomb. He had been part of an archaeological expedition that discovered the lost tomb. Shortly after the discovery, the statue, one of many prized artifacts in the tomb, was discovered in his possession."

Avery did her best to keep her expression passive, not wanting to give Gamil any indication as to her actual thoughts. But inside she was beyond excited. There were simply too many coincidences for her sighting of the man not to be real. There had to be a connection to the pin they were chasing.

"So, Ms. Turner, you see why you are mistaken."

Avery nodded. "I really felt so sure."

"It happens," the detective said. "So, did you finish going through these books?"

"I didn't."

"Why don't you finish looking through the photos for the man you chased today."

Avery left her tea untouched as she looked through the remaining pictures, but she couldn't find the third shooter. When she had finished, Avery pointed out three images that most closely resembled the man who had escaped.

"But none of them are the same man?" Gamil said.

"No," Avery said. "He's not in these pictures."

"Well, there's never any harm in trying, right?" Gamil said as he gathered up the notebooks.

"Can you tell me how much longer I'll be held here? I'd like to get back to my friends and check on Carter."

"It won't be much longer, I promise."

11

Avery paced the room for the next twenty minutes. She had gone from anger at being shot at, to concerned for Carter, to worried about Marco and Harrison, to wholly pissed at the detective interrogating her. Something was wrong here, but the dots weren't totally connecting. At least not yet. She was tired, hungry, and needed to use the facilities. Avery walked over to the door and tried the handle. Locked. The detective had come and gone without the need of anyone unlocking the door for him, leaving Avery to conclude that he must have locked it whenever he left the room.

Avery knocked on the door. When that didn't work, she tried pounding the side of her fist against it. "Hello! Can anybody hear me? I need to use the bathroom."

At last, the door opened and Detective Husani ushered in Harrison. He looked tired but none the worse for wear.

"I was beginning to wonder if I would ever see you again," Avery said.

"The surly detective has been showing me his old family photo albums," Harrison said.

"You too?" Avery said. "I thought I was special. Where is Marco?"

Harrison shrugged. "I haven't seen him since they separated us at the airport."

Avery turned her attention to Husani. "Are you the one in charge?"

"No. That is Detective Gamil. What can I do for you, Ms. Turner?"

"You can let us go. We've been here for hours, and we'd like to leave. With our friend Marco." Avery didn't for a moment believe what the police had said about Marco being a smuggler.

"You and Mr. Harrison are free to go. For now. But you'll need to surrender your passports, and I'd like Mr. Mosley's as well if you know where to find it."

Harrison and Avery exchanged a glance and Harry shook his head the barest bit, pulling his passport out of his back pocket and handing it over. Avery frowned but followed suit. She trusted Harry. He'd explain as soon as he could.

"And Marco?" she asked the detective.

"I'm afraid Mr. Lopez will be staying with us for a while longer."

"I don't understand. Surely we've been here long enough to clear up whatever misunderstanding you might have had."

"On the contrary, he's been formally charged with smuggling."

"What?" Avery's hand flew to her lips, and she could see on Harrison's face that he was as stricken as she. "On what evidence?"

"We have video showing aircraft linked with Mr. Lopez, including yours, moving in and out of several countries at times corresponding with the theft or illegal sale of various artifacts," he said. "We've been waiting for him to come back to Egypt for four years now."

"I—there must be some mistake," Avery said, thinking of the other detective's insistence that the man she knew she'd seen in Washington had been executed here. "Marco wouldn't."

"You should consider how well you really know him," the detective said gently. "Because by using your plane, he has implicated you and forced us to impound your aircraft until further notice."

Avery swallowed hard. No passports. No plane. They were stuck here. And it was her fault.

"On what grounds?" she asked, keeping her voice even.

"This isn't America, Ms. Turner," the detective said. "But even there, I believe if a stolen artifact was discovered it would give your police reason to search the plane."

"You found a stolen artifact on Avery's plane today?" Harrison asked. "That was fast."

"Not hard to check Mr. Lopez's baggage, Mr. Harrison."

Avery's chin trembled. She liked Marco. She trusted him with her life, quite literally, and the lives of her friends, on every trip. He'd rescued them from Antarctica, for heaven's sake. She paid him well, she thought. Could this man be right? Was he a smuggler? If they'd been waiting for him to come back here for four years... Avery hadn't even been a billionaire that long. Had Marco been trafficking stolen goods before she met him?

It tracked with his initial protest about flying here, though he'd given in pretty easily for a guy who was afraid to go to jail in a foreign country.

Avery opened her mouth to protest again, but Harrison spoke before she could. "Thank you, Detective. We appreciate your hospitality."

"Not at all."

The detective stared straight into Avery's eyes for a twenty count. Avery matched him in length and intensity, her lips set in a line, but she didn't argue.

"I'll have one of our officers take you to your hotel," the detective said.

"How do you know where we're staying?"

"I took the liberty of checking."

"Thank you for offering, but we can manage our own transportation. Besides, I want to stop by the hospital and check on Carter."

"We can do that as well. Consider it a goodwill gesture for all you've had to go through here."

A uniformed officer appeared in the doorway. Avery wondered how a man who looked to be about eighteen was old enough to serve on the police force.

"Officer Annan will transport you to the hospital and then the hotel," Husani said. "You must only go where the officer takes you and nowhere else."

"Excuse me?" Avery's eyes flashed, and Harrison laid a hand on her arm.

"Cairo isn't like American cities," Husani said. "I implore you not to go wandering around on your own. It is not safe."

Harrison nodded when Avery glanced at him.

"Fine. Anything else?" Avery asked.

"One more thing. I don't want to offend you, but you might think about covering your head while you're out in public."

The detective handed her a pretty robin's-egg blue scarf. For at least the fifth time since they left Washington, DC, it occurred to Avery how little preparation they had done. The trip had been thrust upon them with almost no warning.

"I'm sorry," Avery said. "I didn't give much thought to your customs before flying here."

"It happens a lot to people coming from other countries. Your linen shirt and pants are acceptable. The scarf is the only thing you need."

"What about me?" Harrison said. "Am I dressed appropriately?"

"You are fine," the detective said.

Avery held the scarf in her hand, looking at it. "I honestly have no idea how to wear this."

The detective smiled. "I will show you, if that is okay?"

"Please," Avery said as she passed it back to him.

Ten minutes and one bathroom stop later they followed the young officer out to the police vehicle. All their possessions had been returned to them save for the firearms and passports.

"We'd like to stop at the hospital first, if that's okay," Avery said, realizing that she had no idea which hospital they had taken Carter to. "But I don't even know where he is."

"It's okay, Ms. Turner," Officer Annan said. "I know where to find your friend."

As the marked police vehicle pulled out of the lot, Avery turned back to look out the side window. Detective Husani was standing alone in the doorway watching them. And he was talking on a cell phone.

12

Their young police escort drove them directly to the hospital. Despite the exhaustion, Avery felt a little boost at the prospect of seeing Carter.

The As-Salam International Hospital was nothing like Avery had imagined, more closely resembling a high-end Las Vegas hotel than a hospital. Multiple connected towers, that looked like blocks stacked atop each other in overlapping patterns, gave the structure a distinctly Aztec vibe. The façade was composed of square windows arranged into Tetris-style formations amid long concrete bands painted in varying shades of tan and ochre. Atop the main structure sat a large neon sign consisting of the hospital name in Arabic along with a lavender-colored symbol Avery didn't recognize.

"If the inside of this place is half as nice as the exterior, I'd say Carter is in good hands, Ave," Harrison said.

"As-Salam is a state-of-the-art hospital," their driver said in perfect English, albeit with a thick accent. "Your friend will get the best care available. You will see."

Avery prayed that was true. The guilt she felt at having led everyone into this nightmare was practically claustrophobic.

The officer said that he would wait outside until they were ready to be driven to the hotel.

They located Carter in an area of the hospital that most closely resembled an intensive care wing. Avery counted twenty-six beds, and nearly all of them were full. Several triage nurses scurried about while a tall, bearded man who Avery took to be the doctor stood at the foot of one of the beds updating information on a tablet.

"Excuse me," Avery said. "I was wondering if you could tell us how our friend is doing?"

"The American?"

"Yes. He was shot at the airport."

The doctor moved toward Carter's bed, barely giving Avery or Harrison a glance.

"Your friend was very lucky. The bullet shattered two of his ribs but missed most of his vital organs."

"Most?" Avery's voice went up an octave.

"Yes," the doctor said, turning to look at them for the first time. "It nicked his liver. We are monitoring him. The pain medication will make him sleepy, but it's necessary."

"But he's gonna be okay, right?" Harrison asked.

The doctor made eye contact with each of them before he spoke again. "He is not, as you say, out of the woods yet."

Avery's heart sank to her toes. Harrison wrapped an arm around her shoulders.

"Thanks, Doc," Harrison said.

Avery sat down beside Carter as the doctor moved off to tend to other patients. Carter's eyelids fluttered when she took his hand.

"Hey, guys," Carter said, his voice low and raspy.

"Hey, buddy," Harrison said.

"How are you feeling?" Avery said.

"Like I got shot." He tried to smile and managed a wince. "Sorry, Avery."

"You have nothing to apologize for. I'm the one who got us into this mess."

"You didn't get us into anything," Carter said. "We're a team, right?"

Avery blinked hard. With her mom gone, these guys weren't her team, they were her family. And Carter was "in the woods" because she jumped into an adventure at a powerful woman's invitation without even reading enough to realize she shouldn't go out without a headscarf.

Avery hated nothing more than she hated feeling stupid. And right then she was thinking she'd learned nothing from Antarctica.

"Right," Harrison said. "Like the Three Musketeers."

"Four, technically," Carter said, shifting his eyes around the room without moving. "We couldn't get in nearly as much trouble without Marco. Where is he?"

Avery exchanged a glance with Harrison. "They're holding him at the police station."

"Why?"

"Just a misunderstanding," Harrison said smoothly. "I think they want to make it clear who is in charge here."

Avery's thumb rubbed the back of Carter's hand absently, her thoughts flitting from Marco to Carter and back again. She got that Harrison was trying to avoid upsetting Carter by glossing over what was happening with Marco, so she stayed quiet about their impounded plane and passports.

Harrison rose up on his tiptoes, adding to his already imposing height, and looked around the ward.

"What's up?" Avery asked.

"I'm wondering what happened to the other shooters."

Carter tapped Avery's palm to get her attention. "The one who was in the ambulance with me was still alive, but badly wounded," he said, barely above a whisper. "I don't know if he survived or not."

Avery's eyes scanned the room, looking at the other patients. Surely, they wouldn't have placed them in the same area of the hospital.

"Well, assuming he made it, they've probably got him stashed somewhere under heavy police guard," Harrison said.

"Let's hope so," Avery said as she scrolled through her phone.

"What are you searching for?" Harrison said.

"Local news stories. According to this, one of the gunmen was killed."

"Any other details?" Carter croaked.

"It just says that two other gunshot victims were transported to a local hospital."

Harrison tugged on Avery's sleeve. "Um, don't look now, but I think Nurse Ratched is pissed at you."

Avery looked across the room at the nurse glaring at them. The woman pointed at her, then at the wall placard of a cell phone with an X over it.

"Sorry," she said sheepishly before sliding the phone back into her pocket.

The nurse returned to her duties.

"I can't keep my eyes open, Avery," Carter mumbled as they drifted shut.

Avery stood and leaned over the bed, brushing her lips over his forehead while being careful not to jostle him. "Get some sleep. We'll check on you tomorrow."

"Um, Ave, it is tomorrow," Harrison said.

Carter grinned, his eyes still closed.

Avery touched the back of his hand one more time, leading Harrison out of the unit before the duty nurse could read them the riot act for staying longer than the posted fifteen minutes.

"If looks could kill, huh?" Harrison said as they returned to the hall.

"Where do you think they would keep the other shooter, Harry?" Avery said as she looked at the directional signs hanging from the hallway ceiling.

"Not a clue. It might help if we could actually read what the hell those signs say."

Avery dug out her cell phone. "I might have an app for that."

She snapped a photo of the sign in front of them and instantly got a translation.

"Well?" Harrison said.

"Come on. This way."

"I'll catch up with you," Harrison said.

"Where are you going, Harry?"

"I figure we'll be less conspicuous if we split up. I know you're about to do something crazy, so I'm going to buy you some time. I figure I might be able to scrape up some professional courtesy from T. J. Hooker out there. Besides, he's only going to wait out there so long before he comes in to see where we are."

"Thanks, Harry," Avery said.

"You can thank me by not getting caught."

13

Harrison found their police chaperone standing outside the black-and-white police van with a bored look on his face.

"Thought you might like some company," Harrison said.

"How is your friend?"

"Carter? He's a tough kid. He'll be okay. Thanks for asking."

Annan nodded.

"So, what do they call you, Officer Annan?"

"Mahmoud."

"Good to meet you, Mahmoud. I'm Harry. You probably won't believe this, but I was on the job too. Almost thirty years."

"Where?"

"The Big Apple, my newfound friend."

Mahmoud looked confused.

"New York City."

"Ahh. I've never been to the United States."

"Well, if you ever get stateside, let me know. I'll give you a tour of my city."

"Thank you, Harry."

"So, any word on what happened to the men who attacked us?"

"I've been told not to talk about that with any of you."

"Nope, I get it," Harrison said, holding his palms up. "I totally get it. You've got your orders. Makes perfect sense. Boy, that's the one thing I don't miss though."

"What is that?" Mahmoud said, taking the bait.

"The brass."

"Brass?"

"Bosses. They're the same everywhere, aren't they? If your department is anything like mine was, you've got more brass than real cops."

Mahmoud nodded his agreement, grinning for the first time.

"You know the worst part? Most of the brass never really were any good at the job. But man can they give orders. I bet you'll be one of the good ones though. How about it?"

"How about what?"

"Have you taken any steps toward promotion? Tests or something?"

"Not yet. I'm still just a private. I hope to be a corporal someday."

"Well, I bet you'll be a good one."

"Where is Ms. Turner? I need to get you two to your hotel and myself back to the station."

"She's still with Carter, but I can't imagine she'll be much longer." Harry leaned on the car. "I was a homicide detective, you know. Once, my partner and I tracked a serial killer almost to Canada. Stopped him two miles from crossing the border after he murdered four bartenders in the city."

Mahmoud's eyes popped wide. "How did you find him?"

Harry grinned and launched into a story complicated enough to buy Avery all the time she should need.

Avery did her best to look like she belonged in the hospital, but even with the headscarf she looked exactly like what she was: an American aimlessly wandering the halls of an Egyptian hospital.

The hospital was huge, and she was beginning to wonder if she would ever find where they had taken the shooter. She checked the wall signs using the translation app until she located the surgery wing.

Not far past the ambulance entrance, Avery located a back hallway with several private rooms. Avery peeked into the rooms one at a time. The third was the charm: The first gunman was lying in a bed hooked to machines with wires and breathing oxygen from a nose cannula. He was either unconscious or sleeping. There was no way to tell which.

Avery pulled away from the door as someone approached. She pretended to look for something in her bag until the employee passed. She found it strange that the room wouldn't be under guard. The man inside had just tried to kill four people.

She peeked into the room again. Nope, not even handcuffed to the bed. Something was seriously amiss. She took one last look down the corridor, then slipped inside the room.

Avery kept one eye on the shooter while she searched the room for anything that might identify him. The small room was quite sparse: Aside from the bed, the monitors, and a large wall-mounted cabinet—empty save for a stack of plastic bedpans, some gauze, and bandage wraps—there didn't seem to be any place for his possessions to be stored.

Turning back, she paused and stared at the man's face, peaceful in sleep. The room was still except for the low whir and beeping of the electronics monitoring his vital signs. It was hard to believe that a man they had never met, and had no connection to, had actually tried to kill them.

Avery shivered, wondering if maybe the police had confiscated his things. Stepping toward the hallway, she figured she might as well be thorough and stepped inside the cramped bathroom, where she located a white plastic bag on a shelf next to the sink—the kind of bag the hospital staff might have thrown the man's belongings into on the off chance he survived.

Avery reached into the bag, shuffling past several items of cut-away clothing until her hand fell on a leather billfold. She removed the wallet from the bag and opened it, her jaw loosening.

"Oh. That's not good," Avery whispered to herself, eyes wide.

Avery couldn't read anything in front of her, but she was the only daughter of a workaholic police detective—she knew credentials when she saw them, and the brass-colored badge opposite the government ID could only mean one thing. The man lying in bed in the very next room—the man who only hours before had tried to kill them—was a cop. At least now she understood why there were no restraints and no one guarding the room.

Fumbling her phone out, Avery snapped several pictures of the ID and badge before slipping the wallet back into the plastic bag.

"What are you doing in here?" The voice behind her made her jump. Her phone clattered into the sink and she let out a small yelp as she turned. If the shooter was awake he'd surely recognize her.

Thankfully he was still sleeping, the machines beeping in rhythm. The man scowling at her wore scrubs, so had probably popped in to check on him.

"I am so sorry," Avery said, her breath catching in her throat. She hung her head slightly as if in shame, but her real intent was to keep her face hidden.

"You can't be in here," the man said, sounding serious. He spoke flawless English.

"I—I was just trying to find a bathroom and I figured that man wouldn't mind."

"We have restrooms in the corridor for public use. These are for patients. Now get out of here or I will call security."

"Of course. Again, I'm really very sorry," Avery said as she slipped past him and into the hallway.

As she hurried down the hallway, Avery's mind focused on her discovery. *A policeman?*

Clearly, she didn't know everything there was to know about this little excursion.

14

Mahmoud dropped them at the hotel Avery had booked from the plane with a promise to check in on them the following afternoon. Harrison thanked him and waved as they watched him depart.

"Well, you and Officer Annan certainly got chummy, Harry," Avery said as they lugged their bags into the hotel lobby.

"And you certainly took your sweet time in there. Did you find anything helpful?"

"Not sure *helpful* is the word I'd use."

"Why do I get the impression you're about to ruin my evening after the day we already had?" Harrison said.

"I found one of the shooters."

"That's good news. Means Detective What's His Name won't be trying to pin a murder rap on us."

"The guy's a cop, Harry," Avery said.

"What guy's a cop?"

"The shooter."

Harrison stopped walking and stared at Avery. His mouth opened but no words came out.

"That was pretty much my reaction." Avery nodded.

"How do you know he's a cop?" Harrison said.

"Here," Avery said, holding out her phone. "I photographed his ID."

"I can't read this, Ave," Harrison said with a frown.

"Scroll to the previous photo."

"Now *that* I recognize," Harrison said.

"He wasn't handcuffed, had no guard. They even had him in a private room," Avery said. "Pretty far cry from what they gave Carter."

"And totally against protocol for a suspect, no matter where we are," Harrison said. He paused before returning Avery's phone. "This badge isn't the same as the one Mahmoud was wearing."

"Different rank?" Avery said.

"More like different branch or agency," Harrison mused. "What have we gotten into here, Ave?"

"I wish I knew."

"I know one thing," Harrison said, glancing around the lobby before he made a beeline for the front desk.

"What are you doing, Harry?" Avery hissed.

"Trust me. Just follow my lead."

"Welcome to Le Passage hotel," said the only man working behind the counter. "May I help you?"

"Yup, we're checking in," Harrison said.

"Do you have a reservation?"

"Do we ever," Harrison said. "It's been one heck of a trip, hombré, and we're in serious need of some shut-eye."

"I understand," the man said with a grin. "What name is your reservation under?"

"Turner," Avery said. "Avery Turner."

"Ah, yes, Ms. Turner. I have it right here. Four king-size singles."

"I'm afraid we will only be needing two," Avery said. "Last minute change of plans."

"I understand. And how will you be paying for your rooms?"

Avery handed him a credit card.

"Very good."

"Any good restaurants in the area where we could rustle up some grub?" Harrison said.

The man checked the time. "We happen to have an excellent restaurant right here in the hotel. The kitchen will begin serving breakfast at six."

"Whoa, that's only two hours from now," Harrison said. "Guess our trip was even longer than I thought."

"You have come from America?" the man asked.

"Land of the free and home of the brave, muchacho," Harrison said, a little louder than necessary.

Avery fought back a smirk at his theatrics.

"Here are your room cards. Unfortunately, I had to put you on separate floors. I hope that is okay."

"Works for me," Avery said, cocking a thumb at Harrison. "You wouldn't believe how badly this guy snores."

The concierge stifled a laugh. "You will find the elevators just around the corner. Enjoy your stay."

"I'm sure we will," Avery said. "Thank you."

As soon as the elevator doors slid shut and they were alone, Avery confronted Harrison. "Okay, what was the Foghorn Leghorn routine about back there?"

"You picked up on that, huh?"

"You weren't subtle, Harry," Avery said.

"About as subtle as your snoring comment. What was that about?"

"Sorry. I just need some sleep. Doesn't this thing go any faster?"

"Not here you aren't," Harrison said.

"What are you talking about?" Avery said.

"I'm talking about this shit show we've been thrown into. First Senator What's Her Butt—"

"Byers," Avery said.

"Byers, thank you—practically bribes you with the promise of a quick and painless government contract, greasing the skids to bait us into saving the planet from an impending Middle East skirmish of some unknown origin by finding some ancient lapel pin. All we've got to do is fly to Egypt and meet with some academic brain trust who was supposed to help us but so far hasn't even bothered to ask why we didn't show up. Instead, our reception committee consists of Egyptian cowboys with itchy trigger fingers, at least one of whom might well be part of the National Police force. They nearly kill Carter, but we fight back better than they gave us credit for, clearly. Enter Inspector What's His Name who grills us for hours about why we're here, takes our guns, our passports, and your plane, then arrests Marco on some trumped-up smuggling charge, but lets us go with a police escort—i.e. babysitter. Are we all caught up?"

"I was there too, Harry." Avery scowled. "In case you've forgotten. What does any of that have to do with when and where we sleep?"

"Something is rotten in Cairo, Ave. And I'm not waiting around to see whether we end up back at the police station for defending ourselves again, or we land next to Carter in the hospital—or worse. It's time we took the bull by the horns. I wasn't sure about your plan to dive into this, but now that we're stuck here for God knows how long, that little jewel Byers told you about seems to me to be our best shot at getting back home alive. Even if we don't know why these powerful people want it, they do want it—so if we have it, we have leverage. And since we can't go anywhere, a little leverage would be okay by me."

The elevator doors opened on Avery's floor. She pressed the Hold button. She knew Harrison thought she was too impetuous about as often as she thought he was too stodgy—it worked for them, because they balanced out. And she needed to let his caution win this one.

"What's your plan, Harry?"

"We check in to our rooms, turn on lights, pull the drapes, put the televisions on any English-speaking channel, loud enough to be heard from the hallway. That should convince anyone that we're here."

"But we're not going to be?"

"We need another hotel. I don't trust anyone here. They've had two plainclothes men on our tails since we left police headquarters."

"Seriously?" Avery glanced around even though she knew they were alone in the elevator.

"Yup. The short clean-shaven guy drives a black BMW sedan, and was sitting on a couch in the hotel lobby pretending to read the paper when we came in."

"And the other guy?" Harrison said.

"Tall, close-cropped beard, driving a white Mercedes SUV. He drove past the hospital twice while I was stalling Private Mahmoud. I don't know what's going on here, but it seems pretty clear that the local police are knee deep in trying to prevent us from ever locating that antique trinket."

"And here I thought you were retired," Avery said.

"Once a cop, always a cop."

Avery took a minute to process what Harrison was saying. "Okay. Let's meet back here in five minutes. We'll take the back stairwell down to the street and flag down the first cab we see to another hotel. Pay cash for everything and figure out our next move. That work for you?"

"Works for me," Harrison said. "And we need to get you a different headscarf, Ave. All the ones I saw outside the hospital were white or black. The police basically marked you with that thing."

Avery snatched the scarf off her head. "I'll find another one."

"See you in five," Harrison said as the elevator doors closed.

15

Less than ten minutes later Avery and Harrison met with their first piece of good fortune. They were sneaking through the hotel's rear exit onto a back street when they nearly ran out in front of a passing taxi. Avery piled into the back of the cab with her bags while Harrison took the front passenger seat. She knew he wanted to be able to check for a tail.

"Where would you like to go?" the driver said, looking at Avery in the rearview mirror.

"A good hotel," Avery said.

The driver's eyebrows knotted in confusion. "But you just left a good hotel."

"Ever tried to sleep in a room next to a screaming baby?" Harrison said.

The driver smiled. "Ah, I understand. I raised two of my own. Not to worry, I know a good hotel just close by here. Very quiet. I will take you."

"Great," Harrison said. "Now maybe we can get some sleep."

As they rode through the darkened streets, Avery thumbed out a quick message to MaryAnn along with the photographs of the badge and ID. As an afterthought she also requested that MaryAnn research the treason case that the detective had mentioned earlier.

As if she'd been awaiting Avery's message, MaryAnn responded almost immediately.

How goes the hunt?

Avery wanted a more secure line and environment before she gave too many details—Harrison's paranoia was finally starting to rub off on her, it seemed.

Can't talk now. Fill you in later. —A

While Harrison made small talk with their cabbie, Avery stared out the window without really seeing the city and tried to piece together what was happening.

She was pretty sure that she had made a serious error in judgment. Beginning with trusting Senator Byers. Avery had assumed from what Byers had said that the Egyptian government wanted their help, but she realized that Byers had never actually said that. And Avery was certainly rethinking it based on everything that had happened thus far.

She had been caught up in the excitement of another treasure hunt and that the request was coming from a powerful woman she admired in the United States government. She hadn't bothered to fully consider that their "help" might not be appreciated in Cairo.

Byers had dangled several proverbial carrots under Avery's nose, suggesting that the missing pin could somehow ignite hostilities here and she needed Avery to find it. Offering to expedite a government contract for the DiveNav. But it had been more than that. Byers had played on Avery's patriotism, suggesting that it was her duty—to her country, maybe even to the memory of her mother—to assist in finding the pin.

Avery replayed their private conversation with Byers. Had the offer of a ride in a government jet been a ruse? Had the senator known all along that Avery would probably want to travel by way of her own jet? Was that how the gear they'd been sent with got loaded into the Gulfstream so quickly? Avery gasped, drawing Harry's gaze to the rearview mirror. She shook her head at him as she considered silently that someone could've planted whatever artifact the police said they found in Marco's bag before they ever left Washington. Avery was beginning to think that maybe Harry was right. Perhaps the senator had played them. While that didn't explain the videos or longstanding warrant the Egyptian detective claimed to have, it might have been engineered to ensure Marco's immediate arrest here. Following that rabbit down a conspiracy-riddled hole, Avery questioned everything that had happened in the past few days: Had the entire Senate committee hearing been a setup? Had pulling their passports been the decision of the Egyptian police or was Byers behind that as well? It would certainly keep them from getting cold feet and returning to the US.

By the time the cab stopped, she was shaking. Harrison paid the man and gathered their bags, and Avery surveyed the new hotel. While it wasn't as grand as the one Avery had already booked and paid for, it was anonymous, at least for now. How long it would take for the police to realize they weren't in their other rooms was anybody's guess.

After paying the driver in cash, Avery and Harrison entered the hotel and walked toward the registration desk.

"I've been thinking," Harrison said.

"About?"

"About why they kept us at the police station so long. Remember the detective said he had already located your hotel so he could give Mahmoud our destination?"

"Yeah."

"Well, we could have told them where we were staying if they'd just asked. I don't think it's a stretch to say they delayed our leaving the police station so they could bug our rooms."

"Meaning they had already told the staff which rooms to give us," Avery said. "The whole separate floors thing."

Harrison nodded. "That television trick won't work for long. Pretty soon, whoever is monitoring those rooms will wonder why they haven't heard us. Even Mr. Beamer in the lobby will get suspicious when we don't come down for breakfast."

Avery nodded, approaching the registration desk alone with a handful of local currency and asking for two rooms.

"Welcome," the man behind the counter said as he handed her their room cards.

"Thank you," Avery said, crossing the lobby to sit next to Harrison on a velvet sofa.

"Any problems with the registration?" Harrison asked.

"None. The guy seemed thrilled that we were paying cash."

"This isn't quite as high-end as the last place. Ten bucks says he did it off the books and splits the money with the cleaning staff," Harrison said.

"Dammit," Avery said as she trudged toward the elevators shaking her head.

"What?" Harrison said.

"If you think the cops bugged our rooms at the other hotel—well, they took our phones at the station, too. Shut yours off and keep it off. I should've thought of that sooner." She powered hers down.

"Don't be too hard on yourself," Harrison said, following her direction. "Your mother was a cop, Ave. It's not like you're predisposed to suspect them of being dirty."

They retired to their respective rooms with a plan to meet up in four hours. It wouldn't be enough sleep, but it was something. Avery knew they needed clearer heads and some food in their stomachs if they were going to stay ahead of the Egyptian police, or whoever was behind what was happening.

After setting the alarm on the nightstand clock, Avery fell into a deep slumber almost before her head hit the pillow.

16

Avery and Harrison walked separately to a nearby coffee shop for breakfast, hoping that the authorities would be less likely to spot them if they were searching for two American travelers.

"Hey, I'm digging the new headscarf, Ave," Harrison said as she pulled out a chair and sat down at the inside table wearing muted cream linen from head to toe.

"Thanks. There was a gift shop in the hotel and I bought a couple different ones. This look like the ones everyone else has on?"

"Does to me."

Harrison had arrived first and grabbed a table near the window. Avery knew he had chosen his seat specifically to watch for possible tails.

"How long do you think we should stay off the grid?" Avery said.

"At least until we can safely move Carter," Harrison said. "Do we have enough cash?"

"For now. Eventually, I'll have to get MaryAnn to send a wire."

"Let's hold off on that as long as we can. No telling what they know or who they'll be watching."

"I'd feel better if I could use my phone," Avery said.

"MaryAnn is probably wondering what happened to us," Harrison said.

"I don't even want to turn it on to check for spyware."

"Can't you text with her by Wi-Fi?" Harrison said. "And just keep your cellular service off?"

Avery stared at Harrison.

"What? Do I have something on my face?"

"Since when do you know how to use Wi-Fi to communicate?"

"Well, can't you?"

"I can. That is assuming this place has free service." Avery scanned the nearby wall signs.

"Don't look at me, Ave," Harrison said. "I can only read the menu because it has pictures."

"Found it," Avery said. "Now let me see if I can use my encryption."

Flashing a thumbs-up, Avery typed out a short message to MaryAnn. As they awaited her response, they made small talk over a breakfast of pastry and cappuccino.

"This isn't quite as hearty as what I was picturing for breakfast," Harrison grumbled.

"Maybe not, Harry, but there's enough caffeine in that cup to fly us back home."

"Great. I'll be shaky all day."

"I was thinking about Byers again this morning," Avery said. "Do you think you might be able to find out what her interest in this is if you reached out to some of your intelligence sources?"

Harrison gave Avery a look she couldn't quite read. "I can try, but don't get your hopes up. It might be a lot harder this time than it sounds. We already have good reason to believe that Mr. Smith is in the employ of the Central Intelligence Agency. I'm not sure I can reach out through my usual channels without raising a flag on this whole thing. As soon as I start poking around, Smith may get tipped off."

"If we can't risk contacting our own intelligence people, why not go outside?" Avery said.

"I'm not sure I follow," Harrison said.

"Our new friends in London," Avery said. "Duval might be able to get us some intel from whoever stole the pin, maybe, without tipping off anyone that the request is coming from us."

"That's not bad, kid." Harrison looked impressed. "Not bad at all. That is unless you think Duval wouldn't answer your call." Harrison gave her a wink. "It's been a while now. He might not even remember you."

Avery snatched her phone off the table.

"Nobody forgets the woman who talked him into breaking into the Tower of London." she said with a wry smile, standing and moving to the door.

"Where are you going?" Harrison said.

"To make that call."

"I thought you were going to stay off cellular service."

"I can make the call with Wi-Fi too, Harry. Finish your food and I'll be right back."

Avery reentered the café ten minutes later. Harrison was still seated at the table, anxiously awaiting word.

"Well?" Harrison said. "Did you get ahold of him?"

Avery nodded.

"So, what did he say?"

"He said he would put feelers out through the usual channels, but he sounded worried about what I could and couldn't tell him."

"That makes two of us."

"MaryAnn called too."

"Did you tell her about Carter and Marco?"

Avery nodded. "She's worried sick."

"They'll be okay, Ave. We'll make sure of it."

"I hope you're right, Harry."

"So, what did she find out?"

"She said she couldn't find very much online about the pin. Certainly nothing that could account for what has happened so far. She said being so small it would have far more historical value than actual value. Her best guess was that it couldn't be worth more than a million dollars, even to a collector. A more realistic value would probably put it closer to several hundred thousand."

"That's not exactly chump change," Harrison said.

"But it's not enough to murder four people over."

Harry nodded. "Did she find anything about the treason case?"

"She did," Avery said. "The detective told me the case was sealed, right?"

"That's what you said."

"Well, according to MaryAnn, the details weren't sealed so much as erased. Not redacted, or protected, just gone."

"Did she get a name?" Harrison said. "I mean the guy was supposedly executed."

Avery slid a napkin across the table. On it she had written five different aliases and a birth name. "An erased treason case, a suspect with five different aliases, and a man executed by his own country who apparently now works as an airport hack in Washington, DC. Who can do all this, Harry?"

"I told you, Ave," Harrison said. "Something is rotten in Cairo. This thing has spy written all over it. And they pulled us in because we had a good cover and we're expendable—I'd bet the house on it. Did MaryAnn say anything else?"

"Not yet, but she was expecting a call from a political history scholar. She'll be in touch when she knows more."

17

Following breakfast, Avery located and deleted the spyware on both of their phones—the program was identical on each and installed less than twenty-four hours before. After two more searches to make sure she hadn't found the horse but missed the Trojans, she returned Harrison's phone.

"They're safe," she said.

"For now anyway," Harrison said.

They left the café one at a time, walking through the busy streets back to their hotel. They had just reached the lobby when MaryAnn rang back.

After checking to make sure nobody was listening in on them nearby, Avery answered her phone.

"Any luck?" She kept her voice low.

"Yes. One of my old colleagues is a political history scholar at the King Salman International University in Sharm El Sheikh. His name is Guy Malik, and he specializes in terror cells and how they form, grow, and ultimately die out. Guy has conducted extensive research on a group who claim to have the pin you're looking for."

"That's great, MaryAnn. Who are the group?"

"Well, that's the thing. The professor is more than a little paranoid about security. He won't share the information remotely. But he's willing to meet with you in person."

"How far away is Sharm El Sheikh?"

"About five hours by car."

Avery checked the time on her phone. It was nearly ten o'clock. "I want to check on Carter first, and we'll need to arrange for a car—"

"I'll take care of the car and send you the particulars. What time should I tell him to expect you?"

"Tell him we'll be there by six. Anything else?"

"Yeah. He said to tell you to be very careful."

———

"There is no way we can go to the hospital to check in on Carter, Ave," Harrison said. "The second either of us is spotted at the hospital, the cops, or whoever is after us, will be all over us again. Staying off the grid means just that. They've got us at a real disadvantage here. We can't go to see Carter, or Marco, and we can't go back to the airport."

"Then what *do* you suggest?"

"Do you trust me?"

"With my life. You know that."

"Okay, then pack up your things and meet me in the lobby in twenty minutes."

"What about the car to the university, Harry?" Avery said.

"I'll take care of our transportation. You just get packed."

———

The transportation Harrison had promised was nothing like what Avery had pictured. It was a battered, primer-colored Land Rover driven by a burly unshaven man named Amal who had at least as many miles on his odometer as the SUV he was driving.

"I can't thank you enough for doing this, Amal," Harrison shouted over the engine noise from the passenger seat.

"Nonsense, Harry." Amal waved away the comment with one large meaty hand. "I am more than happy to assist you and your friends."

"How do you two know each other?" Avery asked, clinging to the roof strap as they swerved through traffic at a speed she was less than comfortable with.

"That is a long story, Ms. Turner," Amal said. "Let's just say I owe Harry several times over."

"I actually just figured we'd rent a car," Avery said.

Amal laughed aloud. "That might have been okay if you were still in America, but here things are very different."

"How so?" Avery said.

"The cities, they are not safe."

"But we're on the highway now," Avery said.

"Even more dangerous. We have what you might call 'old-fashioned highwaymen.'"

"You mean like Kris Kristofferson and Waylon Jennings?" Harrison said.

"I know this group," Amal said with a big belly laugh. "And Johnny Cash. No, these highwaymen are like stagecoach robbers from your Old West. They roam the highways and rob unsuspecting travelers."

"Why don't the Egyptian National Police do something?" Avery said, dumbfounded.

"Or the military?" Harrison said.

"It's mostly organized crime here. Many in the police and military get kickbacks for turning their heads."

Avery arched an eyebrow. "How do you know so much about that?"

"Everybody knows. This is why I am always armed." Amal removed a large semiautomatic handgun from his waistband and held it up. "I will make sure you get to Sharm El Sheikh safely."

"What if we run into more than a couple of robbers?" Harrison asked.

"Don't worry, Harry. I have plenty of weapons." Amal leaned over and popped open the glove box, revealing a small munitions hold.

Harrison whistled. "Do you have permits for all of these?"

Amal laughed. "You are very humorous, my friend."

Avery exchanged a worried look with Harrison.

18

They'd been on the road for a couple of hours and the traffic had thinned out substantially once they'd put a few miles between them and Cairo. Avery was just beginning to relax when a dark sedan raced past them. Amal and Harrison were chatting and appeared oblivious to the passing car.

Avery turned to look out at the passing scenery. She knew it would only be a matter of time before the adrenaline rush wore off and she and Harrison succumbed to exhaustion. They needed a safe place to crash where they wouldn't be found. By anyone.

Her eyes returned to the road just in time to see the black sedan lock its brakes and come to a stop, blocking both lanes of travel.

"Hand out some guns, my friend," Amal said to Harry, slamming the brakes. "We've got company."

"What's happening?" Avery said as she turned to look behind them and saw another dark-colored sedan right on their bumper.

"I think we've found the highwaymen," Amal said.

"And I don't see Willie Nelson anywhere," Harrison said as he passed a firearm between the seats to Avery. "Here."

"What do you need us to do?" Avery said as Amal brought the Land Rover to a stop.

"Nothing for now. Keep your guns hidden from sight and wait here. I will try and talk to them. Harry, you wait for my signal."

Harrison nodded as Amal opened the door and squeezed his large frame out of the SUV.

Avery and Harrison watched as Amal approached the two armed men standing beside the dark-colored sedan. Despite the menacing look on both of their faces, Amal approached with his arms out and empty hands extended as if he were preparing to hug old friends.

"Do you really trust this guy, Harry?" Avery said. "How do you know he isn't going to hand us over to them?"

"He wouldn't," Harrison said confidently.

"That two-word endorsement doesn't inspire a whole lot of confidence, Harry," Avery said.

"Maybe not, but you don't have any history with him. I do."

Avery was focused on the hands of the two men Amal was engaging. It was something she'd learned from her mother long before she'd begun training in martial arts. *The eyes can't hurt you, Avery. Only the hands can do that. If you're ever in a fight, keep your focus on the hands of your attacker.*

Avery wondered if her mother had any idea at the time how beneficial that advice would be to her only daughter. A daughter who had learned to factor her feet, knees, and elbows into the fighting equation.

"Um, Harry?" Avery said.

"What's up?" Harrison said.

"One of the men from the car behind us is standing next to my door."

"And I've got the other one walking up next to mine," Harrison muttered, checking the mirror.

"Still sure of yourself, Harry?"

"Is he standing behind your door or right beside it, Ave?"

"Next to," Avery said.

"Good," Harrison said. "As soon as I get the signal from Amal, I want you to slam your door into that guy and knock him off balance."

"Gotcha," Avery said as she slowly wrapped her hand around the inside door handle.

"Now, now!" Harrison yelled as he leapt from the SUV surprisingly quick for a retired cop with bad knees.

Avery smashed the door into the man as hard as she could, knocking him down a steep grade into the ditch at the road's edge. Before he could recover his gun, she aimed hers at his chest.

The man froze, as if trying to decide his next move.

"Don't even think about it," Avery said as she stepped forward and kicked his gun away.

Avery heard a punch land, followed by what sounded like a body slamming into sheet metal.

"Harry, are you guys okay?" Avery called as she glanced toward them.

"Never better," he hollered.

"We're still on our feet," Amal said as he stood proudly over two would-be robbers lying unconscious in the road.

The sound of a scuffle and more punches being thrown continued on Harrison's side of the SUV.

"You sure you don't need any help, Harry?" Avery said.

"Nope," he huffed. "I got this."

Amal laughed as he watched Harrison fight with the fourth man. "He's okay, miss," he called between chuckles.

Avery heard something solid strike the side of Amal's vehicle followed by the thud of a body hitting the ground.

"And stay down," Harrison said, breathing hard.

Avery's man made a half-hearted attempt to crawl toward his weapon when she glanced away, before realizing that she still had her gun trained on him.

"You do not want to test me," she said.

Considering that for half a second, the man raised his arms in surrender.

19

They abandoned the thieves in the middle of nowhere, embarrassed and without the benefit of their guns, but still very much alive. Before they left, Amal disabled both cars with bullets to their respective radiators. Miles passed uneventfully, and Amal continued to regale them with tales that felt far less fictionalized all of a sudden.

Sharm El Shiekh shimmered on the horizon about four hours into the trip, looking like a mirage from an old TV show. The deep aquamarine hue of the Red Sea flanked by never-ending sandy white beaches gave the entire city a distinctly Caribbean feel.

"Am I seeing things?" she asked. "This place is gorgeous!"

"No, Miss Turner. This is one of our most beautiful and serene resort towns, where you are going."

Avery imagined Jamaican music and rum as the stress of their harrowing journey began to fade. "I can't believe I've never heard of this place."

"Now this is more like it," Harrison agreed.

"You can say that again," Avery said as she gazed out over the water, guilt washing over her at the thought of Carter lying in a hospital bed when he should be here appreciating the view and trying to talk her into pausing long enough to dive that gorgeous water.

"It is a very beautiful city," Amal agreed. "You will find far less trouble here. But stay sharp. Danger can follow you anywhere."

Avery had never heard truer words spoken.

Amal drove them along a palm-tree-lined road that bordered the sea. "This is Naama Bay. Tourists come here for the many bars and restaurants. Maybe right up your alley, Harry?"

"Oh yeah," Harry said. "This is definitely my alley."

"Easy there, alley cat," Avery said. "We've still got work to do."

The King Salman International University campus was impressive. At first glance it appeared almost like a small village tucked in amongst the surrounding city.

Before parting, they thanked Amal for getting them safely to their destination. Avery watched as Harrison pulled the big man into a hug. It was the first time she had ever seen Harry show that much emotion with anyone who wasn't her or her mom, making her wonder what the two men had previously been involved in to create such a bond. She knew Harry well enough to know that if he wanted to tell her, he would.

He didn't, staying quiet as they crossed campus to the building where MaryAnn had told them to meet her contact.

The professor was quite different from what Avery had conjured in her mind. Dressed in a white button-down, tan slacks, and sandals, Guy Malik epitomized a middle-aged tourist. He was tall and fit, with salt-and-pepper hair, a well-groomed mustache, and a mischievous twinkle in his chestnut eyes. Avery wondered if MaryAnn and the professor might have been more than just colleagues.

"Welcome to my university," Malik said. "I trust your trip was uneventful."

Avery exchanged a glance with Harrison before answering, "We had the benefit of an experienced guide."

"That's always a good thing around here," Malik said. "Very nice to meet you both. MaryAnn speaks quite highly of you. It was so nice to hear she's doing well."

"I don't know what we'd do without her," Avery said.

"She is good at making herself indispensable," Malik said with a smile that looked just a touch wistful to Avery.

"I appreciate you taking the time to help us, Professor."

"Not at all, though I suppose we should get started. Come with me."

"Where are we going?" Harrison asked.

"I maintain a modest off-site facility not far from here."

Malik led them to a spotless silver SUV. They tossed their belongings into the back, then climbed inside.

When the professor said it wasn't far, Avery envisioned driving another hour. After traversing the desert from Cairo, distance had taken on a whole new meaning. In truth they drove for no more than ten minutes—unmolested by highwaymen.

The modest off-site facility Malik had described turned out to be an actual real-life bunker. He waited for the steel door to roll up before driving them inside. Avery noticed that everything was controlled remotely. She reached for the door handle before Malik stopped her.

"Please wait until I get an all clear from my security sweep," he said, laying a hand on her arm while he watched his phone screen. "Okay, we are safe."

"Why all the intrigue, Professor?" Harrison said as he stepped out of the SUV. "I figured we'd just meet in your classroom or something."

"I teach from here. Remotely."

"I don't get it," Avery said. "You must have the shortest commute of any of the faculty. Why not teach at the university?"

"It is not about the commute, Ms. Turner. I specialize in terror cells and monitoring threats from the West. There are many who would be more than happy to silence me. I leave once a month to get supplies, but never with any kind of routine they could record and study."

Wow. So it was a big deal that he came to get them.

They gathered at the door that led to the compound's inner sanctum and waited while Malik disarmed another security panel.

Harrison leaned close to Avery and whispered, "Is this guy paranoid or is it me?"

Avery fixed him with a look of disapproval before stepping across the threshold. The room he led them to looked like a television production room with control panels and banks of wall-mounted screens, each displaying newscasts from around the world. Avery could feel the heat rolling off the monitors.

"This is my workstation. All these feeds are monitored twenty-four hours a day."

"You have students help you?" Avery said.

"No, I would never subject my students to the danger of working with me."

"Then how do you monitor all of this?" Avery said.

"Each of these global networks is fed through computer software specifically designed to track and flag key words, phrases, regions, and conflicts."

"Gee, Doc, sounds a bit like the NSA," Harrison said with a wry grin.

"You are not entirely wrong, Mr. Harrison."

Avery watched the grin disappear from Harrison's face.

"Come," Malik said as he led the way through the space into another chamber.

Harrison leaned close to Avery again. "You sure this guy is playing with a full deck, Ave? I gotta tell you, I felt safer in the desert with Amal and the highwaymen."

"MaryAnn recommended him. That's enough of an endorsement for me."

"Are you coming?" Malik said from the doorway.

The next room looked like a small conference room with a table and several padded chairs surrounding it, and a galley kitchen off to one side. The walls were covered with large, detailed maps of the entire Middle East. The far end of the space was set up for remote broadcasting, complete with a large desktop monitor, high-tech microphone, specialized lighting, and a green screen behind the seat Malik likely occupied for his teaching.

"This looks like a podcasting station," Avery said.

"I suppose it could be," Malik said. "This is where I conduct my classes."

"Cool," Harrison said.

"Can I get you something to drink? You must be parched from your journey."

"Not half as parched as those four desperados we left in the desert," Harrison said.

This time Avery nudged Harrison in the ribs with an elbow. "That would be great, Professor. What do you have?"

"I can offer you tea, coffee, or water. I also have a fridge full of soft drinks, if you'd prefer."

"Now you're talking," Harrison said. "How about a Diet Pepsi on the rocks?"

"And you, Ms. Turner?" Malik said.

"That sounds perfect," Avery said.

As soon as they were seated around the table, Malik got down to business.

"MaryAnn has informed me that you are searching for an ancient Egyptian artifact."

"It's a small gold pin," Avery said. "We've only seen photographs of it."

Malik pushed a remote-control button and one of the wall maps disappeared, replaced by a high-resolution image of the pin that Senator Byers had shown them. "This pin, correct?"

"Yes," Avery said. "Apparently it's very important to someone."

"Enough to kill for," Harrison said.

Malik's brow furrowed.

"They tried to kill us as soon as we landed in Cairo," Harrison explained.

The professor didn't even look a little surprised. "I am glad you were unhurt," was all he said.

"Our friend Carter Mosley wasn't as lucky, I'm afraid," Avery said. "He is still in the hospital recovering from a gunshot wound."

"I am most sorry to hear that. I will keep a good thought for him."

"And Marco," Harrison said.

"Who is Marco?"

"Our friend and pilot," Avery said.

"He is being held on bogus charges of smuggling," Harrison said.

"I will keep them in my prayers."

"Thank you, Doc," Harrison said.

Malik pushed another button on the remote and the pin was replaced by an informational slide titled Al-Azra. "MaryAnn explained that you weren't sent here with much information, and the contact you were supposed to have at the university in Cairo never materialized."

"Correct," Harrison said. "Though I've wondered all day if that meeting was ever supposed to actually happen. No one has tried to reach us to reschedule it, and if we'd gotten shot at the airport, we would never have been able to ask anyone here about it."

"They took our passports and impounded my plane," Avery said. "Harry and I figure finding this pin that someone wants so badly might give us some leverage since we're stuck here and we've been attacked twice in two days."

"Your logic abilities are above average, Mr. Harrison, Miss Turner," Malik said.

"But we'd like to know as much as we can about what we're looking for and its history," Avery continued, flashing a smile. "I believe in going in prepared."

Malik pointed to the screen. "As you guessed, the pin is extremely important. And not just for historical reasons. This group is a splinter group from a much larger cell. They are small in number, and extremely volatile because of a recent leadership coup. I believe that coup is how they managed to steal the artifact in the first place. It is believed that several members of Al-Azra stole the pin from a collector in Jordan whose family may be trying to get it back. The collector was killed during the attack on his home. Unfortunately for Al-Azra, the man they killed was the father of Abdulrahman Al-Masri, a high-ranking Jordanian political official who has ordered direct military aggression at the terrorists."

"That sounds like danger of regional instability to me," Avery muttered to Harrison.

"Still not really happy about Byers sending us here to retrieve something that was stolen from a terrorist group," Harrison retorted.

Malik raised one hand. "If I may—that is likely because you do not understand the meaning of terrorism, Mr. Harrison. Your Senator Byers knows what most Americans do not. This isn't as simplistic as white hats versus black hats. You have the luxury of that worldview because your government is powerful and does a nice job selling the heroes-and-villains fantasy."

"Is it a fantasy that terrorists kill many people around the world, Professor?" Avery said.

"No," Malik said. "You are correct, and it is regrettable. But you must remember that in order to survive, many smaller countries must resort to what amounts to guerrilla warfare using what you would call terrorist groups to act as their military wing. While distasteful in some corners of the world, these partnerships are the only thing preventing some lesser governments from being run over by superpowers. Much like your colonialists when you fought for your independence against England. Al-Azra is simply another one of many militant groups.

"Where are these Al-Azra guys, Doc?" Harrison said.

"That is the problem. They have been hiding. Gone to ground, I believe you'd say. They pop up with an attack or robbery every few weeks, then they disappear again."

"But if the military is closing in on them, won't it just be a matter of time before the pin is retrieved?" Avery asked.

"Time is not a luxury, I'm afraid. If this artifact finds its way into Egypt and the wrong people find out, it could dangerously disrupt a peace that has lasted for centuries. Which, not coincidentally, is precisely what I think Al-Azra wants. It may have been a heavy factor in their motivation to take the pin in the first place."

"So let me make sure I understand, now that we have someone willing to explain: The real problem here is not that the pin is so valuable, but that these Azra guys killed some bigwig's father getting their paws on it—if you said why they want it, I missed that part." Harrison paused.

"I'm not sure, other than the fact that a skirmish between Egypt and Jordan creates chaos, and chaos is a beneficial environment for guerrilla fighters to gain leverage. But I'm sure there are other reasons I'm not privy to."

"So is there even still a chance this can all be settled down just by returning the pin to its previous owner's family?" Avery asked. "Would he let it go without avenging his father's death? And do you think Mr. Al-Masri would accept our help in finding the artifact?"

Malik shook his head. "Al-Masri is a traditionalist. He would never willingly accept assistance from an American. Especially an American woman."

"Sounds like our boy's a bit of a misogynist," Harrison said.

"And very dangerous. While he would not accept your help, he would be willing to kill you to get the relic back."

"Jeez, he sounds as bad as the terrorists he's after," Harrison said.

"They are not altogether dissimilar. Similarly, Al-Azra will not think twice about killing anyone who stands in their way. But if you can return the pin to the family, it will definitely alleviate the tension between the two governments, which is likely what your government is most interested in."

Harrison shot Avery a look that didn't need interpreting.

Malik tapped his chin with one finger.

"You should not approach Mr. Al-Masri, Ms. Turner. But Mr. Harrison —with the right disguise, you might."

"What kind of disguise?" Harrison asked.

"You must appear to be at the very least, a wealthy European hobbyist. He cannot know you're American."

"We can manage that," Avery said a little stiffly.

Malik smiled sympathetically. "Please understand that these are not my rules. MaryAnn was very clear that the first order of business is for all of you to get home safely, so my advice will consider that first."

Avery nodded. "Thank you."

Malik stood. "MaryAnn also tells me that you are in need of shelter," Malik said. "You must be tired after your journey."

"Which one?" Harrison said, earning a perplexed look from Malik.

"You're correct again, but I'm afraid we left Cairo under less than desirable circumstances," Avery said. "Our bags are all we have at the moment."

"Is it fair to say you are not on the best of terms with the Egyptian National Police?"

"More than fair," Harrison said.

"We believe at least one of their officers was responsible for attacking us at the airport," Avery said.

Malik nodded his understanding. "And this is why you cannot return to the hospital to visit your friend?"

"Yes," Avery said.

"We're pretty sure we've lost them for now," Harrison said. "But if they're anything like the NYPD, it won't be long before they figure out where we went."

"Then you must stay as my guests," Malik said.

"We couldn't put you out like that, Professor," Avery said.

"And we don't want to put you in any danger."

"Nonsense," Malik said. "Unless you told your taxi driver who you were going to see."

"We did not," Avery said.

"He only dropped us at the university," Harrison said.

"Then you are safe here. I have beds, showers, and plenty of food, everything you need here to refresh yourselves. Let me show you to the guest quarters and let you get settled."

"Thank you, Professor," Avery said.

"Please, call me Guy. And you are most welcome. Come."

20

The next morning, Malik served them breakfast.

"This is great," Harrison said of the soup as he refilled his bowl. "I don't know what you call it, but it's great."

Malik laughed. "I'm glad you like it, Harry. It is a traditional Egyptian stew called ful medames."

"That's easy for you to say. What's in it?" Harrison asked.

"Harry!" Avery said.

"I meant no offense," Harrison said.

"It's okay," Malik said. "The dish consists of fava beans, onion, and spices. I have added some fried eggs so you would feel a little more at home."

"Thanks," Harrison said, though his lack of enthusiasm earned him a glare from Avery.

"Have you given any more thought to what I told you about Abdul-rahman Al-Masri?" Malik said.

The previous evening Harrison had told Avery how worried he was that they had clearly gotten into something they were unprepared for. Malik's description of Al-Masri had done little to assuage his fear.

"We've already had one casualty, Ave," Harrison had said. "And one bogus arrest. I know I'm the one who said 'let's find the pin to gain some leverage,' but these are serious players. I can't stand the idea of you getting hurt."

"I know that, Harry—the feeling goes both ways," Avery had said. "And if you don't think I blame myself for getting all of you involved in this, you're wrong. But if we quit now it will mean Carter was shot and Marco was jailed for nothing. And I don't think it makes us that much less of a target from what we've seen so far. I agree with what you said back in Cairo, we could use a bargaining chip."

They'd turned in, both too tired to talk any more.

At the breakfast table, Avery nodded as Malik excused himself to his office and waited for him to leave the room before she turned to Harrison.

"I've been thinking," Avery began, and Harrison rolled his eyes. She paused. "I tend to be pretty good at thinking."

"Carry on." He waved.

"I would bet that about the last thing Byers thought when she sent us here is that we'd go talk to this guy in Jordan that Malik is telling us about."

"And?"

"And that's exactly why you ought to go talk to him. Anything she didn't think we'd find or didn't want us to know is exactly what we should be trying to find out. I wanted to trust her, because I've admired her for years, but there's too much here that doesn't add up, and the fact that she was suddenly unreachable as soon as we got here and were being used for target practice is suspicious."

"She's probably up for reelection and doesn't want to dirty her own hands with this," Harrison said. "Or she wants the pin for herself. Either way, if there's PR to be had here, you can bet, if we're successful in recovering this thing, she'll take all the credit."

"Only if she gets it," Avery said.

"I'm almost afraid to ask what you mean by that."

"You said we needed leverage, right?" Avery said. "Well, if someone in the Egyptian state police tried to shoot us, and the professor said he'd be concerned about the pin being in Egypt ticking off the government guy in Jordan, then I think you're exactly right. The pin might just be the leverage we need to get our passports back and get Carter and Marco out of here."

"I made a promise to your mother that I would never let anything happen to you."

"Then keep me safe, Harry, and let's stay the course and recover the pin."

"It was my idea, I suppose," he said. "And I don't really see where we have much choice."

"Thank you, Harry," Avery said as she wrapped her arms around him and squeezed tightly.

"Just promise me you won't do anything crazy," Harrison said.

"You know me, Harry," Avery said.

"That's what I'm afraid of."

Avery tossed her napkin on her empty plate. "We have decided to meet with Mr. Al-Masri."

"And you understand the risks?" Malik said as he glanced at Harrison.

"We do," Avery said.

Harrison nodded in agreement.

"Okay," Malik said. "Then I will drive you to Nuweiba."

"What's in Nuweiba?" Harrison said as he attempted to hide his uneaten stew beneath his napkin.

"There is a ferry that will take you to Jordan. I have a contact in Jordan who will meet you."

"There's just one problem," Avery said.

"What is that?"

"The police seized our passports and travel documents."

Malik frowned. "There are ways around this," he said slowly. "But they won't be easy—or entirely safe."

"We wouldn't know what being entirely safe felt like these days anyway," Harrison said.

"Very well then. When you've had time to gather your things and rest after breakfast, we will discuss a plan and I will take you to the ferry."

"Thank you again, Malik," Avery said. "I don't know how we'll ever be able to repay you."

"Don't get killed. That will be payment enough."

"That's what I told her," Harrison grumbled. "What about phones and money, Ave? I know you cleaned up the spyware, but the international service is terrible here, so ours aren't reliable."

"I have prepaid phones for you that work on our network," Malik said.

"And money?" Harrison said. "Do we have enough to keep paying cash, Ave?"

Avery and Malik exchanged a grin. "MaryAnn wired money overnight into my account," Malik said.

"We have plenty," Avery said. "Might as well get on our way."

21

The journey to Nuweiba was entirely uneventful, which was a pleasant change from battling the armed bandits they'd encountered on the way to Sharm El Sheikh from Cairo. Avery sat up front with the professor, data mining as much information as she could to prepare them for their meeting with Al-Masri.

Like Sharm El Sheikh, Nuweiba was an Egyptian coastal town located on the shores of the Gulf of Aqaba. Grass-roofed shelters lined the white sandy beaches, and the water was impossibly blue. The locals went about their daily business as camels meandered down the center of every paved road.

"It's beautiful," Avery said.

"Yes," Malik agreed. "This area was once occupied by the nomadic Muzzeina and Tarabin tribes."

"Bedouins?" Avery asked.

"Very good, Ms. Turner. The ferry to Jordan actually runs from Nuweiba Port about four miles south of where we are now. You are all very lucky to have such a pristine day for your voyage."

"How long is the ferry ride?" Avery asked.

"Almost an hour," Malik said. "The water should be calm on a day such as this. You remember the plan we discussed?"

Avery and Harrison nodded as Malik turned into a large parking lot directly across from the ferry boarding dock. The place was a bevy of chaotic activity, reminding Avery of a cruise ship boarding out of Miami.

Carter, whose Instagram following had made his face famous, always said the nicest thing about getting on a ship in Miami was that everyone was too busy to notice him.

Right then, Avery was counting on it.

Malik helped them retrieve their bags from the back of his SUV.

"We can't thank you enough for your help and hospitality, Professor," Avery said. "You're a lifesaver."

"And breakfast was great," Harrison said.

Malik chuckled. "You are most welcome. Any friends of MaryAnn are friends of mine also." Malik removed a folded piece of paper from his pocket and handed it to Avery. "This is all the information we discussed. If you should get into any trouble, my contact information is on there too. I don't trust many people with it."

Avery stepped in and gave Malik a hug, making him blush. "Thank you, Professor."

"Safe travels, my friends."

The *Amman* was much larger than Avery had imagined. It looked like a cross between a cruise ship and a navy vessel—mostly due to the battle-ship-gray elevated bridge—though much shorter. The brilliant white hull sported the company name A.B. Maritime and stood in sharp contrast to the deep blue of the Gulf of Aqaba. The deck of the ship held several rows of outside seating along with dozens of orange-and-white lifeboats of various sizes. Avery knew the lifeboats were meant to represent safety, but given their current situation, the escape craft did little to boost her confidence.

What they needed was a way on the ship. She surveyed the parking lot, looking for the vehicle boarding line.

"There." She pointed it out to Harrison, examining the cars from the back of the line forward.

"Does everyone here drive a clown car?" Harrison muttered, leading Avery to the shade alongside a hut near the back of the lot.

"We're not going to fit into the back of any of those," Avery agreed, biting her lip. The ferry was due to leave in thirty minutes—the cars would start boarding anytime, and if she and Harrison weren't inside one, they'd get left behind.

Minutes ticked by. The sun crept higher. Avery pointed to a Volkswagen hatchback. "Could we try that one?"

"The driver will feel every jostle of us trying to get into that thing," he said. "No chance he doesn't come look."

The attendant began waving people through the gate, and the cars started rolling.

"We're not going to make it," Avery said, her overnight bag weighing heavily on her shoulder as her face fell.

Harrison opened his mouth to comfort her when a small box truck rolled into the lot, the driver beeping its horn, speeding toward the end of the rapidly shrinking line.

"Thank you, and amen." Avery blew a kiss at the sky and started toward the truck, dodging between parked cars and keeping her head low.

"Avery!" Harrison hissed, throwing his hands up and taking off after her.

They reached the row of cars nearest the truck just as it pulled to the back of the line and stopped. Avery pulled out her phone and opened the camera, zooming in on the cab. "Just one guy, muscular but I don't think he's very big. Not that he will know we're there, hopefully, but just saying." Avery looked back at Harrison. "Now what?"

"You're asking me how to stow away? You remember that I worked in law *enforcement*, right?"

Avery examined the back of the truck. "There's no lock on the door." She looked around. "And nobody out here, because everyone's already boarding. I think if we get in there without being seen, we're golden."

"What if there's a tiger in the back?"

"Who would take a tiger on a ferry?"

"A smuggler?"

"You really think that's likely?" Avery's right eyebrow went up.

"About as likely as you getting me to sneak onto this boat."

Avery sighed, putting her hands on her hips. "Did the police have any kind of reason that would pass in the States for taking our passports?"

"Ours, no. Marco's, maybe."

"Well, I'm not trying to get Marco to a meeting in Jordan," Avery said. "I'm trying to get you there. And without a passport, this is my option. We didn't do anything wrong, but they removed our ability to do this legally. That's not our fault."

Harry nodded slowly. "Your mother said you could argue your way into just about anything."

"We're going to miss our chance." Avery darted behind the truck as it started to roll forward again, her eyes on the ferry workers checking tickets just fifty or so yards away.

Harrison followed, his knees making his step a bit slower.

There was a sticker on the back of the truck with the ferry company logo and a bunch of letters Avery couldn't read. She used her translation app and glanced at Harrison. "Blood oranges and lemons. They don't bite."

He rolled his eyes.

When the truck stopped again, Avery threw the latch on the rear door and shoved with everything she had, rolling it open and boosting herself onto the platform just as the truck lurched forward, throwing her headfirst into a large wooden crate.

Harrison and his mile-long legs scrambled up behind her, staying low to keep his balance and peering at the bruise darkening above her eye. "You okay?"

Avery waved one hand and nodded, pointing at the open door. They were third from the boarding gate. Harry grabbed a strap and went to pull it down just as a small boy in ragged clothes darted up and pointed, saying something neither of them understood.

But Avery understood well that it would call attention she didn't want, probably quickly.

Harrison put his finger over his lips, trying to quiet the child, and the boy just ran faster behind the rolling truck and shouted louder. Avery's heart raced. She wasn't sure of the penalty for stowing away, but something told her the same detectives who'd locked Marco up would be only too pleased to see her and Harrison join him.

Jamming a hand into her pocket, she fished out a mint from the hotel in

Cairo and a handful of colorful bills and flung them out the back of the truck.

The boy's cry cut off in mid-sentence like someone turned off the radio, and Harry shot her a thumbs-up as he pulled the door shut and sat down.

"That was too close, Ave."

"Didn't care for it myself," she agreed, touching her bruised forehead gingerly.

A minute later they felt the bump of the truck rolling onto the ferry and exchanged a smile. "We made it," Avery said.

Since the truck was at the back of the line, they didn't go far onto the ferry. Harry pointed to the black Farsi writing on the crates. "I wouldn't mind an orange."

"Stowing away and now stealing?"

"Buying. I'll leave some cash," he said. "Who's going to miss one orange?"

Avery rolled her eyes as he used his pocketknife to pry the corner of the lid up, the nails squealing as they gave way. Harry grinned as he reached into the crate, but it quickly melted into a frown.

"Are those lemons?" Avery pulled out her phone to scan the print on the outside of the crate, which looked different than the script on the sticker.

"Uh. I hope so?" Harry carefully pulled out a hand grenade, his face going a shade of green in the light leaking in around the doorframe.

"Good Lord." Avery scrambled to her feet. "Put that down."

"Carefully," Harrison said, not so much as breathing in the direction of the pin. He replaced the lid and they moved as far from the crate as they could.

"Now what?" Avery asked. "I don't want to sit next to a box of tiny bombs for an hour."

"Me either." Harry nodded.

Before either of them could offer an idea, the back door to the truck rolled up, revealing a muscular man of average height with dark eyes and hair.

He blinked at them slowly three times before he said something Avery was pretty sure meant intruders and turned on his heel, leaving the door up.

"I wouldn't do that," Harrison said, his voice just loud enough to carry. "Unless you want to explain your special lemons in this box here to the guards, too."

The driver turned and came back, poking his head up over the edge of the platform. "So you're thieves, too," he said in heavily accented but perfect English.

"Oh no, I put it right back. I was looking for an orange."

The driver waved one arm. "You have uncanny luck, then, because you could've picked literally any other box." He regarded them with a shrewd set to his thin lips. "What do you want?"

"To get to Jordan in one piece," Harrison said.

"You are American?"

Avery nodded. "We have a meeting this afternoon."

"Could you not afford tickets?" Doubt crept into his tone as the driver looked at their clothes.

"They were sold out," Harrison lied, thinking about what Avery said before they climbed out of Malik's car a thousand years ago now.

"I was the last truck allowed on," the driver said, tapping his fingers on the deck of the truck. "Okay. I will not turn you in. But you cannot stay in my truck, Americans. It won't be safe."

"We—" Avery began and then didn't know what to say. She couldn't tell him that they couldn't go through customs without blowing his trust. "Sure. Thank you for your discretion."

"Likewise." The driver scouted the area and waved them out of the back of the truck.

"Most people leave their cars and go up to the decks," he said, pointing to the stairs. "No one will bother you. Good luck with your meeting."

"Thank you again." Avery didn't want to wish him luck with his arms dealing.

She followed Harrison up to the deck, where they found a bench near the railing that took full advantage of the view.

"My God." Avery shaded her eyes from the sun. "It's breathtaking."

"I gotta admit," Harrison said, "despite the reason we're here, it is pretty cool."

Avery nodded in agreement.

"Do you think we might be able to get an update on Carter now?" Harrison said. "I mean they can't trace these phones Malik gave us, right?"

Avery had been thinking about that very thing. "I can call the hospital using my fake name but they aren't likely to tell me anything."

"I've got an idea," Harrison said. "Do I have to do anything special with this phone to use it?"

"It's already activated," Avery said. "You just have to dial. Who are you calling?"

"The hospital, of course. I just need the number."

Avery pulled out the notebook Malik had compiled for them. Among the recorded information was the number to the As-Salam International Hospital. She transposed the number onto a clean piece of paper, then handed it to Harrison. "Here you go, Harry."

"Thanks. Be right back."

No sooner had Harrison climbed down the stairwell to a lower level than he was confronted by a young man dressed in dark clothing. The man wordlessly stepped in front of him, blocking the way forward.

"Help you with something, friend?" Harrison said.

The man remained silent, but Harrison caught the slightest shift in his eyes as they moved beyond his shoulder.

Harrison glanced back to see another nearly identical male blocking his retreat.

"You must be Thing Two," Harrison said as he turned his body slightly and spread his stance. "I don't suppose you're with the crew. Here to offer me free drinks, maybe?"

The man in front of him grinned and withdrew a double-bladed stiletto knife from his waistband. The polished blade looked deadly, with a length of about six inches. Enough to cause significant injuries no matter how it was used. As his eyes flicked back to the second attacker, Harrison saw that he, too, was armed with a knife. Harrison pocketed the phone and turned his body even further, allowing himself a peripheral view of both men simultaneously. His eyes fixed on a point halfway between them as he prepared to react to the first sign of movement.

The man in front moved first, smoothly stepping toward Harrison and holding the knife slightly hidden behind his other hand. Harrison had seen this type of combat before—it was typical of well-trained street fighters. As Harrison moved to block the first thrust of the knife, he caught movement from behind as the second man engaged. Without taking his eyes off the first man, Harrison moved backward and drove an elbow into the side of the second man's head, but not before he felt the edge of the knife slice through the side of his jersey. The first man moved again; snakelike, he came at Harrison from a different angle. Harrison knew what they were planning. Goon number one would keep him occupied while the attacker at his flank would slowly and methodically slice him up.

Harrison quickly scanned the walls for anything he could use to defend himself. There: Directly in front of him was a clear plastic sign mounted above a brightly colored flotation ring. Harrison couldn't read the words on the sign, but he only cared about the material itself. The thick polymer would break under pressure leaving him some nice shards to choose a weapon from. He stepped across the hallway between the men and punched the sign at its center as hard as he could, shattering it. The smaller pieces rained onto the floor while several larger, knife-shaped pieces hung limply from the mounts. Harrison tore two free, giving himself one for each hand. Armed, Harrison turned to face his attackers again just in time to see the second man come at him. Harrison slashed at his face with the broken plastic, narrowly missing only because the man leaned back like a boxer. Harrison could feel air against the exposed skin of his side where the second man's knife had sliced through his shirt.

Harrison watched as the men regrouped. Though armed, Harrison knew he was no long-bout match for two smaller and quicker men—they would wear him down before moving in for the kill. What he needed was a distraction, something to pull their attention away from him.

"Harry, I was thinking," Avery's voice came from the steps, stopping mid-sentence. "What is going on here?"

That was not the distraction Harrison had in mind.

"Watch yourself, Ave," Harrison shouted as one of the men turned toward her.

Harrison watched Avery size up the situation before her eyes narrowed into slits.

"I picked that shirt out for him myself," she growled.

The second attacker charged Avery, shielding his knife as the first man had done.

Avery didn't hesitate. She dropped down and swept the man's legs out from under him. He landed awkwardly on the steel floor of the ship's hallway, losing his grip on the blade in the process. Harrison watched the knife skitter across the floor and out of reach. Before the man could regain his feet, Avery softened him up with a knee strike to the chin, then spun on the ball of the other foot, delivering a devastating elbow strike to the side of the man's head. Harrison watched the man's eyes roll back before he collapsed unconscious on the floor. Avery snatched up the knife and turned toward the remaining attacker.

"You want some of this, Bruce Lee?"

The man's attention pivoted between Harrison and Avery a second before he fled down the corridor and out of sight.

22

The breeze and sunshine on the topside deck was enough to make the ferry seem like the safest, most tranquil place on this side of the globe. Grenades and knife-wielding ninjas notwithstanding.

"You sure you're okay?" Avery asked, glancing worriedly for the tenth time in three minutes at Harrison's side. They'd returned to the bench to sit while they figured out how to get off the boat and through customs. Harry was bleeding, but not profusely, the gash in his side about a foot long.

"It's a scratch. I need some ointment and a handful of Band-Aids and I'll be fine."

"You're lucky it wasn't worse," Avery said in an almost prayerful tone.

"I'm lucky, I should say. I can't stand the idea of getting you hurt, too."

"I'm fine. My shirt got the worst of it," Harrison said reassuringly.

"Any idea why those guys came after you?" Avery asked.

"Same reason the ones at the airport did?"

"You're sure we're safe up here?" Avery asked. "Where did they go?"

"Away from you, warrior princess," Harrison said. "As long as we're surrounded by people, we're fine. They waited to get me alone."

"I don't suppose you actually got an update on Carter?" Avery asked.

"I didn't get to place the call." Harrison frowned. "But we'll call from the other side of the gulf. How much longer?"

"About an hour and a half. Should give us time to come up with a plan for arrival since our arms-smuggling truck is out as an option."

"We'd probably have our pick of car trunks right now if we went to check," Harrison said.

"But what if that car gets picked for a random search?" Avery asked.

"Fair." Harry nodded.

Avery gazed out at the gorgeous water, then pulled out her burner phone and started googling. The chip was slow, but forty-five minutes later, she knew everything she needed to, and the shoreline in Aqaba was visible in the distance. She stood.

"Come on," she said.

"Where?"

"You have swim trunks in that bag?"

Harrison was halfway to his feet and paused to glare. "Why?"

"I have a plan." She pointed to a restroom. "Go put them on under your clothes and meet me on the bottom deck."

"Why do I have a feeling I'm not going to like this?"

"Because you won't. But it will get us what we want. Come on, we'll run out of time."

Harrison disappeared into the restroom with his bag, and Avery went into the ladies' room with hers, hoping she was right and this would work.

23

Ancient Egypt, 1500 BC

The women, led by Zefret, were tired and shaken by what had befallen them at the hands of the new pharaoh's henchmen. But they remained resolute, determined that the idol of Ammit would not advance the fortunes of Abasi.

Prior to sealing the entrance to the tomb, they placed the bodies of Abasi's band of thugs along the walls of the tunnel outside, no honor conferred on their traitorous souls. After offering one last prayer to their queen, the women carefully removed several of the support columns, releasing a cascade of sand and quickly burying the entrance to the tunnel and the tomb beyond.

The women followed Zefret to her modest mudbrick home. When they arrived, they found a woman waiting with her young son. The boy needed treatment after breaking his arm tumbling down a flight of stairs. As the local doctor, Zefret's skills were often needed. She and her friends were used to interruptions. As Zefret treated the child, the remaining women waited patiently in another room.

The boy's arm wrapped and his mother smiling, Zefret saw them out and returned to her friends.

"The stolen idol must be recovered and returned to the tomb," Zefret said, following another prayer for their fallen queen.

"How will we find it?"

"If I know the new pharaoh, the idol will not be far from him," Zefret said. The power of the idol would be something Abasi would want to surround himself with.

"But he is well guarded, and we are few in number, Zefret," another woman said. "Surely we will be slaughtered long before finding the idol."

"I would not attempt to deceive you," Zefret said. "Recovery of the idol will be a monumentally difficult task, and we may perish trying. But the idol must be recovered and restored to its rightful guardian, our queen."

"But we have sealed the tomb," the first woman said. "Even if we manage to recover the idol, how can we return it to the queen?"

Zefret nodded. She had thought of that while setting the child's bone.

"Trust me. We will find it and return it to her temple. As long as the idol rests inside her temple, its power will be restored to the queen. We must perform this task regardless of the cost to our group, for the cost to every woman of Egypt will be far greater if we fail. Abasi seeks to erase the queen's existence from history, saddling the women of Egypt with the same limitations that our Greek sisters came here to escape. Recovery of the idol is our sole destiny. As long as we possess the strength and the will to fight, as long as our daughters and their daughters down the line remain resolute, the idol will be returned to our rightful queen, restoring her power—and protection over us and our customs—throughout time."

"Here, here," the women said in unison.

"This will be our sacred oath," Zefret said. "We will never rest until the idol has been recovered and returned to Heba."

24

Present Day

Harrison watched Avery climb over the rail on the lower deck of the ship in a modest blue tank suit, shaking his head.

"We'll drown trying to haul our stuff with us once it gets soaked," he complained.

"That's why I put both our bags into garbage bags I swiped from the bottom of the hand towel bins in the ladies' room," Avery said. "Everything will stay dry and they'll float along behind us." She hefted her own bag over the rail, balancing on a four-inch ledge about two feet above the water. "I checked everything. There's a beach just about a mile that way. It should be nice and crowded on such a beautiful day. And I've never in my life seen a customs desk at the beach. Any beach, anywhere. We'll blend in well enough in our suits."

"Have you ever swam a mile?" Harrison asked.

"The currents are all going that way today. We just have to stay afloat. We'll get pushed along."

He considered that.

"We have to jump before the ferry gets too close to the shore, Harry," Avery said.

"I don't know how I let you talk me into this stuff," he grumbled, putting one leg over the railing and dropping his bag.

The water was cold, but not freezing, just a little bracing.

Avery surfaced quickly, already looking for Harrison, who had both of their bags in hand and was swimming with his right arm.

Taking her bag from him, she pointed. "We should stay out here, parallel to the shore, until we're closer to the beach, then veer in."

He nodded. "What about local wildlife? I'm still bleeding a little."

"I read about that, too—no chance of a close encounter with Jaws here, Harry. The tiger shark is the most bothersome one here, and they're more afraid of us than we are of them. But we're more likely to see babies or a surfacing whale shark than anything else swimming at the surface like this. No worries."

"No worries, she says, swimming thousands of feet offshore in international waters to sneak into another country. What could I possibly be worried about?" Harry muttered.

"It's pretty quiet out here, Harry." Avery got a mouthful of water and paused to spit it out. "I can hear you."

"I meant for you to hear me," Harrison growled.

They swam in silence until Avery's arms started to ache, and she turned to check on Harrison, who was floating on his back. Damn. Maybe a mile or so really was a lot farther than she'd thought. Pulling in a deep breath and looking around at the water, the shore in the distance and the port finally behind them, she knew above everything that she couldn't panic. This was a surface swim, but diving had taught Avery well that panic in the water was a shortcut to drowning.

Think, Avery.

She was good at solving problems. More than good—the skill had made her a very wealthy woman before she was thirty. She would get them to the beach, because there was simply no alternative outcome here. But right then she'd never missed Carter more. Avery couldn't have told anyone when Carter's simple presence started to make her feel calm, like anything that came their way was simply an obstacle for them to scale together—but she knew floating in that gorgeous blue water that if he'd been there, she wouldn't have been scared.

Closing her eyes, she pictured his face: easy smile, mischievous eyes, and strong jaw. Maybe she could just pretend he was there.

On the backs of her eyelids, conjured-up Carter grinned and tapped his temple. "I'm right here, Avery. I taught you everything you need to know about dive safety, and this is just a swim. Just breathe. Watch your surroundings. Look for help. You can do this."

Avery opened her eyes, noticing that Harrison's face was getting pink in the sun. "You okay, Harry?"

"Just floating with the currents like you said," he said without opening his eyes.

Avery smiled, but it faded when she spotted four dorsal fins about twenty yards away and closing fast. "Harry, we have trouble incoming," she said.

He opened his eyes and righted himself, swearing when he saw the fins. "I thought you said... Never mind. Do we have anything that even resembles a weapon?"

"Our fists?" Avery was having a harder time fighting back panic. "Carter says punch them right on the end of the nose and then shove their head down and move them away from you."

"Carter chases adrenaline for a living," Harrison said.

"Is that really all that different than what you and Mom did?" Avery asked.

The animals were only about five feet from them. She moved her legs, treading water, and drew her right fist back to punch. Harrison did the same just as the two in the front popped their heads above the surface for air. Spotting the smooth gray skin and blowholes, Avery let out a whoop, letting her arm fall back to the water.

"They're not sharks, they're dolphins, Harry!" She glanced over. He still didn't look thrilled about being in the water with very large mammals, but Avery's tension melted right away. She and Carter had encountered plenty of dolphins on their dives, and they were always delightful.

She kept treading water as the small pod surrounded them, two more dolphins joining the others from under the water. The one directly in front of Avery raised her head and opened her mouth, chattering excitedly, her face looking like she was smiling.

Avery waited until she stopped and then laughed. "Is that so?"

The dolphin squeaked twice.

"I wish I could tell what you were saying, sweetie," Avery said, putting up a tentative hand and laughing when the dolphin stuck her nose under it. Avery stroked her slick skin and grinned at Harrison. "This is definitely not part of the regular tour."

"It really was like she was trying to talk to you," Harrison said, his face plainly giving away his disbelief.

"Some people think they're smarter than we are, you know."

"I bet she's smarter than quite a few people I've met," Harry said, raising his hand. "Can I? I mean, would they let me?"

Avery nodded and Harrison touched the chatty dolphin's back, gasping when a smaller one to his left swam up and rubbed its whole side along his arm. "What are you, a cat?"

The dolphins circled them, five of the six seeming to want turns to be petted. After playing for a few minutes, the chatty one sat up and squeaked at Avery again.

Avery laughed. "I'm suddenly not as tired." She turned toward the shore. "And look!" She pointed. "The beach!"

Chattering, the dolphin dove under a wave and started swimming. The other animals followed. Grabbing their bags, Avery and Harrison found it much easier to follow their new friends toward a shoreline they could actually see.

About thirty feet from the shore, the dolphins stopped suddenly, and Avery found a sandbar with her feet just in front of where they paused.

She stood and turned to smile. "Thank you."

The dolphins chattered at them one more time before they turned and dove under a small wave, waggling their tails as they headed back to deeper water.

Harrison lifted his bag and stared after them with a loose jaw.

"It's like an episode of *Lassie*," Harrison said. "But in the water."

"What?" Avery asked.

"You know how to make a guy feel old, you know that?"

"Sorry," Avery said.

A wave pushed them a few more feet inland, where the water quickly grew shallower.

The sea was clear, and relatively crowded close to land, as Avery had figured it would be on such a lovely day. They waded in the sand parallel to the shore until they were exactly between lifeguard stands, then turned for the sand. Once out of the water's reach, Harrison dropped to the sand, resting his head on his knees. "The things you drag me into, kid."

"You never got to swim with dolphins working as a cop," she said, sitting next to him.

"I suppose you have a point there."

They watched the water and the swimmers in silence until they'd caught their breath and the sun started to get uncomfortably warm.

"Shall we?" Harrison asked, getting to his feet.

"Sure seems like it," Avery said, letting him pull her up. Carrying their bags, they found a restroom near the boardwalk with an outdoor shower. Taking turns rinsing off sand, they ducked in opposite doors to dry off and change. It took half a roll of paper towels to stop Avery's hair from dripping, but the dry linen of her clothes felt lovely against her waterlogged skin, and she stuffed the trash bag that had kept her duffel dry down into the garbage can on her way back outside, where she spotted a coffee café.

"Yes please," Harrison said when she pointed.

Forty minutes later, Avery and Harrison walked past the port customs office in dry clothing, looking for a cab.

"You think anyone's following us?" Avery asked as they neared the taxi stand.

"Not that I've been able to spot," Harrison said.

Avery hoped Harrison was right, but the truth was someone was already onto them before they jumped off the *Amman*, or they wouldn't have been attacked.

"If there's some kind of international or, God forbid, terrorist APB, we stick out like a broken thumb," Harrison said. "No matter how we try to disguise ourselves, a crazy-tall American man of a certain age gallivanting about with a woman who could be his daughter and looks like you means if somebody wants to find us, they will. Those guys on the ferry ran, but they were working for someone, and that someone knows where the ferry was headed."

"So you're saying what we need is an ally."

"And where might we find such a person here?" Harrison asked.

"I was thinking we might start with Abdulrahman Al-Masri."

"You think this guy whose father was just murdered is just going to invite us to the inner circle because we can look enough like Europeans instead of Americans?" Harry shook his head. "I know what Guy said, but I think that's a long shot, and with our track record so far this trip, it might be a dangerous one."

"Harry, we don't have many options left," Avery said. "Not if we want to locate the pin and get the target off our backs. I think Mr. Al-Masri is our best bet, Harry. He wants to get his hands on that pin as badly as we do. According to the professor, he'd do anything to keep it from falling back into the hands of Al-Azra."

"Including putting us in harm's way," Harrison said. "Don't forget that part of what the professor said."

"Based on the attacks so far, I'd say we're already in harm's way."

"Assuming for a second that I'd be willing to take part in such a crazy scheme, I don't remember the professor saying anything about how to get an appointment to see this bigwig. But I do remember him saying you should stay away from the guy."

"Come on," Avery said with a laugh as she raised her hand to hail a taxi. "I've got an idea. Sometimes, you have to flip everyone's expectations upside down."

25

"Take us to the museum, please," Avery said. With a nod from their taxi driver, they were off.

"Sure," Harrison said. "Still not tracking on how we get in to see Al-Masri, though."

After punching in a number, Avery placed the phone to her ear.

"You have reached the office of Abdulrahman Al-Masri. My name is Fazul. How may I help you?"

"Good afternoon. My name is Jenny Smith and I am calling on behalf of Carter Mosley. He is traveling throughout the Middle East and he would very much like to meet Mr. Al-Masri while he is in Jordan."

"*The* Carter Mosley?" The shriek was so loud Harry jumped. "Treasure hunter and deep-sea diver?"

"The one and only," Avery said, grinning as Harrison rolled his eyes.

"I'm quite sure that can be arranged, Ms. Smith. When was Mr. Mosley hoping to visit Mr. Al-Masri?"

"Tomorrow afternoon. But we'd need some time within the hour, if that's not too much of an imposition," Avery said. "Mr. Mosley's on a very tight schedule, and his agent and I must fully brief Mr. Al-Masri before they meet, as I'm sure you understand."

"Of course. Let me check with Mr. Al-Masri and see if he would be willing to rearrange his afternoon schedule. Please hold."

Avery covered the microphone and grinned at Harrison. "She's asking."

"What is it with Carter? Now we've got Jordanian heads of state fawning over him?"

"Malik said the guy's dad was a treasure collector," Avery said. "I wanted a way to get us both in, which means the meeting has to be something he thinks he wants more than we do." She held up crossed fingers. "Here's hoping it works."

The assistant removed Avery's call from hold. "Ms. Smith, are you still there?"

"Right here," Avery said.

"Mr. Al-Masri is a fan of Mr. Mosley, and he will be awaiting your arrival."

"Thank you so much. See you soon."

"Pretty smooth, Ave," Harrison said as Avery ended the call. "So I'm supposed to be the agent? I can't talk like that Hollywood kid Carter uses. Who is thirty years younger than me."

Avery pocketed the prepaid phone with a grin. "First of all, no one here knows any of that. Second, in this part of the world, people keep things in their families. Therefore, you're his father—Harry Mosley."

The taxi stopped and the driver looked at Avery in the rearview mirror. "We have arrived."

Avery reached for the door handle. "Come on, Mr. Mosley."

Avery and Harrison were led to Al-Masri's office located on an upper floor of the building.

"Salam alaikum," Al-Masri said as they entered. "Welcome to Jordan."

"Thank you, Mr. Al-Masri," Harrison said.

"My assistant said you want to talk with me about an audience with Carter Mosley," Al-Masri said. "Exactly who are you?"

"My name is Harry Mosley," Harrison said. "Carter is my son, and we are traveling together."

"Where is Carter?"

"He had diving commitments today, but an opening has come up in his schedule tomorrow and he wanted us to arrange for a meeting with you," Avery said.

Al-Masri nodded without really looking at her. "I look forward to that." His attention returned to Harrison. "I am a big fan of your son's videos, Mr. Mosley."

"Thank you. Carter is very talented."

Without looking directly at Avery, Al-Masri tilted his head toward her. "And who is joining us today?"

"This is Carter's assistant, Jenny Smith," Harrison said. "My son couldn't do any of the things he does without Jenny's help."

"A pleasure, Ms. Smith," Al-Masri said before gesturing to the chairs in front of his desk. "Please, sit."

"Thank you," they said in unison, obliging.

"I understand you are touring our part of the world, Mr. Mosley."

"Please, call me Harry. Yes, we are doing a bit of sightseeing. I've always wanted to visit the area. You might say it's on my bucket list."

"Bucket list, yes, I know this phrase. Things you hope to accomplish before you die, correct?"

Avery and Harrison exchanged a nervous glance. Maybe that wasn't the best choice of words.

"I'm hoping to delay the dying part for a while yet—I keep adding more things to my list." Harrison winked.

Al-Masri laughed. "That is wise. I like you. So, what do you and Carter think of Jordan so far?"

"To be honest we haven't seen much of it yet. We're hoping to get to the museum next."

"Ah, the Jordan Museum. It is the largest in the kingdom. You will find many cultural artifacts there. Some are nearly ten thousand years old. I will see to it that you have guest passes waiting for you at the door."

"Decent of you, sir," Harrison said as he flashed his best imitation of the famous Mosley grin. "Thank you."

"I must tell you; I was very excited to receive your call today. I have watched many of Carter's exploits. His ability to recover lost treasures is very impressive."

"He's gotten lucky a few times."

"I imagine luck has very little to do with it. It is all about intelligence, skill, courage...and manipulation." Al-Masri leaned his elbows on the desk. "What are you really doing here, Harry?"

"To be honest?" Harrison figured, like Avery said, maybe flipping their expectations upside down was best. "We've come here to recover a lost artifact."

Al-Masri smiled. "I suspected as much. Which lost idol is Carter Mosley looking for in Jordan?"

Avery spoke up, doing her best to describe the pin without giving too much away. She studied Al-Masri's face for signs, but the man remained stoic.

When she had finished, Al-Masri turned his attention to Harrison before he spoke.

"I know of this idol of which you speak and the goddess it represents. And I too have heard the stories about it having been stolen from Al-Azra. First, let me tell you that I have no idea who may have stolen the golden pin, or if it was even actually taken from them. The truth has many faces in this land, Mr. Mosley. Secondly, you should know I intend to find out where the idol has gone and restore it to its rightful owner."

"And who is the rightful owner?" Harrison asked.

"I am, Mr. Mosley. Or perhaps I should say the people of the Kingdom of Jordan are. It is a national treasure in every sense of the phrase."

"I believe we might be able to assist you in that endeavor, Mr. Al-Masri," Avery said. "Finding lost artifacts is what we do best."

"And I believe you would do well to stay clear of things that are not your concern, Ms. Smith." And with that, Al-Masri stood and gestured toward the door. "We're finished here, and I'm afraid my afternoon tomorrow is unavoidably booked up. I have a number of appointments that I pushed back in order to meet with you. Ma'ssalaame."

"If I didn't know better I'd say Mr. Al-Masri wasn't happy with the idea of us getting involved in the search," Harrison said. "You think he bought our cover story?"

"I couldn't tell," Avery said. "Don't suppose you happened to notice the golden statue in the corner of his office."

"You mean the one that looks exactly like the head of the pin we're looking for?"

"Very observant, Mr. Mosley," Avery teased.

"Must be why I picked up the two guys tailing us as soon as we exited the elevator."

"What do you say we try and lose them?" Avery said as she raised a hand. "Taxi."

26

Avery was floored by the sheer number of artifacts displayed at the museum. Coming from a country that didn't exist 260 years ago, Jordan's rich cultural history encompassing thousands of years of humankind was hard to wrap her brain around. Several of the pieces dated back more than nine thousand years. The one thing she could not find was any reference to the pin or how it made its way to Jordan from Giza. Nothing on display even began to resemble the piece in question.

"What do you think, Harry?" Avery said.

"I think we lost them, Ave. At least for now."

"I meant about the museum."

"Oh, it's big."

"That's all you can say?"

"Really big?"

Avery stopped walking long enough to check her burner phone, but there were no missed calls. Maybe no news was good news. Her grumbling stomach reminded her that they hadn't eaten since they arrived, and the coffee had long since worn off.

"You hungry?" Avery said.

"Famished."

They left the museum and wandered the nearby streets in search of a café when they stumbled upon what appeared to be a local newspaper office.

"Would you mind waiting on the food, Harry?"

"Do I have a choice?"

Avery pointed to the building. "If there was anyone who would know whatever dirt there was to be had on Al-Masri, it would be a reporter. Come on, Harry."

"May I help you?" a young woman asked as Avery and Harrison wandered the hallway. "You look lost."

"We are," Avery confessed.

"Oh, my," the woman covered her mouth as recognition lit her features. "Are you—you're Avery Turner, aren't you?"

"Guilty as charged."

"But you're not Carter," the woman said to Harrison.

"This is Harrison," Avery said.

"Pleased to meet you, Mr. Harrison."

"Likewise."

"Wow, I've been following you since the Discovery special about the *Fortitude* and the lost treasure from Norway. You and Carter Mosley are my don't-miss Google alerts."

"Thank you." Avery still didn't quite know what to say when people recognized her, so she kept it simple.

"What are you doing in Amman? Is Carter here with you?"

"Yes, he is. And it's a long story."

"That's just my business. Have you eaten lunch yet?"

"We have not. But we'd really love to."

"Come with me. I'll treat you to lunch and you can tell me why you're here. Deal?"

"Deal."

The reporter led them to a nearby delicatessen and bought them each a plate of meat over yellowish rice.

"What is this?" Avery said after her fourth bite. "It's delicious."

"It's called mansaf. It is lamb and jameed over rice."

"Jameed?" Harrison asked after he swallowed.

"Like...a dried yogurt."

"Well, it's delicious."

"I'm glad you like it. Now, back to my original question, what are Avery Turner, Carter Mosley, and Mr. Harrison doing in Amman?"

"How well do you know Abdulrahman Al-Masri?"

The reporter grinned. "I write about politics. I probably know Mr. Al-Masri better than most. What do you want to know?"

Avery recounted some of the story that had led them to Amman, leaving out the clandestine meeting with Senator Byers and the real reason behind their search for the pin. She was familiar with the reporting game from some of the coverage she and Carter had received following their discoveries. Some outlets reported honestly about their reasons for finding lost treasure, while others painted her and Carter as greedy young adventurers. Having only just met this woman, Avery had no idea which type of reporter she was.

"And that's about all there is to tell," Avery finished.

"That's quite a story," the reporter said. "You never mentioned how you came by this information to begin with."

"I'm not at liberty to share that," Avery said.

"Fair enough." She didn't push, which Avery thought was a good sign. "Well, I can tell you that Al-Masri is one of those political types who cares more about power than he does about people."

"I was led to believe that he's already one of the most powerful politicians in Jordan."

"He is. I would list him as the country's third most powerful politician. There's the king, obviously, and the prime minister, then Al-Masri."

"You'd think that might be enough," Harrison said.

"Not with Al-Masri. I've never known him as the type to be involved with terrorists, but if the relationship was a pathway to power—who knows? I can't say for sure I'd put it past him."

"And the idol alleged to have been stolen from his family?"

"This is the first I've heard of that, Ms. Turner. But I can tell you that Al-Masri is not a sentimental man. If he is chasing something that was taken from his family, it's personal. And if his ego is on the line, he'll stop at nothing to retrieve it."

Avery nodded. The reporter pulled out a business card and scribbled something on the back of it before handing it to Avery. "Here. That's my personal email address. If you need anything, you can contact me that way. I wish you the best of luck in your hunt. Maybe if you're successful you'll consider giving me an exclusive?"

"That sounds fair." Avery smiled.

"And I'll get a chance to meet Carter Mosley."

Avery laughed as she and Harrison got up and headed for the door. "That I think I can definitely arrange. I can't thank you enough for your honesty—and your discretion." She held the young woman's gaze to drive her point home a bit harder.

"Of course. It's a pleasure to speak with you both. And I'll keep a good thought for Carter, of course."

27

"You really trust a random reporter?" Harrison said.

"More than I'd trust Al-Masri," Avery said.

"Touché," Harrison said. "So, what's our next move?"

"We need to get back to Egypt. I cannot stand this. I want to check on Carter. Somehow."

"Just tell me we're not going by ferry," Harrison said as he touched his side.

"No, I got a text through to MaryAnn and she found us a back door courtesy of another fan of Carter's," Avery said as she hailed a passing taxi. "When I was kicking myself about you getting hurt on the ferry today, I remembered an article I read last year about ways for private flights to skip customs when you're in a hurry, and MaryAnn dug through Carter's followers until she found us a plane."

"Who is it this time, the Queen of England?" Harrison laughed.

Avery did not.

"Close. The princess of the Kingdom of Saudi Arabia. In this part of the world only a few private planes are exempt from customs interference—so you have to have the right blood or know the right people."

"Royalty? Now you're talking," Harrison said.

Avery only thought her new plane was nice, it seemed—the princess's jet had everything from a lavish marble bathtub to a fireplace, and that didn't count the TVs that dropped out of the ceiling, the calfskin recliners, or the virtual reality headsets and fully stocked bar that only had a top shelf.

Harrison sat across the aisle from Avery, leaning his seat back and sipping his drink before settling a sleep mask in place.

"You good, Harry?" Avery said.

"Possibly never better. And I've got a foot-long knife wound in my side still, so that's saying something."

Avery laughed. "This is pretty great, isn't it? Makes my plane look like economy class, that's for sure."

"Not economy. But maybe that business class upgrade."

"How are we going to get in to see Carter?" Avery chewed on her bottom lip. "I don't think the police in Cairo will be too pleased that we gave them the slip, so just showing up seems unwise."

"You can bet on that," Harrison said. "But since they have our passports, I'd bet they're currently busy trying to figure out where we've gotten off to, and you said this thing doesn't require us to check in with anyone when we land, so maybe we can use the chaos our absence should have created— plus your theory about flipping expectations on their head—to our advantage where Carter's concerned."

"What do you mean?" Avery asked.

"I mean head straight to the hospital and walk in like we own the joint. A confident manner has a weird way of making authority figures ignore you, especially if they don't think you'd be dumb enough to show up in a place."

Avery blinked. "But they shot at us last time."

"The guy lying in the hospital shot at us," Harrison said.

"Yeah, and his ID said he's a cop."

"I don't think he's with the Cairo police though," Harrison said. "If they wanted us dead, we never would have made it out of the interrogation rooms alive."

"They couldn't just kill us in the police station," Avery gaped.

"From what Malik said, they can do pretty much whatever the heck they want," Harrison said. "And what they chose to do was let us go and watch us. We want to check on Carter. I say we take a taxi directly to the hospital and see what happens."

Avery didn't have a better idea. "Okay, Harry. We'll play it your way."

Their jet landed without incident, and they disembarked and were shown through a back hallway that led out into a posh lounge outfitted with leather furniture and a buffet that smelled like heaven.

Avery's phone rang. She picked up when she recognized MaryAnn's number.

"I was just thinking about you," Avery said by way of hello.

"Well, I've been thinking about you guys constantly. Are you all okay?"

"At the moment, everything is fine."

"Gotcha," MaryAnn said. "I have a couple of pieces of information that should make you feel a bit better—one about your friend from the airport the other day who's in the hospital with Carter, and one about how you're going to get out of that airport."

"Get us out of here first, then tell me about the shooter."

"That will be as easy as going outside, friend."

Avery waved for Harrison to follow and pointed to the sliding glass doors. Out in the terminal, they couldn't walk four feet without someone pausing to look at them.

Avery could tell that Harrison was weirded out by all the stolen glances. Even she couldn't tell if the looks were just because they were Americans or because of something nefarious. After two attacks, it stood to reason that they would be on high alert for another ambush.

They stepped out onto the sidewalk in front of the airport and Avery was about to ask MaryAnn what to look for when she heard a familiar voice. "Fancy a ride, love?"

Avery said a hasty goodbye to MaryAnn and spun around, her face spreading into a grin as she came face-to-face with Duval.

28

Avery started to raise her arms for a hug before she caught Duval's slight head shake. He was here undercover.

"Hey, it's—"

"A dashing taxi driver," Avery said, cutting Harrison off. "We'd love a ride, sir."

"Your chariot awaits," Duval said, gesturing toward the curb with his hand.

After helping them with their bags, Duval climbed behind the wheel of the charcoal-colored Mitsubishi SUV. Harrison commandeered the rear seat while Avery sat next to Duval.

As soon as they pulled away from the curb, Avery reached over and gave Duval's hand a squeeze.

"I can't thank you enough for coming to help. Honestly, all I was hoping for was some intel about what we've gotten into here."

"Yeah, it's good to see you," Harrison said. Avery knew how much it took for Harry to genuinely like Duval given his background.

"How did you find us?" Avery said.

"You two stick out, I'm afraid. And don't thank me too quickly. Word is that you've stirred up a shitstorm here. Did you get a call from MaryAnn yet?"

"Yeah, I cut her short when I saw you."

"I'm flattered, but you need to call her back."

Avery pulled the prepaid phone out of her pocket and began to dial MaryAnn when Duval stopped her.

"Not that phone. Use this one."

"But this one's clean," Avery said, putting up a mild protest.

"Really?" Duval said, giving her a raised brow. "Where did you get it?"

"From a professor MaryAnn used to work with at the King Salman International University in Sharm El Sheikh."

Duval stared at her a moment without speaking.

"Fine," Avery said as she accepted the phone from Duval.

"Now, give me the phones the professor supplied you with and I'll make them safe," Duval said, holding out his hand.

"What about our own phones?" Harrison said as he passed the prepaid cell over the seat to Duval.

"I deleted the spyware I found, but we've kept them mostly off just in case," Avery said.

"Smart move."

"What are you gonna do with these?" Harrison said as he handed over his phones.

"Give me a second and I'll show you how to make them safe again," Duval said as he activated the four-way flashers and pulled to the side of the road.

"What are you doing?" Avery said.

"Back in a sec," Duval said as he jumped out of the SUV.

Avery watched as he circled the vehicle, bending down as he passed each wheel. When he finished his inspection, Duval jumped back inside the Mitsubishi.

"All set?"

"What were you doing out there?" Harrison said.

"Disabling your phones."

"How?" Avery said.

"It's a tried-and-true method," Duval said as he looked at Harrison's reflection in the rearview mirror and grinned. Duval put the SUV in Drive and pulled back into traffic. "If you look behind us, you'll see two piles of broken plastic." Duval turned to Avery. "They just don't make cell phones like they used to."

Avery smiled at him again.

"Now, about that call to MaryAnn," Duval said.

"Right," Avery said as she put the call on speaker and dialed the number.

MaryAnn picked up on the second ring. "Oh, thank God, Avery. Are you guys really okay? I'm assuming since this is from a different number that the cavalry arrived."

"I certainly did," Duval said before Avery could answer.

"I'd hardly call one man a cavalry," Harrison grumbled from the back seat.

"Don't believe everything you see, mate," Duval said.

"Can someone tell me what is going on here?" Avery asked.

"The ID you sent me from the man in the hospital."

"Is it genuine?" Harrison asked.

"Oh yeah," MaryAnn said. "It's not a law enforcement ID though. It belongs to the Mukhabarat."

"What is that?" Harrison said.

"It's General Intelligence Service," MaryAnn said.

"The Egyptian equivalent of your CIA," Duval added.

"Sure," Harrison said. "I can't even pretend to be surprised anymore."

"No wonder he got his own private room," Avery said. "Do you think the Cairo police know?"

"You can count on it," Duval said.

"MaryAnn, were you able to get anything on the charges against Marco, either way?" Avery asked.

"What are they saying about Marco?" Duval asked.

"He's being held for smuggling. Like long-term, they say they've had a warrant out for him for years for smuggling. And they impounded my plane because they say he uses it."

"Preposterous," Duval said. "I can have someone run it down in an hour if you want, but I don't buy it. He's a scapegoat because they need to be able to control you."

Avery wasn't sure if that made her feel better or worse.

"I knew this was a bad idea, Ave," Harrison said. "These are heavy hitters, not amateur treasure hunters. First we had Senator Byers's spy guy in the mix—"

"Mr. Smith," Avery said, using her fingers to make air quotes.

"Now we've made Mr. Smith's Egyptian equivalent as the guy who was trying to kill us," Harrison said.

"And he's staying in the same hospital with Carter." Avery sat straight up and grabbed Duval's arm, wide-eyed. "We need to go there. Now."

"Way ahead of you, love."

29

Duval parked near the entrance to the hospital after dropping Avery at the front door.

"I'm not sure it's a good idea to send her in alone," Harrison said.

"Who said she's alone? Besides, with her headscarf, she's the only one of us who looks like she belongs here."

"You sure she'll be okay?" Harrison said.

"Trust me, Harry. Avery's safer inside that hospital than we are sitting out here."

Avery followed the route to the Intensive Care ward and found an elderly woman in Carter's bed. Her heart nearly stopped as she looked around for her friend. No sign of him. She grabbed the closest nurse she could find.

"I'm looking for my friend but he's not here. Can you help me find him?"

"What is your friend's name?"

"Carter Mosley. He was brought in two days ago with a gunshot wound."

Suspicion registered in the nurse's eyes. "And you say you are a friend?"

"Yes, we're business partners."

"Wait here a minute while I check."

Avery watched her walk to the far side of the room. The nurse spoke in hushed tones to a man who appeared to be the attending doctor. They took turns eyeballing her as they spoke. Avery was doing her best to look calm, but it wasn't working. She watched as the doctor picked up a wall phone and spoke to someone at the other end. After a moment he hung up and approached her. Was Carter dead? Or was she about to be? Or both?

"I understand you're here about the patient who was shot."

"Yes, Carter Mosley. He was here two days ago. Where is he?"

"And you are?"

"Avery Turner. I'm his friend."

"Ms. Turner, your friend is still here but we've moved him to another part of the hospital."

"Is he okay?" she said, only partly relieved.

"Mr. Mosley isn't stable. We are continuing to monitor him for low blood pressure."

"May I see him?"

The doctor gave her directions to his room, along with the caveat that she wouldn't be able to speak with Carter as they were keeping him sedated.

Avery located Carter's room in the wing the doctor had described, but as she approached she noticed a man sitting outside the door. He was dressed in a dark suit and drinking a cup of coffee. She couldn't tell if the man was with the police service or the intelligence service, but it was obvious he was on guard duty. As she approached, he looked up at her. Avery lowered her head slightly and continued past without slowing as if she was headed somewhere else. Her ruse seemed to work as his attention shifted to one of the nurses who engaged him in conversation. As Avery passed the room, she only caught a quick glance through the half-closed blinds, but it was enough to recognize Carter lying in the room's only bed. The bed was slightly inclined, and he appeared to be sleeping. Her heart felt heavy as she noticed the IV bag and the monitors beside his bed.

Avery continued along the corridor and around the corner until she reached the elevators and pressed the down button. She had planned to try and find out if the other wounded patient was still in the hospital, but it was obvious that she had already pressed her luck by checking on Carter. She was battling a mixture of guilt over Carter's condition and exhaustion. What she really needed now was a safe place to crash and regroup. Maybe now that Duval was here, things would begin to look clearer.

The elevator doors slid open and after checking to see that it was empty, Avery stepped inside. Intending to press the lobby button with her index finger, she paused. What if the man guarding Carter's room had recognized her? What if his conversation with the duty nurse was just a ruse to convince her she was in the clear? Avery pressed the button for the first floor instead. If she had been made, they would likely have a reception committee waiting for her in the lobby. No sense in making whatever these guys had planned next easy for them. As the elevator stopped on one, Avery exited and quickly walked to the stairwell at the far end of the hall. As she walked, she fired off a quick text to Duval.

Meet me at the east side emergency exit.

———

"What happened?" Duval said as Avery jumped into the passenger seat of the SUV.

"Were you followed?" Harrison said.

Before she could answer, Duval pulled away from the curb and pointed at the hospital. "I'd say the answer to that question is a resounding yes."

Avery followed Duval's gaze. Standing in the open doorway was the man who had been sitting outside Carter's room. And he didn't look happy.

"Look familiar?" Duval asked.

"Yeah, he was stationed in the hall outside Carter's room."

Avery explained what the doctor had told her about Carter's condition and the fact that they had moved him to a private room. She was worried about his blood pressure after the gunshot.

"Don't get too stuck in that, Avery. He may be perfectly fine," Duval said.

"What do you mean?" Avery said.

"I mean they may simply be using him as bait. They lost you and they aren't happy about it. But they know you'll only stay away so long with your mate injured. The easiest play would be to move Carter to a private room and monitor who comes to see him. That's what I would do, if this was my op."

Avery hadn't considered that. "Then his blood pressure might be okay?"

"Maybe. Maybe not. The doc told you they were keeping him sedated, right?"

Avery nodded.

"They may think it's necessary for some reason, or it may simply be to keep him here. They know you guys won't abandon him."

"Um, don't look now, but we've got company," Harrison said.

Avery glanced in the side mirror to the sound of tires squealing on pavement.

"Hang on," Duval said. "Things are about to get bumpy."

30

Duval whipped the SUV onto a side street, teetering on two wheels and drawing yelps from both passengers.

"Let's try to keep all four on the ground, huh?" Harrison yelled from the back seat.

"Sorry, mate," Duval said. "I got this thing in case we had to go off-road, but it's not quite as good in a slalom."

The quick turn hadn't shaken their tail, either. Avery twisted in her seat to confirm that without the mirror. Looking around, she spotted a sandy embankment straight ahead.

"Why don't we go off-road, then?" she asked as she grabbed for the handle above her door.

"That's a great idea, love. Hang on."

As they came onto the next intersection, Duval crossed directly in front of oncoming traffic without slowing. A cacophony of squealing tires and blaring horns erupted around them.

"Truck!" Harrison shouted.

"Got it," Duval said as he swerved, barely missing a box truck coming from their left. He gunned the accelerator, and the SUV shot forward, forcing all of them back in their seats.

"This thing's really got some kick," Harrison said.

Duval was focused on the road, and Avery was too busy trying to avoid vomiting to reply.

Avery pressed both hands firmly against the dash as she saw the approaching ditch. The SUV momentarily left the ground as it bounced up and over the curb, landing hard in the dirt wash beside the highway. As they rocketed down the incline to the bottom of the dry bed and up the other side, Avery glanced in the right-hand mirror to check on their pursuers. The dark-colored sedan was hung up on the curb that Duval had jumped only a moment before. The front end of the car was badly damaged, making it obvious that they were no longer a threat, whoever they were.

"I think we lost them," Avery said.

"For now," Duval said as he gunned the accelerator, forcing the SUV up and over the opposite bank and back onto the opposing highway. He spun the wheel and pulled over to the side of the road, then looked back at the sedan. "I told you this thing was better off-road."

Avery could see the two men who had occupied the other vehicle standing beside it staring at them.

"They look pissed," Harrison said.

"No worries," Duval said. "They'll just have to get used to disappointment is all. Now, we've got to get you somewhere safe."

"And where might that be?" Harrison said. "Home?"

"Close," Duval said. "Think of it as your home away from home, for now." And with that he pulled back into the travel lane and sped down the highway.

Half an hour later Duval pulled into the parking lot of a nondescript hotel. It wasn't the kind of place Avery had become used to staying since her app sale changed her life two years ago, but it didn't look dangerous, either. Very middle of the road and forgettable.

Avery turned a wrinkled brow to Duval. "I thought we were trying to get out of public places?"

"Yeah," Harrison said. "I figured you'd take us to a safe house or something."

"You've been watching too many movies, Harry," Avery said.

"No," Duval said. "Harry is right, or at least he would be if this was a normal op."

"It isn't?" Avery said.

"Far from it. I told you, you have stirred up a hornet's nest here. There are people on all sides of this thing that will stop at nothing to prevent you from finding that idol."

"Then why not a safe house?" Avery said.

"Because my friends aren't willing to burn their entire network protecting you." He winked. "Even for me."

"So we're on our own?" Avery's voice went up an octave.

"Of course not. Why do you think I'm here? But we need to draw the players out into the open so we know who we're dealing with."

"You want to use us as bait?" Avery couldn't decide which was worse.

"You were bait the minute you stepped on Egyptian soil."

"Great," Harrison grumbled.

"We'll keep them at arm's length," Duval said. "But we can't afford to lead them to any of our safe houses."

"You have more than one?" Harrison said.

"Welcome to my world, Mr. Harrison. It has been an interesting year so far."

"This isn't so bad," Harrison said as he looked around a much higher-end hotel lobby than Avery had expected.

"I couldn't put my friends up at any old dump," Duval said.

"Don't we need a reservation?" Harrison said.

"Already taken care of," Duval said.

"Let me guess," Harrison said. "Mr. Smith?"

Duval grinned. "You missed your calling mucking about with the NYPD, Harry."

Duval and Avery walked to the registration desk, leaving Harrison to keep an eye on their surroundings. They returned a short time later with room keys.

"We got three rooms, each with connecting doors," Duval said. "It will give us at least a fighting chance in case of an ambush."

"Which based on our recent history is pretty damn likely," Harrison said.

"Now, who's hungry?" Duval said.

"More like famished," Harrison said.

"Me too," Avery said. "We've practically done a whole Ironman race today and all we've eaten was some meat and rice. Let's dump this stuff in our rooms, clean up, and meet back in the restaurant in a half hour?"

"Perfect," Duval said.

"Wait a minute," Harrison said. "What about the lobby? If we're all upstairs, who will keep an eye out?"

"Got that covered, mate."

"You mean you've got people inside the hotel working with you?" Avery lowered her voice.

"Why do you think I brought you here?" Duval smiled. "The spider never chases the fly."

31

The three of them looked like ordinary tourists, seated at a table in the far corner of the hotel restaurant perusing menus written in several languages. Harrison and Duval had their backs to the wall, allowing them to keep an eye on the entrance and the rest of the dining room.

"I don't suppose you've got a picture of this thing that people seem so willing to kill for," Duval said when they'd settled on food.

"I do." Avery reached into her bag, removed a torn piece of paper, and handed it across the table.

"Hey, I thought Byers said we were supposed to keep the files in the Gulfstream's safe," Harrison said.

"Since when have you known me to follow a rule I see no reason for?"

After studying the image, Duval handed it back to Avery. "I must say, it is quite striking, but it hardly seems like something that would warrant all this attention. I mean it's not quite the crown jewels of England, is it?"

Avery laughed. "True, but this particular piece has been in existence far longer than any of the crown jewels. Best I can tell, it symbolizes something important for the people of this entire part of the world."

"Apparently," Duval said.

"I just wish we knew exactly what and why," Avery said. "The story goes that the idol was an object of obsession for a pharaoh who ruled somewhere around 1500 BC. Abasi was his name, and from what MaryAnn found, he searched the known world for it for years, even sacrificing soldiers' lives, but he never found it. It turned up in a grave a couple hundred years ago and has changed hands several times since."

"Sounds to me like if we want to find out who thinks this thing is so important now, we ought to see if someone can tell us why that guy thought it was so important then," Harrison said. "I don't know a lot about that period, but I thought all of the pharaohs had a whole lot of gold and jewels."

"You're right, Harry," Avery continued. "It is very odd that this small artifact would have mattered so much to a king."

"Nothing on who it belonged to before he started looking for it, or where it came from?" Duval asked.

Before Avery could answer, she caught a glimpse of a familiar face across the room.

"What is it?" Duval read the worry on her face.

"I just saw our driver from DC heading for the lobby."

"The guy you thought was following us the day before your Senate presentation?" Harrison said.

"The very same. You know, the guy the local PD said they executed here?"

"I don't see him," Harrison said.

Avery turned, but the man was gone.

"Are you sure it was the same guy?" Duval said.

"I'm ninety-nine percent positive."

"So much for him just being our airport driver," Harrison muttered.

"Any chance he works for this Senator Byers that sent you into this mess?" Duval asked.

"For or against, who can tell at this point?" Harrison asked.

Duval nodded. "Would you be able to pick him up on hotel surveillance, love?"

"You have access to that?" Avery asked.

"I told you there was a reason I brought you here."

Following breakfast, Avery and Duval went to the hotel manager's office to review the video, while Harrison hung out in the lobby.

It didn't take long before Harrison noticed a woman checking him out from across the room. Dressed head to toe in black linen, she was pretending to work on a tablet but Harrison was sure she was watching him.

Before he could decide what to do next, Avery and Duval returned, shooting him a double thumbs-up.

"You got lucky, I presume?" Harrison asked.

"It's definitely him," Avery said.

"Any idea who he is?" Harrison asked Duval.

"I've just sent a couple of still shots of his face to my people. If he's a known quantity, we should hear something shortly."

"Good," Harrison said. "Because we've drawn the attention of a woman now, too."

"Where is she?" Duval asked.

"She's right over—" Harrison pointed, then stopped mid-sentence. "She's gone."

"What did she look like?" Avery asked.

Harrison gave them her description.

"So, what now?" Harrison said. "If we really did shake those guys from the hospital, we've picked up at least two more tails."

"That's assuming the two here are working together," Duval said. "Any chance this Byers woman sent a friendly to keep watch over you guys?"

"I guess she could have," Avery said. "We were supposed to meet her contact at the university as soon as we landed."

"Instead, we were met with gunfire," Harrison said. "And at least one of those shooters was a member of that Mukrack group."

"It's Mukhabarat," Duval said with a chuckle.

"That's what I said."

Duval checked his phone when it buzzed, looking up at Avery after he read the screen. "As I said, Marco is clean. No suspicion of illegal activity or open cases on record with Interpol. If he was a wanted smuggler, they'd know."

She hugged him impulsively, feeling guilty for doubting her friend. "Thank you. Anything you can do about getting him out?"

"Actually, my sources say he's safe and well, and I'd like to let the police believe they have their thumb on you with this for the time being. We should have MaryAnn be noisy about burning up phone lines at the embassy for show, though."

Avery pointed to his phone. "Text her. She'll do whatever we need."

Duval sent the message and turned the conversation back to Byers. "Anything else go differently than the senator planned?"

"Actually, it did," Avery said. "She wanted us to take a government plane to Egypt, but I insisted we use my jet."

Duval nodded. "So maybe you made it harder for her to keep tabs on you."

"You just said maybe she just sent people to keep us safe," Avery countered.

"If she did, they're doing a pretty crappy job," Harrison said.

Duval fell quiet.

"What are you thinking?" Avery asked.

"I'm thinking maybe what we need to do is go on the offensive."

"How's that?" Harrison said.

"Do the one thing they wouldn't expect."

"And that is?" Avery said.

"Knock on their front door."

32

Duval drove them directly to GIS headquarters. At the gate they were asked to state the purpose of their visit and who they were there to see.

"We don't have an appointment," Duval said. "But I'm pretty sure your bosses will want to see us."

"And why would you think that?" the guard said.

"Because I'm Avery Turner," Avery said as she passed him her Florida driver's license from the passenger seat.

The guard studied the ID for a second, comparing her face to the photo. "Just a minute," the guard said as he stepped away from the car to consult with another member of the security staff.

"You think they'll really go for it?" Harrison asked from the back seat.

"We'll know in the next few minutes," Duval said.

The guard stepped out of the booth and approached the SUV. He leaned in and handed Avery's license back to her. "Park over there," he said to Duval.

"And then?" Duval said.

"Walk through the main lobby doors to the reception desk. Someone will meet you there."

A balding middle-aged man dressed in a gray suit was waiting for them at the front desk. He watched silently as they each emptied their pockets and passed through the magnetometer. Harrison, who missed his money clip when emptying his pockets, had to walk through a second time followed by a security pat down.

As they picked up and pocketed their belongings, the gray-suited man approached Avery directly.

"Good day, Ms. Turner. My name is Ismael. I understand that you wish to speak to someone here."

"That is correct," Avery said.

"May I ask to what it pertains?"

"Certainly. I'm wondering why your people have been trying to kill us since we arrived in Egypt?"

Ismael smiled but there was no warmth behind the gesture. "I assure you, Ms. Turner, no one from our organization has been trying to kill you."

"Thank you for clearing that up so convincingly," Duval said. "Maybe we still have time to tell the reporter not to run the pictures we gave her of your agents."

"And you are, Mister—?"

"Just call me Trouble," Duval said.

Ismael's face reddened immediately. "Perhaps you all will accompany me to my office where we can discuss this in private."

"Lead the way," Avery said.

———————————

"It sounds like you have had much bad luck since arriving in my country, Ms. Turner," Ismael said after Avery told him about the attacks they'd thwarted so far. "But I can assure you that none of my people were involved in any way in your troubles."

"Spoken like a true intelligence bureaucrat," Duval said.

"Excuse me?" Ismael snapped, growing red-faced again.

"Let me ask you a question," Avery said. "If you were trying to stop us from locating a certain object, would you tell us?"

"Obviously, my position doesn't allow me to share classified information with those who have no need to know. But since you brought it up, what object would you be talking about, specifically?"

Avery glanced at Duval. He gave an almost imperceptible nod. Her attention returned to Ismael. "Hypothetically?"

"As you wish," Ismael said.

"All right, hypothetically, it might be a small idol, a pin, stolen from one group by another, with many different groups trying to be the next to get their hands on it."

"And assuming for a moment that this hypothetical idol was real, what exactly would your interest be?"

Avery hesitated a moment before answering. "You know who we are, correct?"

"It's not exactly a secret what you do."

"Well, all we want is to locate this object and return it to its rightful owner."

"And what if the owner of this hypothetical idol objected to your involvement? Would you simply leave the country?"

"Probably not now. You see, we have one friend who was shot and is still lying in a hospital, even as we speak, and another who's being held by police."

"And the local law in Cairo took our passports," Harrison added.

"But the idol—" Ismael began.

"Hypothetical idol," Duval corrected, earning a frown from Ismael.

"The hypothetical idol," he repeated, "is none of your concern."

"I might have agreed with you," Avery said. "Until your men shot at us and wounded my friend."

Ismael sighed deeply. "I do not feel like we're getting anywhere here."

"If I may weigh in," Duval said. "The way I see it, you know you're not going to scare us off, and you know we are both looking for the same outcome."

"Which is?"

"To recover the idol before this situation devolves even further. It would really be a shame to see photographs of your operatives plastered all over the news."

"Maybe even in the US," Harrison added.

"You're bluffing," Ismael said, even as a worried uncertainty creased his brow.

"Try us, mate," Duval said.

"What are you suggesting?"

"I suggest we either work together on this, or you stay out of our way and let us do what we came here to do," Duval said. "You know how good Avery is at hunting down lost artifacts."

"Stolen artifacts," Ismael snapped, momentarily losing his composure.

"I stand corrected." Duval raised his eyebrows.

"I don't have the authority to make that kind of deal," Ismael said.

"Run it by whoever does," Avery said. "In the meantime, we need a couple of small favors."

"I'm almost afraid to ask," Ismael said.

33

After leaving the GIS headquarters, Duval cashed in the first favor, driving them directly to Avery's Gulfstream to retrieve the rest of their belongings along with the bags that Senator Byers's men had loaded before they left Washington. Avery never took her eyes off the mirror until they arrived at the airport. She saw no sign that they'd been followed.

"I gotta admit, Ave," Harrison said. "I thought you guys overplayed your hand a bit back there."

"Nonsense, Harry," Duval said. "It's not very often in this business that you have the upper hand. I learned a long time ago to shoot for the moon when you have the chance."

"Even if your upper hand is BS?" Harrison said.

"Especially then," Duval said. "You've got to sell it to make it believable."

"You really think they'll leave us to it?" Avery said.

"Time will tell, love. Our threat of exposure was a good one. With no way to confirm what we said, they don't have much choice but to play along."

"For now," Harrison said.

"What about the museum?" Avery said. "You think the contact Ismael gave will really help us?"

"I still can't figure out why you asked him about that," Harrison said.

"The thing was stolen from a terrorist group—of sorts, anyway, given what the professor told us about them. Why would anyone connected with a museum risk getting cross with terrorists?"

"Because they thought this was an important piece of history?" Avery shrugged. "But I don't think some real-life Indiana Jones swiped the thing so much, as I've been thinking about everything we've learned so far, and here's where I landed: If I stole a valuable artifact from scary people and I didn't want to die, I would probably try to find a place to hide it. And something this small, tucked in among a museum-sized collection of ancient gold artifacts... Well, I thought that might be a good hiding place."

"Does your brain ever stop running when it has a puzzle to solve?" Duval asked.

"Nope," Avery said. "I'm hoping Ismael's contact will be able to let us see artifacts that aren't on display."

"And we've got free passes waiting," Harrison said. "Try that in DC."

After securing their belongings with Duval's people at the hotel, they drove directly to the museum. Again, there was no sign that they were followed.

"You really think they've backed off?" Avery said as they walked toward the museum entrance.

"The GIS have," Duval said. "But remember, they aren't the only ones who've been following us."

"That's true," Harrison said. "We've still got Avery's secret admirer from DC."

"Don't forget the lady in black," Avery said.

"Speaking of which." Avery turned to Duval. "Any word from your contacts on the man I picked out on hotel surveillance?"

"Nothing yet. But if he's a known player, we'll make him. Don't worry."

They entered the museum, then waited in a short line to speak with a ticket agent.

"May I help you?"

"Yes," Avery said. "My name is Avery Turner, and I believe you have entry passes waiting for us."

"Let me check," the woman said. She returned a moment later carrying an envelope with three passes inside. "Here they are."

"Thank you so much," Avery said.

"Of course. Is there anything else I can help you with?"

"Yes, we were told that we should ask to speak with the museum's head curator."

"Mr. Avanti. I'm afraid he's on a conference call at the moment. But I'm sure he'd be happy to speak with you as soon as he's free."

"When do you expect him to be free?" Duval said.

"Um, looks like Mr. Avanti should be available in about—ninety minutes."

"Perfect," Avery said. "That will give us a chance to check out the exhibits."

"Where should we start, Ave?" Harrison said.

"Well, the idol is half bird and half crocodile, so let's try and find artifacts that incorporate one or both of those," Avery said.

"Sounds like a plan," Duval said.

"Let's split up to cover more ground."

"Great," Avery said. "Come on, Harry."

34

After nearly an hour of wandering through the exhibits, Avery realized that there were simply too many places to look, and they didn't have enough information to know which things were helpful.

"I feel like we're not getting anywhere, Harry."

"I was thinking the same thing. I mean, it isn't like the pin is going to be inside one of these exhibits."

"We need more information," Avery said.

"Agreed. Where do you suggest we look?"

Avery missed Carter's easy smile and frequent quips—they'd developed a routine on their adventures where she overanalyzed things and fretted about time, and he kept her grounded by making her laugh and occasionally saved the day, either with a brilliant idea or a daring feat. What would he say if he were there?

"The locals always know." She heard the words in her head as clearly as if Carter was standing there.

Avery looked around until she noticed an older kind-faced female docent standing alone. The woman fixed them with a smile as Avery and Harrison approached.

"May I help you?" the woman asked.

"I hope so," Avery said. "This is such a beautiful museum, and I am fascinated by all the artifacts and history."

"Thank you. This museum is one of the finest in the world."

"It is a bit overwhelming," Harrison said.

"It certainly can be. Do you have a specific area of interest?"

"I'm working on a book about little-known ancient lore and small objects that were of significant importance to the cultures here," Avery said.

"Are you looking for anything in particular?"

"Truthfully, we're trying to uncover some information about a few specific artifacts. Do you know anything about this one?" As she pulled out the photograph of the idol and handed it to the docent, Avery noticed Duval approaching. She motioned for him to hold his position.

Duval nodded and stopped to look at a nearby display.

"Have you ever seen any pieces like that before?" Avery asked the woman.

The docent nodded. "Not this exact piece, but I have seen similar ones."

"Many?" Avery said.

"Maybe ten altogether? All of them are very old."

"Where would we find pieces like this one?"

"I have seen a few like this in storage at the university, a few inside the pyramids, and there is one in the next gallery." The woman raised her gaze from the photo and pointed.

"How much of the museum's collection is in storage?" Avery asked.

"Not as much as people think," the woman said. "We have a big space here, and tourism is an important industry, so they try to keep most things on display."

"Oh." Avery's face fell. "That makes sense."

Harrison patted her back, looking around, while Avery focused on the marble floor tile, which was how he saw the man first.

"Ah, Ave," Harrison said.

"Just a minute, Harry."

"I don't think this can wait. Isn't that our DC driver?"

Avery looked up. "It sure is."

Avery glanced at Duval, nodding toward the man following them and signaling for him to circle around behind the man.

"I don't think he knows we've made him yet, Harry."

"He's about to," Harrison said as he strode directly toward the driver.

From the corner of her eye, Avery watched Harrison close to within twenty feet of the man, as Duval was almost upon him from the rear. She could tell the man was about to bolt. Harrison nearly had him when he took off, both of Avery's friends in pursuit.

"Is everything o—" the docent began, her eyes widening as she watched.

"Thanks so much!" Avery snatched the photograph from the woman's hand and sprinted after the others.

35

Avery was glad she had chosen her running shoes that morning. While they didn't really match her outfit, they were handy for chasing a possible enemy combatant through a museum.

She sprinted after them, but they had a pretty good head start. As she moved through the next museum gallery, Avery occasionally lost sight of them as they raced past the throngs of visitors. Even without visual contact, Avery was easily able to follow their progress as they jostled the patrons, parting them like predators through schools of fish. The occasional apologetic shout from Harrison or Duval was handy, too.

The chase continued through another large exhibition space inside the museum until finally the men crashed through an emergency side exit. Avery got to the door an instant before the crash bar latched, shoving it wide and running out into the brilliant sunshine.

The pathway from the exit led directly into the large outdoor marketplace they had seen on the way in. As Avery hurried past the tents and vendors, caught up by the intoxicating aroma of exotic spices and baked goods, it was all she could do not to stop and shop. Some of the tables she ran past were even packed with rows of supposed ancient statuary. Avery wondered if they were anything like the hucksters in the US who tried to pass off weathered wooden furniture as antiquities to unsuspecting tourists. She imagined that many of the miniature statues probably still sported the "made in China" labels on their bottoms.

The angry shouts of shoppers and shopkeepers alike drew Avery back to the task at hand, apprehending the man who had been shadowing them since day one. She focused on her breathing and maintaining an even pace, dodging human impediments as they appeared like she was in some kind of living, breathing video game.

After several minutes, Avery realized she had nearly caught up to them. She could now clearly see Duval and the back of the target just up ahead. She noticed that their pace seemed to be slowing either because their quarry was tiring or because of the thickening throngs of people impeding their progress. Avery spied a thinly populated corridor between the booths to her left. Without slowing, she veered left and picked up her pace again, intending to flank the rest of them. Harrison suddenly appeared about thirty feet ahead, apparently attempting to do the same thing. *Great minds*, she thought fleetingly. Just then a large, bearded man carrying a stack of fruit trays appeared out of nowhere in front of Harrison. The subsequent violent collision caused both men to hit the ground hard, trays flying into the air.

Avery caught the guttural bark of what could only be cursing in Arabic as the angry man staggered to his feet. She heard Harry trying to apologize as she slowed down to help.

"You okay?" Avery said.

"Don't stop," Harrison yelled. "He's right ahead."

Avery sped up, taking full strides now and yelling out warnings to those ahead of her. She'd somehow lost Duval in the chaos, but she had a direct line of sight to the target.

The DC driver continued to slow as he glanced over his shoulder. She stayed right with him as he grabbed various items off tables and threw them back into her path. Avery easily hurdled the obstacles and continued to close the distance. She was nearly within reach of him when she saw Duval waiting up ahead. He was grinning, hunched over like a lineman preparing for a tackle. As the man turned his head one last time to check

Avery's progress, he ran into Duval's arms and went down hard in front of a crowd of people at a frozen fruit ice stand.

Avery pulled up behind them as a winded Harrison arrived. The driver continued to struggle but his exhaustion made the effort all but useless.

Harrison grabbed the driver's collar and half dragged him toward a nearby alcove as people gawked around them. As soon as Harrison let the driver go, they watched him scamper toward the back of the alley, running aimlessly like a trapped bug. He took about five awkward steps before his progress was stopped by a brick wall. As Avery and the others walked calmly toward him, he grabbed the handle of a nearby door but found it locked.

"Time to give it up, Slick," Harrison said.

"Only way out of here is through us," Duval said.

The man's shoulders slumped and he leaned back against the door and slid down into a seated position on the ground. He was clearly too winded to talk.

"We know you've been following us," Harrison said. "Why?"

The man continued to pant even as he shook his head.

"I'm surprised to find you so tight-lipped," Avery said.

"Yeah, you wouldn't shut up on the ride from the airport," Harrison said. "Cat got your tongue?"

"You know, I've never understood that expression," Duval said. "I mean why would a cat have your tongue in the first place?"

"You never worked a murder scene with a houseful of hungry pets," Harrison said.

"Gross, Harry," Avery said.

"Sorry I asked, mate." Duval shuddered.

"So, you must be a real hard case, huh?" Harrison said, turning back to the driver.

"What do you want to do with him, Harry?" Avery said, playing along.

"I was just thinking, if he won't talk to us, maybe he'd be more comfortable discussing things with the guys who shot at us the other day."

"Yeah," Duval said. "I bet they'd be real interested to know that there is another American in Cairo with connections to DC."

Avery watched as the man's eyes widened. She placed her hands on her hips and moved closer to him. "Well?"

Beaten, the man hung his head and muttered, "You were supposed to be on the other jet."

36

"What difference could that have possibly made?" Avery felt anger rising inside her. She felt guilty enough over Carter's condition without this guy picking at her choice to fly in her own plane.

"This is where you're going to want to take your turn to speak," Duval said as he handed the man's wallet to Harrison. "I've seen Avery get mad. Believe me, you don't want to be on the receiving end of that."

"If you had taken the government jet, you could have landed at an American airbase in Jordan, where the security is tighter."

"Why didn't the senator tell us that?" Avery asked.

"Would you have come if she'd told you that flying directly to Cairo in your own plane might get you killed?" The driver kept his eyes on the ground.

"Fair point," Duval said.

"Doesn't sound to me like anything about this was fair," Avery said.

"Does sound to me like they knew all along this was a dangerous mission," Harrison said.

"Of course they knew," the man said. "Why do you think they sent American celebrities instead of soldiers? Or spies?"

"Because they couldn't risk getting American soldiers or spies killed," Harrison said quietly. "But Avery and Carter are expendable."

Avery knew Harrison was beating himself up too.

Harrison pulled a photo ID out of the wallet and held it up. "According to the chauffeur license his name is Ben Mosul."

"Ben?" Duval asked. "You don't look like a Ben."

The man shrugged.

"He doesn't look much like a chauffeur either," Harrison said.

"I don't know who you are, Ben," Avery said as she looked at the man's ID. "But you'd better start talking before we hand you over to the authorities and let them sort you out."

"My name is Benzion," he said. "Cairo is my home."

"Sure it is," Duval said with an eye roll.

"It's true. My cousin works at the pyramids in Giza. My mother works at the central hospital where your friend is being treated."

Harrison leaned forward. "If anything happens to Carter—"

Benzion held up his hands. "I assure you he is in good hands."

"He'd better be," Harrison said.

"What were you doing in DC driving a limo?" Avery said.

"Gathering intelligence. You wouldn't believe the things powerful people will talk about openly in front of their hired help."

"I can attest to that," Duval said.

Avery nodded. "Someone in Washington sent you back here to keep an eye on us, though. Who?"

"Probably that Smith guy," Harrison grumbled.

"Or Byers," Duval said.

"No, no. I assure you, no one in America sent me to follow you."

"Then why are you following us?" Avery said.

"I'm here because I want to stop a bad situation from getting worse."

"What bad situation?" Duval said.

"There are two things about your circumstances that could cause big trouble for a lot of innocent people here, but they are both preventable for those who are paying attention. I am very good at paying attention."

"The senator said this pin had the ability to cause instability, though we haven't been able to figure out why," Avery said. "What else?"

"You or your friends getting killed. Just because the Americans were willing to risk it doesn't mean they'd let it go."

"Oh good," Harrison said. "So we're revenge-worthy at least."

"Don't you mean four?" Avery ignored Harry as she pointed to Duval.

"I don't know who he is."

Duval grinned. "And you're not going to find out either." He turned to Avery. "This makes sense to me. And assuming he's telling the truth, then maybe this senator was on the up and up, for the most part. Takes a worry off your plate, right?"

"How do you figure?" Harrison said.

"She's not after you, or running some big nefarious scheme, you see, she's just out to cover her own ass. Sending you three gives her deniability if you get yourselves killed—Avery and Carter have gotten famous for jumping into stuff like this, after all."

Avery snapped her fingers. "There's no paper trail, either. Which all by itself makes us more expendable than US soldiers."

Benzion laughed. "Do not fool yourself, Miss. There's nothing more expendable to a politician than a soldier."

"Normally, I'd agree with Captain Jackrabbit here," Duval said. "But this situation is volatile. If the senator was responsible for sending troops, even with solid reasoning, and things went bad, she could kiss the next election goodbye. But nobody even knows she sent you."

"Except Mr. Smith the spook," Harrison grumbled.

"Right," Duval continued. "Tell me, have you been able to get the senator on the horn since you arrived?"

Avery shook her head. "No."

"More for my point: If you fail, Byers can say you did this all on your own. Simply some half-baked attempt at finding another lost treasure."

"And if we should manage to find it?" Avery said.

"Then the senator will take all the credit for having the foresight to send us," Harrison said.

"Precisely." Duval nodded.

Avery felt her eye twitch with anger at the thought of having been used.

"Would Byers really send us over here without eyes on, though?" Harrison asked, nudging Benzion with his foot. "Are you working for her now?"

Benzion shook his head. "I just saw a storm brewing and wanted to minimize the impact."

"But Harry's right," Duval said. "Byers would've sent someone to monitor you."

"Maybe a woman," Avery said, thinking back to the woman Harrison had seen watching him at the hotel. "We tend to get overlooked here."

"I wouldn't at all be surprised," Duval said.

"I still don't understand something," Harrison said. "Why does Byers want this pin so badly?"

"What if she doesn't?" Duval mused.

Benzion nodded. "The game is more about who doesn't possess it than who does."

Avery nodded as she thought it through.

"Speaking of secrets, we shouldn't still be standing here out in the open." Duval eyed the crowd that had largely returned to shopping.

"If you are planning to let me go anyway, I could still be your driver," Benzion said.

"We already have a driver," Avery said.

"Your guide, then. I grew up here and I know my way around the city."

"Having a local on the team is never a bad idea," Duval said.

"Even a local the police think is dead?" Avery held Benzion's gaze as she spoke. "They gave me mugshot books to look through, and I spotted you. But the detective insisted you'd been executed."

Benzion's jaw flexed. "You must have been mistaken."

"I never forget a face," Avery said. "It was you. I just don't understand how you're standing here."

Benzion sighed. "My brother. You saw a photo of my brother. My twin—they planted smuggled artifacts in his room and arrested him because his research was too close to something they wanted hidden."

"What?" Avery croaked, her mind going to Marco, and Duval's assurances that he wasn't a criminal.

"The ancient world had some very ineffective kings. There are scholars who think that there may have been women who stepped in after particularly disastrous kings and cleaned up their messes, only to be erased from history by the kings who came after them."

Avery leaned against the wall. "You're saying the modern police didn't want your brother to research the history of powerful women here, so they killed him?"

"It was not local police. It was high-ranking government officials."

"Why should we trust you?" Harrison asked.

Benzion pointed to his wallet. "There's a photo of us in there. He was my best friend. I just want to help whoever is going to finally figure this out and make it too big to go away, and right now my bet is that you are that person, Ms. Turner."

"The man's got a point," Duval said. "It's not wholly unlike what we saw last year in the UK. It's not that the government cares about an old lie or who was in charge—at least, probably not. It's that they care about their people finding out what expert and thorough liars they are, lest people quit trusting them."

Harry opened the wallet and studied the photo.

"Is there anything you can do that would actually help us?" Avery asked.

"You are looking for information about the idol," he said. "And my cousin who works at the pyramids knows more about history than anyone I know."

"Take us there." Avery handed Ben three American twenties. "You're our new guide."

As they made their way through the throngs of market goers back to the SUV, Harrison leaned close to Avery and Duval. "Do you really think this is wise?"

"We need information if we're ever going to find the pin," Avery said. "It's tiny. But it was supposed to be the object of a pharaoh's obsession. What better place to look than the pyramids?"

"I still don't like it," Harrison said.

"Look at it this way, Harry," Duval said. "Far better to have this git under our watchful eyes than to wait around for him to stab us in the back."

37

It took Duval nearly an hour and a half to make the trip to the Giza pyramids. The traffic was snarled to a crawl almost the entire way.

Benzion's cousin turned out to be a woman named Padama: Petite and gorgeous, she had the largest eyes and longest lashes of any woman Avery had ever seen.

A tour group had assembled by the time Avery and the others arrived, bringing the total number of tourists to twenty, the most allowed for a single guide. Avery scanned the crowd for familiar faces but saw none. She exchanged a quick glance with the others, confirming that they hadn't seen anything unusual, either.

Padama led them first to Khufu, the northernmost and largest of the three pyramids. For all the times Avery had viewed photographs of the stone temples, no image could do justice to the sheer size of the real thing. *Colossal* was the only word that came to mind. Yet for something built on such a grand scale, the interior spaces by comparison were very small. The burial chamber in particular was both hot and cramped.

"How long have you worked here, Padama?" Avery said after sneaking her a five-dollar tip.

Padama turned and fixed Avery with a beaming smile. "I have been conducting tours of the great pyramids for the last three years while I continue my archaeological studies at the university."

Duval leaned in close after Padama returned to her place at the front of the group and continued her well-practiced narrative. "Easy with the tips there."

"What's wrong with tipping?" Avery said. "It brought a smile to her face."

"Nothing, except you just handed her the equivalent of two weeks' pay."

"Jeez, Ave," Harrison said. "No wonder she's smiling."

Avery looked at the contents of the tomb in amazement as Padama continued her speech. It was mind-boggling to contemplate how much time had passed since the events that led to the creation of the pyramids.

After the tour was over and most of the group moved on to explore the area on their own, Avery and the others hung back with Padama.

"Thank you for such a wonderful tour, Padama," Avery said. "Benzion told us that you were very knowledgeable about Egyptian history."

"You are much too kind. I am still learning."

"Well, I was impressed," Harrison said.

"And it takes a lot to impress Harry," Duval said.

Padama laughed.

"I wonder if you might be able to help us," Avery said. "We are trying to locate a very specific object, and a kind docent at the museum told us we might have some luck here."

"I can try," Padama said. "What does it look like?"

Avery produced the folded photo from her pocket and handed it to Padama.

Padama studied the picture for a moment before returning it to Avery. "I am sorry, but I am not familiar with this particular piece."

"I had hoped you might have seen even a drawing of it in one of your classes."

"I don't believe so, but it does remind me of the golden idol of Ammit."

"What is that?" Harrison said.

"Ammit is the crocodile goddess guardian of the underworld," Padama said. "The ancients looked to her as a source of great wisdom and foresight. If I might ask, how old is the piece you're looking for?"

"We think it dates at least to 1500 BC," Avery said. "Beyond that, we're not sure."

"And where did you get this photograph?" Padama asked.

Benzion spoke for the first time since they entered the temple. "I don't want to see my cousin drawn into something that could get her hurt."

"Relax, Bennie," Harrison said. "They're just questions."

"Questions about something that got you shot at," Benzion grumbled.

"He has a point, mate," Duval said.

"My cousin has always been too protective of me," Padama said, patting his forearm. "But I am a woman now and I will make my own decisions, Ben."

Avery watched as Benzion nodded his resignation. "Yes, you are correct."

Padama turned her full attention to Avery. "What else can you tell me that might help?"

"I know that the pin was located for the first time in several centuries in a mastaba in the western cemetery here at Giza in the early nineteenth century. But I've been wondering if it may have been removed from another burial site first. It's hard to find anything online from so long ago."

Padama laughed again. "Online yes, but the 1800s are like last week in a place like this where our history is so long and well documented."

"Where are all these documents?" Avery said.

"Yeah," Harrison said. "Could you take us there?"

"They are all over, but none of you would be able to read them if I did. They are all written in Aramaic."

"What about Avery's theory that the idol could have come from another place before it turned up in the western cemetery?" Duval said.

"It is quite possible," Padama said. "Many sacred objects were stolen by tomb raiders. It wasn't uncommon that these prized possessions would then be reburied with the thieves when they passed."

"Is there anything about the goddess you mentioned that might make something so small particularly valuable or sought after?" Avery said.

"If we assume your information about the age of the idol is correct, in the Middle Kingdom, small objects like this one, especially when they belonged to royalty or religious leaders, were often blessed and believed to possess magical powers."

Avery and Harrison exchanged a glance. Benzion's eyebrows went up.

"Do you believe that?" Harrison asked.

"In magic?" Padama said. "I'm not sure. But there are others besides you looking for this idol, no? Perhaps they believe in the old ways and desire to harness this magic."

"Maybe," Avery said absently as her eyes wandered about the space. She spotted a stairwell hidden in one darkened corner of the chamber. "Where does that go?"

Padama turned to see where Avery was pointing. "There are tunnels below."

"Tunnels?" Duval said, his interest clearly piqued.

"What's in them?" Avery said.

"Mostly they are used for storage. The burial chambers can't hold all the original objects housed here and accommodate crowds, so the objects in the displays are stored below and changed out a few times a year."

Avery had noticed right away that the space was small. But she wasn't excited about it until right then. "Are there a lot of objects in the storage area?"

"Oh yes. Many, many crates of priceless history."

"I don't suppose we could get a look down there, could we?"

"Um, Ave," Harrison said as he prodded her in the arm. "Don't look now, but the mystery woman from the hotel is back."

Avery and Duval both turned to look for the woman.

"I don't see her," Avery said.

"Got her," Duval said. "She's in the back. Too tall to hide in the crowd."

"I'd really like to get a glimpse of whatever is down there." Avery turned back to Padama, worried that the opportunity might not present itself again.

"Legend says the spirits of the pharaohs and their courts protect the treasures of their kingdoms. Many terrible things have happened even to scientists who disturb ancient idols."

"We're not afraid of ghosts," Avery said.

"Perhaps you should be." Padama looked unsure. "You promise not to touch anything?"

"Cross my heart."

Shaking her head, Padama lifted the rope, and Avery quickly ducked under.

Avery looked at Duval. "You coming?" Duval took one last glance at the mysterious woman, then followed her.

"What about us?" Harrison asked as he pointed to Benzion.

"You two keep the woman in black occupied," Duval said.

"We won't be long," Avery said. "I promise."

38

Duval pulled two small, powerful flashlights out of his pocket and handed one to Avery. The stone steps seemed to continue infinitely into the inky subterranean blackness, swallowing up the light. As they continued their endless descent, the air cooled until Avery had goosebumps—a far cry from the sweltering heat of the tomb.

"How far beneath the pyramid do you think we are now?"

"No idea," Duval said. "I'm too busy trying to picture anyone volunteering to carry storage crates full of heavy artifacts down here."

"Or back up," Avery said. "A few times a year, she said. That's one long climb."

Avery's memories of searching mining tunnels in Virginia with Carter came screaming in to take over her thoughts like the cartoon Kool-Aid pitcher busting through a brick wall. There, she and Carter had found a forgotten mass grave of sorts. What was waiting down here?

"People go in and out several times a year," she muttered. "Not at all the same situation as Virginia."

"What?" Duval asked.

"Just a prayer," Avery said.

They reached the bottom and stepped off into the sandy floor of a tunnel. A tunnel underneath the freaking desert. Avery swung the beam of her flashlight around, in awe of their surroundings.

"This is just incredible," Avery said.

"Jackpot already?" Duval sounded so hopeful it was endearing.

"No, I just meant..." Avery swept one arm around. "This. The tunnels, the pyramids, all of it. It's just amazing that it's all still here. Most estimates put this manmade room we're standing in at four thousand years old."

"Makes you realize that our own history is really just a blip on the world's timeline," Duval said as they moved away from the steps.

"When I was little, reading about the pyramids, I never could've imagined I'd be standing here someday, you know?" she said.

"Same," Duval said as he moved forward and waved for her to follow him.

As they moved deeper into the tunnel, the beam of Duval's light picked up an alcove in the stone. They poked their heads inside to find a deep recess packed floor to ceiling with unmarked wooden crates.

"How exactly are we supposed to examine anything down here if it's all packed away and we can't touch it?" Avery said.

Duval fixed her with an impish grin. "Surely Padama knew how it was stored. Which means we can interpret 'don't touch' as 'don't swipe,' I think. Besides, who's going to know?"

Avery hesitated, replaying Padama's warning in her head.

"The other choice is to climb back up those ten million steps we took to get down here without so much as a glimpse," Duval said.

Avery did not want to do that.

"Come on," Duval said, waving her forward. "If anyone hid it down here recently, it ought to be in a place we can find it easily, right?"

Some of the crates were open on top, others could be accessed from their sides. Avery and Duval each took one side of the alcove to conduct a brief search. Many of the pieces stored inside the crates were made from precious metals, and some of them were jewelry.

"Any luck?" Duval asked after several minutes of rummaging.

"Lots of cool finds but nothing even resembling the pin we're looking for. Keep an eye out for a logbook or a journal, too—anything that might give us a clue to where some of these artifacts originated—maybe that can help us figure out where the pin came from and why anyone wants it so badly. And try and put everything back the way you found it, okay?"

Duval laughed. "You aren't worried Padama will come down here to check up on us, are you?"

"She's not about to leave a tour group unattended. Besides, she would send Harrison or Benzion down first."

"Good point."

After exhausting their search through the crates in the first alcove, Avery and Duval moved down the tunnel, looking for the next storage space. About fifty feet down the passageway, they discovered another alcove similarly packed with crates.

"This could take all day, love."

"At least nobody is shooting at us down here."

"Good point. Let's swap sides this time. I'll take the left."

"Works for me," Avery said.

They had been searching for several minutes when Avery discovered a solid gold cuff bracelet with a mosaic of the bird/crocodile goddess Ammit in jewels.

"Guardian of the underworld, beneath the pyramids," Duval said. "Fitting."

Avery couldn't disagree. She snapped a quick photo of the bracelet before returning it to its crate. They searched through half a dozen more crates before Avery stopped and stood up to stretch her back.

"What do you think?" Duval said. "Had enough?"

Avery sighed. "I knew finding the pin itself down here was probably a long shot. Just because I might hide it in a place like this doesn't mean anyone else would think to. But I hoped we might find something that would give us a little direction, you know?" She threw her hands up. "A log or ledger that would give us something on where a similar item—like that cuff bracelet—came from."

Duval's brow wrinkled. "But we know the pin has been found and relocated many times."

"Yes, but we haven't been able to definitively trace it backward farther than the mastaba. Carter and I have found that knowing the origin of a treasure often provides important clues, and when Padama mentioned ancient magic as a motive for having the thing, I really thought maybe knowing where it was before it resurfaced after thousands of years might help us figure out who could possibly want it so badly, and why."

"I haven't seen anything that looks like a ledger down here," Duval said. "They probably keep those in an office somewhere."

"I guess." Avery's chin dropped to her chest. "Let's head back."

They walked past the first alcove again and had nearly reached the first tunnel intersection when Avery stopped dead in her tracks.

"Did you hear that?" she said.

"Yeah," Duval said. "A rat maybe?"

"I don't want to see the kind of rat that could survive down here." Avery quickened her pace. "Something feels off."

"Maybe it's the mummy coming after us for poking around in his stuff," Duval teased.

Avery glared at him. "Is that supposed to be funny?"

"Just trying to lighten the mood."

"Try harder."

Avery stepped into the tunnel intersection and something whizzed past the end of her nose, striking the wall beside her head.

Duval grabbed her by the shoulders and pulled her back.

"Please tell me that wasn't a flying rat," Avery said, her voice an octave too high.

"Not a rat. An arrow!" Duval pointed his flashlight at it. "Jesus."

Avery crouched into a defensive position. They both shined their lights in the direction of the stairs where the arrow had come from.

The woman they'd seen upstairs, that Harry had spotted at the hotel, was standing several steps from the bottom holding a bow, and appeared ready to fire another arrow in their direction.

"Is that who I think it is?" Duval asked.

Avery nodded, counting five more nearly identical figures staring back at them.

39

The women slowly advanced toward Avery and Duval.

"How do you want to play this?" Duval whispered.

"Two on six isn't something I've ever practiced," she whispered back.

"Well, it looks like we're about to learn on the fly."

The women split up, two moving toward Avery and three others descending upon Duval. The woman with the bow stayed near the base of the stairs, trapping them in the dungeon.

As Duval moved to block the first punch thrown, his legs were buckled by a kick to the back of his knees followed by another to his lower back. As he dropped to his knees, the first attacker swung her elbow in a wide arc, striking him squarely across the jaw and snapping his head back. They were outmatched here, in a way they hadn't been before even when their attackers were armed. These women were warriors—skilled, unrelenting fighters who showed no weakness or remorse. The next flurry of punches and kicks left him seeing stars. Duval staggered backward to regroup before he lunged forward, blocking an incoming kick before being set upon from both sides by sharp jabs to his rib cage.

"Avery, you okay?" he croaked.

"I've been better. You?"

"Getting my ass kicked."

Duval staggered back to his feet and continued to fight, but the more he tired, the wider his punches sailed, missing their mark more often than not. He caught a glimpse of Avery as the leader approached her, bow in hand. Before he could warn her, a woman with sharp fingernails connected a loaded punch with the side of his head, stunning him. He watched in slow motion as Avery's legs were swept out from under her, sending her to the ground on her back and momentarily knocking the wind out of her. As the three women continued to pummel Duval, he saw Avery spring to a standing position and snatch the bow from the leader, breaking it and throwing it down the tunnel, drawing a primal scream from the smallest of the women, who scampered after it.

Duval focused on blocking incoming blows and felt like he was making progress when one of his attackers grabbed him in a chokehold from behind. With an arm curled around his neck below the jaw, she held his head while the other two grabbed his wrists, forcing him to watch while the leader thrashed a battered Avery, finishing up with a high kick to her solar plexus that doubled her over. Another leg sweep sent Avery to the ground again, stunned. Duval tried to shout as the leader straddled Avery's hips and grabbed her by the hair, pulling her face close to her own. The woman shot Duval a glare before her attention returned to Avery, the choke hold on his throat tightening.

Now lacking oxygen, Duval struggled to free himself, earning several more blows to his ribs for the effort. When one felt like it snapped, he sagged, watching helplessly as Avery's attacker spoke to her in heavily accented but perfect English.

"I could kill you both before I leave here," the woman said.

"But you won't?" Avery said.

The woman nodded only once in response.

"Why?" Avery asked.

"You are a worthy opponent, Avery Turner, yet you have been drawn into something you don't fully understand. This is not a prize to be won in a race. This is our history. Ammit is safe. Take your meddling back to America before you and your friends get yourselves killed. There are forces at work here you couldn't possibly comprehend."

"We were sent here to help keep peace in the region, not to find a prize," Avery choked out.

Duval knew Avery had meant only to explain, but her words seemed to anger her attacker. As the woman stood, she flung Avery's head to the ground with a sickening *thump* that Duval could almost feel inside his own skull.

"Choose wisely," the woman said, her attention shifting between Avery and Duval. "I will not offer a second warning."

As the strong arm unwrapped from his throat, Duval pulled in a deep breath, doubling over. Before he could fully recover, a devastating kick to his ribs dropped him to his stomach on the tunnel floor. Through bleary eyes, he watched the warriors depart, gliding almost ghostlike out of sight. Fighting through his own pain, Duval crawled toward Avery. Just before he reached her, she turned her head to one side and vomited into the sand. The last thing he remembered was his face landing in the cold sand.

40

Avery regained consciousness in the hospital emergency ward. At first everything was out of focus—her head practically felt detached from her body; there was no pain, but also no memory of how she had gotten there.

Gradually the room came into view. She became aware of the repetitive beep of electronic monitors nearby, along with another unidentifiable noise: a low grumble, like a growl or labored breathing. Breathing...snoring? She tried to turn her head to see. Mistake: Her entire body, including her head, lit up with pain that flared out in every direction. She must have screamed, because the snoring became a loud snuffle that abruptly ended with a familiar voice.

"Avery?" Harrison scrambled to his feet.

Avery whimpered, blinking twice.

"There she is." Harrison stepped to the edge of the bed and smiled. "The former lightweight champion of Cairo, Avery Turner."

"Don't make me laugh," Avery whispered.

"How are you feeling, killer?"

"Like a piñata after a birthday party. For a baseball team."

"Then you'll be happy to hear the doctor says nothing's broken."

"Except my head?" Avery asked.

"You've got a mild concussion. They're going to keep you here overnight to monitor you."

"Mild, my foot. What happened?"

"You don't remember being attacked in the tunnels under the pyramid?" Harrison leaned closer, concern knitting his eyebrows together.

Her eyes widened as the memory of the ghostly encounter flooded back. "Oh my God. Where is Duval?" Her eyes filled with tears that spilled over instantly. She could not be responsible for getting anyone else hurt.

"They took him for X-rays."

"How bad is he hurt?"

"He looks a little worse than you. And I'm trying to help Ben and his cousin figure out how this happened. You can take me at hand to hand, and Padama said no large men had even been inside the chamber today."

Avery started to shake her head and thought better of it. "We got our asses handed to us by a group of six women, Harry. Did you find them?"

"Who?"

"The women who attacked us. The one dressed in black from the hotel, she was the leader."

"What?" Harrison gaped. "I mean, we saw her in the crowd about the time that you and Duval headed down the steps."

"Didn't you see her follow us?"

"No. We were keeping an eye on her, she was hanging out, and then she just sort of vanished into the crowd. One minute she was there and the next she wasn't."

"You must have passed them leaving when you came looking for us, though," Avery said.

"We didn't see anyone."

"How *did* you find us?"

"We got worried when you didn't come back to the tomb. I tried calling you both, then figured you didn't have a signal down there, so we went looking."

"But you didn't see our attackers?"

"All we found were you and Duval, unconscious and bloodied."

"How could they have gotten past you?" Avery said as much to herself as to Harrison.

"I don't know. Maybe there are other tunnels that lead somewhere besides the tomb."

"Maybe," she said. Or maybe they were ghosts? She'd never have considered it until right then. Logic, reason, science, computers—Avery's world had always had room only for what she could see and understand. But all the talk of magic and curses and mummies plus a wicked ass-kicking and concussion broadened her capacity for the supernatural. Six flesh-and-blood women didn't just vanish under a hundred feet of sand. She shut her eyes. Her head hurt and thinking was making it worse.

"So, who are these women?"

"I don't know, Harry. The one we keep seeing is clearly the leader and the only one who spoke."

"What did she say? Do they know where the idol is?"

"She said that Ammit was safe."

"What the hell does that mean?"

"I think it means they have the pin. Those chicks back there were some kind of badasses—I'd give them warrior goddesses, even. I could absolutely see them taking on terrorists with no fear."

"Swell," Harrison said. "So what did they want with you?"

"She told me she didn't want to kill me but she wanted me to leave. She said I'd been pulled into something I don't understand."

"Clearly," Harrison said dryly. "If only we had the ability to comply." He paused. "Do we? What about the swanky jet we took back here from Jordan?"

"I'm not going anywhere without Carter and Marco."

"Of course. I wasn't thinking about that." Harry sighed. "So...now what?"

"We know who has the pin now. So the mission is to figure out who they are and get it back, I guess."

"You're kidding me." He gestured widely to the bed and monitors. "I'm not a fan of the idea of round two."

Avery shook her head in response and was rewarded with an explosive pain behind her right eye. Gingerly she laid her head back on the pillow and tried to still herself. "Clearly I'm not suggesting taking the fight to them. This will require smarts, not strength—they might have kicked my ass, but I'm smarter than the vast majority of people."

"That's true." Harrison looked relieved.

"Where is Benzion?"

"He stayed at the pyramids to watch after his cousin. Said we'd put her in danger because she was seen talking to you. I don't trust that guy, Avery. Too paranoid, and too cagey. For all we know he tipped those women off that you were there."

"I believe his story about his brother. Who would carry a photo of their own self in their wallet? That would make anyone paranoid—and it also leads perfectly logically to him being protective of his family. Besides, I'm the one who told him to take us to the pyramids, remember? And he was sitting with you all the way there. Did he text anyone?"

"Not that I saw." Harrison pursed his lips. "But I still don't trust him."

"Some days I think you don't trust me, either, Harry. You have issues."

Avery started to laugh and grimaced in pain, staying quiet until it subsided to a manageable level. She felt Harrison's gentle touch as he held her left hand between his.

"Is there anything I can do?" Harrison asked.

Avery resisted the urge to nod her head. "Tell Duval I know where the pin is, kind of. And I want him to start thinking on how we can steal it back."

"Are you kidding me?"

"Just tell him, Harry," Avery said.

Harrison let out a long sigh. "Okay. You get some rest now."

"Thanks, Harry," Avery said as she drifted away on a cloud of exhaustion and painkillers.

41

Harrison sat in the corner watching Avery sleep. He couldn't help but admire her drive and determination, even in the face of what seemed like insurmountable odds. Just like her mom, in all the ways that counted most. The same attention to detail, analytical mind, and never-say-die attitude was the reason they had the highest homicide clearance rate of any NYPD detectives before or since. As he watched the peaceful rise and fall of Avery's chest as she slept, Harrison couldn't help but wonder what Val would have to say if she were here watching over her daughter's battered and bruised body.

"I thought you promised to keep her safe, Harry." He heard her as clearly as if she was standing by the chair.

"I'm trying, partner," Harrison whispered, shaking his head. "She got your stubborn streak."

Val had been dying when Harrison made that promise, never imagining where life would take them. It was one of the reasons he had agreed to retire from police work and move down to the Florida Keys with Avery. He figured he could keep an eye on her while enjoying a newfound life of leisure. Back when he thought her days were going to mostly consist of swimming, running, and keeping up her self-defense skills by sparring with him, anyway. Seemed like a lifetime ago from the corner of a hospital room on the other side of the world two years after Mark Hawkins got himself killed and turned Val's little girl into a world-famous treasure hunter.

It was nearly noon the following day before the hospital released Avery and Duval. Avery had badgered the attending doctor so insistently that he'd finally relented, sending them out the door with a long list of things that should alarm them.

"If any of these symptoms present themselves, you'll need to get back here immediately," the doctor said. "Do I make myself clear?"

"Perfectly," Avery and Duval said in unison.

They checked on Carter again before departing but he was still unconscious. The doctor told them that his vitals looked better, but he had developed a blood infection that had to be treated with IV antibiotics. Avery left her burner phone number and made the doctor promise to call if there was any change in Carter's condition.

"I still don't think this is a good idea, Ave," Harrison said as he wheeled her outside. "You two look like you went fifteen rounds with Mike Tyson."

"I don't feel that bad, Harry," Avery said. "Really."

"Speak for yourself. I feel like I got knocked out in the first round," Duval grumbled.

"I've got some things I want to take care of," Avery said. "And the first thing is—"

"The first thing is you and Super Spy here are going to the hotel to get some more rest," Harrison said, cutting her off. "That's what you promised the doctor and that's what we're going to do."

"But we—"

"But nothing, Ave. The hotel is safe. Duval has seen to it. No one will bother you there. You both need your rest. Look at you. A couple of second graders could lay you out in less than a minute. Is that what you're hoping for?"

"No. I just want to finish what we started."

"Harry's right, love. We need some rest and a plan."

"We know who took it now," Avery said. "The hard part is done. We just have to get it back."

"Something tells me you're underestimating the difficulty ahead of us. But we will," Duval said. "We've just got to be smart about this. Trust me."

Defeated, Avery turned her head and looked out the window at the passing cars. She knew Harrison and Duval were right, but she didn't want to lose momentum. The warrior women were the key, and they already had a twenty-four-hour head start on covering their tracks.

Duval had arranged for an upgrade at the hotel after the presidential suite came open, and the four-bedroom suite was twice the size of the apartment Avery had grown up in. It featured an open-air design with one central gathering area and an adjoining kitchen and dining room. The sleeping quarters were located off two short hallways at either end of the space, each with its own private bath. As Avery dragged herself to her room, she found that someone had taken the time to unpack and organize her clothes. Everything was either hung neatly in the closet or folded in the bureau drawers. Even her toiletries had been arranged along the bathroom countertop. It was almost like being at home.

She paused in front of the bathroom mirror, intending to freshen up, when she caught the first real glimpse of her bruised and swollen face. Gingerly she lifted her shirt to reveal her bare torso. Her rib cage was tattooed with fist-sized bruises the color of eggplants. Harry was right: She did look like she'd lost a boxing match. She dropped her shirt and limped to the king-size canopy bed. She didn't know if it was seeing her injuries for the first time, or just plain old exhaustion setting in now that the adrenaline rush had faded, but as she looked at the plush bedding she knew all she wanted was to crawl underneath the covers and sleep for at least a week. She shuffled to the window, drew the drapes, and did just that.

42

Ancient Egypt, 1500 BC

As the months passed, the women became experts at blending in. Disguising themselves as men allowed them to slip into crowds both unseen and unnoticed. Excitement buzzed through male circles as the new king continued to wield power and expand his kingdom—never mind that the backbone of society at home was slowly crumbling with every new law aimed at controlling women.

Heba's court continued to meet in secret, surveilling their adversaries, never losing sight of their goal to recover the stolen idol and to seek retribution against Amunet's murder. Abasi, on the other hand, became entrenched in building his legacy and grew confident in his victory, and so slowly lost interest in hunting for the resistance.

So much the better.

Fulfilling their regular duties by day, albeit increasingly restricted, the women spent the nights digging a new secret meeting place beneath Zefret's home. The space doubled as a meeting place and a place for Zefret to treat special patients. They were all well aware that although the pharaoh may have gotten distracted building his own fortunes, some of his loyal followers had not, and they kept an eye out for Amunet's women to violate Abasi's laws.

One such law forbade women from being out in public after the sun set. The women continued their surveillance and intelligence gathering by going out disguised, and in groups of two. On one particularly fortuitous night, two of the women followed a small group of men and overheard one of them bragging about having killed Amunet.

They rushed back to Zefret's secret meeting place and recounted what they had witnessed.

"Do you think these men were simply bragging?" Zefret asked.

The most petite of the women shook her head. "I know this man personally and he is not only capable, but he is both brutal and extremely loyal to the pharaoh."

Zefret turned to the other woman. "And what do you think, sister? You have not offered your thoughts on this man."

"I think this man either possesses the pin or knows where it is hidden," she said quietly.

"And if he is Amunet's killer?" Zefret asked the entire group.

"Then we must recover the pin of Ammit," one of them said.

"And exact revenge," another chimed in.

43

It was midafternoon before Avery awoke. Duval had slept too, and though neither was ready to do battle with anything tougher than a room service meal of lamb and rice, both were feeling somewhat more rested.

"That bed is the most comfortable bed I've ever slept on," Avery said.

"I might have to get one for myself when we get home," Duval agreed.

"Speaking of which," Avery said. "Where's my laptop, Harry? I couldn't find it anywhere."

"That's because I hid it."

"Mine too?" Duval said.

"Yeah," Harrison said. "Knew if I didn't, neither of you would rest."

"Well, we're bright-eyed and bushy-tailed now, Harry," Avery said.

Harrison retrieved both of their computers from his room and handed them back.

"Any word from the doctor about Carter?" Avery said as she powered up the laptop and opened her email.

"Not yet."

She opened the computer and they heard the email tone bing.

"Well, here's some good news from MaryAnn," Avery said.

"Spill it," Duval said.

"Yeah," Harrison said. "I could use some good news."

"Seems she has a friend in Minya who can authenticate the pin if we locate it."

"That doesn't get us any closer to finding it, Ave," Harrison said.

"She goes on to say that this friend has some military connections should we need them to help us get everyone home safely."

"That is very good news," Harrison said. "Home doesn't sound bad right about now."

A soft knock came from outside the hallway door to the suite.

"We expecting company?" Avery said.

"Nope." Harrison stood and pulled a pistol from his waistband.

"Where did you get that, Harry?" Avery said.

"I've got connections now," Harry said simply as he crossed the room to the door, carrying the gun at the low ready. "And if you think I'm going to continue waltzing around this place without a gun, you're crazy. Bow and arrows, crazed bands of thousand-year-old ghost women, what's next?"

"Dirty Harry," Avery said with a smirk.

"Who is it?" Harrison said as he reached the door and stepped off to one side.

"It's Javier," a familiar voice said. "Let me in."

Avery turned to look at Duval. "Did you?"

"Thought it was time to call in some friends."

Harrison snatched the door open to find his friends Javier, Reggie, and Oscar, who'd saved Avery and Carter's operation in England last year, standing in the hallway carrying duffel bags.

"Heard you gringos might be in need of assistance," Javier said with a smirk.

Avery hugged each one of them as they filed into the room, Duval warning them to be easy with her.

"Good to see you again, Harry," Oscar said, giving him a fist bump.

"Took you guys long enough," Duval said.

"Hey, maybe you haven't heard, mate," Reggie said. "Air travel has gotten nuts again."

"I can't believe you guys flew all the way here to help us." Avery blinked back tears of joy.

"A friend in need, right?" Javier dropped his bags on the rug.

"Yeah, maybe this gesture of goodwill will finally square things with that whole revolution snafu between our countries," Reggie said with a wink.

"Don't push it," Avery quipped.

"Where's Marco?" Oscar looked around.

"They arrested him," Harrison said.

"Using him as bait, I'm afraid," Duval said. "The local cops even had Avery wondering if her friend was a smuggler, so they're convincing buggers."

"And desperate ones, then." Oscar clapped his big hands. "This is where it gets really fun."

"I guess we'd better get started straightaway," Javier said.

Avery, Harrison, and Duval brought the others up to speed on what had happened so far, beginning with the strange request in Washington, DC, from Senator Byers and the mysterious Mr. Smith.

"Mr. Smith, huh?" Reggie said. "Sounds like someone we're familiar with."

"And not in a good way," Javier added.

Oscar punched his fist into an open hand.

"So, they basically set you up," Javier said when Avery had finished speaking. "This Byers and Smith."

"We still can't tell," Harrison said. "I think that for a while and then I think maybe she's just not as smart as someone with her job ought to be."

"What do you say we help you guys recover this trinket and get you back to your own side of the planet?" Javier asked.

"I say that's the best idea I've heard all week," Avery said.

"So, what do we know about this idol?" Reggie said.

"Not a whole lot," Avery said. "It's a representation of the goddess of the underworld, and for some reason was an object of obsession of a little-known pharaoh who ruled during the Middle Kingdom. His name was Abasi. But the history we've been able to find doesn't say he found it, only that he searched. Yesterday, we learned that in those times it was common for objects like this one to receive blessings that gave them magical powers."

"A magic bauble people are still willing to kill for after a millennium," Javier said.

"Three and a half millennia," Avery corrected.

"Okay," Javier said. "Three and a half. Does this sound like a movie to anyone else?"

"Welcome to my world, friend," Harrison said.

"So if the king was all focused on finding this thing, does that mean someone might have stolen it from him?" Oscar asked.

Avery tipped her head to one side. "I honestly haven't given that much thought. It's not like these pieces have hallmarks like the crown jewels that allow us to find out who made the thing. But MaryAnn is looking for any information she can find, so if she figures it out, she'll let us know."

Duval put up one hand. "I had a thought yesterday when I was wired up to the pain meds that I lost until just now, but here it is again: You said that woman said the pin was safe."

Avery put her index finger up, her forehead creasing with a thought of her own. "Actually, exactly what she said was 'Ammit is safe,' like it was more of a person than a thing."

Duval nodded, smiling. "That tracks with what I was wondering. Remember how you said the pin turned up in a grave in the 1800s? Well— I'm wondering whose grave that was. Those ladies we met yesterday sure seemed dead set on keeping us away from this thing."

"I think they have it, though," Avery said. "The more I think about it, the less possible it seems to me that they don't. They were there yesterday to warn us to stay away. A preemptive strike of sorts."

"But if they're afraid you might take their trinket, why didn't they just shoot you?" Harrison said. "Seems like that would have been a whole lot easier."

"They tried," Duval said. "Nearly got Avery with the bow and arrow."

"I don't think the 'nearly' part of that was an accident. She called me a worthy adversary." Avery wrinkled her brow. "Said I didn't understand what was going on."

"Um, I distinctly remember the tall scary woman telling you they would kill us next time if we didn't leave the country," Duval said. "Right before she bounced your head off the ground."

Avery ignored him.

"But just by virtue of showing up and attacking you, they've tipped their hand," Javier said. "What purpose does that serve for them? They gave away where it is. If they really have the idol, why not just stay hidden?"

"That's a good question, Ave," Harrison said.

"Maybe we were getting too close," Avery said. "Harry noticed this woman hanging around a couple of days ago, but there were several of them in the group. Who knows how many have been following us without being noticed, or what they've overheard?"

"We need to figure out why they thought we were getting close, then," Duval said. "We must know something we don't know we know."

"Exactly." Avery pulled her laptop over in front of her and swiped the screen open. "But now that the cavalry has arrived, until we figure out what that is, we might be able to do a little recon of our own."

44

Forty-five minutes and a room service delivery later, Avery had managed to hack into the security camera systems of both the hotel and the museum, obtaining several images of the woman who'd told her to go home.

"That's definitely her," Duval said as he looked at the images.

"I wonder how long she's been following us?" Harrison said.

"You've gotta teach me that trick some time," Javier said.

"Now I'll send these to MaryAnn to run through some facial recognition software I've been working on. And we'll see if we can find out exactly who she is."

"Assuming she isn't a thirty-five-hundred-year-old ghost," Duval said.

"A ghost couldn't do all that damage to you." Oscar shook his head.

"How about six ghosts?" Harrison said.

"Maybe," Duval said. "You know I've got people who can run those pictures through software too."

"No offense," Avery said. "But the stuff I'm working on is much quicker and much more accurate."

"Why am I not surprised?"

"Because she's brilliant," Harrison said.

"That she is, mate. That she is."

It took less than two hours for MaryAnn to confirm that the woman was very much a living, breathing—beatable—human. She sent an email with several attachments and followed up with a phone call.

"Great work, MaryAnn," Avery said.

"Don't thank me. It's your software."

"How sure are we that this woman in the pictures you sent is her?" Duval said.

"Ninety-nine-point-eight percent sure."

"That sure sounds like beyond a reasonable doubt," Harrison said.

"These pictures I sent you are all from news photos. She isn't mentioned by name in any of the stories, so I still don't know who she is, but that is definitely her. As you can see, she frequents museum events, political rallies, and the pyramids. But it seems she excels at making herself invisible in a crowd."

"But we still don't have her identity," Harrison said. "How does this help us?"

"I'm working on that," MaryAnn said. "I've circulated her photo to a couple of my museum curator friends since she spends time at cultural events, and I'm waiting to hear back."

"Thanks, MaryAnn," Avery said. "What would we do without you?"

It took less than an hour for MaryAnn to text Avery a name.

"Kabrirah?" Duval said when she read it to the group. "That's it? No last name?"

"Nope," Avery said. "Two of MaryAnn's sources knew of her by first name only. Apparently she's some kind of a radical who lives totally off the grid. Which is sort of the equivalent of a twenty-first century ghost, when you think about it."

"So, how do we find this Kabrirah?" Harrison said.

"Sounds like she's more of a find than be found lady," Duval said.

"She certainly found you," Reggie joked.

"This is where my people shine," Duval said. "Let me circulate her photos and first name through my network and see if anything shakes out."

Duval's intelligence contacts located an address in Cairo in less than an hour.

"Impressive," Avery said with a smile.

"I do aim to please," Duval said, drawing snickers from his old friends.

"Let's go." Avery stood—slowly.

"Wait a minute," Harrison said. "You aren't going anywhere yet, young lady. Have you forgotten how bad a beating you two took?"

"He's right," Oscar said. "You and Duval need to stay here and rest up. Harry and I will check out the address and report back."

"And what are we to do?" Javier said.

"Make sure nothing happens to them," Harrison said.

"Thanks, Harry," Avery said, smiling. "You and Oscar be careful, okay?"

"I promise we won't get up to anything good without you," Oscar said.

Harrison and Oscar took Duval's SUV, figuring if there was any trouble they would at least have the ability to go off-road. The address, just outside the city limits but only a couple of miles from the hotel, appeared to be an ordinary townhouse. A long row of tan-colored apartments sat back from the road upon a steep short rise behind a cement retaining wall. The front yard was a two-tier well-maintained combination of grass and stone and several scrawny-looking deciduous trees that Harrison couldn't identify. Stone steps spaced approximately one hundred feet apart rose from the sidewalk to provide access to the front entrance of the units.

"That doesn't exactly look like Haunted Mansion," Harrison said as they drove past.

"I agree," Oscar said. "Not entirely sure what I was expecting, but after the way Avery and Duval described the women, a normal little nondescript flat wasn't on my radar."

"I was looking for Bruce Wayne's bat cave," Harrison said with a chuckle.

Oscar laughed.

"Let's swing around and see what the back of the property looks like," Harrison suggested.

Avery couldn't stop fidgeting as she and Duval waited for a report back from Harrison and Oscar.

"The doc said rest and I'm pretty sure pacing doesn't count," Duval said.

"I'm keeping my muscles from atrophying," Avery said.

"I don't think that happens in a day," Reggie said gently. "But you are probably keeping them from healing."

"Probably," Avery sighed before walking over to the couch and sitting. "I just want to be doing something. I don't like this helpless feeling. We're not any closer to finding the idol. Carter is still not well enough to travel. And the people trying to kill us seem to be multiplying exponentially. At this point I don't think we'd help ourselves if we gave up on the hunt, because I'm not leaving Carter and Marco alone here, and all the people keep telling us to go home. At least when we're looking for the pin, we're on the offensive." She waved one hand. "This is making me feel like a sitting duck."

"Can't argue with any of that," Javier said.

"Maybe we need to refocus your brain on a different puzzle," Duval said. "Do you mind if I ask you a personal question?"

"Shoot."

"Why aren't you seeing anyone?"

Avery opened her mouth, then closed it again. That wasn't at all the question she'd expected, especially not with Duval's friends—who both suddenly looked intrigued—listening. "I...well, I was seeing someone, though it was a long-distance thing for about a year. Mark Hawkins was his name, and it was complicated, but we were trying to be more than friends," she said. "And then he...well...you know."

"Actually, I don't. What happened?"

"He died before we figured out if we could really be anything."

"I'm sorry," Duval said. "Didn't mean to pry."

"I guess I could ask you the same question, couldn't I?"

"I've had relationships," Duval said.

"One-night stands don't count," Reggie said with a laugh.

"Says who?" Duval said.

Avery laughed.

"I guess if this topic is fair game, I'm surprised you and Carter haven't hooked up, Avery," Reggie said.

"Yeah," Javier said. "Two crazy treasure hunters like you guys should be a perfect match."

"It's been a long time since I found anyone as interesting as Mark Hawkins was," Avery said.

"Maybe you're just not looking at how interesting other blokes could be," Reggie said.

"Maybe," Avery said.

Before she could give it much more thought, Harrison and Oscar walked back in flashing double thumbs-up. "The real live gang leader lives off the grid in a perfectly normal little townhouse." Oscar nodded to Duval. "It shouldn't be any problem to get in and out. We just need to learn her schedule."

45

Avery was thankful to have the conversation—and her thoughts—turn back to deadly adversaries and lost treasure. It was less complicated—and far less dangerous.

"What did you guys find out?" she asked as Oscar and Harry took seats in the winged armchairs facing the sofa.

"Broad daylight makes it difficult to get a look inside a stranger's home without drawing attention to ourselves," Oscar said.

"Luckily, I was with a professional," Harrison said.

"I'm almost afraid to ask," Avery said.

"We made entry, surreptitiously," Harrison said.

"You mean you broke in?" Avery said. "You, Harry? I'm kind of impressed and kind of horrified."

"We just picked the lock and let ourselves in," Oscar explained.

"That sounds an awful lot like breaking in," Avery said, keeping her eyes on Harrison.

"After the beating they gave you, Ave, I'm not as concerned about their right to privacy as I might otherwise be," Harrison said.

She smiled and nodded in understanding. "Tell me they won't know you were there."

"They won't," Oscar said.

"Oscar even had me take my shoes off," Harrison said.

"Did you find anything that might shed light on who these people are?" Avery said.

Harrison and Oscar exchanged a glance.

"There are idols and statues of this afterlife chick, Ammit, literally all over the place."

Avery sat back. "Really?"

"Like, stalker-serial-killer obsessive, cult-level stuff. Altars in every room, paintings, sketches, I wouldn't be surprised if this woman who came for you has a tattoo or five of this goddess."

"Which means they're not going to give up," Duval said.

"Yep. That is exactly what that means," Avery said.

"Anything else that we might be able to use?" Duval asked.

"Yeah, almost the same level of infatuation with someone called Heba," Oscar said. "There was a separate altar in the living room and everything."

"Heba," Avery repeated, pulling her computer into her lap and typing the name into Google.

"Babynames.com says it means 'gift' in Arabic." She scrolled. "I have a twenty-something poet, a makeup influencer, and a healthcare company here. Nothing deserving of an altar."

"Maybe the significance predates the internet?" Harrison asked. "It was pretty creepy in there."

Avery tried searching for Ammit and immediately got a dozen artifacts and the story of the goddess of the underworld.

"There's not much the internet doesn't know, no matter how old it is," she said.

Avery's cell rang before anyone else could speak. "It's MaryAnn," she said as she answered the call on speaker. "Hey, MaryAnn. What did you find out?"

"According to government records, the townhouse is owned by Kabrirah Farouk. There is no outstanding mortgage, and she has been the owner of record for the past seventeen years."

"The place doesn't look much older than that," Harrison said. "She's likely been the only owner."

"Close," MaryAnn said. "She inherited the property from her grandmother of the same last name, though there's no marriage of record for either woman, or for Kabrirah's mother, who died when she was four."

"I wonder if gram was a certifiably crazy ass-kicker too," Duval mused.

"Anything else?" Avery asked MaryAnn.

"Nope. I'll keep checking though."

"Can you also see if you can find anything on a god or goddess called Heba? I'm striking out with Google, but I know your network casts a wider net, especially about ancient subjects."

"Sure, I'll see what I can dig up for you."

"Thanks, MaryAnn," Avery said. "How are things back home?"

"Better than they're going in Cairo. Any word on Carter?"

Avery looked at Harrison. "Nothing yet."

After ending the call, Avery turned back to Harrison and Duval. "So they're not ghosts after all, but they are maybe some sort of religious sect." She tapped one finger on the arm of the couch. "I don't love this."

Harrison's brow wrinkled. "Doesn't it mean we're on the right track?"

"I think it means they're more serious about keeping the idol safe than I originally thought." Avery sighed. "This kind of worship isn't at all about money or power, it's about reverence. Which means this is a matter of honor for them." She looked between the guys. "I don't suppose you happened to notice the pin lying on one of the altars and picked it up, did you?"

"Sorry," Harrison said.

"But we have an idea where it might be," Oscar said.

Avery sat up straighter, wincing when her ribs twinged. "That's the kind of thing we lead with, usually."

Harrison pointed at Oscar. "Your friend found two safes inside the house. One downstairs and one up."

Avery's eyes widened. "You think they might be hiding the pin in one of them?"

"Not in the one on the first floor, it was right out in the open," Oscar said. "But the one on the second floor was hidden. A wall safe. If I were a betting man, that's where it would be. Humans are pretty predictable creatures."

"You say that like you're not one of us," Javier said.

Oscar winked.

"We need to go back and check," Avery said.

"A minute ago, you were ashamed of me for breaking in and talking about how these women had honorable reasons for wanting this bauble," Harrison said.

"I've never been ashamed of you for a minute of my life," Avery said. "And just because I can see why they want it doesn't mean I want them to let people die in the name of protecting their principles." She looked at Duval and his friends. "How long will it take you to prepare?"

"Prepare? This is a bloody wall safe, not the Tower of London," Duval said. "Give me forty-five minutes and I'll go get it myself, bruises and all."

"Assuming no one is home," Reggie said.

"Goes without saying," Harrison said.

"You're not going alone," Avery said as she struggled to stand.

"Where do you think you're going?" Harrison said.

"Harry's right," Javier said. "You need rest. This will be child's play for us, Avery."

"You didn't see these women in action," Avery said. "They are highly trained and proficient in combat, and I don't think they'd take kindly to having men break into their sanctuary. She had some kind of respect for me—I'm going with you and that's all there is to it."

Oscar looked to Harrison. "Can't you talk some sense into her?"

"Not so far," Harrison said.

"Why don't we just invite the bloody cops along?" Reggie sighed.

"Okay," Avery said. "Harry, you're coming too."

46

It was dark when they returned to Kabrirah's house. They parked across the street under a blown streetlamp, allowing Duval to use his night optic binoculars.

"You see anyone?" Avery said.

"No," Duval said. "Aside from a light over the kitchen stove, the entire house is dark."

"Doesn't mean no one is home," Harrison said.

"Yeah," Javier said. "What if they figured out you guys were here earlier and they're waiting?"

"We didn't leave a trace," Oscar said.

"That you know of," Reggie said. "Maybe they did that taped-hair trick to see if anyone broke in while they were out."

"You've been watching too many movies," Duval said as he lowered the glasses and looked back at Reggie.

"Trust me, they don't know we were there," Oscar said. "I'm a professional."

Avery wished she was as sure as Oscar seemed to be. She didn't know if it was Javier and Reggie's chatter that was making her uneasy, or some kind of post-traumatic thing because of what Kabrirah and her friends had done to her and Duval.

"So, what's the plan?" Harrison asked Oscar. "You want me to come with you again?"

"No, we've got this one, Harry. You just keep an eye on these two. We don't want anything happening to them."

Dressed head to toe in black, Javier and Oscar slipped quietly out of the SUV and into the darkness. "Be right back," Javier said as he gently pushed the door closed.

Avery's anxiety doubled with each passing minute. By the time fifteen had passed, she was crawling out of her skin with worry. "Where are they?"

"Relax, Ave," Harrison said. "They know what they're doing."

"Truth," Duval said. "They are the best."

At thirty minutes, Avery opened her door. "I'm going in there."

"That's crazy, Ave," Harrison said. "You heard him. He wants us to stay put."

"Something's wrong," Avery said. "It's been too long."

"Then I'm going too," Duval said as he opened his door and stepped outside. Before he had taken even one step, he fell back against the doorframe.

"Are you okay?" Harrison said, taking ahold of his arm.

"Just got a bit dizzy is all."

"Neither one of you is in any condition to do this," Harrison said, his tone firm.

"Nonsense," Avery said before throwing a couple of phantom punches. "See? As long as there isn't a crowd inside, I'll be fine."

"I'll go with her," Reggie said.

Before either Harrison or Duval could offer up further protest, Avery and Reggie were gone.

They found the back door unlocked just as Duval said it would be and snuck in. Inside, the house could've been found on any typical middle class American street. The streetlights spilling through the windows lit up more than she would have imagined—she could clearly see where Oscar and Javier's feet had scuffed the shag carpet, but the trails split and went in different directions. After several moments, she and Reggie found Oscar crouched inside an understairs closet on the first floor.

"Christ and crackers, mate," Oscar whispered, laying one hand on his chest. "You scared the heck out of me. What are you doing here?"

"I was worried," Avery said. "You were taking too long. What is that?"

"This is the third safe," Oscar said as he went back to work on a keypad safe buried in the floor. Avery stepped over the crumpled rug that was usually used to cover the safe and leaned on the wall, ignoring the pain in her ribs.

"I thought you said the pin was probably in the upstairs safe."

"I was wrong."

"You checked?"

"Yeah," Javier said from behind them. "No pin in either of the others. But there was a user guide for another safe in the upstairs one. This one. It must be here. I did find some papers you may find interesting upstairs, though."

Oscar glanced at Avery. "Were you really worried about us?"

"Of course. I thought maybe you were hurt."

"I'm touched."

"Hurry up," Javier said. "Before we get ourselves hurt."

"Okay, okay."

"I don't suppose there was a combination written somewhere on that book you found?" Reggie asked.

"Got it," Oscar said as the door popped open. He lifted it and shined a small penlight inside, revealing a rolled piece of paper—and a small gold pin with a jeweled head.

"Oh my God, you found it." Avery snatched up the idol, staring at it for a moment before plopping it into a velvet bag.

"Don't know what this is," Oscar said as he handed her the only other thing in the safe. It looked to Avery like an ancient scroll. "But it's probably important."

Avery slipped the scroll inside the bag too.

"I thought we were only supposed to recover the pin," Javier said.

Avery paused a moment. "Like you said, it's probably important. I want to know what it says."

"You're the boss," Oscar said as he latched the safe door and replaced the carpet. He stepped out of the closet and closed the door. "Come on. Let's get out of here."

They were halfway to the rear entry door when the sound of footsteps came from the floor above them.

"Quick," Avery said. "Someone's coming."

They raced across the living room rug toward the door. Reggie pulled the door open and motioned the others past him. They sprinted out into the night to the sound of raised angry voices coming from inside the apartment. In the distance Avery could just make out the outlines of Harrison and Duval standing beside the SUV waiting for them.

47

The adrenaline rush Avery had felt at holding the small idol and while fleeing Kabrirah's lair waned quickly, allowing every one of her aches and pains to demand her full attention. Her leg and left side burned as she struggled to keep pace with the others, the angry shouts from inside Kabrirah's house still echoing in her head. How many of the women had been there? And where had they come from? It had sounded like they materialized on the second floor, almost like a video game, which made no sense. Yet Oscar had managed to break into all three safes, including the one upstairs, before they were discovered. Had Javier overlooked an alarm? Or had the women simply showed up and gotten upstairs without anyone hearing? Avery didn't think that was likely since the closet they had burgled was under the staircase.

They reached the street that ran perpendicular to the housing project, sprinting in front of a large van, the cargo box providing them with cover should their pursuers be close.

"What happened?" Harrison asked, concern dripping from the words. "Are you okay?"

"They're right behind us," Reggie said, winded.

"What?" Harrison backed up, wide-eyed.

"Let's go!" Avery said, louder than she meant to. "Explain in the car."

Harrison jumped into the driver's seat and fired up the ignition. The SUV was already rolling by the time Avery closed the passenger door.

"Did you find it?" Duval asked.

Avery turned around to face him. Breathless and grinning she held up the velvet bag. "We sure did."

———————————

The trip back to the hotel was uneventful, though Avery kept one eye trained on her side-view mirror for anyone tailing them. Several times she focused on a closing vehicle only to have it turn off onto a connecting roadway before reaching them. Though nobody spoke, the energy inside the SUV was palpable. By possessing the idol, they had painted a target squarely across their own backs. Many people would be coming for them now. Avery knew they were all thinking about their next move.

Copying his countersurveillance maneuver at Kabrirah's, Duval had Harrison park the SUV near the hotel but outside of its own lot. No sense in making it easier for their adversaries to find them.

Once safely inside the suite, Avery produced the bag and carefully removed the golden pin.

"It's beautiful," Duval said. "But small to cause all this chaos."

"And deadly," Reggie said.

"Not sure I want to touch it," Harrison said.

"You believe in ancient magic, my friend?" Javier said.

"Not normally," Harrison said. "But that little bugger has been the origin of a lot of pain as of late."

"That's far more to do with the people hunting it than it is with any power the object itself has," Avery said.

"Hard to believe something that tiny can be so powerful," Oscar said absently.

"Not to me," Harrison said. "I felt the same way the first time I met Avery."

"Aw, Harry," Avery said.

"As touching as this Hallmark moment may be," Duval said, "we need a plan, friends. I figure we've got less than an hour before word gets out that we've got the idol and all hell breaks loose."

"He's right, Avery," Harrison said. "We completed the mission but amplified our personal risk by doing so. We need to shift our focus to getting out of here with Carter and Marco—and maybe how this thing could help us do that." He glanced at Duval. "I'd say first that we've got to keep moving if we're to have any chance of getting out of here in one piece, with or without the pin."

"Our first stop should be MaryAnn's other professor friend in Minya."

"Can we trust him?" Harrison said.

"MaryAnn trusts him," Avery said. "And Yazir has offered to authenticate the pin for us."

"You really think those chicks beat the snot out of you two to warn you away from a fake?" Oscar asked.

"I think they might be smart enough to put a decoy in a safe," Avery said. "And like Harry said, we need to move and we need an exit strategy that gets everyone home safely."

"That's good enough for me," Duval said.

"You sure about taking the train, Harry?" Avery said as she studied the pin, turning it over in her hands.

"Yeah," Duval said. "If memory serves, you gave your last excursion by rail a two-star review."

"Well, I gave the stabby ninjas aboard the ferry a one star," Harrison said. "I figure if we at least mix it up a bit, we can keep these people on their toes. Plus, the train obfuscates the risk of highwaymen with you two in no condition to fight."

"Sound advice, mate," Reggie said.

The Ramses Railway Station, named after Pharaoh Ramses II whose statue once graced the entrance, was the central station of Cairo, a beautifully designed mecca connecting rail passengers to anywhere in Egypt as well as bus transport and taxi services.

The seats Harrison booked were for the midnight train to Minya. They were all feeling the exhaustion of the trip. Even Reggie, Javier, and Oscar, the most recent arrivals, looked in need of rest. The station was sparsely populated. Avery was surprised, given the dense population of the city, but enjoyed the peace and quiet. Despite the colorful design of the station and the foreign feel of the area, travel was still travel, and there was a familiarity about waiting to board, much like anywhere else she had traveled.

The tired treasure hunters trudged up the steps onto the train and handed their boarding passes to the conductor. The conductor smiled and exchanged a wordless nod with Avery. She momentarily tightened her hold on her travel bag before realizing that he was only one of a handful of people she had met over the last several days who hadn't wanted to harm them. It was a pleasant change of pace, and she relaxed her grip.

They each picked a seat in the private cabin car, close enough to each other to feel comfortable but far enough away to allow some privacy. Avery took a window seat directly across from Duval. She stared blankly through the glass as the train lurched forward, then began to roll out of the brightly lit station into the dark starlit night.

"Do they serve food on this train?" Harrison said after they'd gotten settled. "I forgot to check."

"Do you always think about your stomach, Harry?" Javier said.

"No. Sometimes I think about why I let Avery talk me into all these crazy adventures."

"You'd be bored otherwise, mate," Duval said.

"I could stomach a little boredom, I'll tell you."

A light knock came from the other side of the hallway door. Reggie got up and opened it to find the night porter standing there with a tray of finger food.

"Would any of you care for a snack?" the porter said.

"You bet your bippy," Harrison said, getting to his feet. "What do you got?"

The porter listed off the various treats, including something called basbousa.

"That is delicious," Avery said as she tried a bite.

"No kidding," Harrison agreed.

"What's in it?" Oscar asked.

The porter opened his mouth to answer but Harrison cut him off before he could. "Don't tell me. I don't want to know."

"Why not?" Duval asked.

"Because he'll say something like scorpion brain pâté, and it will ruin it for me."

Avery laughed as the porter departed with a confused expression. She returned to gazing at the night sky until she felt the first tugs of sleep. She hadn't realized just how exhausted she was until the gentle sway of the train car began to take hold.

Twenty minutes later, they were well outside the city, and the only sound inside the cabin was the faint rhythm of Harrison snoring. Avery was still awake, though her eyes were closed, and her head had begun to bob up and down as she fought the overpowering urge to slumber. She had nearly drifted off when another knock came from the hallway door.

Harrison gave a loud snort as he awoke. "What now?"

"Maybe it's the dessert course," Reggie said.

"Ha-ha," Harrison said as he stood and opened the door. "What can I do for—?"

Avery looked up to see why Harrison had paused mid-sentence.

"Gun!" Harrison shouted as he tried to slam the door in the man's face.

The man, stronger than he looked, pushed back against Harrison, pushing his gun hand through the door, and trying to fire blindly into the walls of the cabin. Duval grabbed the gun and pulled the man's arm farther through the opening while Avery and Reggie jumped up and helped Harrison with the door. Duval twisted the gun free of the man's grasp before he could fire a single shot. Realizing that they couldn't close the door on the burly intruder, Avery changed tactics and whipped the door open. Charging past Harrison, she delivered a kick to the center of the man's chest that sent him backward into the opposite wall of the hallway. Before the man fully recovered, Avery moved in and swept his feet out from under him, and he crashed to the floor of the rail car. As she turned to deliver another strike, she saw two more men closing quickly on her position from the far end of the hall.

"Need a little help out here," Avery said as she squared her shoulders and prepared for the next wave of attackers.

"I'm with you," Oscar said.

"Me too," Duval and Reggie said in unison.

"Guess I'm the odd man out," Harrison said.

"Not necessarily, Harry," Avery said before delivering an elbow to the first assailant's head, dropping him unconscious to the floor. "There's two more coming from behind."

"Got 'em," Harrison said as he and Javier moved to cut them off.

Avery stepped forward as the first of her attackers approached, closing the distance before the man could set himself for a punch. She ducked his attempt at a roundhouse and drove her foot into his kneecap while Oscar delivered a devastating uppercut. The man cried out and went down with a thud. Before Avery could turn her attention to the second man, he moved in from behind and grabbed her in a bear hug. He was taller than Avery and barrel chested. He lifted her feet off the floor and pinned her arms against her sides, hurting her bruised ribs and making it impossible for her to mount any kind of counterattack. She was about to ask Oscar for some help when he reengaged with the first attacker as the man regained his feet. Farther down the hallway, every person in her group was squared off with another attacker. Realizing that she was on her own, Avery lowered her head to her chest and drove it backward. As she felt the back of her head connect with the man's chin, his arms loosened their hold on her slightly, but before she could slip free, the arms tightened around her again and he began shuffling her toward the open doorway at the end of the car.

Avery continued to struggle, kicking the man in the calves and delivering face strikes with the back of her head, but to no avail. The burly man didn't seem to be fazed in the least following her first strike. Avery realized to her horror that she was quickly tiring and unable to cry out for help. The man's python-like hold on her prevented her from being able to draw a full breath. Each time she exhaled, the man squeezed tighter.

Avery felt the chill of the night air as the man stepped out onto the platform and moved toward the railing. It was clear that he intended to throw her off the train. She made one last effort to stop him by wrapping her legs around the doorframe and slamming the back of her head into his nose. She couldn't hear the impact due to the sound of the wind whipping past, but she felt the satisfying crack of bone and cartilage. The man's arms loosened again and this time she was able to slip free. She turned just in time to watch as Oscar delivered an uppercut to the man's chin that knocked him from the platform out into the night. One moment he was there and the next he disappeared into the darkness.

Avery stayed on her knees for a beat, taking deep breaths.

"You okay?" Oscar asked, holding her shoulders and studying her face after he helped her up.

Avery nodded. "I won't be in about an hour, but adrenaline is the most effective painkiller there is. Thanks."

"Don't mention it."

Avery and Oscar hurried to the far end of the hallway, where Harrison, Javier, Reggie, and Duval were fighting with three other men.

For the next several minutes, the hall was filled with the sound of grunts and groans and things breaking as punches were thrown and kicks delivered until the only people left standing were Avery, Harrison, and the four Brits.

The empty train and red-eye skeleton crew combined to offer them absolutely no help. Lucky for them, they didn't need it.

"Everyone okay?" Avery said.

"I'm good," Javier said.

"Me too," Reggie said.

"Right as rain, love," Duval said. "Though I'd say we'll pay for that later."

"What about you, Harry?" Avery said.

"Still standing, but I'm giving this train two stars as well."

49

They dragged the four unconscious men inside the sleeper cabin and bound them with duct tape from Duval's go bag.

"You always carry duct tape?" Avery said with a smirk.

"Never know when I might be needed to fix something," Duval said.

Avery and the others thoroughly searched each of the men, looking for anything that might identify them, but came up empty.

"I'll take first watch," Oscar said.

The rest of the trip was uneventful. After the fight, everyone had far too much adrenaline to sleep, and it was nearly dawn by the time they arrived at the station in Minya.

All four of the attackers had regained consciousness by the time they pulled into the station. Reggie and Oscar added more duct tape, securing them to each other inside the cabin. All four glowered at them, eyes drawn low over their taped mouths.

"If looks could kill, huh?" Javier said.

"That should hold them until we're well away from here," Avery said. "Thank you, gentlemen."

Harrison shook his head as he looked at the men. "I sure wish we only had one group coming after us, Ave. I'm beginning to think this doohickey might actually be cursed."

Avery couldn't disagree.

As they disembarked, Avery felt every one of her injuries.

"You okay?" Oscar said again.

"I'm fine," Avery said. "I just really need some rest."

"And maybe a full day of nobody trying to kill you," Harrison said.

"That too."

They piled into the first taxi they found that was large enough to accommodate all of them. Avery noticed one of the police officers patrolling the station eyeballing them as they got situated. She worried for a moment that he might stop them or summon other officers but after several long moments the officer turned and continued on his way.

"Where are you going?" the taxi driver said in broken English.

Avery recited the address MaryAnn had sent them.

The driver nodded his understanding and pulled away from the curb.

"Well, I don't know how, but we made it," Harrison said.

"Just barely, mate," Duval said. "My bruises have bruises."

"I hope this little trinket is worth all of this trouble, Ave," Harrison said.

As Avery touched the velvet sack holding the pin, she hoped so too.

The house at the address MaryAnn had provided was unremarkable. A beige-colored single-story flat on a postage-stamp-sized lot, consisting of sand and overgrown weeds. It didn't look to Avery like anyone had ever cared for the exterior.

"You sure this is the place?" Reggie said as they climbed out of the taxi and Avery paid the driver.

"It's the right address," Avery said.

"It may be the right address, but it doesn't look like he was expecting company," Javier said. "What a dump."

"Maybe he's just one of those blokes who sits at his computer all day," Duval offered.

"Maybe," Avery said as she stepped through the gate and walked toward the front door.

As she reached out a hand to knock, Harrison stopped her.

"The door's been forced, Ave."

"Harry's right," Duval said. "It would appear we aren't the first ones here."

Avery looked around for something to use as a weapon, finding a rusted piece of iron bar that had once been part of a window grate leaning up against the outside wall near a faucet. She picked it up and pushed the door open. A quick look inside confirmed that the place had been ransacked.

"Professor Yazir," Avery called out. "It's Avery Turner, MaryAnn's friend. Are you here?"

"Doesn't look like anyone's home," Oscar said.

"And it doesn't look like he left of his own accord, Ave," Harrison said.

"Harry's right," Duval said, pointing to a crimson splash of blood on the floor next to an overturned chair.

Harrison knelt down for a closer look. "This is fresh."

"First order of business is to make sure there's no one here," Duval said.

"Exactly," Harrison said. "Let's split up."

They searched every inch of the ransacked interior of the house, but the man they had come to meet was gone.

"I think we're gonna need another way to authenticate this thing, Ave," Harrison said.

"Or we need to figure out where they've taken him," Reggie said.

"He must still be alive. Otherwise, why not simply kill him and leave him here?"

"Makes sense," Duval agreed. "But only if he has something they really want."

"But what?" Oscar said.

"Maybe they knew we were coming here," Harrison said.

"Or thought we already had," Javier said, completing his thought.

"That would certainly explain the mess," Duval said.

"So, what's our next move, Ave?" Harrison said.

"You can start by putting your hands in the air," a voice commanded from the next room.

Avery complied and turned to see two uniformed police officers pointing weapons at them.

"Great," Harrison groaned. "More guns."

50

Avery and the others were handcuffed and separated before being escorted to the back of several police vehicles. The officer who appeared to be in charge questioned each of them at length on the scene.

"I told you, we came here to visit the professor," Avery said. "Everything was like this when we arrived."

"How do you know the homeowner?" the officer said as he glared at her accusingly.

"I don't. But we have a mutual friend who suggested that we stop by and say hello while we were in Egypt."

"Hello?"

"Yes."

"And who is this mutual friend?"

Avery toyed briefly with the idea of making up a story instead of giving him MaryAnn's name and phone number, but she knew getting caught in a lie would only make their situation worse. Besides, she had no way of knowing what the others had already told him.

The officer exited the vehicle after obtaining MaryAnn's contact information. Avery noticed that one of the neighbors had gone from merely watching the proceedings to becoming an active participant. The woman was speaking to one of the other officers and pointing animatedly at the house.

Oh, please let her say that she saw what happened before we got here, Avery thought. The officer in charge, waved over by the other officer, began speaking with the woman. Avery shifted in her seat, hoping to get a glimpse of Harrison, or the others, but the sun reflecting off the windows kept her from seeing inside the other cars. After what seemed like an eternity, the officer in charge stepped away from the woman and made a cell phone call, presumably to MaryAnn.

Avery continued to shift around in the back seat, trying to find a position that prevented the handcuffs from digging into her wrists, but there didn't seem to be one. She wondered if it was possible for every single part of her body to hurt at once. She felt like one big bruise.

Complaining, even in her own head, brought instant guilt over Carter's condition. Just the thought of him pulled her thoughts from her own injuries as soon as she realized they'd never received an update from his doctor. And poor Marco, sitting in jail accused of something Duval said he didn't do—had it really been two days since they talked about how to get him out? Avery wondered if any of Duval's intelligence friends had made progress on that front. There was so much going on, it was hard to remember to check everything.

Avery was pulled from her reverie by someone opening the rear door to the police car. It was the officer in charge.

"Step out of the vehicle, Ms. Turner," he said.

The officers freed Avery and the others after MaryAnn confirmed Avery's story about the professor, and the neighbor told the police that she had watched the professor forced out of his home by three figures dressed in black shortly before Avery arrived.

"My apologies for the confusion, Ms. Turner," the officer said.

"You're just doing your job," Avery said. "My mom was an officer. I understand."

"It seems that you are a victim of circumstances."

"And bad timing," Harrison grumbled.

"Yes," the officer said. "I've been on the phone to several other members of the National Police force. Trouble seems to follow you wherever you go. You might be the unluckiest tourists I have ever met. It seems that there was also some sort of altercation on board your train last night."

Duval widened his eyes. "Really? We didn't hear anything."

"We were all asleep," Javier said.

The cop didn't buy a word of that. "Perhaps Egypt just isn't your cup of tea."

"Good one, mate," Reggie said.

"When will you be returning to America?" the officer said.

"We need our plane and our passports back to do that," Avery said. "The Cairo police took them last week. And we have some friends we won't leave who aren't able to travel right now."

"I see," the officer said. "I hope you all make it home in one piece, then."

———————

The police summoned a taxi for them, and Avery directed the driver to take them to the closest hotel. She knew if they didn't get some proper rest soon, none of them would be much good to anyone.

"You sure about this place, Ave?" Harrison asked as the taxi pulled into the lot.

"Not at all. But I don't think we've got many options at this point, do you?"

They piled out of the taxi and Avery paid the driver. They booked the only four-room suite the hotel had, along with two adjoining rooms, then dragged their bags up to the rooms.

"This isn't half-bad," Duval said as he moved about the main space.

"I'm glad you approve," Avery said.

"I'll take the room closest to the door," Harrison said.

"Why you?" Duval said.

"Because the way I'm feeling right now, no bad guy in his right mind would want to mess with me."

"Or bad gal," Avery said, thinking of Kabrirah.

"Which reminds me," Harrison said. "How long do you figure it will be before the ladies show up to reclaim their pin? If they stole it from actual terrorists, we must look like babies with a shiny lollipop to them."

Avery looked at Duval.

"I can't imagine it will be long," Duval said. "Kabrirah didn't strike me as the forgiving type. She has to know we have it, so it's just a matter of how long it takes her to catch up to us."

They ordered a huge room service breakfast of falafel, eggs, cheese, and bread. Even Harrison, who was usually fussy when it came to eating strange foods, gobbled up his meal with gusto. Avery only ate half of the food in front of her, before quietly sipping her coffee.

"Aren't you hungry?" Duval said.

"Not particularly," Avery said.

"Do you mind?" Harrison said as he reached for her plate.

"Help yourself, Harry."

"Penny for your thoughts," Reggie said as he pushed his empty plate away and leaned back into the sofa.

"I'm just wondering how it is that I've gotten us all so far in over our heads."

"You mean we, don't you?" Duval said. "How we got so far in over our heads? We all walked into this willingly, remember?"

"Well..." Harrison said.

"Duval's right," Javier interrupted. "None of us would be here if we didn't want to be."

"Thanks," Avery said as she opened her bag and fished out the idol. "I just keep wondering if this little guy is worth it. And what craziness will knock on the door next."

"I suggest we get some rest while we can, before we find that out," Duval said.

"Duval's right," Avery said. "But I have to admit that I'm worried about who's going to show up next if we try. I mean, those guys last night found us on a train. That we didn't book in advance. And then someone took Mary-Ann's contact out of his home before we got near the place. If people you two can't make are tailing us, even anticipating our moves...well, like you said—they aren't amateurs."

Reggie and Oscar raised their hands. "Don't worry about a thing," Reggie said. "You get some rest and we'll take the watch."

51

They slept until early afternoon. Avery awoke feeling refreshed for the first time since they'd landed in Cairo to a hail of bullets. She turned on the shower in her private bathroom, adjusting the spray until the water was as hot as she could stand it. Peeling off her T-shirt, she checked herself in the mirror. Avery frowned as she took in the field of multicolored blotches that comprised the skin of her arms and torso. Several of her ribs were badly bruised, but at least nothing was broken. She checked to make sure the idol was still safely concealed beneath the mattress in her room, then climbed into the shower.

Clean and dressed, Avery joined the others in the common room. Oscar stood near the window looking out for trouble like a sentry.

"Thank you for keeping us safe," she said, patting his shoulder.

"Of course," Oscar said.

"Better?" Duval asked her from the corner of the sofa.

"The restorative powers of a hot shower really can't be overstated," Avery said.

"Okay, so we slept, now we need food," Harrison said.

"I checked with the front desk," Duval said. "There's a place not far from here that's supposed to have the best lamb on the planet."

"As hungry as I am, I don't care if it's only second-best," Harrison said. "Let's go."

They caught a taxi to the restaurant. Avery watched as Reggie and Oscar kept their heads on a swivel. It was obvious that they took their security assignment seriously.

Before leaving the hotel, Avery had made another attempt at dressing to conceal her identity—and some of her bruises. Her accessories included two scarves and oversized dark glasses. As they traveled along, she caught Javier staring at her.

"What?"

"Nothing."

"Um, you weren't staring at me for no reason. What is it?"

"Fine. I know you're trying to blend in, but it's not working. You look more like a young Audrey Hepburn on vacation."

"Wow, thanks." Avery beamed.

"I'm impressed that he knows who Audrey Hepburn is," Harrison said.

"I used to love watching those old American movies," Javier said. "Sabrina is a favorite."

"There may be hope for you guys yet," Harrison said.

"We're here," Duval said as the driver turned into the parking lot.

Avery, Duval, and Harrison sat at a table near the rear of the restaurant while Duval's men waited outside keeping their eyes peeled for trouble.

"You sure the guys don't want to eat with us?" Avery asked as she perused the menu.

"They ate at the hotel while we slept. Trust me, they are far happier on guard duty than they would be in here."

The lamb was certainly the best Avery'd ever had. As they ate, Avery kept track of everyone coming and going from the dining room.

"What's wrong?" Harrison said.

"I just keep getting this weird feeling that we're still being watched," Avery said.

Duval scanned the room. "As long as I don't see six women dressed in black seated at the same table, I'd say we're okay in here."

"You're probably right," Avery said.

"So, what's the next move?" Duval said. "I mean, without MaryAnn's contact, what are you planning to do with the idol?"

"I honestly don't know," Avery said as she reached into her bag and touched the idol through the false compartment. Despite its small size, there was something comforting about it. As if it really did hold some kind of ancient magic. "I'm expecting MaryAnn to call back with another option any time now."

They were nearly finished eating when Harrison nudged Avery's leg under the table.

"What?"

"Don't be obvious about it, but I think we've got company."

"Where?" Avery said as she lifted her glass and took a drink, allowing herself a view of the dining room.

"The two women seated at the far-left side of the dining room and two others near the front," Harrison said. "I can't swear to it, but I think they've been checking us out."

"Did they come in together?" Avery asked.

"About four minutes apart," Duval said.

"Is there anything that gets by you?" Avery said.

"Not much."

"Is it them?" Harrison said.

"I can't be one hundred percent," Avery said.

"Believe it or not, we didn't get a good look at their faces when they were beating us up, Harry," Duval said.

"Except for the leader, Kabrirah," Avery said. "I'll never forget her face."

"Do you see her now?" Harrison said.

"No," Avery said. "But that doesn't mean she isn't close by."

"So, how do we find out if these are the same women?" Harrison asked.

"See if they take the bait?" Avery said as she wiped her mouth with a napkin and stood up.

"Where are you going?" Duval said.

"The restroom to see if anyone follows."

Duval pursed his lips and nodded. "Sound strategy. Harry and I have your back."

Avery had barely disappeared down the hallway to the restrooms before two of the women from the closest table rose and followed.

"I guess that answers that question," Harrison said as he pushed his chair back and stood up.

"Either that or they're trying to pull the old chew and screw," Duval said.

"How is it you can even make that sound regal?" Harrison said.

Duval winked. "It's all in the accent, mate."

They turned the corner to find the hallway empty. The door to the women's room was closed and no sound came from inside.

Harrison hesitated at the door. "What if we're wrong? I don't want to go barging in on three women simply using the bathroom."

"Avery might be in trouble, Harry," Duval said. "I'll take the chance."

He shoved open the door, the scene too alarming for him to revel in the fact that he'd been right. The larger of the two women had her hand around Avery's throat, pinning her against the wall, while the other rifled through Avery's bag.

"Let her go," Duval yelled.

"If it isn't the pretty boy who can't fight," the woman holding Avery sneered.

"I said let her go." Duval stepped closer, though wary of the injuries they were capable of inflicting.

The woman holding Avery's bag dropped it on the floor of the restroom and assumed a defensive stance. "Why don't you make us?"

Harrison pushed past Duval and pointed a gun at the woman holding Avery. "Let her go."

The woman holding Avery released her and backed away with her hands raised. The other woman stared at the gun in Harrison's hand like it might bite, then backed away too.

"You've got quite a way with the ladies, Harry," Duval said as he stepped in and retrieved Avery's bag.

"You okay?" Harrison asked Avery, who was gulping air and rubbing her neck.

"I am now. Thanks. Any idea where the other two are?"

As if in response to her question, the bathroom door burst open, striking Harrison's arm, sending the gun skittering across the tile floor. The two women from the other table rushed in and engaged Harrison and Duval. Avery scrambled after the gun but one of the women kicked her in the chin before she could recover it, knocking her to the floor. Amid a blur of punches, kicks, and elbows the fight spilled out into the hallway as the bathroom door was torn off its hinges when Harrison knocked the tallest warrior woman through it.

Duval was barely holding his own against the woman who'd been going through Avery's bag when a quick glance confirmed that Avery was now taking out her anger on the woman who had been choking her and had clearly gained the upper hand. Harrison's gun was nothing but a dark blur as it slid around the floor between feet like a hockey puck.

The lavish bathroom was quickly destroyed as the melee continued. Every mirror shattered, a pedestal sink was ripped from the wall, and water sprayed out into the room, wetting the floor. As Avery made another grab for the gun, she was rewarded with a hard kick to the ribs for her trouble, the pain buckling her knees and dropping her where she stood. Fighting to regain her feet, she heard approaching sirens. So did everyone else—the four women fled through the kitchen, leaving Avery and her friends battered and bruised but alive.

"Never thought I'd love that sound," Duval quipped, rubbing a jaw that was already turning purple.

"It grows on you," Harrison said.

"Everybody okay?" Avery asked.

"Not sure what okay is anymore," Duval said as he grabbed Harrison's gun and climbed to his feet. "Here, Harry. You might want to hide this before the cavalry arrives."

Harrison tucked the gun in the back of his waistband.

"How will we ever explain this?" Duval asked. "Those dames are grade A warriors."

Avery picked up her bag and removed a stack of bills. "I'm thinking we buy our way out with a bathroom remodel."

52

The restaurant's surveillance cameras had footage of the women following Avery into the restroom, and audio picking up the scuffle, so the owner tripped over himself apologizing to her and tried to refuse to let her pay for the damage, but Avery insisted. The sirens belonged to an ambulance that drove right by, but Avery was sure thankful they'd come along when they did.

Duval said something to the driver that Avery couldn't understand.

"You speak Aramaic?" Avery asked.

Duval nodded.

"Is there anything you guys can't do?" Harrison shook his head.

"We didn't do such a great job of protecting you," Oscar said.

"It's not your fault they snuck up on us," Avery said.

"Still, we should have picked up on that possibility," Reggie said.

"It's not your fault," Avery repeated. "The one thing we've been good at since we got here is underestimating the people who are after this pin."

"Can you believe they actually thought you'd have it inside your bag?" Duval said, laughing.

Avery removed the idol from the false compartment and held it up. "I did. Harry and I haven't had great luck securing things in hotel rooms."

"You've got brass ones, Avery," Javier said.

"What?" Avery said. "It was the safest place I could think to keep it."

Before anyone could say more, Avery's cell phone rang.

"What's new, MaryAnn?" Avery asked, clicking the speaker button.

"We've got more trouble here than I know what to do with, Avery," MaryAnn said. "I'm not even sure where to start."

53

Ancient Egypt, 1500 BC

Though the women of ancient Egypt enjoyed more freedoms and rights than many do in much of today's world, they were not warriors. And society had never meant them to rule as monarchs, a line that Heba had dared to cross.

Women were not trained to fight. They were expected to be scholars and scribes, teachers and doctors. To nurture society while the men fought the battles. Zefret knew this better than most. But as she sat in the dark amid the flickering firelight, looking out upon her group, the group she had never even wanted to lead, she knew that things were about to change. They would either effect the change they wished to see or go down trying. She wondered if the cost of failure might be too great to bear.

As she and the others prepared for what was to come, the new pharaoh was busy stripping the women in their society of the very freedoms they had long taken for granted. Abasi's fear of strong women was precisely why Heba had chosen to ascend the throne following the death of her husband. She had seen something evil in his son, something unfit to lead. She had known that under Abasi's rule, unchecked, her kind would wilt and wither.

Under Heba's rule, Egyptians had made great leaps and discoveries.

The country's wealth had nearly tripled. But Heba and Amunet had been wise enough to predict the scheme Abasi was planning far enough in advance that much of that wealth was hidden away inside the temple before the coup. If Zefret had been honest with herself, even she hadn't believed a coup would be successful. But somehow, Abasi had turned enough soldiers' opinions against women to plot an attack, and it had taken the lives of two of her dearest friends. Now it had fallen to them to keep the dream of a better future alive. A doctor and her rogue band of misfit warriors. Unskilled but driven. Would drive be enough?

Zefret knew that time was short. Abasi's men were growing angrier by the minute. Their king was focused on expanding his reach, which had been a welcome distraction but was now a problem, because plunder, war, and imperial reach take money. Abasi had begun looking for ancient treasures of the kingdom he remembered from his childhood, and grown furious when he couldn't locate them. He sent his best soldiers in search of the secret temple of Heba. After weeks of searching, they were frustrated that they couldn't locate and desecrate the temple, and furious that they didn't know where the treasure was hidden.

Zefret and the others had gone into hiding. She knew that Abasi had ordered his men to focus on Heba's inner circle. Zefret could see the determination in each of the women's eyes. She prayed that each of them would remain loyal, and not fall prey to the false whispers of a traitor.

The shadow of one of her most loyal followers approached in the dark. It is Dendera.

"Why are you sitting here away from the others, Zefret?"

"I am in contemplation."

Dendera sat down next to her and gazed back at the others. "It is a great burden that you must carry. Leading us through a hostile time in search of a return to the better life."

Zefret only nodded at her friend's ability to read a situation so clearly.

"But you need not shoulder the load on your own," Dendera continued. "We are all ready and willing to do what must be done."

Zefret knew the importance of each of their nightly sessions, whether the recovery of materials to fashion their own weapons of war, or training to fight like men. Both of these pursuits were necessary to their cause if they were to have any hope at prevailing.

At last, Zefret spoke. "I am worried that our followers, loyal though they may be, don't have a true appreciation of the sacrifices they may have to make in order for our cause to be successful."

"Sister, I assure you that each one of us knows the cost. We have seen the price Heba paid. But when it comes to the future survival of our own daughters, no price could ever be too high."

Zefret smiled at her friend's confidence, and prayed she was right.

54

Present Day

"I shouldn't be on speaker," MaryAnn said. Avery picked up the phone and switched the audio as Harrison made a face. She patted his hand and mouthed, "I'm sure it's fine."

"Are you sitting down?" MaryAnn asked after confirming that everyone was okay.

"Yes, I'm sitting down." Avery suddenly didn't want to be.

"I think I know why the idol is in such demand, Avery. If this information is correct, that pin is the key to the location of an ancient lost treasure. The lost treasure of Heba."

"Well of course it is," Avery blurted without even really thinking. She was almost annoyed that she hadn't put that together herself, having ridden this horse three times now—as soon as MaryAnn spoke, Avery didn't even bother to ask her source. She just knew in her bones it was as true as the sky was blue. There had to be a bigger treasure at stake to invoke this level of madness.

"You took that well." MaryAnn laughed.

Avery removed the pin from its hiding place and examined it closely. If this tiny idol was some sort of map to another treasure, it was well concealed. There was nothing that would outwardly point to the golden pin as being anything but a tribute statue to the keeper of the underworld.

"Well, that makes a lot more sense," Avery said. "It has been nonstop crazy since we got here. If you could see the size of this thing, you'd know it couldn't be the only thing so many cutthroat killers are after. Now—who in the world is Heba, and how could they bring about so much chaos?"

Harrison and Duval leaned forward awaiting an update, and Avery held up an index finger.

"Are you someplace I can send you some secure documents?" MaryAnn asked.

"Not at the moment," Avery said. "But we're getting on the first train back to Cairo."

Harrison groaned at the mention of another train.

"Let me know when I can forward what I have," MaryAnn said. "Any update on Carter?"

"He's the other reason we're going back," Avery said. "We haven't heard anything about him, and I want to see for myself."

"My new friend Amir at the embassy says Marco is okay," MaryAnn said. "He's not happy, but he is being fed and left alone."

"If there's any way for you to get him a message, tell him it won't be long. And that I'm so sorry."

"Will do. Wait until you see this story. I've studied ancient history for decades and I was absolutely enthralled—and completely flabbergasted."

"Looking forward to it." Avery ended the call.

Fifteen minutes into an as yet uneventful train ride, everyone was settled and still enough in a private car for Avery to relay MaryAnn's comments about a larger treasure. She got two words out—"So, anyway..."—before Duval's cell phone chimed with an incoming message. Avery watched as he read the text, his eyes widening.

"What is it?" Avery asked.

Duval smiled and shook his head. "Now its your turn to wait."

Avery fixed Duval with a *what gives* look.

"Ladies first," Duval said.

"Would somebody mind telling me some part of what the heck is going on?" Harrison grumbled.

"MaryAnn thinks there might be more to this little pin than we think."

"Meaning?" Javier said.

"Meaning that it might be the key to locating a big, fat, three-thousand-year-old treasure."

"Brilliant." Duval clapped his hands. "Now, the message I just received makes a lot more sense."

"Well?" Avery said.

"An offer just came through a back channel for that famous little lass."

"What back channel?" Reggie asked.

"Shannon."

"I always liked that guy, kind of in spite of myself," Harrison said.

"How much?" Oscar asked.

"Five hundred million pounds."

Avery's jaw dropped open as she tried to process the figure. "Five hundred...million?"

"That's the offer," Duval said.

"What's that in real money?" Harrison said.

"I'd have to check on the current exchange rate," Duval said. "But it's pretty favorable at present. I'd guess it would be about six hundred and fifty million."

"Dollars?" Harrison said, pointing to Avery's bag. "For that little trinket?"

"Key to another treasure, remember, Harry?" Avery patted his hand.

Duval nodded. "And the buyers want to meet."

"Put them off, but politely," Avery said, opening her laptop. "MaryAnn had more. That altar y'all found in the townhouse? Whatever this is supposed to lead to is called—I feel like I need a drumroll—"

"The treasure of Heba?" Duval asked.

"Thunder stealer." Avery shook her head at him.

"I thought we were supposed to guess."

"You just wanted to say it first," Javier said, turning back to Avery. "So do we know who this person was?"

Avery held one hand out to Duval. "I know you have to be traveling with a secure hotspot."

He smiled. "Can't get anything past you. May I?"

She handed him a computer and he connected it to the hotspot and gave it back.

Avery opened the first attachment to MaryAnn's email, frowning. "I don't suppose any of you read hieroglyphs, do you?"

Everyone shook their heads. Avery clicked around in the document, trying to figure out why MaryAnn sent it, finally noticing a page tab at the bottom of her screen, slightly obscured because the window was too large. She clicked to page two and found what she figured was a translation, skimming the words as her jaw loosened.

"What?" Harry and Duval asked in unison.

"You guys aren't going to believe this," Avery said. "Heba wasn't a goddess at all. She was a queen. An ancient queen of Egypt."

No one spoke for at least fifteen seconds.

"I feel like that's the kind of thing they'd tell you in school," Harrison said. "It's been a while, but I'm pretty sure all the kings were...well, kings. Wouldn't a woman be interesting enough to warrant her own chapter in history books?"

"That's the thing, Harry," Avery said. "She was erased. Long before there were books to put her in."

Duval snapped his fingers. "That guy, the one who took us to the pyramids. Ben?"

Avery pointed, bouncing slightly in her seat. "Yes, he said his brother was researching women who...What did he say? Cleaned up messes after ineffective kings?"

Harrison's lips set into a grim line as he nodded to Avery's computer. "He also said his brother was executed for doing that research. In this century. Is this one of those things we're going to wish we could unlearn?"

"Too late now," Avery said, reading more. "The kingdom prospered under Heba's rule, expanding, advancing science, and enjoying a long period of peace. It says women came here as refugees from Greece because Egyptian women could own property and study and work as doctors." She blinked hard. "Wow. The vast riches of her kingdom were hidden because her stepson...aww, man." She glared at the screen like it had offended her.

"What?" Duval asked.

"Abasi. The pharaoh who wanted the pin so badly—he was her stepson. He orchestrated a coup as soon as he was old enough to recruit some soldiers to follow him, and he killed Heba and assumed the throne. And proceeded to scrub all evidence of her from history."

"Probably a lot easier to accomplish then than now," Oscar said.

"Sure," Harrison said. "Knock down a couple of statues and burn some scrolls and voila. Heba never existed."

"That's about the size of it. Only trouble was, Heba had many loyal followers and this idol everyone's still chasing was said to have magical powers bestowed upon it by her high priestess—who some said was also her consort. It wasn't just a cherished possession of Heba's—it was *the* cherished possession. The one thing she always had with her and prized above all else."

"Is this history or a TV soap opera?" Harrison asked.

"Couldn't be that magical," Duval said. "Not based on what happened to the queen."

Reggie nodded.

"This history is fascinating, but I still can't tell how useful it is here," Javier said. "If her stepson erased her from history, then there's no tomb or temple we can search for treasure, right?"

"Maybe not," Avery said. "But MaryAnn said the pin is supposed to somehow be the key to the treasure, which explains why so many people are so desperate to get ahold of it—maybe especially why Abasi was, that close to Heba's death." She held up the bag. "I say in for all these pennies, in for the pounds. We go for broke and find the treasure ourselves."

"If they don't even want anyone to know there was a queen, what do you think they'll do to keep the existence of a treasure that belonged to her quiet?" Harrison asked. "I haven't wanted to believe that they were just drugging Carter to keep you here, Ave, but this makes it make sense— nobody does this like you do, and you won't leave without him. So they follow us until you find the treasure and then swoop in and yank the find out from under you so they can keep it quiet."

Avery laughed. "Let them try. We'll negotiate our way out of here in the court of public opinion."

"Meaning?" Duval asked.

"I mean leverage the on-camera discovery of an ancient Egyptian treasure to Carter's Instagram following while we plead for Marco's freedom and ask people to pray for Carter's recovery so we can go home," she said. "Egypt makes more than twelve billion dollars a year on tourism. Risking tarnishing their history with a hidden queen was enough to get Benzion's brother killed, whether that was the actual government or a rogue agent or two. They will not want an audience as big and dedicated as Carter's to think they're in the business of drugging or detaining tourists."

"That sounds suspiciously like a plan, love." Duval didn't try to hide the admiration in his voice.

"We are getting our friends back and everyone is getting home whole and breathing," Avery said firmly. "If finding a treasure nobody knows exists is the ticket, so be it."

Duval waved his phone, reminding her of the mind-boggling offer. "Someone knows it exists. But I think I can handle it."

55

The train pulled into Ramses Station ninety minutes later. Duval had ordered a car to meet them and took the keys to a large silver SUV from a man out front while Oscar and Javier insisted on carrying Duval's and Avery's bags out into the blinding sunshine and oppressive heat.

"Just how many 'friends' do you have, Duval?" Harrison asked.

"What can I say. I'm an exceptionally charming lad."

"Charmed is more like it," Avery said.

Duval raised his hand in greeting as they crossed the lot. Both men nodded.

"So, what are we going to do about the offer, Ave?" Harrison said.

"String them along as long as we can without making them mad, giving Duval time to try to ID them," Avery said. "Anyone willing to pay that much for the pin has to be pretty sure the lost treasure is worth many times that —and probably wants to hoard the value for themselves. I don't want that —that treasure and this history belong to the women of Egypt, not anyone else. But before we start the hunt, we're going to check on Carter. I'm tired of vague reports of concerns I haven't seen evidence of, and if they're just keeping him drugged, someone is going to be sorry. I'm not afraid of the Cairo police anymore—if they wanted us locked up, they'd have come for us already. I'm not leaving that hospital again without speaking to Carter myself."

"I've missed you," Carter said, sitting up in the bed playing solitaire on the tray table, when she appeared in his doorway. Avery let out a screech and ran to him, grabbing his hand because she wasn't sure throwing her arms around him wouldn't injure them both.

"It's good to see you, Carter," Harrison said from behind her.

"Likewise, Harry. I see you found some help while I was out of commission."

"Good to see you, mate," Duval said as he stepped into the room. "Reggie and the boys are watching the doors and the car. So, how soon can we bust you out of here?"

"At least several more days," a voice said from behind them.

Avery turned to see Carter's doctor approaching.

"But he looks great," Avery said, her eyes narrowing.

"He is improving, but the healing will still be a slow process. A long flight back to America brings danger of relapses as well as deep vein thrombosis—which could be fatal. I am sure none of you want that."

"Carter's health is our first priority, Doctor," Harrison said.

"I'm glad to hear it," the doctor said, pausing a moment to look over the group standing before him. "And if you don't mind my saying, you all look like you could do with some rest."

"Thanks, Doc," Harry said.

"Free medical advice is rare in your country, isn't it?" The doctor grinned. "I've got to finish my rounds. Don't stress my patient."

"We won't," Avery said.

"Well, you guys should catch up," Duval said, tapping Harrison on the arm and earning a curious glance from Avery.

"Where are you going?" she asked.

Harrison spoke first. "We—um, we're gonna go find some coffee."

"That's right," Duval said. "You guys want anything?"

"I'm fine," Carter said.

"Me too. Now." Avery squeezed Carter's hand, not buying a word of their story. But also not caring a bit what they were up to—her heart had never felt so full as it did with Carter holding her hand and smiling at her, and mostly all she could think was how she might get her chair closer to his hospital bed.

What the heck was that about?

"What are we really doing?" Harrison said as soon as they were out of earshot.

"I want to find out more about this Egyptian bloke you shot," Duval said.

"He's probably not even here anymore," Harrison said.

"If you guys got him as good as Avery thinks, he'll still be here. Come on."

They found him resting in the same private wing Avery had previously described, though the hospital staff had moved him one room down the corridor.

Duval spotted an abandoned laundry cart with several white coats draped over it. After a quick glance to be sure no one was watching, he walked over and snatched up a doctor's smock and shrugged it on.

"What do you think?"

"You don't exactly look like the local doctors," Harrison said.

"That's because I'm a specialist, Harry. Now watch me operate. And keep an eye out for me."

Duval strolled into the room and closed the door behind him. The patient lying in the bed glanced over in his direction but said nothing. Duval picked up the chart hanging from the footboard.

Duval switched to his flawless Arabic without missing a beat. "How are we feeling today, Mr. Fawzi?"

"Like I got shot. How are you?"

Duval grinned. "I haven't been shot, so better than you, I guess?" While it was clear the man was not going to be overly cooperative, at least he was talking.

Duval donned a pair of latex gloves, then pulled back the sheet to expose the bandage.

"Let's take a look at your wound, shall we?"

Fawzi grimaced as Duval tugged on the tape holding the bandage in place.

"Easy, Doc."

"Well, it isn't the prettiest wound I've ever seen, but you'll have a great story to tell the ladies."

Fawzi grinned at Duval's attempt at macho humor.

"How did the Americans manage to shoot you anyway? If you don't mind me asking."

He flashed a disarming smile when Fawzi looked shocked that he knew so much about the wound. "Your superior filled us in when he came to check on you," he explained. "You were unconscious. He said you were his best officer. Those Americans must have been something else."

Duval kept his smile in place. He'd read this guy in less than two minutes—flattery mixed with a bit of challenge would get him talking.

"Amateurs." Fawzi waved one hand. "It was just bad luck. It was supposed to be a straightforward operation. But I guess nothing ever goes according to plan, does it?"

Duval smiled at the irony. "No, it does not, my friend."

"Is the one they call Carter Mosley still here in the hospital?"

Duval nodded. "Trust me, I'm trying to get him out of here as fast as possible."

"Not so fast," Fawzi said.

Duval frowned for effect. "I don't understand. I thought you would want him gone from here."

"I am hoping for a more permanent end to his meddling."

"What did they do exactly, these Americans?"

"What do Americans always do? They stuck their nose into something that does not concern them. They are part of an assassination plot. Sent here to destabilize our government and make us vulnerable."

"Who are they here to assassinate?" Duval had to work to not sound too worried.

"Sorry, Doc. Classified."

"And you, a National Police officer, were assigned to stop them?"

Fawzi scoffed. "No one would send a police officer. Egyptian intelligence. I was not tasked with stopping them but with killing them. Before they could execute their plan."

"And that's why they shot you?"

"Me and my less fortunate colleagues."

"The one who died." Duval nodded.

Fawzi sighed. "The bosses pulled back on the operation because of the casualties and the risk of exposure after we failed to eliminate the target. The whole thing has been in limbo while I've been trying to not die here. But finally, they're moving forward."

"What can I do to help?" Duval said.

"Keep Mosley here for another twenty-four hours."

"And if I do that?"

"We will take care of the rest."

A knock came from the door and Harrison stuck his head inside.

"Yes?" Duval said in English, still in character.

"We gotta go," Harrison said.

"Okay, Harry."

Fawzi's eyes narrowed as he looked back and forth between the two men. Before he could react, Duval clamped a hand over the man's mouth and pressed against the artery supplying blood to his brain. It was a well-practiced maneuver, and Fawzi stopped struggling after only a few seconds.

"Jesus, Duval. Where did you learn to do that?"

"I'll tell you when we have more time," Duval said, pointing to the door. "Relax, Harry—I didn't permanently damage him. But Carter won't be as lucky if we don't get him out of here before this guy's friends arrive."

"You're kidding, right?"

Duval shook his head as he moved toward the door. "My sleepy little man told me himself. We've gotta bust Carter out of this place. Today."

56

"You know, Avery, you're one of the smartest people I know," Carter said when she quietly gave him the CliffsNotes version of their situation and her plan. "Which, given my background, might not be saying all that much." He scooted his legs to one side. "Come sit on the bed. That hard plastic chair can't be good for your injuries."

"Your background is fine," Avery said, moving gingerly to perch on the bed, facing him. "And thank you. Where's that coming from?"

Carter shrugged. "I don't know. It was just something I felt needed saying, so I said it. I just admire you, that's all."

"Well, thanks. I admire you too. The worry—and guilt—has been utterly overwhelming the past several days. I'm not sure I've ever felt so relieved as I did when you were sitting up talking when I walked in. How long have you been awake?"

"Since this morning. I tried to call you and Harry, but it went straight to voicemail."

"Our regular phones are off. We have burners, but I left the number with the doctor." Avery scowled.

"That dude—he's a good doctor and all, but I don't think they let him sleep. He's always here and always running. I'm sure he forgot."

"I suppose with you looking so much better, I'll let it go," she said, putting a finger on his jaw. "They even let you shave."

"I got to take a shower in the tiny bathroom there," he said. "It might go down as the best shower ever. I've never been so glad to be clean."

Avery laughed. "I said something similar just this morning. I have missed you this week, Carter Mosley."

"So, getting shot and being told by a doctor that you could've died is a good way to take stock of your life, it seems," Carter said. "Do you mind if I ask you a personal question?"

"Another one?" She smiled. "Duval asked me the same thing the other day. I answered his, and right now I'd pretty much give you the moon if you asked me."

"Why don't you ever...you know...date? I know people ask you out. But you never go."

Avery stared, blinking, for what felt like an impossibly long time. She cleared her throat. "Pretty much the same question Duval asked, too."

Carter frowned, just for a second. "I'm not trying to make you uncomfortable."

"You're not," Avery said. "Though I haven't really given this enough thought to have a good answer. I lost Mark and found a life I'm happy with. I haven't found dating interesting in a while, I suppose." She winked. "Or maybe you just find it interesting enough for both of us."

"What? I don't play the field that much. These days."

"How many women made the effort to stalk you online and send you undergarments in the mail in the last month?"

"That's not me playing the field, that's them being inappropriate. And kind of gross. The number of them that arrive unlaundered is... disturbing."

Avery wrinkled her nose. "Yuck. Seriously?"

"It's not as glamorous as rock stars always made it sound." Carter laughed. "Let's leave it at that."

Avery covered her ears. "Say no more. For real."

When Carter mimed zipping his lips, she moved her hands.

"My point stands. It's not like you have a shortage of offers," Avery said, unsure when she went from deflecting to data mining with this line of questioning, but desperate to hear his answer all the same.

"I'm starting to think maybe I've just been looking in the wrong places," Carter said, holding her gaze long enough to make her fidget.

Carter leaned toward her, resting one hand gently on her knee.

Sparks skated from that knee to every hair follicle and toe in the time it took to blink. Not that Avery dared to blink right then.

"It's been a long time since I found anyone as interesting as Mark Hawkins was." Avery rested her hand on top of his, increasing the pressure on her knee, her head swimming from the electricity shooting through her nerve endings.

"Anyone I know?" Carter half whispered.

"Maybe." Avery wasn't sure she said the word out loud as she stared at Carter's lips, wishing her face didn't look like she'd gone ten rounds with Evander Holyfield.

Carter's grip tightened on Avery's knee as his face inched closer to hers. Avery let her eyes fall shut and held her breath.

The door opened, Harrison and Duval's voices sending them springing apart before anyone noticed how close they'd gotten.

"Thought you two were getting coffee?" Avery said in an accusatory tone that made everyone's eyebrows pop up.

"We've gotta go." Duval said. "Now."

Avery shook her head. "You're as bad as Carter. I tried talking the doctor down, but he still wants him to stay here another day or so. And I'm not ready to leave yet." She had a feeling the moment had passed even if she could get rid of Duval and Harrison, but she was willing to give it a shot.

"We're just going to have to hope he's good to go, Ave," Harrison said, examining Carter's IV for a way to disconnect it.

"What are you talking about?" Carter asked, looking alarmed and waving Harry away from the bed.

"They're sending someone here to kill you, kid," Harrison said.

Avery's eyes widened. "Who?"

"Egyptian intelligence," Duval said.

"We've gotta split, Ave. Like right now."

"How did you guys find this out?" Avery asked.

"Doesn't matter," Duval said before turning to Carter. "Where are your clothes?"

"I don't have any idea."

They availed themselves of the confusion of hospital shift change to sneak Carter out of the ward, dressing him in the bathroom in scrubs Duval swiped from the same cart as the lab coat while Harrison called Javier and the boys to bring the SUV around.

"What about my shoes?" Carter said as they hurried past the nurse's station.

"Too late for fashion," Oscar said.

"Excuse me," a voice called out from behind them.

"Don't stop," Avery said. "We're almost to the elevator."

"Wasn't planning to," Duval said.

"Excuse me," the nurse said again, closer and angrier now. "Where do you think you're taking him?"

The elevator doors chimed as they slid open, and they hurried Carter inside.

"Just needs some air and sunshine," Duval said.

Avery quickly punched the lobby button.

They hurried through the doors toward the SUV where Javier and Reggie were waiting.

"Took you guys long enough," Reggie said.

"Yeah," Javier said. "We thought you got caught."

"We did," Harrison said. "By a rabid nurse."

"Luckily, I was too fast for her," Carter said.

"Good to see you still have your sense of humor," Avery said. "Now let's get out of here."

They returned to the Cairo hotel, where they still had rooms, to regroup.

"How much time do you think we bought?" Harrison asked, waiting until Carter was in the bathroom to avoid worrying him.

"I wouldn't think much," Duval said.

"We bought enough," Avery said. "You said they were sending someone to the hospital to kill him. He's no longer there. And we've got the pin."

"Or key," Javier said.

"Or whatever this thing is," Reggie said. "But now we're not looking for the treasure anymore?" He looked like a little boy who'd just dropped his ice cream cone.

"With confirmation that the secret police are trying to kill us? Are you insane?" Avery asked. "It was one thing to think we were being followed, but their spies have literally been told that we're here to murder someone and they have orders to kill us. Let someone else find the treasure. Our mission now is escape. We get Marco and we get out of here."

"Sounds like a plan to me," Carter said as he reentered the room.

"Only one problem with that," Duval said.

"Why does there always have to be a problem?" Harrison groaned.

"And what exactly is that?" Avery said, hands on her hips.

"Your plane is still in plane jail."

"Duval's right," Harrison said. "Even if we bust Marco out, he has nothing to fly us home in."

"Then what?" Avery said. "We can't just sit here waiting for them to come in and start blasting."

"Maybe we can try flying out on a commercial airline," Carter said.

"Look at you, Boy Wonder," Harrison said.

"That's actually not such a bad idea," Javier said. "The last thing I'd be looking for would be to see my prey walk onto a commercial airliner."

"Except the Cairo PD has our passports," Avery said.

Duval waved one hand and pulled out his phone. "I'll have excellent fakes here in ninety minutes."

Harrison and Carter looked impressed. Avery just pressed her lips into a thin line. "I'll make the reservations," she said.

"What do you mean we can't fly out until five days from now?" Avery barked into the phone.

"Why can't anything ever just be simple?" Harrison asked.

"That's not how the universe works, Harry," Oscar said.

"Indeed," Duval agreed.

Avery held up her hand and shushed them.

"You're telling me there are no available flights out of here until Thursday," Avery said. "Look, I need four tickets on the earliest available flight to Washington, DC."

"I'm telling you, there are no flights available with seating for four people until Thursday," the airline agent said.

"What about private charters? There must be other options. I'll pay any fee."

"I'm sorry, Ms. Turner, but the schedules are all backed up."

"Wait," Avery said as her eyes widened. "I never gave you my name."

"Hang up, Ave," Harrison said.

"They're onto us, love."

Before Avery could do more than return the handset to the receiver, there was a knock at the door.

"That can't be good," Reggie said.

"Tell me one of you ordered room service," Harrison said as the knocking came again.

Avery shook her head and walked toward the door. "Who's there?"

"Ms. Turner, it's Detective Gamil. I have your passports."

Avery opened the door, immediately recognizing the young detective who had shown her the mugshots. Standing behind him were two uniformed officers she did not recognize.

"What can I do for you?" Avery asked.

"I am very sorry, Ms. Turner," he said. "But we have come to arrest Mr. Harrison."

"For what?" Harrison said.

Detective Gamil held up the warrant. "Archaeological looting."

"You're kidding," Duval said.

"I wish I were," Gamil said as the two officers pushed past him and into the room. "I'm afraid Mr. Harrison must come with us."

"I feel terrible that I ever doubted Marco for a second, but I know in my bones Harry has done nothing wrong." Avery stood up straight and stared the detective directly in the eye. "If you take him out of here, I will make you sorry."

"If I don't, I'll lose my job," Gamil said, moving past her.

"They know you tried to book airfare. They think Marco isn't enough, and they know how much you love Harry. This is how they mean to keep us here." Duval kept his voice low behind Avery.

"What can we do?" she whispered.

"At the moment, nothing. We play along."

Avery didn't like that answer, but she didn't want to risk getting anyone else arrested or hurt.

"Please just let us do our jobs, Ms. Turner," Gamil said.

Avery caught Oscar moving to flank the officers who were busy hand-cuffing Harrison. She shook her head as they locked eyes and mouthed the word *don't*.

They watched helplessly as the officers marched Harrison toward the door.

"How do we arrange for bail?" Avery asked.

"If you'll come down to the station, everything will be explained," Gamil said.

"They're not going to let us leave, are they?" Carter asked.

"It's like that bloody awful Eagles song about the hotel," Reggie said.

"'Hotel California'?" Javier said.

"That's the one."

"Um, that song is not about a hotel," Avery said.

"Whatever. The point is, they have no intention of letting us out of here."

"Not as long as we have this thing," Avery said, holding the pin up again.

Another knock came at the door. This time Duval pulled out his handgun, accompanying Avery to the door.

"Yes?" Avery said.

"Valet service, ma'am. I have been instructed to deliver a note."

Duval steadied himself behind the door and nodded to Avery.

She opened the door to find a male valet standing there holding an envelope.

"Are you Ms. Turner?"

"I am. Who is the note from?"

"It doesn't say," the valet said as he handed it to her.

"Thank you," she said, accepting it before closing the door.

"What do you think?" Carter said.

"Instructions, I'd guess," Duval said.

Avery tore the envelope open and removed a single sheet of paper written in the same scrawl as her name on the envelope.

"What does it say?" Reggie asked.

Avery could feel tears threatening. "It says if we want to see Harrison again, we will wait here for further instructions."

"So much for going home," Carter said.

57

"We've got to get this thing someplace safe," Avery said as they sat around her laptop FaceTiming with MaryAnn.

"Like yesterday," Carter said.

"It's the only thing guaranteeing Harry and Marco's safety at this point," Duval agreed. "I'm not even sure all the different agencies who are in this have been told the same story, but I am sure that everyone around here with a badge or a gun sees us as public enemy number one."

Avery already knew that, but somehow hearing the words made the situation feel more dire.

"Before I say anything else, Carter, it is so good to see you I'm about to cry," MaryAnn said.

"It's very good to be seen," Carter said. "Thank you."

MaryAnn cleared her throat. "Now then. Back to the many problems at hand: I've had less than no luck with the embassy," MaryAnn said. "But I will keep trying, and I can help you by digging up more information on Ammit and the history behind the pin. I've already engaged the help of another expert in the field of ancient Egyptian history. Her name is Ullah and she is a research specialist at a museum right there in Cairo. I know you don't want to broadcast the possibility of treasure, so we have to be delicate, but perhaps she can find something that will help."

"We'll take whatever help we can get," Carter said.

"Thanks, MaryAnn," Avery said.

"Don't mention it. I'm on it. I'll call as soon as I have something to share."

After ending the video call with MaryAnn, Avery turned to Duval. "We're playing an away game here and I don't like that the odds are stacked against us."

"Neither do I," Carter said. "Where are we supposed to hide this thing that nobody will be able to get to it?"

"I may have an idea about that," Duval said. "We need to take a little trip."

"What about the note?" Carter said. "The instructions said to wait here."

"And you will be right here when they contact you," Javier said.

"You're not suggesting that we leave Carter alone?" Avery looked horrified. "That's not going to happen."

"Take it easy," Duval said. "Nobody's leaving anyone alone. We're all in this together, and we'll be smart about splitting up. Carter is injured, and Avery, the note was addressed to you. Reggie will stay with you."

"When are you going?" Avery asked.

"After dark."

58

MaryAnn called back two hours later with a bit of background information.

"This really is so exciting," she said. "The history is so scant it's widely believed among people who know about it—and there aren't many of them —to be a myth or a legend. But it looks like the little evidence available suggests Heba was married to the pharaoh back around 1500 BC, when he died. She took over the throne," MaryAnn said. "There was a power struggle that may have resulted in the death of Heba and rise to power of her stepson, a guy named Abasi."

"Sounds like a long time to hold a grudge," Javier said.

"You haven't met my ex," Reggie quipped.

"Can we stay on point here?" Avery said.

"Sorry," Duval said. "Please, MaryAnn, continue."

"So, before Heba died, her high priestess, a woman named Amunet, is said to have put a blessing on that pin. Abasi grew obsessed, hunting it to the detriment of his kingdom and his duties to his people. He believed the blessing on the pin was a curse on him and his reign."

"When really he just messed things up his own self by focusing on the wrong thing," Carter said.

Avery glanced at him but said nothing.

"Some blessing," Carter went on. "Saves my life one day and sends Harry to prison a few days later."

"It looks like Abasi tried to erase all references to his stepmother from the pages of Egyptian history, and he did a good job, too," MaryAnn said.

"We saw that in the document you emailed," Avery said. "So how sure can we be that any of this is accurate? I mean, I took archeology in college and didn't know ancient Egypt had a queen."

"The Greeks. They were out of Abasi's purview. Here's where the excitement comes in: When I sent out my request for information about this last week, a friend of Malik's who works at the Al-Assad National Library in Damascus remembered a tome that came to them from one of the monasteries—an ancient Greek history text the monks copied from the original scrolls and into a book during the Byzantine empire, to preserve the history. It took him a few days to find it, but he did today, and it includes mentions of Heba and her empire, though she is sometimes referred to as a man and sometimes as a woman."

"Uh. She was transgender? In 1500 BC?" Duval asked.

"I guess that's possible," MaryAnn said. "There have been transgender or 'two spirit' people throughout world history. But I'd bet this is simpler than that. Since only men were allowed to rule, she found a work around by disguising her gender as she prepared for leadership."

"That makes sense." Carter glanced at Avery. "Though it's sad and frustrating that women were treated that way."

"Especially since according to the legends, Heba was a far superior leader to her husband and her stepson both," MaryAnn said. "And that's not all—I thought this was especially interesting given your experiences there this week—this collection also included writings that mentioned a group of women who created scrolls before Abasi banned women from learning to read or write. These women were bound by an ancient power to keep the old history alive for their future generations of daughters."

"Oh, blimey." Duval snapped his fingers and looked at Avery. "The warrior chicks. How much you want to bet?"

"Nothing, because you're right." Avery sighed. "Which means their motive isn't greed. That's why all she said was that the pin was safe. They're not treasure hunters or killers, they're guardians."

"The women who attacked you?" Carter asked. "So we're kind of on the same side?"

"This complicates things." Avery shook her head. "No, they're not exactly our enemies, but a group that idolizes the dead queen won't part with that for love or money—or threat of international incident. That's why nobody looked like they cared when I mentioned that in the tunnels under the pyramid. For once, we're not up against someone who cares about the material value of the treasure we're hunting. Good on them?"

Duval nodded. "But bad for us. No deal to be made."

Oscar sat heavily in an armchair.

"Peachy," Reggie said.

"And the treasure?" Oscar asked. "Avery said there was treasure."

"The Greek text supports that, too," MaryAnn said. "It details a vast fortune that went missing right before Heba's death. A fortune that may have been part of the reason Abasi was after Heba's followers."

"I appreciate all this, MaryAnn, thank you," Avery said. "I just don't know what to do with it, exactly."

"I understand, and sympathize. One thing you could do is go talk to the Greek text expert Guy Malik knows—he says she's there, at the national museum, for a translation conference," MaryAnn said. "Her name is Riva, and Guy already told her to expect you."

"Are we that predictable?" Avery asked, making a face.

"You're smart. Smart people go talk to the source when they can."

"Maybe that thing is good luck." Reggie pointed to the pin.

"They've definitely been shot at more than they've been helped," Javier said.

"But wasn't most of the shooting before they found the pin?" Reggie countered.

"Fair point," Carter said.

MaryAnn laughed. "I'll let you know what else I can find, or if I hear back from anyone who can help with Marco and Harry."

"Thank you." Avery ended the call and surveyed the room.

"So, what exactly is the plan?" Reggie said.

"I think we have to find the treasure," Avery said. "I know I said two hours ago it was time to get out of here, but I won't leave Harry and Marco, and a jailbreak is at least as dangerous as treasure hunting. So I say we focus on what we know how to do." She took the pin out of its bag and held it up to the light. "We'll need to figure out what this pin is the key to, exactly. Then we'll get Harry and Marco out of jail. Someone will trade the treasure for their freedom, whether it's our government or theirs. And then I'm going home to my island and my beach and I may sell my plane."

Duval nodded slowly. "Sure. The only thing stopping us is a band of women who think it's still 1500 BC, Egyptian intel assassins pretending to be cops, and every hired thug from here to Jordan."

"Piece of cake," Oscar said.

"What about Mr. Smith and Senator Byers?" Javier said. "Where do they fit into this slippery equation?"

"We still don't know," Avery said.

Avery wondered to herself if perhaps the man Harry trusted the most, his former NYPD commander Roger Antonin, might have the contacts necessary to provide a peek behind the curtain on Smith and Byers. It was for Harry's sake, after all.

"Not to sound too self-serving," Reggie began.

"But?" Avery asked when he paused.

"Well, you guys know we love you, but I was wondering about maybe some kind of reward if we succeed."

Avery grinned at his obvious motive. "*If* we're successful, I'll personally make it worth each of your time, even if I have to do it from my own bank account."

Oscar rubbed his hands together. "Where do we start?"

59

Ancient Egypt, 1500 BC

Zefret had identified their target weeks prior to the planned attack. The guard she had selected out of all of Abasi's men was perfect. Self-confident, cocky, and too enamored with himself to keep his eye on the ball. Preferring to regale the local men and women with stories of his exploits as opposed to doing the job he had actually been charged with, which was locating Zefret and the others and ending the threat posed by them.

As with all things her son and his charges did, the details of their nightly duties were unimaginative and predictable. It was just one more thing that made the man a perfect candidate for their purposes.

She trained the growing group of women over the following weeks intentionally searching for the bravest and most skilled members of their little band of warriors. Zefret had modified their sessions to focus on the skills that would be needed to overpower the guard and to locate the missing pin that she knew he possessed. It was another detail gleaned from listening to him bragging about the trust Abasi had placed in him.

Finally, the night came that Zefret had deemed the most suitable, the night of the new moon. When the lunar god known as Lah was renewed and devoid of light, casting the vast landscape of Egypt in full darkness. The only light not of man would be the cold stars above.

Zefret and a handful of her best-trained women had hidden themselves among the shadows where they knew the guard would be. As he passed by each of his scheduled stops, he drew closer to the trap they had set for him, while Zefret followed from a safe distance to avoid detection. Several times during the night he met up with and accompanied other guards, but Zefret had planned for this, as it was a typical occurrence, and each of the meetings was brief.

Finally, when the guard was alone at the far edge of his assigned area, Zefret and the others closed in on him. Zefret was nearly upon him when one of the other women mis-stepped, giving herself away to the guard, who removed his bronze sword and prepared to attack her. Before he could do more than draw back his arm, Zefret pounced on his back, pummeling him repeatedly about the head and neck with her dagger. The guard's lifeless body dropped to the sand without so much as a sound being uttered. The other women paused to stare at Zefret, who was wild-eyed and covered in the man's spilled blood. One by one the women began to nod until it was clear to Zefret that there would be no going back. They had crossed a line, and she had earned their trust. Abasi would never give up the hunt for her or her band of warriors, but it mattered not. The only thing that mattered now was finding and recovering the pin of Heba.

While the others kept watch, Zefret rifled through every inch of the guard's clothing, but the pin was not on his person. Frantically she searched the ground around the attack but there was no trace of the small idol. Having followed the man for weeks, Zefret and the others knew that the guard's quarters were near the palace gates. She rose to her feet and signaled the others to come in close.

"Come," Zefret said in whispered tones. "We must search his quarters. There is no time to waste."

The handful of women disappeared, swallowed up in the shadows cast by flickering nearby torches.

60

Present Day

Following their conversation with MaryAnn, Avery decided it would be a better use of her time to visit the museum, rather than simply waiting around to see if further instructions were forthcoming from whoever sent that note about Harrison. On the off chance they were contacted with instructions, Duval, Carter, and Reggie remained at the hotel.

Duval sent Avery with Javier and Oscar for peace of mind. Malik's friend Riva met them just inside the main entrance lobby.

"You must be Avery and Carter," she said.

"Actually, this is my friend Javier," Avery said.

"A pleasure, ma'am," Javier said.

"Carter had another commitment today," Avery said. "Thanks for agreeing to assist us."

"And you are?" Riva said as Oscar moved closer to them.

"This is Oscar," Avery said.

"We all go way back," Javier said with a grin.

"Very nice to meet you, Oscar."

Oscar nodded and blushed, which made Avery smile. Riva was pretty, with a curvy figure, long dark hair, and wide, bright green eyes. It was funny to see a guy as big and confident as Oscar knotted up over a pretty woman.

"If you'd care to follow me, I can find us a place to talk, and show you a few things I gathered up after Malik's message came through. This is all very exciting—when you study ancient history, you don't really get to find new information very often."

They followed Riva across the polished checkerboard marble floor to an elevator that led to the research labs beneath the main museum. Avery noticed that Oscar's eyes never stopped moving. Despite being enchanted by Riva, he clearly was on the job.

"MaryAnn said that you're visiting for a conference?" Avery asked as they stepped into the elevator.

"More like a university study," Riva said as she pushed the button marked 4B. "It's a six-week residency that began this morning—I arrived yesterday. My field of study is anthropology and ancient dialects. It was while cataloging some fragile Byzantine texts hand-copied by monks that I first stumbled upon these Egyptian references. After a bit of study, I dismissed the stories as legends, which is how most academics view them. But Malik's message came several days ago and made me wonder, and then I arrived here and made a new friend and she helped me realize the importance of what was contained in that book, and how they might be beneficial to the Egyptians. To the whole world."

The doors opened into a well-lit corridor that seemed to stretch out forever.

"How big is this museum?" Avery said.

Riva laughed. "Enormous. Right this moment, we are moving under the main courtyard that you crossed to enter the museum. Believe it or not, there is more going on below the museum than inside it."

Avery grinned at the irony in Riva's statement considering their current predicament.

"I have read about you, Avery," Riva said. "Given the tedious nature of my work, I can only imagine how exciting hunting treasure must be. Never knowing what waits around the next corner."

"You have no idea," Javier said.

"It has its moments," Avery said, giving Javier a light jab in the ribs.

"Here we are," Riva said as she used a passkey to gain entry to a temperature-controlled workspace. Once inside, Avery was astonished to find one side of the room completely covered in state-of-the-art tech while the other was stacked high with crates of brittle-looking parchments and books.

"Wow," Avery said. "I never imagined so many ancient documents still existed."

Riva smiled proudly. "Against all odds and time, they have remained. And more are discovered every day in various parts of the world. Some say civilization has forgotten more about history than it will ever know."

"Wait until they look back at social media," Avery said.

"Oh, it isn't all bad," Riva said. "I follow Mr. Mosley's page."

"So you're the one." Avery winked, earning a laugh from Riva.

It took Riva several minutes to get set up so she could show them what she had been working on. She had already pulled the correct references after receiving word through MaryAnn that Avery and Carter would be paying her a visit. While Riva chatted up Javier, Avery checked her phone to see if Roger Antonin had responded to her message yet. There was zero cell service due to their subterranean location, but a single line of text from Roger had been delivered at some point before they came down.

I'm on it.

After exchanging a glance with Oscar, Avery pocketed her phone and returned to the conversation.

"I was shocked to discover this after I heard from Malik," Riva said. "Given what he told me what you were looking for. I sent him the text from the Byzantine book, but I walked in here this morning and found a scroll waiting, written in ancient Greek with a bit of Arabic slang thrown in. I was excited to learn you were coming because all day, I have been translating a newly discovered scroll that tells much about Pharoah Heba and her cult of followers."

"Cult?" Javier said. "That sounds like a bad thing."

"You'd think so," Riva said. "But like all dialects, the meanings of words change constantly. Guess that's a good thing for someone with my skill set."

"So cult was good back then?" Avery said.

"It was. The literal meaning of the word in ancient times was more akin to loyal or loyalist. Even after the passing of Heba, her core group of loyalists stayed true to her beliefs, going so far as to protect something that had great value to her."

"A pin?" Avery asked, swapping a look with Javier.

"Yes, the small idol carried by Heba is frequently mentioned. But even more intriguing is the reference to priceless riches and their connection to the idol. There was brief reference to the idol being a key in the Byzantine tome, but this is more."

"The hidden treasure," Oscar said absently, earning a curious glance from Riva.

"Perhaps," Riva said. "Although treasure in those times may well have had a very different connotation than what we would consider valuable today."

"That's true," Avery said.

"Exotic spices and tapestries were often sought-after commodities in ancient times," Riva explained when the guys looked confused.

"Can you tell us more about Heba's cult?" Avery asked.

"They were very much like any other religion you might have practiced," Riva said. "Devout, loyal, protective of their queen. Possibly warriors, if protecting her or her temple was called for."

"We know the type," Avery said.

61

"So, these women were more like a religious sect?" Avery asked as they watched Riva work on translations through the computer.

"Very much like that. Some of the sects, consisting entirely of men, worshipped male deities, while women did the same for their deities. Heba's cult was fiercely loyal to their queen."

"I don't suppose you've heard of any of these cults still in existence?" Javier asked.

Riva turned and fixed him with a curious expression before laughing. "Not after thirty-five hundred years, silly." She turned to Avery. "For a second, I actually thought he was serious."

As soon as Riva's attention returned to the computer screen, Avery shot Javier a glare. "That's Javier," she said. "A regular laugh riot."

"What are those words?" Avery said after watching the computer skip over several during the translation process.

"They are unknowns," Riva said. "Despite the expertise of our staff and the highly technical software we employ, there were so many variables in language back then that we still uncover symbols and sentence structures that aren't easily translatable. Different geographical areas and different sects often employed their own words that don't translate even among the same time period or tribal affiliations. It just means we're still learning."

"So, the meanings of some passages remain a mystery?" Avery said.

"Sometimes. But other times we can make a highly educated guess as to the meaning based off the surrounding syntax."

"But it's still just a guess, right?" Javier said.

"I like to call it a best guess," Riva said. "I suppose the similarity in our jobs is that we both rely on some luck. Speaking of which, I wanted to tell you about my new friend Kate—she's an archaeologist, about to begin a dig in Giza."

"That's neat," Avery said, looking at Javier, who shrugged.

"She's employed a kind of sonar technology in the discovery that she thinks has found the entrance to subterranean tombs lost for thousands of years."

"Okay, now that's cool," Javier said.

"Cooler still is the fact that one of the texts she found at her last dig site helped lead them to this location. She showed me images last night to ask me to help with some unknown words. Turns out, I knew one of them because of you and your search: That scroll contains several references to your Pharaoh Heba."

Avery's eyes widened. "Where did you say this dig was again?"

62

Avery's cell service returned as soon as she, Javier, and Oscar returned to the main floor of the museum. Avery heard the chime of multiple messages dumping into her phone from the server.

"What is it?" Javier asked as they quickly moved toward the exit doors.

"Duval and MaryAnn."

"Everything okay?" Oscar said.

"No news is good news at the hotel, and MaryAnn was checking on our meeting. The bad luck we had here last week has shaken everyone up."

Oscar drove them back to the hotel. When they arrived, they found the rest of the group waiting like they were due home from battle.

"Still no word on Harry?" Avery said as she searched their faces.

Carter shook his head. "Nothing."

Before Avery could respond, her cell rang with an incoming call. It was Roger Antonin.

"I've got to take this," Avery said as she scurried into her bedroom and closed the door.

"Thank you for agreeing to help, Roger," Avery said by way of a greeting.

"Agreeing to help and actually being able to provide assistance are two entirely different things, Avery."

"You can't help?" Avery felt her heart sink.

"I didn't say that, but we're not there yet. I've put in several calls to friends in the State Department who might be able to do something. Now I have to wait to hear back. Who do you think is behind this?"

"I have no idea. It feels like everyone we meet has some reason for trying to take us out over this piece of history."

"Seems like overkill. Especially if this pin is no bigger than you said it is."

"There may be a lot more to it than we first thought."

"Oh?" Antonin said.

Avery explained about the exorbitant back-channel offer they had received to sell the pin.

Antonin whistled. "You think it's legit?"

"I do."

"Who would drop that much money for an old gold trinket?"

"Someone who will stop at nothing to get their hands on the treasure that it might unlock," Avery said. "And something else occurred to me today—we've been trying to figure out where Senator Byers fits into this, and I'm beginning to think her reason for sending us here might be less about preventing a war than recovering a treasure so valuable it could be used to fund one."

Avery waited for Roger to say something, but he remained silent. "Did you hear what I said?"

"I'm starting to get worried you guys may have stepped into something too big to escape from this time, kid."

"You sound like Harry."

"I mean it, Avery. I don't like this. You need to be very careful about who you trust."

Avery paused a moment to consider the noisy group of people occupying the next room. It sounded like an unruly classroom. But they were like family to her. And not only her, but to Carter and Harrison too. Would any of them try to sabotage what they were doing? It didn't seem likely. Especially given what they had already been through and risked for each other. Besides, in a strange land far from home, trust was something earned, not given. Duval, Reggie, Javier, and Oscar had earned her trust and then some, many times over. And Carter, Harrison, and Marco's loyalty weren't even a question. No, the only question now was who was pulling the strings. And why?

"So, what's your next move?" Antonin said.

Avery opened her mouth to fill him in on the news of the dig, then stopped. While she had no reason not to trust Roger Antonin, her mother's former boss, he hadn't actually done anything she could prove except call her and ask about their next move. So taking his advice meant not trusting him either.

"I'm not sure."

"What do you mean?"

"I mean I want you focused on how you are going to get Harry and Marco out of jail, not on what I'm doing while I wait."

63

"How did it go with Roger?" Carter said as Avery perched next to him on the edge of the sofa.

"He's working on a plan to get Harry and Marco out of jail," Avery said. "Or he better be, anyway."

"Why don't we just go down there and bust them out?" Oscar said. "Like the old days."

"Because it isn't the old days anymore," Javier said. "Cameras and electric fences make that a bit more dicey these days."

"Maybe for you," Oscar said.

"For any of us," Reggie said. "We've got to be more subtle about how we do things now."

"I hate subtle," Oscar said. "Harry is a chill old dude for being a copper, and we all know what they do to cops in jail—"

All the color drained from Avery's face.

"Come on now, mates," Duval interrupted smoothly. "The fight is out there. Let's not turn on each other, okay?"

Avery watched as they each took turns nodding their heads. Even Oscar finally relented.

"Good," Duval said before turning back to Avery. "What's the plan going forward?"

"We need to take a ride to an archaeological dig site."

"What are we looking for there?" Reggie asked.

"Answers, Reggie," Avery said.

"Answers to what?" Carter said.

"Maybe everything."

The dig site was located less than an hour from the hotel. Reggie drove one of their SUVs while Duval piloted the other. Avery rode with Duval, while Javier rode shotgun with Reggie. Oscar remained behind at the hotel, guarding Carter. Anyone foolish enough to come looking to do more than deliver a message to their hotel room's occupants would quickly find themselves in the fight of their lives.

Avery had kept her conversation with MaryAnn from the others, but the excitement was making it difficult to concentrate on the task at hand. There was next to no conversation during the long drive as everyone kept their eyes peeled for trouble. If there was a perfect time to stop them from moving forward, this was it, and everyone seemed to know that in their bones without it being said.

64

The site itself reminded Avery of something she had seen in nearly every one of the *Jurassic Park* movies. Dusty, barren, and full of possibilities. She wondered if whatever was waiting beneath the sand portended something as catastrophic as the resurrection of dinosaurs. Nothing above ground would have given any indication that something significant was buried below, and she was almost as excited to talk to the team lead about the tech that she'd used as she was to learn the suspected history of the area and what they'd find.

The area was a bevy of activity. Vehicles coming and going, large canvas tents and makeshift shelters quickly erected to protect both personnel and equipment from the elements. Avery was glad she had remembered to wear her dark glasses and headscarf. They offered at least some protection against the sun's unrelenting rays.

A man in a bright orange vest directed them toward a roped-off area where a number of other off-road vehicles were parked. Avery was surprised to find no one checking credentials of those entering the site.

Duval and Reggie parked the SUVs beside each other. Avery noticed that both men backed their respective vehicles up against the ropes, allowing for a quick escape from the area if that was required. Growing up with Val had taught Avery that this was second nature to anyone in the getting-out-of-Dodge-quickly business. She felt a pang as she realized Harrison would have done the same if he were here now instead of locked up in some godforsaken Egyptian prison.

"Ready, love?" Duval asked, tugging Avery back to the here and now. His smile said he understood that she was worried.

"Ready," Avery said as she hopped out of the vehicle. A five-minute walk through the encampment brought them to a structure that was half plywood and half canvas. Inside they found renowned UK archeologist Dr. Kate Granderson. Granderson looked exactly as Riva had described, right down to her piercing and inquisitive eyes.

"Avery Turner," Granderson said, greeting her with a warm handshake. "I watched your TED talk a dozen times. It is such a pleasure to meet you."

"Likewise, Doctor," Avery said as she felt her cheeks blush.

"Please, drop the formalities. Call me Kate, and thank *you* for being here today."

Avery introduced the rest of her party by first name only, calling them her entourage.

"Come, let me show you what we've done," Granderson said after the formalities had been completed.

The doctor led them to a larger tent filled with stacks of high-tech electronics similar to the equipment they'd seen in Antarctica.

"What is all this?" Duval said.

"This is our base of operations. We're using a combination of subsonic shock wave technology and state-of-the-art mapping systems that incorporate artificial intelligence to map out manmade structures beneath the ground."

"You're kidding," Avery said, her voice going up with excitement.

"I thought this might be up your alley—I couldn't believe when Riva said she'd met with you today. We've been constructing blueprints, for lack of a better term, of a tomb that likely hasn't seen the light of day in thousands of years. Older than the pyramids, I suspect. And with a little luck, even more interesting."

Avery studied the equipment and exchanged the occasional nod with the people staffing each station.

"We're on the trail of an ancient mystery of our own," Avery said. "Riva said you might know something about the Pharaoh Heba?"

Kate's brows drew down, her face flushing as she looked around. "Who put you up to this?" she hissed. "I realize you probably have no idea what you're asking, but whoever sent you here…"

Avery raised both hands in mock surrender. "I'm not sure what I said to upset you, but I assure you I meant no offense."

The men looked more intrigued than alarmed or apologetic.

"I've spent years being ridiculed in every academic and archaeological circle for believing in fairy tales about an ancient queen," Kate said, her expression telling Avery her guard was still up.

"I see," Avery said. "And can relate. I made a wildly expensive vanity app that allowed people with more money than they had sense to chase clout more efficiently. I might know a thing or two about people not taking my work seriously."

Kate's face and shoulders relaxed. "I didn't think of it that way."

"We've met with Riva, and our research director has talked to linguists and Greek historians about Heba and her followers. We believe she was real. And honestly, I'm hoping you're about to find her tomb."

Kate nodded, her face stretching into a smile. "I hope so, as well. And I'm glad to have some believers here to witness what I hope will be a day for the history books."

Avery and Duval exchanged a glance.

A particularly sunburned fellow stuck his head inside the tent and waved to get Granderson's attention.

"Yes, Felix, what is it?"

"Doctor, I think we've done all we can to prepare for tomorrow's entry. Thought you'd want to know."

Granderson turned to Avery and the others. "How about it? Would you like to see the spot from which we will make history tomorrow?"

Avery and Duval followed Dr. Granderson while Reggie and Javier walked along behind them keeping an eye out for trouble.

"Tell me more about what led you to this discovery, Kate," Avery said.

"It really has been a monstrous undertaking. Years of research and setback after setback. Writing grants and fighting with bureaucrats. I'm sure you know how that goes. Nobody wants anything to do with it until they think you might actually be onto something. Then everyone wants to tell you what to do, how to do it, and how they want their own piece of whatever you may uncover."

Avery was all too familiar.

"Truthfully, none of this came together as more than just speculation until my new friend Riva tripped over a Byzantine copy of a Greek text that mentioned Heba. I had a single scroll I bought at auction five years ago that led me to suspect that Heba's hidden resting place might be here at Giza, but there were so many unknowns in the text. I believe that Heba's stepson went to great lengths to wipe out any mention of her in Egyptian history. I found one writing from fifty years after her death that indicates that she never even existed. Scant references—like ghosts whispering they were so thin—to a hidden tomb without mention of an occupant were about all we had to go on. Whose tomb? Hidden for what purpose? It wasn't until I found a paper written in 1942 by a linguist in Greece about the Byzantine translation text that I began to truly believe. I have traveled this part of the world hunting down any scrap of information for years, being laughed out of my profession for the trouble, and honing my technology. We've spent months mapping what's under our feet, and then just days ahead of making entry, I happened across Riva, who had just seen the very Byzantine book that started this for me. She was able to fill in some of the gaps in my scroll, as well. I believe the queen is watching over us, and I am beyond excited about the prospect of actually finding her tomb and sharing her legacy."

Duval whistled. "That is a lot of hard work for something that might only have been an urban legend. Didn't you ever doubt what you were chasing?"

Granderson stopped walking and turned to face Duval. "Not for a moment," she said. "I would think that you, a treasure hunter, of all people, would know that even urban legends are usually rooted in fact. While the stories may grow grander over time, they tend to spring from reality."

They followed the doctor until they reached a collection of heavy equipment, piles of sand, and stacks of heavy timbers. Construction workers and engineers dressed in bright reflective vests milled about the site. Amidst all of this was a large gaping hole in the ground that seemed to lead nowhere.

"Reminds me of that Oak Island reality television show," Javier said as he looked down into the timber-reinforced sandy maw.

Granderson laughed. "Not altogether different. We've taken great care to try and prevent a cave-in."

"And you've identified this as the entry point?" Avery said.

"The most likely entry point," Granderson said. "As you know, with AI, everything is about probability. Even the mapping we have been doing has a degree of chance associated with it. Our job has been to find the site and then, using mathematical calculations, come up with the best way inside."

"That almost sounds ominous, love," Duval said.

Kate's eyebrows lifted, and Avery waved a hand. "He calls everybody that."

"Not exactly everybody." Duval smiled. "And I never mean to offend."

Kate nodded. "Ominous is sort of at the heart of what we do, isn't it, Mr. Duval?"

"Indeed, it is."

Avery watched the men working in the hole at their feet. Her thoughts oscillated between the scroll she had hidden in the hotel room, the one discovered in Kabrirah's floor safe, and the fact that both she and Granderson had availed themselves of AI as a way to fill in the informational gaps leading to their discoveries. She wondered if perhaps the DiveNav might prove useful in the next phase of Dr. Granderson's search.

"What do you think is down there?" Reggie said.

"Best we can tell, lying about thirty to forty feet below the surface is the top of a very large structure of some kind. The structure itself is composed of hallways and chambers, some of which appear to intersect while others look like they might be sealed off."

"Any idea what the structure is?" Javier said.

"I'm afraid all we can do at this point is speculate. It might be a tomb, or possibly a monument, or even a storage shelter of some type. We don't really know yet."

Duval cocked a thumb over his shoulder toward the pyramids. "Any chance it's connected to those?"

"Could be? What we're doing here isn't an exact science. Using instruments to bounce signals off buried stone only gets us so far—until we can actually see and touch what is buried beneath us, most of this is simply speculation."

"I bet you can't wait to get a peek," Avery said.

"You've no idea," Granderson said. "So, what do you say? Would you all like to join me tomorrow on what I hope will be a memorable day for the history of the world?"

"We'd be honored," Avery said.

"We should celebrate this impending discovery," Kate said. "Would you also like to join me for dinner? I have an idea that I'd like to run past you."

"We'd be honored," Duval said a bit too quickly for Avery's liking.

"I don't have any formal wear packed," Avery said. "We've been living on the run as of late."

"Not to worry," Kate said. "I know just the place."

65

Avery and Duval sat across from Dr. Granderson in a cozy restaurant while Reggie and Javier people-watched outside, insisting they weren't hungry.

"You must be very excited about tomorrow," Avery said as the waiter topped off her glass of wine.

"Excited. Nervous. Worried. Take your pick."

"A find like this could set you up for life in the academic world," Duval said.

"Or finally break me," Kate said, holding up her own wineglass for the waiter. "You remember that American journalist with the big nose and mustache?"

"Geraldo Rivera?" Avery said.

"That's him. Well, he did a show years ago about the discovery of Al Capone's safe. Do you remember that?"

Avery shook her head. "I don't."

"I do," Duval said.

"What happened?" Avery asked.

"Nothing," Kate said. "It was a complete bomb. They found this safe hidden in some walled-off room under the Lexington Hotel in Chicago. Built it up that Capone had hidden some top-secret mind-blowing stuff in there—people thought they'd find guns or jewels or incriminating papers

—there was even speculation about a human skull. The whole thing, like two hours of lead-up and then the actual safecracking, was televised live with something like thirty million viewers."

"And?" Avery said.

"Nothing. When they finally opened the safe at the end of the show, there was nothing inside but dust. It was hilarious."

"A PR disaster for the network and the reporter though," Duval said.

"And you're afraid that might happen to you because we're here?" Avery asked. "We don't have to livestream. Or record at all."

"That's kind, except—that's the price of being an explorer," Kate said. "Every discovery comes with its own risks and rewards. Making new discoveries is great, but they are still unknowns. Investors are just speculating when they hand us research checks. Nobody really knows if we'll find anything."

"But it's the thrill of the hunt that keeps you coming back, right?" Duval said.

Kate grinned over her wineglass. "I knew I was going to like you. Are you sure your friends don't want to join us for dinner?"

"Trust me, they are much happier outside," Duval said, earning a curious look from Kate.

"You must have some ideas about what it is that you've found," Avery said, attempting to draw Kate back into the discovery conversation.

"Oh, believe me, I have plenty of thoughts, but nothing concrete. My research has shown that most of what was constructed on a larger scale back then was to honor their kings or gods. But there is nothing to suggest that any kings were ever buried in that location."

"Maybe it's the resting place of a god?" Duval joked.

"If it is, I hope they're in good humor tomorrow when we wake them."

"It's still mind-boggling," Avery said.

"What is?" Kate asked.

"The amount of time that this thing, whatever it is, has been sealed up. You might be the first person in thousands of years to set foot inside it."

"It is an amazingly romantic notion," Kate agreed. "If only I didn't feel like I was going in with one arm tied behind my back. It would be nice to have at least some idea what I'm walking into and where I should focus my attention."

Avery had been wrestling with when or even if to bring up the DiveNav. This seemed as good a moment as any. "Funny you should say that. I might have something that could help."

"I'm intrigued," Kate said as she set her glass on the table and leaned forward.

As they ate, Avery gave an overview of how the DiveNav functioned, employing similar AI technology to what the doctor had used to map out the buried structure.

"So, it's an odds-based system," Kate said.

"I suppose," Avery said. "More than an educated guess. The data used to populate the fields where odds of success are calculated is drawn from historical as well as present day mapping and knowledge. Think of it like DNA threads with gaps that could lead to new discoveries. Each time a new piece of information is obtained, it gets uploaded into the self-learning CPU, filling in those gaps and increasing the likelihood of a successful find."

"And you think your DiveNav might help me avoid becoming the next Geraldo?"

"It can't hurt," Avery said, though secretly she'd been wondering for most of the meal whether the scroll at the hotel that she'd nearly forgotten about in all the chaos might hold a secret they needed.

"What's the catch?" Kate asked.

"No catch," Avery said. "You wouldn't even need to mention the Dive-Nav, unless it ends up being instrumental in a significant discovery. If that happens, I would of course expect to be credited for assisting."

Kate nodded.

"Still your discovery," Avery added.

"Of course," Kate said.

"But a successful find in the desert would do a lot to bolster the versatility of the DiveNav."

"What about the monetary value of any treasure discovered?" Granderson raised an eyebrow.

"Not our concern," Duval said.

"We have no need of it," Avery added.

"How very altruistic of you," Kate said, her speech just beginning to show the first signs of a slur. "If you're not careful, both of you may need to add archeological research assistant to your resumes."

"More wine?" the waiter said as he stopped by the table.

"No more for me," Kate said, holding her hand over her glass. "I need to keep a clear head for tomorrow."

"All set," Avery said.

"None for me either, mate," Duval said.

Avery waited until the waiter had left before speaking. "So, would you like us to bring the DiveNav?"

"Why not?"

66

After dinner, Reggie and Javier drove Avery and Duval back to the hotel, bringing takeaway for Carter and Oscar, who were playing cards in the hotel room.

The journey was again uneventful, and Avery wondered what—if anything—that might mean. Given the absolute train wreck this trip had been, and the vigor so many people involved had shown in trying to deter or murder them, Avery figured there was little chance everyone had suddenly given up. It was far more likely that their adversaries had simply decided to play the long game with more patience. One of the things Avery had learned from their previous experiences was that once people realized how smart she and Carter were together, they were content to sit back and let Avery and Carter do the heavy lifting. And as their reputation grew, the time it took to get there on every hunt seemed shorter.

Avery went directly to the room safe and found the scroll still locked inside. She removed the document and placed it on top of her bed, carefully unrolling it and studying the symbols. Contained within the ancient text were some of the same symbols she had seen when talking to Riva. Symbols the computer could not decode.

The scroll on Avery's bed was nowhere near as old as the ones she'd seen in Riva's lab. This was clearly someone's attempt to copy what Avery hoped was an original document. Perhaps the original was in such bad shape that a copy was needed to preserve it—this was still very old, just not ancient.

As she studied the symbols, she thought about Kate's researchers. Could they be trusted? Since they'd arrived in Cairo, they'd learned that they couldn't trust the Egyptian National Police, the local detectives, politicians. How hard would it be for someone with half a billion pounds they could toss away on a pin to bribe one of Kate's people with the possibility of a big payday?

Avery pulled out her cell and dialed MaryAnn.

She spent a couple of minutes outlining her worries and then took a deep breath. "So, what do you think? Can you put us in touch with someone trustworthy who might be able to help decode this thing?"

"What if I could take a crack at this myself?"

"Oh?" Avery couldn't hide her surprise.

"I have an idea. If you send me jpegs of the scroll in order, I'll stitch them into a single document, which should work fine for my purposes."

After ending the call with MaryAnn, Avery called Roger Antonin again.

It rang six times, and Avery was beginning to think Roger wouldn't answer the phone when finally, he picked up.

"Avery?" He said with a gravelly voice. "Do you have any idea what time it is?"

She didn't. Nor did she much care.

"Anything new on getting Harrison released?" Avery asked, ignoring his protest.

Roger sighed. "Hang on a sec. Let me go to the other room so we don't keep my wife awake too."

Avery listened to the shuffling of Roger's feet and imagined him moving from the bedroom down the hall to his study.

"Okay," Antonin said. "I'm doing the absolute best I can here, Avery. But you've gotta understand what kind of mess this is."

"I don't care how messy it is, Roger. They've got Harry and Marco, and they're only holding them to keep Carter and me in this country. Do you have any idea what the weight of that guilt is doing to me?"

"Be that as it may, the official word from the State Department is that the Egyptian government believes Harry is some kind of tomb raider. We're talking Indiana Jones, for crying out loud. They say he stole some significant artifact."

"That's ridiculous," Avery said. "Harry has been with us the entire time we've been here. If he was stealing artifacts, I think I'd know about it. What are they alleging he stole?"

"I didn't say I believe them. All I know is what my contact told me."

"They delivered a note to the hotel, Roger, right after they took Harry away, telling us to sit tight and await further instructions. Does that sound like everything's on the up and up to you?"

"No, that sounds like a kidnapping," Roger agreed. "But I don't know what you want me to do, Avery. I'm more in the dark about what might really be going on there than you are."

Avery could feel her frustration building. She was angry that Roger wasn't getting anywhere, and she was still upset with herself for dragging all of them into this mess in the first place.

"What about Senator Byers? Did you find out anything about her?"

"According to my contacts, Byers is a real piece of work—slippery as an eel and just as likely to bite. She's been investigated multiple times dating back to her time in the US House of Representatives, but nothing ever sticks. But given where you are and her references to instability, it's worth mentioning that some of the charges pertained to meddling in the oil market. Whenever the press tries to pin her down on anything leaked, she chalks it up to partisan politics and calls it a witch hunt. I don't know what her endgame is here, but I'd say you shouldn't trust a single thing she's told you. When was the last time you spoke to her?"

"When we left her office for the airport. She won't return my calls."

"Stop trying. I'll keep stirring the pot. In the meantime, don't take any unnecessary chances, okay? Just wait until you hear from me."

67

The sky was cloudless as Avery, Duval, and Oscar made the drive from the hotel to the dig site. The weather forecast called for temperatures to reach triple digits. Avery was nursing an extra-large coffee, having managed no more than a few hours of sleep. Between her conversations with Roger and MaryAnn, her brain was stuck in problem-solving mode, killing any chance at actual rest.

Carter had begged to go with them, but with his injuries, Avery figured he would be more of a liability than an asset. Besides, as long as he was tucked away under guard with Javier and Reggie at the hotel, he was one less person for her to worry about.

MaryAnn and Avery had chatted via FaceTime several times throughout the night, and each new piece of information the scroll offered had been uploaded into the DiveNav. Avery wasn't sure how much help the device would be once the search ensued, but she felt much better armed with information that nobody else had.

"How are you feeling?" Duval asked from the driver's seat of the SUV, snapping Avery out of her own thoughts.

"Tired," she said.

"Valid," Oscar said.

"But I'm excited about today's search."

"I'm sure I don't have to tell you that we have to be careful. Up until now it has been crazies chasing us all around. If we actually get inside this tomb, or whatever it is, God knows what we may run into."

"Luckily, I'll have you two watching out for me," Avery said.

Duval grinned. "We're not going to be much match for a ghost or a mummy." His voice was light, but was that worry she read in his eyes?

"Is that the DiveNav device I've heard so much about?" Kate asked as Avery removed it from her bag.

"It is," Avery said. "Would you like a look?"

"Please," Kate said, accepting the device as if it were as fragile as an egg. "I did some reading last night and I'm fascinated."

"Don't worry," Avery said. "It's tough. You won't hurt it."

"It doesn't look like much," Duval said. "But Avery has used that baby to make some huge discoveries."

A burly, deeply tanned man stuck his head through the tent flap. "Dr. Granderson, we're ready when you are."

"Thank you, Aaron," Granderson said before turning back to Duval and Avery. "You ready to help me make history?"

"After you, Doc," Duval said.

Several members of the crew were around for the dig, though only a few people would actually accompany them into the opening. Avery noticed that additional staging and ladders had been added to the excavation since the day before. The stone blocking the opening had been lifted from the structure and now hung above the dark rectangular entrance to whatever lay beneath them.

The search party consisted of Dr. Granderson, her assistant, three of Aaron's men, Avery, Oscar, and Duval. They were each fitted with a high-tech hard hat, each with built-in headlamps and wireless high-definition cameras allowing them to record everything they saw in real time. Kate said there would be extensive Hollywood-type editing if anything came from the search. In addition to the cameras, each of them also had a belt-mounted receiver that allowed them to monitor in real time what everyone else was seeing.

"I'd rather not have such a large exploration party," Granderson said. "The last thing we need is a bunch of your people trampling everything, Aaron."

"While I understand your reticence, Doctor, I have been involved in a number of these around the world and you're going to want my people there to monitor the situation and protect you." He glanced at Avery. "And you are the one who added three people at the last minute."

"You're expecting booby traps?" Oscar's eyebrows went up.

"Yes," Aaron said. "On the first entry to an ancient tomb, that is exactly what I expect. The people who built these underground tombs or vaults or whatever this turns out to be were very aware of future generations of looters who might be tempted to get their hands on all the valuables. It was considered a vital part of their faith to guard against that."

"And how do you propose to keep us all safe, mate?" Duval asked.

Aaron turned toward him. "My people will lead the way, looking for anything suspicious. If they find something, they will stop us and attempt to make it safe to proceed."

"And if the booby-trapped section works?" Avery said.

"Then it will be my people injured and not any of you."

Aaron's words did little to comfort Avery. A quick glance at the others told her they felt every bit as vulnerable as she did.

Aaron turned back to Kate. "Shall we go then, Doctor?"

68

The air inside the sandstone structure was stale and strange, the smell of sand and musk edged with a bit of decay. Sound traveled differently than Avery had expected, likely a result of being under tons of sand. The small party was joined together by a nylon tether that ran through carabiners hung from their belts, the idea being that if one of them got into some kind of trouble, the others would be able to pull them to safety. The last person into the tunnel was tethered to a monitor topside, who was responsible for helping them find their way back out.

Avery listened as Granderson excitedly narrated their descent into the structure. She hardly resembled the cool, fact-driven scientist they had met yesterday—standing at the mouth of the chamber, she looked more like a kid who'd just been handed the key to Disneyworld.

"I can only see about ten feet in front of me," Kate said. "The darkness seems to swallow up the light beams."

"Hold up a second, Doc," Aaron said from the front of the line.

"What is it?" Duval asked.

"Not sure. There is a pattern engraved on the floor."

"Let me see." Kate unclipped herself from the tether line.

"That's not a good idea," Aaron cautioned. "That line is meant to keep you safe."

"Can you read ancient script or symbols?" Granderson snapped.

"You know I can't."

"Then you need me to decipher the design."

Aaron stepped to one side.

"Thank you."

Avery watched as Kate shuffled to the front of the line and knelt to study the floor. Avery held up her own monitor, watching in real time what Kate was seeing. Unlike the previous sections of sandstone floor, the one in front of them contained a number of cobblestone-sized pieces into which symbols had been carved. Each of the stones stood out of the tunnel floor by an inch or two as if they were triggers of some type.

"What do you think they are?" Avery called.

"I'm not sure," Kate said before radioing up to the surface. "Are you seeing this, Riva?"

"I am, Doctor," Riva said. "Give us a minute and we'll see if we can decode them for you."

Avery wasn't sure what any of the symbols represented, so she was studying the way the stones were laid out. The pattern wasn't entirely random, though Avery's adrenaline level was so high she was having trouble solving the puzzle. The eye was the key—it was the one carving that repeated at various intervals. Avery's eyes compared the other symbols around each one.

After what seemed like an eternity, the linguist radioed back. "It doesn't appear to be a warning of any kind. The stones themselves indicate that the tunnel is a holy place, but nothing further."

"What about the positions of the stones?" Avery said, keying her own microphone. "Do you see a pattern? I feel like there's something there I just can't quite unlock."

"We do not, Miss Turner. Our suggestion is that the eye stones very likely point out the position to be followed. Step carefully only on the eye stones. They should lead you through."

"Great," Duval said. "I don't want to be down here any longer than necessary."

"Spooked, are you?" Aaron asked.

"Bored," Duval countered.

"Okay, everyone," Kate said as she returned to her place in line and clipped her carabiner onto the tether cord. "We're moving on."

One by one they each moved forward, giving the person in the lead enough slack to control their progress. As soon as the first man had cleared the stones, stepping only on the eyes, the next person moved into position and so on. They continued the maneuver until they had reached the end of the line where one of Aaron's men brought up the rear. He was halfway across the stones when he stopped.

"What's wrong?" Kate asked. "Why are you stopping?"

No answer. Avery turned in time to see the man rear back and let out a violent sneeze.

"Thanks for that, mate," Duval said. "I don't even want to think about where that landed."

No sooner had the words escaped Duval's lips than the man lost his balance, stepping down on a stone with a crescent moon carving. A hollow thud sounded above them, and the stone disappeared into the floor, clearly setting something in motion.

Avery looked on in horror as the floor beneath the man seemed to fall in on itself, pulling him down with it. What had previously appeared to be solid flooring now looked like sand cascading down inside an hourglass.

Realizing he was in trouble, the man screamed for help as he struggled to find something to grab onto, coming up with handfuls of sand as the floor of the tunnel seemed to swallow him whole.

He had sunk nearly to his waist in seconds and showed no signs of slowing. Avery felt the first tug on the tether.

"Pull," Aaron screamed. "We must keep him from going under."

Kate unclipped herself again and ran to the back of the line, wrapping her hands in the tether cord and yanking even as her feet slid slowly toward the edge of the trap. Everyone fought, but it was no use. Something unseen was pulling the man down, something more than gravity or his own weight.

"Cut the line, Doc!" Duval shouted.

"I can't," Kate said through gritted teeth as she tried to inch backward. "He'll die."

"If you don't, we'll all die," Duval said.

It was an impossible choice for almost anyone to make.

Avery realized that Kate, feeling the weight of responsibility for the expedition, wouldn't act until it was too late. Unclipping herself from the line, Avery pushed past Kate and drew her own knife, quickly sawing away at the nylon separating Kate from Aaron's man. The man reached up and tried to grab at Avery, but she feinted out of his reach and kept cutting. Finally, the cord snapped, and the end of the line fell into the cascading sand.

Avery watched helplessly, tears streaming down her cheeks, as the wild-eyed man continued to scream. She felt Duval's arms encircle her shoulders and heard Aaron urge them to go on as Kate turned away and vomited into the sand. Avery wasn't leaving this man to die alone if she couldn't save him. The screams came to an abrupt end as he slipped beneath the surface of the floor and out of sight. The last thing Avery saw were his gloved hands clawing at the sifting sand that now covered the floor where the stones had been.

69

An eerie silence settled thick over them. Avery looked around to see the shocked faces of their party as each carefully climbed back to their feet. Aaron moved back to re-examine the floor, which appeared whole and benign. The steppingstones had vanished as if they were never there to begin with, and only the sand remained.

"Well then. I don't want to be tethered to any of you," Aaron's other "expert" said. "Whatever that was nearly dragged us all down there. If the civilian hadn't stepped in, we'd be buried alive."

"Anyone no longer wishing to be tethered, feel free to unclip from the line," Kate said hollowly.

"I wish that had happened before we all walked across it," Duval said as he removed his carabiner from the rope.

"I agree with Mr. Duval," Aaron said. "It would seem as though retreat isn't a very viable or enticing option. I suppose I can't speak for everyone, but I'm not excited about trying to walk back across that ground just now, and I was never good at the long jump."

"You can't seriously be thinking about pressing on." Kate's assistant looked horrified. "You saw what just happened to that man."

"We did," Aaron said. "And though it is unfortunate, my man understood the risks, as we all do."

"I agree," Kate said. "We came down here to find something, and I am not leaving until we find it."

Duval turned to Avery and whispered, "Shades of Captain Ahab?"

Avery nodded. None of them knew Kate well enough to know what made her tick, but the fact that she had invested years of her young life into pursuing a noteworthy archeological discovery that had made her a laughingstock, and might now be on the verge of proving the doubters wrong, meant she was likely feeling the rush most treasure hunters felt as they neared the finish line. Avery read the wild look in Kate's eyes as a sign the doc would be happy to sacrifice all their lives if it meant vindication awaited her.

"It's safe to say we have no idea what other fun surprises might be waiting for us around the next corner," Duval said. "For the sake of the group, let's slow down and use our collective brain power."

"Still bored, Mr. Duval?" Aaron said.

"All set now, thanks," Duval retorted.

Avery turned to Aaron. "How much of this type of thing have you done?"

He glanced at Kate before answering. "Not all that much. I am an engineer by trade. I have done three other digs, and signed on to this project because the doctor promised to make me famous."

Avery sighed, shuddering when a large black beetle skittered over her shoe. "Well, if we don't do a better job of navigating our way through here, you may just get your wish."

They continued on through the twisting tunnel of rock. Each of them focused on the sandstone seams where the walls met the floor and ceiling of the passageway. Most traps would have to spring from one of those intersecting surfaces.

Avery paused to take a sip from her water bottle. The air wasn't overly warm, but it was dusty, and the stress of the enclosed environment raised her body temperature, causing her to sweat.

"You okay?" Duval asked as he moved up beside her.

"I think so?" Avery tried to smile. "You know what I keep thinking about?"

Duval shook his head, uncapping his own bottle of water.

"I'm thinking about how much I hate tunnels."

"The coal mine you told me about?"

"Yeah, the coal mine. I keep waiting for the lights to go out."

"Well, with this many lights, I don't think you need to worry about that."

"How about skeletons?"

"That I can't guarantee. I mean, truthfully, isn't that what we're hoping to find down here?"

Avery nodded before sliding the bottle back into her belt and moving forward.

Several minutes later they came to the first split in the tunnel.

"Okay, everybody," Kate said. "Let's stop here while I figure out our next move."

"Aye, aye, Captain," Duval whispered. Avery managed a genuine smile this time.

Aaron and Kate examined the two different passageways. One of them broke off to the left and appeared to maintain the same level upon which they had been walking, while the floor of the right-hand tunnel pitched sharply downward.

Oscar joined Avery and Duval. "I'm betting on the left passage."

"I'll pick the other one, then," Duval said before turning to Avery. "What about you, love? Got a favorite?"

"Not a favorite, per se, but I think the doctor will go with the right one."

"Why?" Oscar asked.

"Because the tunnel descends sharply. She'll see it as a quick route to whatever is hidden down here."

"What if the people who built this godforsaken hole planned on that?" Duval asked.

"To make it more tempting?" Oscar asked.

"That is a reasonable assumption," Avery said.

"Okay, everyone," Kate announced. "We'll continue forward in the right passage."

"Shocker," Duval said with a wink.

"Hey, Doc," Avery called.

"Yes?"

"We've been discussing it," Avery said. "And we think we should stick with the left-hand tunnel."

"Why?" Aaron said.

"Because the one on the right could be a trap," Duval said.

Kate put her hands on her hips. "Is this based on some scientific theory or more of your layman's conjecture, Mr. Duval?"

"One heck of an educated guess," Duval said.

"As much as I value your wit, this is still my exploration, and you are only here as a guest. And I say we move down the right-hand passage."

Kate turned to Aaron, and he waved another of his men forward. Avery could see the fear in the man's posture as he studied the entrance to the tunnel.

Kate and Aaron decided to tie a rope around the man's waist before he entered the passageway while the others hung back gripping the rope in case of trouble.

"Sure, because that worked so well last time," Duval whispered. Avery just shook her head, eyes glued to the activity at the mouth of the tunnel.

"Now, if anything goes wrong you shout and we'll pull you out," Aaron said to the man.

"And if you can't?" Duval asked.

"It will be fine," Kate said, but her words rang phony to Avery.

The man carried an extra light to supplement the one on his hard hat. Using it to inspect every inch of the space, he moved forward one careful step at a time. Avery and the others gradually fed more line, maintaining a hand-over-hand grip on the rope as they followed his progress from the main tunnel. The angled floor continued downward until the man was standing well below them.

"I think I found something," he called as he stopped to inspect one of the tunnel walls.

"What is it?" Aaron said.

"Some type of metal grate. Copper maybe. Big. Set into the wall."

"What would that be used for?" Avery asked Kate.

"Could be anything, really."

"With all due respect, Doc," Duval said, "only two things I've ever known a metal grate to be used for. Keeping something out or—"

"Wait, there's a crack in the floor." The man stepped farther into the tunnel and a metal-on-stone shriek had everyone covering their ears.

"Keeping something in," Avery shouted. "Come back!"

He didn't move, and they watched in horror as the grate swung neatly across and into a niche on the opposite wall, trapping the man at the lower end of the tunnel.

"Help," the man began to shout. "I can't move this thing."

Avery detected the panic in his voice.

"Wait a minute," the man called. "I hear something."

"I hear it too," Duval said. "It sounds like—"

"Snakes!" Avery screamed as she pointed to a hole in the ceiling from which a steady stream of large, brownish-colored snakes poured into the tunnel. Each of the oversized serpents slithered quickly toward the man.

"Jesus, I hate snakes," Duval said.

"What kind of snakes are those?" Kate's assistant asked.

"Egyptian cobra," Aaron said, his voice faint.

"Their venom is a mixture of neurotoxins and cytotoxins." Kate looked horrified.

"English please," Duval said.

Aaron shook his head. "She means he is about to die from respiratory failure."

"Oh my God," Avery said.

Aaron withdrew the knife from his belted sheath and quickly sawed through the nylon connecting them to his man.

"What are you doing?" Kate's wide-eyed assistant said. "You can't just leave him down there."

Aaron sheathed the knife and tossed the severed end down the tunnel. "Perhaps one of you would like to go down there and get him?"

"Not on your life," Oscar said.

"Where did the snakes come from?" Duval asked, rounding on Kate. "I thought you said there hadn't been anyone down here in thousands of years?"

Kate's assistant pushed her glasses up and raised one hand. "Snakes are remarkably adaptive and survival oriented. They could conceivably have been put in a chamber above this one long, long ago and bred new generations underground eating insects. The burrow a snake would use to go to the surface would be insignificant and likely not noticed by anyone out in the desert."

"This is why I say she's the best assistant in the business," Kate said faintly.

Avery felt her heart racing as she watched helplessly from her position in the main tunnel.

More screams echoed around them as the snakes attacked.

Avery turned toward Kate, hoping she might finally see something resembling compassion, but found only greed and determination etched upon the doctor's tanned features.

"Now can we try the left tunnel, love?" Duval said.

Kate fixed him with a look of contempt but said nothing.

"Come on," Aaron said. "Let's get this done."

70

They traversed the other tunnel through countless turns and switchbacks but met no further booby traps. Aaron and his remaining man led the way, followed by Kate and her assistant.

Avery kept pace with the others but felt detached, like the entire thing was nothing more than a bad dream.

"You okay?" Duval asked as he moved up beside her.

"Not really," Avery said, half laughing at the absurdity of their situation. "You know what I keep thinking about?"

"What?"

"I keep wondering how many more people Dr. Granderson and Aaron will sacrifice before they get to us."

"You stick close to me."

"How is it that these traps still work after so much time?" Oscar said.

"Because they're rather uncomplicated," Aaron said. "Rudimentary, but effective if your goal is to keep someone out. They just didn't count on people coming in a large group. Grave robbing was a shameful and therefore solitary pursuit."

Avery's thoughts turned to the idol they had taken from the floor safe and the scroll that accompanied it. What were Kabrirah's warriors protecting?

"I think I've found something," Aaron's remaining man shouted.

Avery exchanged a wordless glance with Oscar and Duval.

"Can't wait to see who gets sacrificed next," Duval muttered.

The group looked on as Aaron and his man checked out the find. Unlike the previous anomalies in the tunnel, this one didn't look ominous at all: In fact, it appeared to be nothing more than a large thin slab of sandstone covering an opening in the tunnel wall. Human skulls were mounted to the stone ledges on either side.

"It can't be this simple," Aaron said.

"Not true." Kate's voice was an octave too high with excitement. "The ancient people were a suspicious lot who believed in the power of magic and curses. Those deeply held beliefs would have been enough to scare off most Egyptians. And those who weren't deterred likely wouldn't have made it past the traps."

"Almost as effective as watching members of your exploration team getting picked off," Duval said.

"Let's get this stone moved," Kate said.

Aaron signaled for his remaining man to help.

"I'd stand back if I were you," Oscar said to Avery.

Avery took several steps back from the stone as Aaron and his man used steel bars to loosen it.

It took several minutes before they were able to pry the impediment loose from the surrounding rock wall and slide it to one side. Avery peered into the passageway but was unable to see anything but darkness inside.

"I half expected some ancient flame thrower to blast us," Duval said.

"Really, Mr. Duval," Kate scoffed. "A flame thrower?"

"Yeah, love, really. It's about the only trick these ancient people of yours haven't thrown at us."

"Don't forget crushing us under a stone fulcrum," the assistant said.

Duval turned to the bespectacled researcher. "I'm really beginning to dislike you."

Aaron picked his last remaining man to attempt navigating the uncovered tunnel. He looked every bit as nervous as the colleague who'd been bitten to death by cobras. Once again, the nylon rope was tied around the man's waist before he shuffled into the passageway.

"This is how Captain Kirk used to treat the guys with red shirts," Duval said.

"Who?" Aaron asked.

"Never mind, mate."

"If you find anything that looks even remotely suspicious, get back here, okay?" Aaron said.

The wide-eyed man only nodded as he stared into the darkness.

"Okay then. Good luck, my friend."

Avery stood with the others as the last explorer slowly moved down the tunnel. Her heart raced, and her stomach felt like it had taken up residence in her throat. It was like watching someone march toward their own death in slow motion.

"Jesus, I hate this." Duval sighed.

"Be thankful it isn't you in that tunnel," Oscar said.

They continued to monitor the man's progress as he moved farther along the tunnel.

"Anything?" Aaron said.

"No," the man yelled back. "It's clear. I don't see any—wait a minute. I think I might have found something."

"What is it?" Granderson demanded.

Avery felt herself tensing as they awaited an answer. Seconds passed before the man responded.

"It looks like steps that lead to another chamber below the tunnel floor."

"Can you see down very far?"

"No. Not without descending into the chamber."

"Okay," Aaron said. "Don't do anything else until I get there."

"You mean until we get there, right?" Kate snapped. "This is my discovery, and you'll not beat me to it, Aaron."

Avery exchanged another glance with Duval.

"This bird is certifiable," Duval said.

"By all means, Doctor," Aaron said. "After you."

Avery and the others moved down the tunnel. Avery took great care in checking her surroundings as she moved, not wanting to trigger another calamity by rushing into the unknown.

They gathered at the top of the steps where their companion stood waiting. The cavern was just as he had described, but deeper than Avery had imagined. The beams from their headlamps did not light even six steps in front of her.

"Well?" Granderson asked impatiently. "Is anyone going to check it out?"

Aaron turned toward her, his eyes narrowing. "We can't see where the stairs end, Doctor. I'm not about to risk another life."

"Then how do we explore this?" the assistant asked.

"Hang on," Duval said. "I've got an idea."

Avery watched as he removed a small plastic glow stick from the pocket inside his pack. He twisted the stick until it made a *snap*, then shook the contents until the thing gave off a greenish glow.

Duval tossed the stick down into the darkness. It sailed past the steps, finally coming to rest about thirty feet below them. The floor was wide and flat, and at the very least there wasn't a trap sensitive to motion or light—or a few ounces of glow stick.

"I half expected it to be crawling with more snakes," Oscar said.

"Let's get on with it," Kate said as she turned her attention back to Aaron.

"Good with this?" Aaron asked his man.

He nodded. "Not sure I trust the stairs though."

"He's right," Avery said. "Let's give him a secure point to rappel from. If the steps are rigged in some way, he'll be able to stop his own fall."

"Good thinking," Aaron said.

"You sure you want to do this, mate?" Duval asked as he and Aaron tied the waistline tether to a sandstone outcropping. "What's your name, anyway?"

"Jamal," Aaron's man said. "And I'll be careful."

71

Jamal took one step at a time, testing each stone platform with his shoe before putting his full weight on anything. He kept a tight grip on the tether, wrapping it around his gloved hands to keep from slipping.

"It looks good so far," he called without looking back.

"Keep an eye peeled," Avery said.

"What am I looking for exactly?"

"Anything out of place or that feels wrong."

"Like crumbling stairs, mate," Duval said.

Avery and Aaron turned toward him and gave him a dirty look.

Duval shrugged. "Just trying to help."

"The next step below me looks funny," Jamal said.

"Funny how?" Kate asked.

"It just looks off, like there are seams that shouldn't be there. All the other steps seemed solid."

"Don't move, Jamal," Avery said as she grabbed a loose stone from the tunnel and moved down the steps.

"Whoa, whoa," Duval said. "Where do you think you're going?"

"To help," Avery said.

"That could be dangerous," Oscar said.

"You should listen to your friends," Aaron said.

"And you should stop volunteering yours," Avery snapped back before continuing down the stairs to Jamal.

"Here," she said, handing him the stone from the step above the one he stood on.

"What am I supposed to do with this?"

"Drop it onto that step," Avery said. "If I'm right, it will set into motion whatever trap they installed here."

"And if that trap brings down the entire staircase?" Aaron called from above them.

"He's right, Avery," Duval said. "Come back."

Jamal nodded. "I'll be okay. Go."

Reluctantly, Avery took several steps up toward the main tunnel, then turned to watch Jamal.

"Ready?" Jamal's voice shook.

Avery nodded.

"Here goes nothing."

Jamal tossed the rock onto the step directly below him and it landed with a hollow thump. Everyone stood holding their collective breath. Just when Avery's shoulders started to relax, a deep rumble began somewhere beneath their feet and everything around them began to vibrate, releasing a cascade of sand from the ceiling high above them.

"Come back," Aaron cried from above them.

"Hurry, Avery," Duval hollered.

Avery and Jamal raced up the steps taking them two at a time. Avery didn't need to look back to know that the entire staircase was collapsing in on itself. The wide eyes of their group and the rumble of falling stone told the story.

Avery and Jamal reached the top step at the same moment, diving onto the tunnel floor just as the last of the steps fell into the cavern far below. Coughing and sputtering, the others helped them to their feet.

"You okay, love?" Duval asked.

Avery nodded.

"Here," Oscar said as he handed her his water. "Drink."

Avery rinsed out her mouth and spit before taking a large gulp of cool water. "Thanks," she said as she handed him the bottle.

Aaron handed Jamal a water bottle too.

"Thank you, Miss Turner," Jamal said.

"Don't mention it," Avery said with a smile.

"Now, how in hell are we supposed to get down there?" Kate stared down into the gaping maw as if nothing had happened.

"Hey, Doc, maybe we should be just a little grateful that Avery and Jamal weren't killed, huh?" Aaron said.

Kate glared at Aaron until she realized that everyone was watching her, including the blinking red light of the camera. Avery watched as the doctor's expression softened. "You're right. Thank you, Avery. I'm glad you and Jamal are okay."

72

Gradually the stone dust began to settle allowing them a glimpse over the edge into the darkness that had returned to the cavern below.

"Got any more of those glow thingys?" Aaron asked.

"A few," Duval said.

"I may have something better," Kate's assistant said before removing the pack from her back and digging through it.

Avery watched her remove a battery-powered lantern.

"Will this do?"

They rigged the lamp with another tether rope and slowly lowered it over the side into the abyss below. As the swinging light moved downward, Avery could see the full level of destruction. The collapsed staircase had left behind nothing but a huge pile of rubble. She didn't want to imagine what that much stone would have done to her and Jamal had they not gotten off the steps in time.

Duval whistled. "Man, that thing was like a house of cards."

"A good description," Aaron said. "Whoever constructed this intentionally made the middle step the keystone to the entire thing."

"I really am glad you're okay," Kate said as she approached Avery.

"Thanks," Avery said, wondering if the doctor had experienced a change of heart, or if her current demeanor had more to do with realizing now that six cameras were recording her every move.

"It's too bad we couldn't get your DiveNav to work down here," Kate said.

"Yeah, I don't understand it," Avery said. "Maybe we just don't have enough information yet."

Even without a satellite connection, the DiveNav should have provided them with some type of guidance. She had used it as an effective locator before when no such uplink existed, simply relying on the internal CPU data combined with state-of-the-art artificial intelligence. It felt like something was blocking it from functioning, but she had no idea what.

"So, how do you propose we get down there?" Duval said.

"Anyone bring a ladder?" Avery said.

"As a matter of fact, yes," Aaron dug into his bag, producing a collapsible rope ladder.

"Brilliant," Duval said. "You're like a tomb raiding Boy Scout, mate."

"Engineers live by the same model of preparedness," Aaron said.

It took them several minutes to figure out how to rig the ladder to the tunnel floor.

"That should work," Aaron said. "I would suggest that we don't have more than one person on the ladder at a time."

"Do you want me to go first?" Jamal asked nervously.

"Why don't I try this time?" Duval stepped up and Avery's heart skipped a beat.

"No," Aaron said. "I think it's time I took some of the risk, don't you?"

"You'll get no argument from me," Oscar said.

"After you," Duval said.

Avery stood beside Kate, watching as Aaron slowly descended the ladder, finally reaching the bottom and stepping off.

"What does it look like?" Kate called.

"Give me a sec," Aaron said as he untied the lantern and began to walk the perimeter of the cavern.

"Well?" the assistant called. "Can you see anything?"

"It's definitely a tomb of some sort," Aaron said.

"I'm going next." Kate pushed past Jamal and climbed onto the ladder.

Duval stepped close to Avery. "Wonder how that will look on camera?"

"She did say she had a good editor."

One by one, they climbed down to the lower chamber. Only Jamal, who'd lost his appetite for adventure, remained topside in case something went wrong.

Avery watched as Kate rushed into another tunnel at the opposite end of the space.

"So much for being careful," Oscar said.

"You think the good doctor has a death wish?" Duval said.

"More like she's blinded by greed," Avery said.

"Or drunk on power," Aaron mused.

They followed carefully, finding Kate gazing awestruck at the mummified remains of two people atop a stone altar.

"Is that who I think it is?" Avery breathed, repulsed and fascinated at the same time.

Kate took her hat off and grinned into the camera. "I, Dr. Kate Granderson, have discovered the tomb of the forgotten pharaoh, Queen Heba."

73

They made it out of the tunnels without losing anyone else, Avery whispering prayers as they passed the points where they'd lost fellow explorers. While Kate rushed to notify the Egyptian government and her research backers of "her" discovery, Avery sat in the shade under a canvas shelter sipping water as she watched people come and go from the entrance to the underground tomb like excited worker bees. Oscar and Duval and several researchers stood a few feet away.

"That's wicked," one of the researchers said as Oscar and Duval told them about the snakes.

Avery tossed the empty water bottle. "It was horrible to watch."

"You're right," the researcher said. "I didn't mean to—"

"I'm sure," Avery said. "Honestly, it doesn't seem real. More like something I dreamt or saw in a movie."

"What do you think?" Oscar said as he sat down beside Avery. "You think that's really Heba's final resting place?"

"I'm not sure," Avery said. "Granderson obviously found someone's tomb down there. But it will take an expert to determine whether the remains are Heba. I don't remember ever reading about a tomb with two mummies on the altar."

"Odd that there isn't some big pyramid marking this spot," Aaron said as he wandered in out of the sun.

"Not really," Avery said. "If that is Heba, her cult needed to hide her from her stepson. A pyramid isn't very discreet."

"Her stepson sounds like a real dick," Duval offered.

"So, level with me," one of the researchers said. "You're here because you think there might be treasure hidden down there somewhere, right?"

"I have no idea," Avery said truthfully. "We didn't get to see much of anything beyond the two mummies."

"Yeah," Duval said. "They whisked us out of there pretty quickly after we risked our necks getting down there."

"I still wager there must be something valuable," Aaron said. "Or why bother with all the booby traps?"

"Those may have just been built to deter the stepson's men from disturbing the tomb," Avery said. "A pharaoh's final resting place was very sacred."

"Who's this now?" Oscar said as they turned to see the arrival of a small caravan of SUVs.

The people spilling out of the silver vehicles had an official air about them. As they approached on foot, Avery spotted a familiar face. It was Ismael, the bureaucrat from the GIS office.

"Hey, isn't that the guy from—" Duval said.

"Yes," Avery said. "It is."

"He sure didn't waste any time getting here," Oscar said.

Avery had been thinking the very same thing. As he and his entourage passed, he regarded Avery with a smug grin.

"Was that a canary feather sticking out of that bloke's mouth?" Duval said.

"It sure looked like he was gloating," Aaron said.

Before Avery could respond, her cell phone buzzed with an incoming call from MaryAnn. "Gotta take this," she said before standing and walking outside the shelter.

MaryAnn asked first about the tomb search, having always wanted to visit a dig site. Avery stuck to the highlights, intentionally avoiding the more graphic demise of some in their party.

"That is so awesome. I wish I could have been there with you."

Avery was glad she wasn't. With Harry and Marco incarcerated and Carter wounded and under house arrest at the hotel, they had suffered enough losses already.

"Okay, I brought you up to speed," Avery said. "Tell me what you've learned."

"I think I managed to decipher some of these unknown symbols on the scroll you found. They are pretty obscure even in Egyptian historical circles."

As MaryAnn explained, two things became obvious to Avery: They had very likely found Heba's remains, though Avery couldn't help wondering who the other body belonged to. But the treasure wasn't down there— MaryAnn said the second thing the scroll revealed was that the vast treasure belonging to Heba was hidden in a separate location.

"It seems clear that her warriors were trying to honor her wishes by hiding everything from her stepson," MaryAnn said.

"Any idea where?" Avery asked even as she wondered how many generations of Heba's warriors there had been.

"Now is the part where I feel like that pin you found is supposed to come in handy," MaryAnn said.

"Maybe that's why they were together in the safe," Avery mused.

Avery wondered again about the true role of the women she and Duval had fought just a few yards away. It was more than a coincidence that one of these women possessed not only the idol but the scroll. They worshipped both the goddess the pin represented and the queen no one knew existed. They could fight. They were smart. And they were singularly focused on guarding the pin. Didn't they have to be direct descendants of Heba's original cult?

Even Granderson, with all her funding, had been driving blind. Whether the doctor would admit it or not, Avery couldn't help feeling that the discovery of Heba's tomb might have been mostly luck.

"Any luck with the DiveNav?" MaryAnn asked, pulling Avery from her reverie.

"No, and I don't know what was wrong with it. I couldn't get it to work while we were underground."

"No signal?"

"That was part of it. Something about the way the tunnel to the tomb was constructed rendered our device useless. But the DiveNav worked in Antarctica even when we were offline. I don't know what happened."

Avery's phone vibrated in her hand as another call came in. She checked the display. Roger Antonin.

"I've got to take this, MaryAnn. It might be about Harry."

"Okay. You want me to keep going with the translation, right?"

"Yes. Don't stop. I'll call you later."

Avery disconnected her call with MaryAnn and accepted Roger's.

"Tell me you've got good news," Avery said.

"I found out where they're holding Harry and Marco. And I managed to pull some strings with someone who works for the Egyptian military."

"Please tell me they're both okay."

"According to my contact, they are being well cared for."

"And when are they going to release them?"

"That will be a lot harder to pull off, Avery. They insist to anyone who asks that Harry's a tomb raider and Marco's a smuggler."

"Harry's not a tomb raider and Marco isn't a smuggler any more than I am, Roger," Avery paused, considering the fact that she had in fact, just walked out of a tomb. She watched Dr. Granderson walk past accompanied by Ismael and several of his men. "But I think I know who might be."

74

Ancient Egypt, 1500 BC

Zefret and her band of female warriors availed themselves of the cover of darkness. Carefully they approached the palace gates, weapons at the ready, watching for the guards. She fed off the surge of nervous energy, nearly palpable as it seemed to crackle in the air around them.

She knelt in the shadows, pausing long enough to pray to Amunet's spirit and the goddess Ammit to keep them safe in this early endeavor to protect the legacy of all their sisters, whether crossing to the afterlife or carrying on in this life. Only vaguely aware of the other women watching her from the shadows, Zefret continued with her short meditation until Eman, a scholar in Heba's court, approached her.

"What is it, sister?" Zefret said softly so as not to be overheard by any of the palace guards.

"I offer a suggestion," Eman said.

"And what is it that you would suggest?"

"Let me go in your stead."

"Why would I do that?" Zefret said.

"Because you are the only leader we have left. We look to you for guidance and strength. If something should happen to you, who will lead?"

Zefret knew Eman spoke the truth, but she resisted. "And what if something should happen to you?"

"The cause is more important than I am, or any of the others, but it is your destiny to lead us forward. To keep Heba's legacy alive for all time."

Zefret couldn't disagree with Eman's assessment, but it pained her to put Eman in harm's way.

As if reading her innermost thoughts, Eman said, "You would not be sending me into the lion's den, sister, for I am offering this to you."

Zefret reluctantly agreed. "Very well, sister. We will wait here until you return."

Eman nodded once, then made for the building that had housed the dead guard's quarters. Zefret and the others split into smaller groups and spread out along the perimeter to wait.

Eman had been gone less than ten minutes when a guard assigned to a roving patrol came around the corner and spotted one of the women. Before any in her group could react, the guard cried out for help.

"Intruders!" the guard shouted. "Stop."

The woman who had been spotted moved quickly to silence him, but it was too late—a dozen men descended upon them.

Zefret stood and fought, taking down two of the responding guards before being wounded herself. The man who had wounded her moved in for the kill.

"Stop," the head guard shouted. "Zefret is to be taken alive."

"Under whose orders?" the angry guard challenged.

The head guard moved in close to the insubordinate man. "By order of Abasi, your pharaoh. Would you dare cross your king, soldier?"

Zefret watched as the guard bowed his head slightly and stepped back.

"A wise choice." The head guard grabbed Zefret by the arm and yanked her away from the gates. A prisoner, she stumbled forward, her eyes catching a glimpse of her sisters racing away into the dark toward what she hoped would be their freedom. Whatever good intentions she had in honoring Eman's request seemed to have been a futile gesture. She had no way of knowing what fate awaited Eman. Her own was clear and it would come at the hands of the man who had betrayed Heba herself. Abasi.

Zefret was dragged, bleeding, into the royal chambers of the palace.

Abasi was summoned from his bed by the head guard. While his disheveled appearance might have been cause for laughter under normal circumstances, these circumstances were anything but normal.

"You and your friends have been a thorn in my side, Zefret," Abasi said as he tied his robe tightly against the night's chill.

"That is unfortunate," Zefret said through clenched teeth, attempting to hide the pain. "Perhaps if you hadn't betrayed our queen."

"Queen?" Abasi spat. "There is no such thing as a queen. I am Egypt's pharaoh now."

"A throne cannot be stolen." Zefret stood defiant. "It must be earned."

"What would you know of royalty, Zefret? You're nothing more than the daughter of commoners."

"And friend to a queen."

Abasi moved in closer and bared his teeth in anger. "When I am through, there will be no recorded history in which your beloved Heba is mentioned. I will see to it that her memory is erased for all time. As will be yours and your followers, along with your pathetic attempt at revolt."

Zefret spat at his feet, attempting to draw him closer. The men holding her gripped her biceps tighter still, while she continued to hold onto her wounded ribs from which blood still flowed.

Abasi took only a half step toward her. "What were you doing outside the palace? And what have you done with the pin?"

"I was out walking, and I know nothing about any pin."

Abasi took another half step toward her. "It is a small golden idol, and I know you have it."

"If you've lost something, perhaps you should ask your lying henchman where it is," Zefret said.

Abasi's eyes narrowed. "What do you know of my henchman?"

"I know one died a traitor's death tonight."

Abasi signaled to two of the guards. "Go and check on my men."

As the guards ran off to check, Zefret exposed her teeth in a wicked smile.

"You and your friends will be executed for your traitorous acts, Zefret. In fact, why wait?" Abasi signaled one of the men holding her. "Hand me your dagger."

Zefret had been awaiting this moment. As the guard on her right removed one hand from her arm, she pounced, pulling the dagger from beneath her own robe, the one she had been using to hold her wound closed. She sliced the throat of the guard on her right. As she withdrew the blade she watched Abasi scamper away from her toward his throne. Without hesitation she swung the dagger at the guard on her left before he could react, slicing his stomach open in one deep cut before plunging the knife into the side of his neck, burying the blade to the hilt.

Abasi yelled from behind his throne for the other guards. Zefret knew she didn't have time to kill the pharaoh before the other guards returned. She pointed the blade at him.

"I will watch you die with my last breath, coward. Mark my words."

"Guards!" Abasi screamed again.

Zefret disappeared into the darkness.

75

Present Day

It was time to call it a day. Avery had long since grown tired of watching Granderson prance around like she was a superstar, stopping to give the occasional interview to the media that had already begun to camp out on the site perimeter.

"Looks like we're yesterday's news," Oscar said.

"At least as far as the good doctor is concerned," Duval added.

"You think she ever really cared about having you guys along?" Oscar said.

"Only as long as she thought we might be able to help her locate Heba's tomb," Avery said absently as she watched the dog-and-pony show playing out before them.

"Or bring her more viewers," Duval added. "But clearly, it was all always about her."

"I agree," Oscar said. "I saw how easily she discounted those who died down there trying to help her find the tomb."

Three things occupied Avery's mind at that moment: getting Harrison and Marco out of lockup, moving Carter someplace safer, and finding the lost treasure that had already cost so many so dearly. Kate Granderson wasn't in this for humanity, she was in it for herself, and Avery wouldn't let her sacrifice anyone else for her pursuit of fame and riches.

"What's the plan, then?" Duval asked.

"We can't do anything more today," Avery said. "We may as well head back to the hotel and regroup."

"Sounds right to me," Oscar said.

As Avery stood, her cell phone rang. It was Carter.

"Everything okay, Carter?" Avery asked, skipping right past the greeting.

The mention of his name caused all of them to turn their heads toward Avery.

"I am okay, Avery," Carter said. "But I think we might need to move. And the sooner the better."

On the road back from Giza, Duval busied himself securing a safe house. Despite the afternoon traffic, they made it back to the hotel in record time, driving by rather than turning into the lot to give themselves a chance to see what Carter and Javier had seen.

"Got 'em," Oscar said from the driver's seat. "The silver Mercedes directly to the left of the entrance."

"Two figures inside," Duval said.

"What about the other vehicle?" Avery said. "Carter said they spotted two." As if in answer to her question, her phone rang with a call from Carter. Avery answered, putting it on speaker for the others.

"We got two out front in a silver Mercedes," Avery said.

"Found ours too," Carter said. "One man seated inside a black BMW in the rear lot and another man standing beside it looking at the hotel."

"How can we get you guys out of here without being followed?" Avery asked.

"I have an idea about that," Duval said. "Carter, can you put your phone on speaker?"

"It already is," Carter said.

"Javier," Duval said.

"Right here, mate," Javier said. "What do you need?"

"Do you remember how we solved a similar problem in Singapore?"

"I do, indeed," Javier said. "Do you really want to give up one of these vehicles?"

"No, I want you and Reggie to procure an option."

"On it," Reggie said. "We'll let you know when we're ready."

Avery disconnected the call. "What happened in Singapore?"

Duval turned in his seat to face her. "You'll see. Now, let's get Carter ready to travel."

It took them less than ten minutes to gather their belongings and move out of the suite while Oscar commandeered a luggage cart from the lobby. As they packed, Duval monitored Javier and Reggie's progress by text message.

"I still don't understand the plan," Avery said as she hoisted Harrison's bag onto the pile. "These guys were either sent to keep eyes on us or to take us out. How exactly do you plan to lose them?"

"We'll handle everything," Duval said, looking up from his phone screen. "We go down to the lobby while you check out, then we'll load Carter and all your stuff into the SUV."

"And how will that fool anyone?" Carter said.

"Trust me, mate. Okay, let's go. Javier just pulled up in front."

Duval stepped out of the elevator first, while Avery, Carter, and Oscar hung back.

Duval turned and gave them the all-clear signal at which point Oscar pushed the cart into the lobby.

Carter stayed with Duval as Avery went to the desk to drop off the electronic room cards.

"I hope you enjoyed your stay, Ms. Turner," the attendant said.

"It's been quite an adventure, that's for sure."

"I hope you'll consider staying with us again the next time you're in town."

"I can't wait," Avery said, while thinking that she couldn't imagine that ever happening. Not willingly anyway.

Oscar had just finished loading the SUV as Avery, Carter, and Duval arrived outside.

Avery and Carter sat in the back seat while Oscar climbed back behind the wheel and Duval rode shotgun.

"All set?" Oscar asked Duval.

"Just another minute," Duval said. "Waiting for Reggie to get into position."

"What position?" Carter asked.

"Okay," Duval said. "Let's go."

Avery kept her eyes peeled as Oscar put the vehicle in Drive and pulled away from the hotel entrance.

"Both of our tails are on the move," Duval said.

"Which exit do you want me to—" Oscar began before Duval cut him off.

"Make like you're going to exit out the front of the lot, then swing around to the rear."

"Got it."

Avery could see the Mercedes approaching from the right. It appeared the driver was trying to time their arrival so that they could fall in behind the SUV as they exited. Oscar's sudden change of direction seemed to throw them off and they made eye contact with Avery as they passed.

"That guy looks pissed," Carter said.

"He knows we've made him," Oscar said.

"You think he's pissed now, wait until Javier makes contact," Duval said.

Avery was about to ask what that meant when she saw a vehicle back up at a reckless rate of speed from a parking spot and ram the Mercedes's front fender, pushing the luxury sedan sideways across the lot into another car.

"Holy crap," Carter said.

"That guy didn't even look where he was going," Avery said.

"That guy is Javier," Oscar said. "And he knew exactly where he was going."

"Vehicle one is out of commission," Duval said.

"How do you know?" Avery said.

"The right front wheel. It's lying sideways on the pavement."

"What about the guys inside?" Carter said.

"Hang on a minute," Duval said, watching his phone screen. "They are out of commission too." He held up his cell phone. The picture on the screen showed two men seated in the front seats clearly unconscious with the smoke from the airbags still floating from the open windows.

"Onward, Jeeves," Duval crowed.

"It's Oscar, you pompous ass."

"I imagine a similar fate awaits our friends in the BMW?" Avery asked with a nervous laugh.

"Now you're getting it, love," Duval said.

76

After taking out both tail vehicles and their occupants, Avery and her entourage continued, unbothered and unfollowed, toward the safe house. Avery's SUVs led the way, while Reggie and Javier followed.

"I gotta hand it to you guys," Carter said. "That was pretty slick the way you shook our tails."

Duval laughed. "It's an old street trick."

"Whose cars were those that Javier and Reggie used?" Avery asked.

"Not a clue, love," Duval said. "Hopefully, they're insured."

"And the guys inside them?" Carter said.

"Sleeping peacefully at the moment, I hope," Duval said. "Reggie and Javi got their guns, too."

"They'll wake up with bad headaches," Oscar said, giving Avery a wink in the rearview mirror.

"Not to mention trying to explain the accidents to the local police," Duval said. "And the loss of their guns to their employer."

Avery wondered who that employer might be.

It took the better part of an hour to reach the safe house. When they arrived, Oscar and Reggie drove the SUV inside an underground garage attached to the main residence. The door closed automatically behind them, triggering overhead lights.

"Honey, we're home," Duval said as he climbed out of the vehicle.

The safe house was big. A sprawling one-story built atop a concrete substructure, which according to Duval had been reinforced to withstand a serious assault.

"Anyone comes looking for you here, we head directly to the basement, capisce?" Duval said.

"But they shouldn't be able to find us, right?" Carter said.

"No reason they should," Javier confirmed.

They spent the next half hour getting settled. Avery took one of the rooms that afforded a view of the ocean, unpacking the few clean clothes she had left in her bag before hopping into her private shower. She ran the water as hot as she could stand, and it felt good on her aching and bruised muscles and quieted her racing mind. She shampooed her hair twice, wondering if the desert sand would never come out.

Clean and dry, she stood in front of the full-length mirror and assessed the damage. Her entire body looked like a psychedelic paint party. The bruises she'd gotten shortly after their arrival had begun to heal, now an ugly shade of green turning to yellow. She was glad there were no keynote addresses on her upcoming schedule. The only wardrobe that would hide her injuries was a full-length snow suit.

A knock on the bedroom door startled her.

"You decent?" Carter called.

"Just a minute," Avery said as she hurried to the bed and slipped into sweatpants and a T-shirt. Smiling, she opened the door.

"What's up?" Her heart thumped harder when she opened the door to find Carter standing there freshly showered and shaved.

"I'm gonna throw in a few of my clothes in the washing machine. Didn't know if you wanted to add anything before I ran a load."

"Thanks, I'm down to almost no clean clothes."

As Avery turned to gather her laundry, her phone rang with a call from MaryAnn. She handed Carter a bundle wrapped up in a linen shirt and picked it up.

"How goes it?" MaryAnn asked.

"You wouldn't believe me if I told you," Avery said as she sat on the edge of the bed and filled MaryAnn in on the afternoon's happenings.

"Jesus, we're going to have to change your name to Trouble if you keep finding so much of it." MaryAnn said. "Any news on Harry or Marco?"

"I know they're being well cared for," Avery said. "Roger Antonin has a source inside the Egyptian government, but they aren't planning to release them yet. They have Roger convinced they really think Harry is really some kind of grave robber."

"That's ridiculous," MaryAnn said.

Avery couldn't agree more. In fact, if there was anyone in their group who was least likely to steal something from a tomb or anywhere else, it was Harrison.

"Are you guys still at the hotel?"

"We decided to change locations to be closer to the dig site. Speaking of which, can you dig up some background on Dr. Kate Granderson?"

"Sure. Anything specific that you're looking for?"

"Just trying to get a handle on her."

Avery wasn't sure what she hoped to find out about the doctor. Maybe she was simply hoping to confirm that Granderson was motivated by greed and her ego and not something more sinister.

"Speaking of Granderson and her discovery, I ran across a friend of a friend of a friend who might interest you," MaryAnn said. "She works at the university library not far from the pyramids."

"Oh?" Avery raised her eyebrows.

"Yeah, she runs the women's history section of the library. Apparently they possess some interesting wax recordings of lectures that the former chair of women's studies gave on the legend of the Pharaoh Heba."

"You're kidding," Avery said, having no idea what a wax recording was but picturing something similar to Harry's collection of pressed vinyl record albums.

"Nope. And my friend said that she'd be more than happy to give you private access if you'd like."

"I'd like. Tell her we'll be there in the morning."

77

Early the next morning, Avery and Carter were driven to Cairo University. MaryAnn's "four degrees of Kevin Bacon" colleague, Amina Saqqara, worked in the Archaeology Conservation Center Library, specializing in women's history.

The university was in a high-traffic area of the city, surrounded by congested streets of cars, buses, and pedestrians. The domed ballroom was located just inside the university's grand entrance. Avery gazed around at the eclectic style of the various structures. Everything from copper-domed buildings to stone clock towers to Greek Revival–influenced buildings that reminded her of Washington, DC. Surrounded by lush greenery and palm trees, the immaculate campus looked like it could have sprung from the creative mind of Walt Disney himself.

"Aren't you coming in with us?" Avery said as Duval pulled up in front and stopped next to the sidewalk.

"I'd rather wait out here in case you and Carter need to make a quick getaway," Duval said. "I'll park in one of the nearby lots."

"You expecting trouble?" Carter gave Duval a wry grin.

"Always, mate."

"Okay," Avery said. "Text me if anything goes wrong out here."

"Likewise."

Avery and Carter entered the air-conditioned lobby and asked one of the students for directions to Amina Saqqara's office.

Saqqara's face lit up when they walked in "You look just like you do on television," Amina said.

"You're too kind, Ms. Saqqara," Avery said.

"As do you, Mr. Mosley. Though I always picture you in your diving gear."

"Thanks," Carter said. "That's where I'm most at home."

"I spoke to MaryAnn yesterday about your research into Heba." Saqqara's eyes lit up. "The news of the tomb is so thrilling! I learned of her as a legend, a made-up story, they said. To think the stories were true... She was generations ahead of her time."

"We're trying to find out all we can about her," Avery said. "In fact, we were actually part of Dr. Granderson's discovery yesterday."

"You were there?"

"I was unable to make it," Carter said. "But Avery was there."

"It was great to be a part of it," Avery said. "I hope it turns out to be Heba's lost tomb."

"As do I. The inspiration she will give to the coming generations of Egyptian women."

Avery waited for Amina to get to the point of their visit.

"I understand you would like to listen to the wax gramophone lectures we have about the Pharaoh Heba."

"Very much so," Avery said. "I must admit, I've never heard of a wax recording."

Saqqara nodded. "They are very old and predate analogue recording on pressed vinyl. Come, I will show you."

She led them to the elevator, then up to the top floor of the library.

As they exited the elevator and stepped into the private space, Avery was immediately overcome by the smells associated with old tomes. There was something distinctly romantic about bound paper, leather, and ink. The feel of the books, the scent, gilded pages, and the infinite lifetimes of historical knowledge contained within.

They followed Saqqara past the rows of shelving to the back of the floor where a fancy soundproof room, constructed of hard wood and glass, stood in one corner of the space.

"This is where we keep one of our most prized possessions," Saqqara said. "The wax gramophone."

Avery and Carter moved in for a closer look. Neither of them had ever seen anything like it. The player looked a lot like an older version of the record player Avery remembered seeing on her mom's old RCA labels when she was little. The unit was an oak box with a hinged cover to protect the player mounted within. Protruding from the outside was a hand crank and fluted metal horn which acted as a speaker. Inside the player looked more like an antique sewing machine than anything resembling an audio player.

"Wow," Carter said. "That looks pretty cool. Where does the recording go?"

Saqqara pointed before she moved to a row of shelves, retrieving two long, thin cases and bringing them to the table. She unclipped the clasps on one of them and opened the lid. Inside were rows of what looked like cardboard spools roughly the size of a removable 35mm camera lens. She brought it to the table where the gramophone was perched.

"The original wax recordings only held about two minutes' worth of information, but these were second generation with smaller grooves."

"How much information do they hold?" Avery asked.

"About four minutes."

"Man," Carter said. "Tough way to record lectures. Maybe they were shorter back then."

Saqqara laughed.

"These two trays contain the lectures about the legend of Heba."

The gramophone itself was easy to use after Saqqara gave them a short tutorial. It was clear that they would be spending as much time changing the recordings as they would listening to the lectures.

"I'll leave you to it," Saqqara said. "Any trouble and you know where to find me."

"Thanks," Avery said.

78

Avery scrounged up a pad of paper and pen and began taking notes from the professor's lecture while Carter manned the gramophone, changing out recordings almost constantly.

Avery jotted any items of interest through five tubes and was listening intently to one recording when Carter began to swap it out with another.

"Wait," Avery said. "Would you replay that one? I want to hear it again."

As Avery listened to the recording a second time, she picked up on something she had previously missed. The professor spoke about the lost queen of the ancient world and her high priestess, who Riva mentioned, but also of a third woman who was a trusted advisor, a doctor and mother. Avery couldn't help wondering how those roles had intersected in ancient Egypt and what they might mean when it came to helping them to locate the treasure. She made a note.

"Okay, you can change it now," Avery said.

"Your wish is my comm—" Carter stopped, tipping his head.

Avery froze, the sound of a commotion coming from downstairs.

"What is that?" Avery said.

"Someone's yelling," Carter said.

Avery picked up her cell phone and checked for text messages. To her horror she saw that she had missed two from Duval minutes earlier:

Police r entering the building.

U 2 scram.

Before Avery could read him the messages, Carter's eyes widened as the sound of shouting drew nearer.

"Duval says it's the—"

"Police," Carter cut her off. "Yeah, and they're coming up the stairs. Come on."

Avery closed and latched the lid on the case of recordings they had yet to listen to and hugged it to her chest.

"What are you doing?" Carter said from the doorway. "We don't have time for this, let alone anything to play those on."

"Doesn't mean we won't find something. I'm not leaving clues behind for someone else to find."

"Let's go. They're almost here."

They raced up the back staircase to the roof, searching for an escape route. After closing the heavy steel door, Carter looked around for something to block it. Leaning against the small dormer next to the door was a four-foot section of two-by-four that appeared to have been used to prop the door open. Carter grabbed it and forced it up under the outside door handle, kicking the lower end into the roofing asphalt to jam it into place.

"You think that will stop them?" Avery said.

"It will at least slow them down," Carter said. "Come on. We've got to find a way down from here."

They quickly moved around the outer edge of the roof. On one side was a metal fire escape that led down to the ground where a uniformed officer was pacing. On the opposite side was another flat-roofed building. But was it close enough to jump to in their banged-up states?

"It's a little lower than we are," Avery said as she backed up preparing to run. "Think we can make it?"

"Are you crazy? That's almost ten feet, Avery. And it's five stories down if we don't. Harry will kill me if anything happens to you."

"Not if you're already dead." Avery's joke fell flat and she put both hands up.

"Sorry. What's your idea?"

"Give me a hand with this ladder," Carter said as he retrieved an abandoned aluminum ladder from the side of the HVAC unit mounted to the roof.

Carter extended the ladder to its full height, then struggled to lower it to bridge the gap between the buildings. The far edge just reached as it clanked noisily onto the other roof.

"You go first, and I'll steady the ladder. Go."

Avery slid the case of recordings along in front of her as she shimmied over the ladder. She was halfway across the expanse when she heard the sound of splintering wood. She turned her head to see the board Carter had used to block the door break in two and the door swing open.

"Don't look," Carter yelled. "Just keep going."

"There they are," a voice cried out from behind them.

"Come on, Carter," Avery yelled as she dove onto the opposite rooftop.

Carter scrambled quickly across the ladder, not looking back. He was halfway to Avery when the police grabbed onto the ladder and lifted, trying to upend it and send Carter to his death.

"Hang on," Avery yelled as she fought to hold her end in place.

Carter held tight and crawled faster toward Avery.

She watched in horror as the officers shoved the other end to one side, angling the ladder until only one rail was still in contact with the edge flashing while the other dangled precariously. What kind of policemen were these people?

"Carter!" Avery screamed.

79

Avery laid her body out full length, bracing her feet against a bulkhead while fighting to maintain her grip on the ladder as she fought to keep the officers from pushing their end completely off the building.

"Hurry, Carter." Avery forced the words through clenched teeth. "I can't hang on much longer."

"I'm going as fast as I can." Carter straddled the rails like they were railroad tracks and shuffled toward her on his hands and knees.

As Avery looked across the expanse, she realized that the officer was attempting to figure out what she was doing to counter her efforts. Carter had nearly reached the rooftop when a second officer joined the first, wrestling the other end of the ladder away from her.

"Now, Carter," Avery yelled. "Jump!"

Carter leapt from his knees toward the roof, his fingertips just managing to catch the elevated lip of the ledge as the ladder clattered to the ground fifty feet below.

"Hold on." Avery ignored the scrape of the hot asphalt on her bruised skin as she shimmied toward him. "I gotcha."

Carter planted his feet against the building's concrete façade and climbed like he was trying to ascend a cliff face as Avery grabbed onto his wrists and pulled him up and over the edge. They landed in a heap, nose to nose with Carter's weight on Avery's injured torso.

Her breath stopped as their eyes met.

It didn't hurt that bad.

Carter licked his lips as his eyes traveled over her face, a light in them she'd never noticed. Avery's heart hammered so hard there was no way he didn't feel it—Avery herself figured it was just going to explode and then she wouldn't have any worries left.

Shouts from the other roof made Carter shake his head, pushing himself to his feet and pulling her up beside him.

"Thanks, partner," he said breathlessly as he looked down at the ladder. "That was close."

They both looked over as the officers began hollering for help from the roof of the other building.

"Looks like they got locked out." Avery laughed.

"Oops," Carter said. "If only they had a ladder."

"Come on." Avery picked up the case of wax recordings and hurried toward the door on their own roof.

As Avery reached for the handle, the door opened, revealing two wide-eyed students.

"Excuse us," Avery said as they hurried past and down the stairs.

"Hey," one of the students yelled after them. "You're Avery Turner."

"Now who has a fan club?" Carter teased as they raced toward the first floor.

They took the stairwell to the lobby, then slowed their pace, attempting to blend in with the students milling about. They pushed through the glass entryway to the front of the building to find Duval parked directly in front. He motioned for them to hurry.

Avery chanced a glance toward the library where three officers were just running into the building.

"Guess it's not just us," Carter said smugly as they hurried toward the waiting SUV.

"What do you mean?" Avery said as she opened the closest door.

"There's never a cop around when you need one."

"You kids have fun at the library?" Duval said as he sped away from the curb.

"It's really never been my thing," Carter said.

"Let's go," Avery said as the officer who pushed the ladder off the roof ran from the library.

80

Back at the safe house, they sat around the dining room table like a dysfunctional family joking around and enjoying Oscar's culinary creation while Avery silently mulled over what she had learned from listening to the professor's lecture. She'd thought they knew all the principal players in the story, but the professor also mentioned not only the high priestess but a third woman who was both a doctor and mother. Who was this woman Heba thought so much of? And how was the story lost and then found and then lost again so many times throughout history?

"You're quiet tonight, Avery," Carter said. "You thinking about Harry and Marco?"

"Yeah," Avery lied, feeling guilty that she had allowed them to slip momentarily from her thoughts.

"I'm sure they're fine," Duval said.

"I was thinking about the lecture we were listening to as well," Avery said.

"What about it?" Carter said.

"First off, I'd love to get my hands on another wax recording player so we can listen to the rest of it."

"Let me see what I can do on that front," Duval said.

"What else?" Carter prompted.

"I'm wondering if Heba had been sick at the time of her death."

"What makes you say that?" Reggie said.

"Well, according to the lecture, one of her most trusted advisors was also a doctor."

"That's interesting," Javier said. "I'd be happy if I could just get my doctor on the phone, let alone have her be my spiritual advisor."

"Don't knock the NHS," Oscar said. "You could be stuck paying a bloody fortune for everything like our friends here."

After dinner, Avery retired to her room to FaceTime MaryAnn from her laptop while the others cleaned up and made a nightcap. Avery filled MaryAnn in on what she had found at the university library and about their close call with the police.

"I'd like to learn more about this doctor friend of Heba's," Avery said. "It feels like there is something there worth exploring. Like why would the pharaoh have a doctor at her right hand unless she was ailing? Could you dig into that for me?"

"I'm on it. Speaking of doctors, your friend Kate Granderson has been all over the news, even here," MaryAnn said. "Her discovery has gone viral. I've been looking into the good doctor as you requested and may have found a juicy little tidbit you didn't know."

"Do tell," Avery said.

"There's behind-the-scenes chatter about her having accepted a position within the Egyptian government," MaryAnn said.

"When did that offer happen?" Avery said.

"About a month ago," MaryAnn said.

"Meaning she may have been playing us." Avery's thoughts went to the traps. "Jesus, what if she took us down there with her to get rid of us in one shot?" She shivered. "Aaron insisting on bringing his men might have saved Duval, Oscar, and me."

Avery's phone rang. Unknown number.

"You need to take that?" MaryAnn asked.

"The number is blocked," Avery said. "And everyone but you who knows I have this phone is in the next room."

"And Harry and his old boss. I'll let you go and get started on my homework," MaryAnn said. "Talk soon."

"Thanks, MaryAnn."

With that, Avery closed her laptop and picked up her phone.

"This is Avery," she answered.

"Wondered if you would pick up." The voice was familiar, but it took Avery a beat to place it after the chaos of the past few days.

"Kabrirah?" Avery said finally, her jaw dropping.

"We need to talk."

"About what?"

"Your friend Harrison for a start."

81

"I've agreed to meet with Kabrirah on neutral ground," Avery said, standing at the end of the table after the shortest, but maybe most eventful, phone call of her life.

"That's a really bad idea," Carter said.

"I gotta go with Carter on this one," Duval said. "Why would you trust someone who tried to kill you?"

"That's the thing, actually," Avery said. "She didn't and she could have."

"Um, in case you've forgotten, she and her friends put both of us in the hospital," Duval said. "Before they attacked you in a public restroom."

"He's right," Oscar said. "I don't even know this woman and I don't like her."

"Why would you risk meeting with her?" Javier said.

"Because she offered to help us get Harry and Marco back. Sort of."

"I still don't like it," Carter shook his head. "Even then. What's to stop her from leading you into a trap?"

"You," Avery said. "All of you. Duval and I were seriously outnumbered last time. But now, we've got the finest thieves and intel people in the business. Right? I mean you saved all of London, didn't you?"

"She's got a point," Reggie said, nodding.

"We are pretty badass ourselves," Oscar said.

"Where and when is this meeting supposed to take place?" Duval said.

"Tomorrow at noon. At the Pyramids of Giza."

———

Avery didn't immediately recognize Kabrirah. It was the first time she had seen the woman not in full warrior mode shrouded in black. She approached on foot, her hands empty. Dressed in a light-colored robe and headscarf, Kabrirah looked like any other local woman touring the ancient pyramids.

"I wasn't sure you'd actually come," Kabrirah said.

"I wasn't sure I wanted to," Avery said. "Not after the ambush Duval and I faced the last time we met."

"I'm only half sorry about that," Kabrirah said. "You were trying to steal Heba's pin. Something you finally managed, I might add. How exactly did you find it?"

"Once I figured out who you were, it was pretty easy to locate," Avery said.

Kabrirah nodded, then turned her head toward where Carter and the others were standing nearby. "I see you've recruited more help to your cause."

Now it was Avery's turn to nod. "I didn't want to be outnumbered again."

"What exactly is your interest in the pin?" Kabrirah said.

"I believe it may be the key to finding a much larger lost treasure. What is your interest?"

"My interest is in honoring the memory of our lost queen. You've met some of my sisters."

"There are more?"

Kabrirah grinned. "Many more. We are all daughters of the cult of Heba. And my sisters are all as driven as I am."

"Don't you mean fanatical?" Avery said.

Kabrirah's grin vanished. "I could have killed you," she said.

"Why didn't you?"

"Because I had done my research on you and Carter Mosley before we met. It seems that your treasure hunting has been for benevolent reasons, at least so far. I figured scaring you off might be easy. It appears I underestimated you."

"Why did you want to meet?"

"Because I think we might be able to assist each other."

Avery studied the woman's face for signs of deception. If she was lying, she gave nothing away.

"How?" Avery said at last.

"I want the pin returned and, like you, I want to find the secret it holds."

"You mean you don't know where the treasure is either?"

"No. But I know it is massive, as is the lost temple where Heba is actually buried."

"You don't think Dr. Granderson found her tomb yesterday?"

"I know she didn't."

"But she's telling the whole world that she did," Avery said.

"She can say whatever she wants, but it won't make it so."

Avery couldn't argue with that sentiment. "So, you're proposing to help us find the missing treasure?"

"I'm proposing we help each other with that," Kabrirah corrected.

"And free Harry and Marco from prison?" Avery said.

"That too."

"In exchange for what?"

"In exchange for you returning the pin."

"*If* we are successful," Avery said.

"Yes. If we are successful."

"Why should we trust you?" Avery said. "You nearly killed Duval and me."

"But we didn't. And I reached out to you. And I have these."

Avery tensed and prepared to give the signal for trouble as Kabrirah reached inside her robe. Over Kabrirah's shoulder she saw Duval and Carter move several steps closer.

Kabrirah removed several rolled-up sheets of paper and handed them to Avery.

"What are these?"

"Blueprints of the prison where they are holding your friends."

"Where did you get these? And how did you know they were holding them at this prison?"

"We hacked the government servers."

Avery stared at her in disbelief. "Why?"

"Because our history is long, and our resources are vast. And because I decided to help you. You were drawn into something dishonorable because someone appealed to your sense of honor. That's wrong."

Avery glanced back at the drawing. "Even if we somehow managed to get inside the prison, we don't even know where they are holding them."

"I have a sister who used to work there."

"Okay," Avery said as she rerolled the blueprints. "I'm listening."

82

"I'm not sure why you would trust these women," Duval said as they drove back to the safehouse.

"Because I don't have a choice. Nobody else seems to have a way to get Harry and Marco released, but Kabrirah says she does. You were in her house. She doesn't care about anything but restoring Heba's legacy—it's been centuries, and their generation finally has the chance to reconcile history."

"And what does she want from you?" Carter asked.

"I might have said that we'll help Kabrirah and the others to find where Heba's treasure is hidden."

"And the pin we worked so hard to get?" Duval said.

"It will be returned to Kabrirah. After the treasure is found."

"Did Kabrirah happen to mention how she would manage Harrison and Marco's release?" Javier said.

Avery nodded. "She has a friend who once worked at the prison."

"And?" Reggie said. "What is this friend going to do?"

"Help us bust them out," Avery said.

Oscar drove Avery, Duval, and Carter to the designated meeting place well before dawn.

"I still don't like this, Avery," Carter said. "What if Kabrirah is just setting us up? Hell, by the time we're through, we'll all be spending the rest of our lives in an Egyptian prison."

The same thought had occurred to Avery, but she wasn't about to admit it.

"What do you want me to say, Carter? She isn't part of the government. Kabrirah wants the pin back. I suppose she could turn us all over to the police and just go take the pin, or trade us our freedom for the pin. Or maybe she does what she says. We have more people here this time, so if there's a chance we can get Harry and Marco back, I'll risk it."

"I hope you're right," Duval said. "We're sailing through uncharted and mighty dangerous waters, love."

Avery hoped she was right about Kabrirah, too.

Kabrirah was waiting right where she said she'd be, along with three formidable-looking women. Dressed all in black, they resembled ninjas.

"I thought you said it was just going to be you and Mr. Mosley," Kabrirah said as they approached. "Who is this?"

"That's Oscar and I'm Duval," Duval said, extending his hand to her. "Your friends beat the hell out of me when last we met. Guess I didn't make much of an impression."

Kabrirah maintained eye contact with him but made no effort to accept his offering.

"It's an old warrior custom," Duval said, keeping his hand out. "Offering my sword hand to show there's no threat."

"They are friends of ours," Avery said. "You can trust them."

"We'll see," Kabrirah said as her attention returned to Avery. "Have you taken care of the ventilation system yet?"

"No. I needed to be close. I'll do that now."

Kabrirah nodded her understanding.

"And your inside friend, have they taken care of their end?" Carter said. "There'll be nobody covering our entry point, right?"

"Don't worry about my friend," Kabrirah said. "You can trust him."

Avery went to work on her laptop, quickly hacking the prison's environmental controls. "I'm in."

"Jeez, that was fast," Duval said.

"It's the government," Avery said. "Some of the easiest stuff to hack into."

"They're all the same," Kabrirah said.

"Low bid ring any bells?" Carter asked.

"Okay, it's disabled," Avery said, stowing her laptop back in the SUV.

"Follow us," Kabrirah said as she and the others turned and headed into the darkness.

The mouth of the tunnel was covered at ground level by a rusted steel grate. A single padlock secured it to the framework. It took one of Kabrirah's women less than thirty seconds to pick the lock and open the grate.

"Where does this tunnel lead?" Carter said.

"Inside the prison," Kabrirah said matter-of-factly.

"I know *that*," Carter said. "I mean what exactly are we crawling through to get inside?"

Avery watched as Kabrirah cracked a toothy smile. It was the first time she'd shown any emotion other than rage.

"You'll see," Kabrirah said before ducking inside.

The other women in her group stepped in right behind her. Avery, Carter, Duval, and Oscar followed. It didn't take long before Avery and the others figured out what Kabrirah had been smiling about. The putrid smell inside the tunnel quickly gave away its purpose.

"Oh my God," Carter said. "It smells like—"

"Shite," Duval said, completing his thought.

"It's a gray water line," Kabrirah said.

"Yeah, well it isn't all gray," Carter said as he shined his light on something floating past.

"How long is this tunnel?" Duval said, gagging.

"Point four kilometers," Kabrirah said.

"Great," Carter said. "Isn't there some other way we could get Harry out that doesn't involve crawling through this—"

"Shite," Duval said again.

"Exactly," Carter said.

Avery turned and stared Carter down.

"I was just asking," Carter said.

83

They reached the point in the tunnel where the first-floor grate appeared in the blueprints.

"There it is," Avery whispered as she pointed up toward the ceiling of the tunnel.

"We are directly outside the prison showers," Kabrirah said.

"Great," Carter said. "I could really use one about now."

Kabrirah moved past to allow two of her group to lift the grate out of its frame. Avery felt her stomach tighten as she watched them angle the grate to allow them to pull it down into the tunnel. She half expected them to slip and bang the metal on something, giving themselves away to the guards as clearly as an alarm. But they executed the maneuver with precision, placing the grate on the tunnel floor without so much as a scrape.

"You ladies must have played a lot of Operation as youngsters, huh?" Duval joked.

The stone-faced women looked at him before silently climbing up through the hole and into the prison. Avery and the others quickly followed.

As soon as they were all through onto the main floor, they made their way silently along the corridors until they came to the correct cell block. As they crouched in the shadows, they heard a group of guards talking and laughing.

"How do we know they haven't moved them?" Carter whispered.

"They haven't," Kabrirah said. "Harrison and Marco are in the third cell on the second level directly above us."

"We're not all going up there, are we?" Duval said.

"No," Avery said. "You five stay down here and Kabrirah and I will go fetch them."

"Tell me again why I couldn't just wait outside," Carter said.

"And miss all this fun?" Oscar said.

"If we are discovered, we'll need you to run interference," Avery said.

"And what exactly does that mean?" Carter said.

"It means take out the guards," Kabrirah said.

"But no killing," Avery said, noticing the disappointment registering on the faces of Kabrirah's group. "We just disable them so we can escape with Harry and Marco."

After a long moment, everyone nodded their agreement.

Kabrirah looked at Avery. "You ready?"

Avery took a deep breath to steady her nerves. "Yup. Let's do this."

Catlike, they ascended the steel steps to the second level of cells. As they moved along the gangway, Avery could still hear loud talking and laughter from the guards interspersed with occasional snoring from nearby cells. As they neared the correct cell, Avery caught the familiar deep resonance of Harrison's nocturnal snorts and grunts.

Kabrirah stopped just before Harrison and Marco's cell and signaled for Avery to do the same.

"What is it?" Avery whispered.

"Stay here for a second while I pick the lock."

"Why?"

"Because if I screw this up, you'll have a head start to get out of here."

Avery crouched down, making herself as small as possible while she watched Kabrirah work. After a moment, Kabrirah returned to Avery and shook her head.

"What's wrong?" Avery said.

"My friend forgot to mention something very important."

"What's that?"

"This is an old prison. The doors don't open individually. They run on a bar that opens the entire row."

"Meaning?"

"Meaning in order to let your friends out, we will also be releasing everyone else on this level."

Wide-eyed, Avery scanned the entire row. Assuming that each of the cells was occupied, they could be releasing as many as twelve prisoners.

"You still want to go forward with this?" Kabrirah said.

Avery nodded. "The other inmates might provide the distraction we'll need to make our escape. You take care of the locking bar, and I'll make sure Harry and Marco are awake and ready."

"You've got two minutes," Kabrirah said before she scampered off.

As Avery moved into position, she could just make out Harrison's bulk atop the mattress on the bottom bunk. She listened to him snore for a moment, then reached into her pocket for the pea-sized pebbles she had filled her pockets with outside. She tossed them one at a time until she found her mark. Harrison let out a loud snort, then sat upright in bed.

"Harry," she whispered.

"Who's there?" he said, rubbing the sleep from his eyes.

"It's me, Avery."

"What the hell?"

"Ms. Avery," Marco whispered. "What are you doing here?"

"We've come to get you both out of here. Get your shoes on."

She watched as they quickly dressed and approached the door.

"Who's we? And how exactly did you think you were going to break us out, Ave? These doors all open together."

As if in answer to his question, Avery heard the sound of squealing metal. She stood back just as the entire row of doors popped open.

"Come on. Let's go."

84

At first, there was only silence after the squeal and clank of the doors opening. Avery heard the guards' conversation come to an abrupt halt as they probably tried to process what they had just heard. Within seconds the prison erupted into chaos: The guards began shouting as they approached the cells, and the occupants began to spill out onto the upper corridor. Avery couldn't make out what the guards were shouting but she was pretty sure it wasn't kind.

Avery, Marco, and Harrison raced past two confused inmates and down the steel steps.

"Jesus, Ave. I hope you brought the cavalry with you or we'll end up being cellmates."

"They don't house the men and women together, Harry."

"Don't be so sure." Carter grinned as he opened the door.

"Carter," Harrison said, surprised. "Duval. Oscar. Man, I'm glad to see you guys. Who are the rest of these people, Ave? And what's that smell?"

"Oh, you're gonna love it, mate," Duval said with a chuckle.

"Let's go," Kabrirah said as she raced toward the showers.

"Hey, isn't that the woman who almost killed—"

"Yes, Harry," Avery said. "Come on. I'll explain everything later."

The shouting intensified as they moved along the hallway. Avery could hear the electric crackle of tasers mingled with screams as the guards looked to quell the uprising. They were nearly to the showers when Avery turned the corner and found Kabrirah and her warriors standing over two motionless guards laid out on the concrete floor.

"Relax," Kabrirah said. "They're just unconscious. Now move."

One by one they squeezed down through the hatch into the tunnel. Avery and Duval were the last two down. As she dropped into the tunnel, she heard the clank of the cell doors being closed again.

"That should buy us some time," Duval said.

"How do you figure?" Avery said.

"Because they'll have to do a bed check before they know who's missing," Harrison said. "But it won't take them long to figure out what happened. After they find those guards, we'll only have a few minutes at most."

"Then we better make every moment count, Mr. Harrison," Kabrirah said.

85

Ancient Egypt, 1500 BC

The women made it back to the secret meeting room undetected, though the bleeding from Zefret's wound was more pronounced and one of the women was working to clean the wound and staunch the flow.

"Did you find the idol, sister?" Zefret said, grimacing through the pain.

"No, and I looked everywhere," Eman said. "I barely made it out without being caught by one of the guards. Perhaps we were wrong about him having it."

Zefret considered this for a moment. No, she was sure she had seen the pin hanging around the man's neck. But if it hadn't been there when he was killed, and if it wasn't in his quarters, where was it?

"Perhaps he knew we were coming and hid it," one of the women offered.

"Perhaps," Zefret said. "But I am almost positive he had it in his possession."

"How did you get away, sister?" Eman asked. "I heard they captured you and took you to Abasi."

As Zefret relayed the story, her eyes lit upon Neith, the youngest of their tribe. Neith, Amunet's late brother's only daughter, looked troubled and appeared to be hanging back from the others. Zefret continued her account of what had happened, and the threats made by Abasi, without drawing attention to Neith.

"We may need to flee our homes in Cairo," Eman said.

"Where would we go that would be outside of Abasi's reach?" one of the women asked.

"I'm thinking Greece," Eman said. "The journey across the desert will be treacherous, but far less so than remaining here waiting for Abasi to find and kill us."

"If we leave here, we will not be able to return," Zefret said. "Abasi will find and destroy our homes."

"I can't bear to think of the palace guards tearing my home apart," Eman said.

"We will make a new home for ourselves," Zefret said. "And work to preserve Heba's legacy."

The others nodded in silent agreement.

Zefret thanked the woman who had finished dressing her wound before turning to the others.

"Now, sisters, we must rest. The journey across the desert will not be an easy one. We will leave in the morning."

One by one the women retired to makeshift beds to sleep.

Zefret waited until the others were asleep before crawling from her bed and approaching a wide-eyed Neith.

"What secret are you hiding, little one?" Zefret said.

"The guard we killed never had the pin, Zefret," she said as she burst into tears.

"How do you know this, sister?"

"Because I took the pin from her body during the attack."

"Why would you do such a thing?"

"The pin is too powerful a talisman to simply bury with the queen. We will need it to stop Abasi."

"You are wrong, Neith. It must be buried in the temple along with Heba and the rest of the treasure for that power to work."

"But what of the chalice? The other half of the pin. Ammit's blessing was upon both of them. If we bury them together and they are found, then Abasi will have complete control over everything."

Eman appeared at Zefret's side. "Abasi will not find the temple, Neith. And Zefret knows how powerful the blessing is, for she is the one who held Amunet's hand as she made it. It is protecting us even now. You must have faith in our plan to pass the writing on. We will keep the story of Heba alive for future generations. You must return the pin to Zefret, child."

Neith wiped away the tears with the back of her hand, then sat up and rummaged through her belongings.

After a moment, she hung her head and held out the pin toward Zefret.

86

Present Day

Avery, Carter, Duval, Oscar, Marco, and Harrison arrived back at the safe house to find Javier and Reggie pacing a path into the living room floor.

"Welcome back, Harry," Javier said as he moved to give Harrison a hug.

"Um, you might want to hold off on that until I've had a chance to change and shower."

Javier gave him a curious look.

"We used a sewer tunnel to gain access to the prison," Avery said.

"Yeah, we're more than a little ripe, mate," Duval said.

"I'm gonna burn these clothes," Oscar said.

"It is good to see you again, Harry," Reggie said.

"It's good to be seen, my friend," Harrison said.

Avery had barely stepped foot out of the shower before her burner phone rang. She recognized the originating number instantly. It was Detective Gamil from Cairo.

"Good morning, Detective," Avery said, doing her best to sound cheery.

"Good morning, Ms. Turner."

"What can I do for you?"

"I'm wondering if you've seen Mr. Harrison or Marco in your travels?"

"Is that supposed to be funny?" Avery said. "You know very well that your men locked them up on false charges."

There was a long pause before Gamil spoke again. Avery began to wonder if he might be trying to trace her phone.

"That is actually why I'm calling. We seem to have misplaced them."

"I'm sorry? How is that even possible?"

"How soon can you meet me at the station?"

Avery agreed to go down to the station to speak with him, giving herself two hours to throw him off. If she'd agreed to drive directly there, he would know approximately how far from the station she was staying. He didn't sound happy that she was going to be a while.

"I'll see you then," he said.

They scrambled to move Harrison and Marco to a hotel using one of MaryAnn's credit cards to rent the room, thereby keeping them hidden while still protecting the sanctity of Duval's safe house. As the others took care of moving them, Oscar and Reggie drove Avery and Carter to Cairo.

Detective Gamil was standing in the lobby when they walked into the station.

"Wasn't sure you'd show," Gamil said.

"Why wouldn't we?" Avery said, trying her best to maintain the façade of indignation. "We've done nothing wrong. You're the ones who lost our friend."

The detective gave a slight grin and nodded as he looked from Avery to Carter and back again.

"Follow me," he said as he led them back to the interview rooms.

"And you're trying to tell me that you had nothing to do with Marco and Harrison's early morning escape from prison?" Gamil said for the fourth time in thirty minutes. The normally reserved detective's frustration was clearly on display.

Avery maintained eye contact and a stoic expression. "Detective, how could I have had anything to do with Harrison's disappearance if I didn't even know where you'd taken him?"

As Gamil stared back at her, Avery's mind wandered to Carter, who had been taken to a different room. She wondered what tricks they might be using on him and how he was holding up under pressure. On the way to the station, she had told him that they would be split up by the police as soon as they arrived. It was Interrogation 101, something Avery had learned well from her mother and Harrison. Avery knew the local police had nothing on either of them. Nothing besides a strong suspicion, anyway. Who else would have wanted to break Harrison and Marco out of prison?

"You're trying to convince me that someone else would want to get your friends out of prison?" Gamil said. "Do you have any idea how far-fetched that sounds, Ms. Turner?"

"I'm not trying to convince you of anything, Detective. As a matter of fact, there have been so many people trying to stop us from enjoying our vacation here that I'm surprised you haven't tried to track one of them down for questioning. Maybe talk to the man who tried to kill us as soon as we stepped off the plane. I assume he's still in the hospital."

Gamil sat back in his chair and stared, unblinking, at Avery. She knew he had nothing on them. And without some type of admission, he couldn't hold them no matter how badly he wanted to.

"Where are you staying, Ms. Turner?"

"That's none of your business. But if you must know, Carter and I are with friends. And we have at least a half dozen people who will be more than happy to provide you with statements saying that we were with them all night."

Avery knew that this was the decisive moment. Either Gamil would take the chance and lock them up, or he would go the safe route and allow them to leave, likely assigning plainclothes officers to track them to see if they led him back to Harrison and Marco.

Gamil stood up and picked up the file folder he'd brought to the interview room.

"Thank you for coming in, Ms. Turner. I'll let you know if we make any progress toward locating the escapees."

"Detective," Avery said, "I've been thinking about what you said, about Marco using my plane. Did you find anything on board?"

"Nothing incriminating."

"Excellent." Avery grinned. "My attorney tells me Egyptian law limits the amount of time you can impound property that isn't evidence of a crime, and your time with my jet is up, I'm afraid. I'd like my jet released and my passport back. You can return Mr. Mosley's to him, too."

Gamil's chin quivered as he stood in the doorway staring at Avery. He knew she was right, but he wasn't happy about it.

She stared back until he looked away.

"Very well," he muttered.

87

Oscar pulled away from the police station as soon as Avery and Carter climbed inside the SUV.

"Wasn't sure you'd be coming out of there," Reggie said.

"It was touch and go for us too," Avery said. "But we got our passports. That's something."

"You think they bought our story?" Carter said.

"Not by a long shot," Avery said.

"You know they'll be following us, right?" Oscar said.

Avery nodded. "We have to lose them. I don't want to compromise the safe house, and I also don't want them to know where we stashed Harry and Marco. I think the best thing for them is to get out of Egypt as soon as they can."

"They? Don't you mean we?" Carter asked.

"We'll catch up when we keep our end of the deal I made with Kabri-rah. She did what she said she would. I'm not leaving without keeping my word."

"I get that." Carter fell quiet, knowing he wouldn't win if he argued.

While Oscar drove a circuitous route to nowhere, making frequent U-turns and stops for no reason, Avery phoned the airport and arranged to have her jet fueled and ready to fly by three o'clock.

They arrived at the airport an hour early to find Duval and Javier waiting with Marco and Harrison. Both Harrison and Marco wore dark glasses and baseball caps pulled down low to hide their identities as they lugged their bags across the tarmac to Avery's Gulfstream.

"Man, I never thought I'd be so happy to see your jet, Ave," Harrison said.

"Me neither," Marco said.

"We're almost home, amigo," Harrison said.

"Don't look now," Carter said. "But we've got company."

Avery turned to see two dark-colored SUVs approaching quickly from the far end of the tarmac.

"Oh, great, who is this now?" Harrison said. "Cops or more hired assassins?"

"I don't think it's the police, Harry," Avery said.

The vehicles pulled up and stopped between Avery's group and the jet, effectively cutting off their route of escape.

The doors on each of the SUVs swung open and multiple men spilled out and surrounded them.

Avery made eye contact with Duval as he reached toward his weapon. Avery shook her head. "Don't," she said. "We can't risk a firefight now."

Duval dropped his hand to his side.

A well-dressed man stepped from the back of the middle SUV and walked casually toward them. Ismael, who they'd seen twice before. "You should listen to her," he said. "There is nowhere for you to go."

"And we were so close to getting out of here," Harrison grumbled.

"Are you with the Egyptian police?" Avery said.

"Hardly, Ms. Turner," the man said with a chuckle. "No, I represent— other interested parties. And we have impounded your jet on suspicion of criminal activity. Come, we will explain everything."

"Here we go again," Harrison said as he exchanged a glance with Avery.

"Hands off, pal," Oscar said as one of the men tried to grab his arm and he shoved him back. Duval and the others reached for their weapons and the men from the SUVs raised theirs.

"There is no need for bloodshed. We only wish to talk."

Avery ran down every conceivable scenario in her head, but there was no way to win this. They were outnumbered, outgunned, and totally exposed. Even if they were able to overpower these men, the resulting shootout, if it didn't leave Harrison and Marco wounded or worse, would draw the attention of the police and they'd all end up in a cell.

Avery signaled for Duval and his men to lower their guns.

"You sure?" Duval asked.

"I'm sure," she said.

Ismael gestured toward the SUVs. "Come, Ms. Turner."

"Avery." Carter's voice hitched with worry. Avery didn't even know Carter knew how to worry.

"It's okay," Avery said, projecting a confidence she didn't remotely feel. Aside from Duval and his men, the only other ally she'd managed to find since this treasure hunting chaos started was Kabrirah and her fighters. And she wouldn't go so far as to call the women her friends. They were driven to the GIS building and left in a room to wait. The minutes ticked by, chipping at their patience.

"I thought our guy was gonna fill us in," Harrison said. "Where is he, Ave?"

Carter tried the door handle, but it was locked.

"That would have been too easy, mate," Duval said.

"They want something from us," Javier said. "Or we'd be dead already."

"Optimism." Reggie pointed at Javier. "I like it."

Oscar and Marco remained silent.

The door to the room opened and all eyes shifted to a man none of them had seen before. His intense eyes scanned the crowd before landing on Avery.

"Ms. Turner, my name is Kazmir. It is a pleasure to finally meet you."

"Wish I could say the same," Avery said.

"Not like we had a lot of choice," Carter snapped.

"Ah, Mr. Mosley. A pleasure to make your acquaintance too."

"Want to tell us what we're doing here?" Harrison said.

"And you must be Mr. Harrison, one of the escape artists."

"I must be."

"I'm not familiar with the rest of your friends, Ms. Turner."

"There's a reason for that," Duval said.

"No matter. What I have to say affects all of you." Kazmir sat down at the table and gestured for Avery to sit across from him.

Reluctantly, she did.

"I want you to locate the treasure of Heba's temple," Kazmir said after a long moment.

"What?" Avery blinked. She wasn't sure what she thought he was going to say, but it wasn't that. "Why?"

"Because it is very important."

"I thought the pin was the important thing," Avery said. "You're not after the pin? Because we don't have it anyway. It was stolen." Avery crossed her fingers under the table. She wasn't a great liar, but this treasure hunting stuff was improving her skills.

Kazmir waved away her comment. "The pin was a means to an end. The real find is the temple."

"You're kidding, right?" Avery said.

"Do you have any idea how many people have tried to kill us over that stupid pin?" Harrison said.

"It's hardly stupid, Mr. Harrison," Kazmir said. "Just not the...big prize... as you Americans would say."

"So, what?" Carter said. "The pin is...like...a door prize?"

"No, Mr. Mosley. The Egyptian government wanted the pin to safeguard it. You see, the Saudi princess is a direct descendant of the Pharaoh Heba."

"Afraid I don't understand," Duval said. "Seems like she'd be entitled to it, then."

"It isn't that simple," Kazmir said. "It is part of Egypt's cultural history. The artifact itself is an ancient goddess."

He stared at the table. Avery watched him for three beats.

"And?" she prodded.

Kazmir looked up. "I read of your brilliance, Ms. Turner. Compounding the problem is that the princess's current boyfriend is part of what your country would call a terrorist cell."

"Great," Harrison said, drawing the word out like he was in pain.

"You can see how bad it would look if terrorists stole such an important artifact, besting the Egyptian government."

"We were told that if the pin fell into the wrong hands, it could start an international incident," Avery said. "Is this what that was about?"

"I'd call it more of a regional instability. You might have been oversold on that point."

"Oversold?" Avery's voice rose as her rear end came out of the chair. "We've almost died ten different ways that no one's ever seen outside an eighties action movie. We've dodged bullets, nearly lost friends, endangered people we love, seen things we can never unsee...and we were... oversold?"

"Sounds more like a lie to me," Carter said. "And someone ought to tell that senator woman that Avery's pretty mean when she gets mad enough to yell."

"Senator Byers is merely trying to get on the princess's good side, Ms. Turner," Kazmir said, raising both hands.

"Why?"

"Why else, love?" Duval shook his head. "Because the Saudis have oil."

"Why does it always come down to that?" Harrison rolled his eyes.

"Because, Mr. Harrison, oil is money, and money is power. Technically what the senator told you is correct, but I'll concede not entirely honest."

"You should be a politician," Duval said.

"Not enough power in politics." Kazmir smiled.

"What is the bottom line?" Avery said. "You want us to find a treasure that no one is even sure exists, and you're not going to let us go home unless we do?"

"I also have the power to make the charges against Mr. Harrison and your pilot, Marco, go away. Something that fleeing this country wasn't going to solve anyway. The greatest treasure the world has ever known exists not in some museum but hidden beneath this very city. Hidden by a selfish woman from an ineffective king."

Avery couldn't say that she had already agreed to help Kabrirah and her band of warriors. Truthfully, she would have agreed to almost anything to obtain Harry and Marco's freedom. The GIS could restore everyone's good name and ability to travel.

And swirling around all the blackmail and subterfuge, there was the truth: Avery actually did have an idea where the treasure was hidden, assuming the DiveNav calculations were accurate. When Granderson discovered the tomb she incorrectly assigned to Heba, Avery started playing with her invention, feeding it all the information she and MaryAnn had dug up, and asking the artificial intelligence to solve the puzzle. The answer it had spit back made sense to her, but she hadn't even told Carter because she wasn't sure what she wanted to do with the information. But now...

She sighed. "If we agree to help you, you'll let us go home and live in peace? No strings?"

"Avery, you can't be serious," Harrison protested. "These people have lied to you at every turn. They arrested me. I had to have a cavity search, for crying out loud."

Carter couldn't hold back his laughter. Avery shook her head as she swallowed her own. "I'm sorry, Harry."

"What do you say, Ms. Turner?" Kazmir asked. "Will you help us by finding Heba's temple and the lost treasure?"

"I can't do it locked in here."

"I won't take up anymore of your time." Kazmir stood and waved for a guard to open the door. "Go and bring me back my treasure."

Avery pushed back the chair and stood up.

"Remember to keep your promise. I'll make sure to keep a good eye on your jet."

88

While Avery had figured Kazmir would either return Marco and Harrison to prison or find some other way to prevent them from leaving if she refused to search for the treasure, she hadn't predicted how angrily Kabrirah would react to the news.

"Is this some kind of trick?" Kabrirah thundered at Avery in her living room nearly an hour after Kazmir dismissed everyone from the station. "You promised to help us find the treasure."

"And I am doing just that," Avery said.

"Why did they catch you attempting to leave the country?" Kabrirah demanded, shaking off the hand of her friend, who hadn't been introduced or said a word since Avery and her team arrived, laid on her arm.

"I wasn't planning to go anywhere," Avery said. "I was merely at the airport taking care of my friends. You held up your end of our bargain, and I will hold up mine."

Harrison's eyes widened. "Not going anywhere? But you said—"

"I said I was going to put you and Marco on the jet and get you out of here," Avery said, cutting him off. "And I was. Carter and I were planning to stay and fulfill the promise we made to Kabrirah for her help in busting you out of prison."

"We really are trying to help," Carter said.

Kabrirah fixed him with a look of disdain. It was clear that if she was going to trust anyone, it would be Avery and Avery alone.

"Tell me again why you think the treasure and tomb are here in Cairo," Kabrirah said.

"I'll show you," Avery said as she slid the laptop from her bag and opened the DiveNav program.

"What is that?"

"This is the program Carter and I use to locate treasure."

"We've used it both on land and undersea," Carter said. "The technology is state of the art."

"It's beyond state of the art," Duval said, pride creeping into his voice.

"Here," Avery said. "I've placed a topical map over the area the DiveNav has indicated as the location with the highest probability for finding Heba's tomb and the hidden treasure."

"But that is right here where we are standing." Kabrirah leaned in for a closer look.

"I believe it may lie directly beneath where we are standing," Avery said. "Do you know the history of this property? I know you inherited it from your grandmother."

Kabrirah stood, pacing. "I am a direct descendant of Zefret, Heba's physician and trusted advisor. This property was purchased by my ancestors specifically because Zefret's home was here."

"And that doesn't make perfect sense to you?" Avery asked. "Where better to hide Heba's treasure?"

"I've lived here for years. If there was something hidden here, I would have found it."

"Not if it was hidden below ground," Carter said. "But it sure makes sense to me that this could be why the property has remained in your family all these years."

"I had to sign an oath that I would never sell it, it must be ours, no matter what," Kabrirah said slowly. "Let's assume for a moment that you are right. What would you suggest we do about that? Dig the foundation out from under my home?"

"I think we need to bring in Dr. Granderson," Avery said. "She has imaging equipment that will tell us if it's really here or if we're chasing shadows."

Kabrirah sighed and turned to the other woman. The woman nodded her agreement. Avery wondered if there was more to the relationship between these two than simply being fellow followers of Heba.

"Okay," Kabrirah said. "Bring her in."

It took less than ninety minutes after Avery's call to Granderson for Kabrirah's doorbell to ring. Avery hadn't been sure how receptive Kate might be to the idea of a long shot search, especially as convinced as she was that she'd found Heba's tomb. But Kate's wild determination to find the tomb under the desert near Giza had told Avery her chances were decent. Avery barely got the word "temple" out before Kate asked for the address.

Following introductions, they set up Kate's imaging equipment in the basement of Kabrirah's home. The group stood around watching as Kate monitored the screen.

"There is something buried here," Granderson said, sounding almost as surprised as Kabrirah looked. "Do you see it?"

Avery and the others crowded in for a closer look.

"What is it?" Duval said.

"It looks like a small chamber," Kate said.

"Whatever that is doesn't look large enough to hold a missing treasure of the ages," Carter said. "Does it?"

"This may well be the mouth of a much larger structure," Kate said.

"Like the mouth of a temple?" Kabrirah asked.

"Possibly," Granderson said.

Granderson called for her assistants to bring excavation equipment from the university, and Oscar and Reggie lugged every bit of it down the narrow basement stairs, refusing to let any of their injured friends help. Not surprisingly, Granderson didn't offer to help.

Kabrirah made the first cut in the floor herself, and Avery's team and various "sisters" of Kabrirah's cut a small chunk of the foundation free.

Kabrirah peered down into the hole using a small, bright flashlight. "A room. There is a room down there."

It took two days of the same cuts and lifting the floor out in chunks, working from the center to the edges so they didn't fall. Once there was a hole big enough for a person in safety gear to slip through, Kabrirah insisted on going first.

"No snakes, Avery," she called.

Avery slipped down and shined her light around.

"It is dark down here," she said.

"Indeed," Kabrirah said. "But I don't see anything, I'm afraid. No treasure. No door to a temple."

Granderson was the third person down, and she wasn't giving up without a fight. Convincing Kabrirah that the larger chamber could be below with what Avery thought were some sketchy readings on her sonar gadget, Granderson brought in hand shovels and brushes to excavate the chamber floor.

Avery spent three days brushing dust and sand off rocks before she dropped her tools and went up the rickety stairs Harry'd made the day before because he was bored.

"Where are you going?" Kabrirah asked.

"I'm done," Avery said. "I'm sorry, but there's nothing down here. We're wasting time."

The chamber they uncovered was longer than it was wide, about the size of a walk-in closet. It was also empty. Not a single artifact—the only thing of note were some ancient glyphs in one corner near the floor.

"What do those mean?" Carter said.

"They appear to reference a hidden entryway or door," Granderson said.

"But there is nothing here," Kabrirah said. "What about the room, Doctor? What do you think its purpose was?"

"It was common for middle class Egyptians to have holy spaces," Granderson said. "It may have been used for prayer, or even preparation for the afterlife."

"Or for meetings of a secret society of women warriors?" Avery mused.

Kabrirah grabbed her friend's hand and nodded at Avery. "I like that one."

Avery checked her phone. Duval and Harrison were late. They were due back with lunch fifteen minutes ago.

"Does anyone have a cell signal down here?" she asked.

"What is it?" Kabrirah asked.

"Probably nothing," Avery said. "It's just that I expected Harry and Duval back by now."

Granderson checked her own watch. "I have to clean up and get back to the other site for a meeting."

"What about this search?" Avery said. "We haven't finished."

"This will keep for now," Granderson said. "But if it ends up leading to something, it will be my second major discovery of the month. I'll be set for life, Avery."

They trudged up the stairs to the main floor of Kabrirah's home, calling for Harrison and Duval, but got no reply.

Avery whirled on Carter, panic on her face.

He put his hands on her arms. "Don't borrow trouble. They're okay."

A car door slammed outside, and Carter smiled. "See?"

"Hey, what gives?" Avery called, stepping out to the porch. Her phone buzzed with several incoming messages now that the signal had returned. "We're practically starving, you two."

"Avery, no!" Harrison shouted.

"Back inside and lock the doors," Duval yelled as Avery spotted the two men behind them. Both held short-barreled automatic rifles.

89

Avery was still trying to decide their best move when Kabrirah pounced. She leapt up onto and over a bench like an acrobat, launching herself directly at one of the gunmen, catching him by surprise. Before he could raise his weapon, Kabrirah landed both feet in the center of his sternum, knocking him backward into the wall. A hail of bullets connected with the ground, wall, and an upstairs window, spraying shards of rock, wood, and plaster everywhere.

Neither Avery nor Carter hesitated, wanting to take advantage of the distraction created by Kabrirah's surprise attack. They closed in on the other gunman, Avery diving at his legs, aiming to knock him off balance, while Carter targeted the man's head.

They both connected before he could react, sending him tumbling over the table and onto the floor. Harrison quickly wrestled the rifle from the first gunman while Duval disarmed the second. In seconds, it was over. Both gunmen lay on their backs, stunned by what had happened.

After dragging both men inside and strapping them to dining room chairs, Avery and Kabrirah questioned the intruders. As Avery took a moment to study both men's faces, she realized that she recognized one of them: She'd seen his photo at the police station with Kazmir a week before.

"I know you," Avery said to the man. "You're the Saudi princess's boyfriend."

"And I know you," the man snarled as he spat in her direction. "Typical American woman, always thinking she knows better than everyone else."

Carter stood calmly and punched the terrorist in the jaw.

"Easy there, Dirty Harry," Harrison said, trying hard to muffle a laugh.

The terrorist spat again. "Nice punch Carter Mosley. It's a shame you and your friends will never make it home."

"What are you talking about?" Avery said.

The man smiled, revealing blood-covered teeth. "The Americans will lose their new oil deal simply because you could not do as you were told. In today's global economy, your government will charge you with treason."

"What is he talking about?" Granderson said.

"They are terrorists," Kabrirah said. "Who knows what they are talking about."

Avery pulled out her cell phone, holding the terrorist's gaze. "Kabrirah's right. Let's let the authorities deal with them. We'll see how many treason cases you can raise from the basement of the Cairo police station."

90

"Thanks for the warning, guys." Avery sat down next to Duval on the top step outside, holding up her phone, where she had several texts warning her that they'd been grabbed and there was an ambush coming. "No signal in the dungeon room."

"We tried," Duval said.

"What happened?" Carter asked from the doorway behind them.

"We didn't even make it off this street," Harrison said, pointing. "They were about five houses that way, and they had the hood up on the car. We stopped to see if they needed help and they hit us with...darts?" He looked at Duval, who nodded. "Knocked us right out. They tied us up. We came to in the back of the SUV. The bozos were outside having a smoke, so Duval had the idea to use the voice thing on his phone to text you a warning."

"Or five," Duval said. "Sorry it didn't help."

"I don't care about a thing except that everyone's okay," Avery said, as Kazmir from the GIS arrived with several of his men, and Kabrirah let them inside.

"You've captured a couple of known terrorists," Kazmir said. "Well done, Miss Turner."

"We were lucky," Avery said.

"You were lucky we didn't kill you to retrieve our pin," the boyfriend said. "I would have enjoyed that very much."

Kazmir laughed aloud at his comment. "Unlikely, because you would have failed."

The boyfriend looked confused. "I don't understand."

"Ms. Turner no longer has the pin. It was stolen."

Avery caught a steely-eyed glare from Kabrirah but couldn't explain in front of the others. She remained silent.

"Who stole the pin?" the boyfriend said.

"Men that he sent?" Carter said, pointing to Kazmir.

"And we could have been killed in the process," Avery said.

"Relax, Ms. Turner," Kazmir said. "Nobody was hurt."

"That was just luck," Carter said.

"At least I didn't send men with rifles to the airport to kill you like my predecessor did."

Avery exchanged another glance with Kabrirah. Clearly, she was incensed by the idea that Avery no longer had the pin. Avery gave a slight head shake that she hoped would hold her at bay, at least until the man had left with their prisoners.

Kazmir ordered his men to take the terrorists into custody.

"Well done, Ms. Turner," he said again on his way out the door.

"Perhaps you can explain that," Kabrirah snarled as she watched the terrorists being loaded into government vehicles. "We had a deal."

"And we still do," Avery said, choosing her words carefully. "We were forced to lie to that man in order to gain our freedom. So we could keep our word to you."

Kabrirah blinked. "So, you still possess the pin?"

Avery nodded. "And I will honor our deal and return it once the treasure is found."

"And the glyphs we found downstairs, will they help us locate the treasure?"

"I think so," Avery said. "And if you'll help me upload the information into the DiveNav, I think it will help us locate the actual site. But we must hurry. Dr. Granderson has the same information we do, and I don't think her scurrying out of here had anything to do with her work."

"Yeah, but she doesn't have the DiveNav," Carter said.

"Or the brilliant Avery Turner," Harrison added.

91

Ancient Egypt, 1500 BC

Zefret and the others remained hidden throughout the day. Sheltered from the heat, and from those searching for them, they rested. Even with the small amount of sleep she managed, Zefret's mind was working hard to solve the problem of where to hide the scrolls of knowledge.

Come nightfall, Zefret led them from the hiding place. Under the cover of darkness, they moved to the edge of the city where the library stood. Creeping inside, they hurried down into the dank basement.

"Wouldn't this be the first place Abasi would look?" one of the women asked.

"Abasi despises knowledge, sister," Zefret said. "This would be the last place he would search."

"Precisely why it was the perfect place for the temple," another woman said.

One by one the group entered the secret passage, then descended to the levels below that led to the hidden temple. Zefret was the only one of them who had ever stepped foot inside before this night. As Heba's most trusted advisor, Zefret had been instrumental in helping to hide the treasure prior to the pharaoh's death.

Upon reaching the temple, Zefret instructed that the scrolls should be placed in a stone alcove near the back of the space.

"Why would we simply not keep the scrolls, sister?" one of the women asked Zefret.

"Because, if we should be captured or killed as we make our way across the desert, then the scrolls will fall into Abasi's hands and be lost for all time."

"And if we should be successful and make it across the desert?"

"Then we will have the story of Heba to share with our daughters and to those who will listen."

"What if this secret temple is found?"

Zefret smiled. "A horrible death awaits any of Abasi's men who dare desecrate this holy place."

She led them in prayer, the entire group unaware, save for several gold statues, that the world's largest treasure was secreted nearby. As the group began to make their way back to the library, Zefret placed the pin in a carved hollow in the center of the altar she had designed for it as a place of honor. Kissing the cool stone, she turned to leave. Unseen, Neith stepped out from behind one of the statues and slipped the pin into her robes.

As they departed from the temple, Zefret led them through a series of carefully constructed and deadly traps designed to keep Abasi and his men from finding the treasure.

92

Present Day

"It doesn't make sense, MaryAnn," Avery said hours later, frustrated with the DiveNav, looking at the pin for the ten-thousandth time, and afraid they were running out of time.

"Everything said the pin was the key. But how?"

"Maybe it's an actual key? Like when you find the place?"

Avery shook her head, then threw up her hands. "It's as likely as anything I'm thinking." She dropped it on the bed and it bounced, landing on the scroll next to her knee.

"Shoot, don't tear that." Avery leaned to pick the pin up and something caught her eye.

"No way," she breathed.

"What?" MaryAnn asked.

"Hang on." Avery picked up the scroll and held the pin in front of it.

"Holy beach week, MaryAnn, you know the diamond in this thing's eye?"

"Yes, just more than half a carat."

"Or a bald-faced lie." Avery waved the scroll. "It's not a diamond at all, it's a freaking magnifier, MaryAnn. And there's a note in the top left corner of this scroll."

"What?" MaryAnn screeched. "What does it say?"

"Humbly seek knowledge," Avery said. "Can you call that map of the ancient city back up? I know where we need to look."

———

After a good night's sleep, a little inspiration, and some food, Avery went back to Kabrirah's, excited to share what she'd found. MaryAnn was on FaceTime so she could be part of the day—she'd more than earned it.

"Did you know your house sits right on top of the ruins of Zefret's home?" MaryAnn asked on a call.

"Pretty amazing, isn't it?" Avery replied.

"It appears Zefret's followers took the task of preserving Heba's legacy quite seriously." MaryAnn sounded almost reverent. "Nothing you've found so far is a coincidence."

"That explains the hollows in the room we found," Carter said.

"There were likely once doors to these spaces that would have been obliterated and buried as the streets were razed and the neighborhood built," MaryAnn said, looking at an ancient rendering of the city on FaceTime.

"Imagine all of that happening without anybody being aware of what was beneath them," Kabrirah said.

One of Kabrirah's sister warriors spoke up for the first time. "This would have been a holy place in ancient times. The land and the house built upon it. Zefret was a doctor."

"A place of healing was sacred," Kabrirah confirmed.

"It's importance to the followers of Heba likely explains why the DiveNav misdirected you in the first place," MaryAnn said. "The information we decoded from the scroll led us to the most obvious location, which is where you are right now."

"I don't understand how that could have happened," Harrison said. "The information contained in the scroll was accurate, correct?"

"It was accurate," MaryAnn said. "But there were parts of the text that were unrecognizable. They matched nothing on record for that time."

"Each of the tribal cultures used some of their own unique language in creating scrolls," Avery clarified. "Meaning that not every part of the text could be translated with what we had for information at the time."

"And now?" Kabrirah said.

"Now we have managed to decode the remaining symbols," MaryAnn said. "Because Avery is brilliant."

Kabrirah turned to Avery. "What does she mean?"

Avery reached into her bag and pulled out the pin and scroll she'd taken from this house. "This belongs to you," she said. "But while I had it, I was thinking about the legend of the pin being the key, and then I dropped the pin on the bed and it landed here." Avery held the two things up so Kabrirah could see the tiny letters.

"Humbly seek knowledge," Kabrirah read. "So?"

"We worked half the night," Avery said.

"And you found the site of the hidden temple?" Kabrirah interrupted.

Avery nodded and pulled up a current map of the area and pointed to the location. "We sure did. It's not far."

"Avery, Google says that's an insurance company," Harrison said, holding up his phone.

"Not thousands of years ago it wasn't," MaryAnn said. "Back then, it was the city's only library."

"It's so logical it's almost easy," Avery said. "Zefret and her friends buried the treasure in the one place a man like Abasi would shun—under the library."

"Like your mother always said, knowledge is power," Harrison said, earning a smile from Avery. "She was one smart cookie, Ave."

"Seems like you take after your mom," Carter said softly.

"How sure are you that thing of yours is right?" Kabrirah asked.

Avery checked the DiveNav display. "Ninety-nine-point-four percent sure."

93

"You can't possibly expect to just waltz in here and destroy my basement," the incensed owner of the insurance company said as he scanned the group and the equipment they carried.

"You need to relax, Mr. Yadish," Kabrirah said. "This is my friend Avery, and she could buy this building many times over."

Avery handed the man her business card. "TreasureTech designs is very interested in your property, sir. Name your price."

"You're *the* Avery Turner? The famous treasure hunter?"

Avery grinned and cast a glance in Carter's direction. "I am," she said.

Harrison jabbed an elbow into Carter's ribs. "Move over, Junior. I think you just got less famous."

"So, can we explore your basement, Mr. Yadish?" Avery said.

"I suppose you can afford to cover damages." He grinned. "And I am insured."

———

"I hope you really know what you're doing with that DiveNav thingy, Ave," Harrison said as he stopped shoveling to wipe the sweat from his brow. "I feel like we're just gonna keep tearing up basements and coming up short. How do we really know this treasure even exists?"

"Oh, it exists all right, Mr. Harrison," Kabrirah said.

"Harry. Call me Harry. After all we've been through, I think we can drop the formalities, don't you?"

"Okay, Harry."

"Just don't go beating up on my friends again, okay?"

"I think I can make that promise," Kabrirah said.

"Glad to hear it," Duval said as he tossed another spade full of earth from the ever-deepening hole.

Avery had availed herself of the scanning equipment left behind by Dr. Granderson before they began to dig. Unless the equipment was malfunctioning, it clearly showed some type of cavern buried beneath the floor. According to the readings Avery was obtaining, the cavern extended deeper than the scanner could read.

Duval's spade made a clanking sound as it connected with something solid. "Think I might have found something here."

"Either that or you hit a sewer line, and we've had enough of those this month," Harrison said.

Avery motioned them out of the hole before jumping in to take a look. Carefully, she brushed away the soil until a stone entryway slowly began to take shape.

"Is that what I think it is?" Carter asked.

"Yeah," Avery said breathlessly. "I think we may have actually found it this time."

It took them the better part of an hour to unearth the entire stone. But based solely on the symbols engraved upon it, it appeared to be the capstone covering the temple's entrance. Using prybars and their shovels, they managed to slide the large stone off the structure, revealing a stairwell that led deep underground into darkness.

"You found it," Kabrirah said softly.

"We found it," Avery said.

Avery could see the tears forming in the woman's eyes.

"So, are we going down there or what?" Javier asked, bouncing on the balls of his feet.

While they had all been focused on the dig, nobody noticed that they had been joined in the basement by Reggie and Javier.

"I thought you were going to keep watch?" Duval said.

"We thought it would be okay if we had a peek at how it was going," Reggie said. "It's been quiet all day out there, and Oscar is still on duty."

Avery waved Reggie and Javier over. She knew Duval's friends got excited by two things: the thrill of the chase, and money. Here, she had both. It was simply too alluring for them to stay away.

"Okay, you've had your peek, now get back upstairs and make sure we don't have any more unexpected guests. We'll let you know when we know what's down there."

"I'm afraid it's too late for that," a voice said from the bottom of the basement stairway.

Avery turned to see Dr. Kate Granderson, flanked by several men carrying guns.

"I'd like to say I'm surprised, but I'm not," Avery said.

"I figure I'm entitled to whatever it is you think you've found," Granderson said. "Especially since you're using my equipment."

"You took off so fast from Kabrirah's when the terrorists showed up that we figured you wouldn't mind," Carter said.

"You're a horrible judge of character then," Granderson said, flashing him a crooked grin.

"That's what I keep telling him," Harrison said.

The men with the guns waved Avery and the others toward the far corner of the basement.

"You can't kill us," Avery said. "This building is full of witnesses."

"Who will believe a scientist who's practically a national hero when she says the greedy Americans attacked and left us no choice." Granderson smiled.

"What did you do to Oscar?" Javier demanded, stepping toward Granderson.

She laughed. "He's big, but not the brightest kid in class, is he? I told him you'd called me for help and kept him distracted while my men walked in behind him."

"You're not a scientist." Avery shook her head. "You're just another greedy treasure hunter."

"Maybe I am," Granderson said as she pulled a handful of zip ties from her bag. "But you're not taking credit for this find. Tie them up."

94

As soon as the first of Granderson's goons got close enough, Avery attacked, stunning him with a head butt to the nose. She didn't need to look to Carter, Harrison, or Duval to know that they were on the same page. Kabrirah leapt into the action, sweeping the legs out from under one of the men, which sent him crashing to the concrete.

When it was over, Avery stood with her group holding the guns that belonged to Granderson's men.

"Nice try, Doc," Avery said.

"I may have underestimated you," Granderson said.

"You wouldn't be the first," Kabrirah said with a smile.

"What do you want to do with them?" Carter said.

"I'm tempted to simply tie them up and leave them here," Avery said.

"Exactly what they had planned to do with us," Kabrirah said.

"But you won't because you'll need my expertise as you explore the temple," Granderson said.

"She's right," Avery said, thinking of booby traps and getting to the temple more than exploring the interior.

"You're not really going to trust her are you, Ave?" Harrison said.

"Not for a minute. But she does have enough knowledge to be of some help when we get down there."

"I don't mean to be a buzzkill, love," Duval said. "But we had a lot of equipment at our disposal when we went into the tomb, and we still lost two people. Aren't we going to need more than we have here?"

"I might be able to help you with that," a familiar voice said from the bottom of the cellar steps.

Avery turned to see Kazmir and his men.

"I knew you'd be the one to find it," Kazmir said.

"Is that why you threatened us?" Avery said.

"Blackmail is the word I think you're looking for, Ave," Harrison said.

"I'd prefer to think of it as providing proper motivation, Ms. Turner."

"We're not really going to let this guy go with us, are we?" Duval said.

"Don't think we have much of a choice," Carter said.

"You are wise beyond your years, Mr. Mosley," Kazmir said as he gestured to the temple entrance. "Shall we?"

One by one, the unlikely group of explorers climbed down into the temple foyer. Each of them carried an electric lamp, and many had digging tools as well. They continued down one seemingly endless flight of stone steps after another, far below the basement floor. The chambers were cramped at the start but gradually began to open into a huge area the farther down they went.

"How the hell did they manage to build something so massive underground?" Harrison said.

"How did they build the pyramids above ground, Harry?" Avery said.

"We're still trying to figure that one out," Granderson said.

Kabrirah moved in close to Avery and whispered, "Beware of traps, Avery. The closer we get to whatever awaits, the more likely it is we will find them."

Having already considered this, Avery nodded. She pointed to the front of the group where Dr. Granderson, the GIS man, and their respective goons had congregated, rushing forward without any thought about the dangers that awaited them. Kabrirah grinned. She well understood the power of greed, having been part of a cult that had defended against it for countless generations.

Avery moved toward Duval and Carter, intending to give the same warning, when one of the GIS men cried out from the front. Everyone froze in their tracks, watching as the stone floor seemed to rotate slightly. Canting to one side, it sent the two men standing upon it sliding toward a hole that had opened in the wall. Avery watched in horror as the men clawed at the smooth stone trying to find purchase against the gravity that was threatening to send them into an unknown abyss.

"We've got to help them," Kazmir yelled back at the others.

"What would you suggest we do?" Granderson asked coldly. "Follow them through?"

Avery wasn't surprised to see the doctor have so little regard for the men in peril. She had been just as callous when it came to her own people.

As soon as the two men slid out of sight beneath the chasm in the side wall, the floor began to revolve back into its original level state, locking back with a loud grating thump. The screams fell immediately silent.

"You don't see that every day." Reggie's eyes were wide.

"What do you think happened to them?" Javier swallowed hard.

"I'd rather not think about it," Avery said.

"They were probably crushed between the stones," Harrison said.

"Thanks, mate," Duval said. "Wanted that delightful image imprinted on my brain."

"How do we move forward?" Kazmir asked.

"That's what you're worried about?" Carter said. "After losing two of your men?"

"Reminds me of one of the guys your mom and I worked for on the NYPD, Ave," Harrison said.

"A real knob?" Duval said.

"Close enough," Harrison said.

Granderson spoke at last. "I watched the movement of the floor and it's some kind of cantilever system. If we can move one of these stones to the left side of the floor it will block the movement." She pointed at the massive stones lining the walls.

"How are we going to move something that big?" Reggie said.

"Perhaps we can help," a high, sweet female voice said from behind them.

Avery turned, her jaw loosening.

"You're...you're a princess," Avery said. "Like a real princess."

"And you are Avery Turner," the princess bowed. "It was my honor to help you, and it is now my honor to know you."

Carter poked Avery and pointed. Behind the princess, Avery spotted her boyfriend and his friend who had been escorted away by the GIS the night before.

Kazmir hung his head, refusing to meet her gaze.

"We can't trust anyone," Carter said.

95

"I thought you had these guys in custody?" Harrison rounded on Kazmir.

"They, as you say, 'made bail.'"

"Since when do you bail out terrorists?" Carter said.

"This is not America, Mr. Mosley," Kazmir said.

"Apparently it isn't the UK either," Duval said.

Avery stepped toward the princess, causing both of her men to raise their weapons. The princess held her arms out to the sides, stopping their approach.

"I would say it's a pleasure, but after our last run-in with your friends, I can't be sure that it is," Avery said.

"You must forgive Pim's overzealous nature," the princess said. "He has a tendency to shoot first and ask questions later. But he means well."

Avery wasn't sure she agreed with that, but arguing it at gunpoint or starting a firefight in an enclosed space replete with booby traps didn't seem smart, so she just glanced over at Carter, who was now standing beside her. "I'm familiar."

"Perhaps you and I can come to some mutual understanding," the princess said.

"I'd like that." Avery paused, looking at the man who'd told her the night before how much he'd enjoy killing her. "You didn't hurt our friend Oscar, did you? He was outside."

"He's still outside."

Avery's eyes widened with panic. "Is he alive?"

"He is simply sleeping," the princess said. "You have my word."

Avery and Kabrirah spoke quietly with the princess for several minutes while the others waited in an uncomfortable silence. When they had finished, they approached the others and announced that they would work together for the common good.

"What if we're not happy with that?" Kazmir said.

Kabrirah spoke up before Avery or the princess could. "Seeing as how you have already lost two of your men to greed, I'm not sure you're in any position to bargain."

Kazmir looked to Dr. Granderson for support, but she refused to meet his gaze.

"Shall we go, then?" the princess asked.

They continued cautiously, stopping each time they came to something that looked wrong. Both the princess and Granderson deferred to Avery's analytical mind to solve the puzzle that would help them bypass each trap. At last, they came upon a section of the temple that appeared to be a dead end. Upon the wall were carved a number of ancient symbols.

"Well, that's just great," Kazmir said. "You've led us to absolutely nothing, Ms. Turner."

"Hey, let's go easy there," Carter said, a dangerous edge to the words.

"Yeah," Harrison said. "Don't take it out on Avery that you didn't get your damned treasure."

"This is a lot farther than you would have managed without her," Duval said.

"Avery, look out," Kabrirah yelled.

Avery caught the flash of movement a second too late as one of Granderson's men flanked her and grabbed her from behind, wrapping his arm around her in a choke hold.

"Now, each of you will drop your weapons," Granderson said. "Or I'll have my man snap her pretty neck."

The princess's boyfriend moved toward the man, causing him to squeeze Avery's neck tighter.

"Don't test me," Granderson said. "Drop them."

The boyfriend looked to the princess for guidance, and she nodded. One by one, each of the guns was dropped to the ground.

Harrison shook his head as he tossed his. "You're gonna regret this."

Granderson's other man moved close and retrieved Harrison's gun.

"How do you figure, Mr. Harrison?"

"I just know Avery. It's not a good idea to get on her bad side."

"I think I'll risk it."

As Granderson's second goon turned to pass one of the guns to her, Avery lifted her feet off the stone, throwing off the balance of the man holding her. As he shifted backward, Avery drove the back of her head into his chin. The sudden move caused the back of his head to strike the stone wall, stunning him. As she felt his hold on her loosen, she grabbed his arm and flipped him over her back onto the floor. A shot rang out, ricochetting off the floor near Avery's feet.

She glanced up in time to see Carter charging Dr. Granderson. As the doctor swung the gun in Carter's direction, Kabrirah came at her from the other side, landing a kick to the back of her knees. The impact caused her to lose her balance just as she pulled the trigger and the shot sailed wide, striking one of the ornamental stones protruding from the wall. The ground beneath their feet began to shake, sending a cloud of dust down from the ceiling.

"It's caving in," Javier shouted. "We gotta get out of here."

Avery dodged a falling stone as she picked up one of the guns. She turned to run, but stopped in her tracks as she caught sight of the princess, standing wide-eyed in the center of the tunnel. Her first thought was that she had been hit, but as she approached, the princess pointed behind Avery.

Avery turned to see what had previously appeared to be a dead-end wall crumbling before their very eyes into a pile of rubble. When at last the dust cleared, a cavernous space gaped beyond the tunnel. Dusty but slightly gleaming gold and silver stretched as far as any eye could see. As they stepped over the debris and into the hidden room, their lights shone brightly off the treasure laid out before them.

EPILOGUE

One Week Later

Avery and Carter sat on the veranda sipping coffee, both staring out at the ocean. Lost in thought, after a week of sleep and good food and walks on the beach, they were still trying to decompress. Avery spied Harrison aboard her boat tied to the dock and gave him a wave.

"What's Harry doing out there, anyway?" Carter asked.

"Puttering. He is retired, after all."

"Have you heard anything from Kabrirah since we got back?"

"As a matter of fact, I just messaged with her last night." Avery flipped her laptop open.

"And?"

"And she and the princess have started a project: They're building a museum to honor Heba's history."

"That sounds like a lot of governmental red tape," Carter said.

"Something tells me that if anyone can get through it, they can."

Carter nodded. "Two strong-willed women right there."

"With a strong bond."

"Speaking of bonds, how's Duval?"

Avery lowered her glasses and turned to face him. "I don't know. I haven't spoken to him since we got back. Why?"

"I just figured, you know, you two spent a lot of time together in Egypt, and..."

"You figured what?"

Carter fidgeted nervously in his chair, then cleared his throat. "That maybe you were finally going to start dating?"

Avery stared at him. "You good, Carter? I've seen you face a dark cave full of skeletons, fight off two-ton seals, even jump out of perfectly good aircraft. Why do you look scared sitting on this balcony with me?"

"It's just—"

"It's just what, Carter? You weren't this nervous in the Senate chamber."

He turned toward her, took a deep breath, making his muscular shoulders look even broader than they were. After a moment, he turned back toward the water.

She waited in silence while he wrestled with whatever it was he wanted to say.

At last, he spoke. "I know you think I'm just a shallow playboy, Avery. There's plenty of reason for that, before you go defending yourself—I'm aware. And I'm not as high society as most of your friends, even Duval."

Avery couldn't breathe, waiting for him to continue, nothing in her entire universe but Carter's voice.

"The truth is that I've looked everywhere for the right woman, when for the last two years she's been living just down the beach from me."

Tears sprang to Avery's eyes. She bounced up from her deck chair, touching his shoulder before she settled herself onto his lap.

"I guess that's one way to answer me." Carter laughed, touching the end of her nose.

"I'm nothing if not direct. Usually." Avery leaned her forehead against his, staring into his wide, dark eyes like she'd never be able to stop.

She giggled when she realized she didn't have to stop.

"What's funny?" Carter asked.

"We have the whole rest of our lives to stay right here like this if we want," Avery said softly, her gaze going to his lips.

They closed over hers in a single heartbeat, and time stopped spinning.

For the first time in her life, Avery Turner, computer genius, couldn't think. She could only feel. Fireworks colored the backs of her eyelids, and every inch of her skin felt like it was on fire. Avery had kissed other men—once at a Christmas party, she'd even kissed Mark—but nothing had ever stolen her senses like Carter Mosley's lips devouring hers under the Florida sun.

Later, neither would be able to say who kissed who, but both would agree that it was downright magical. Nobody would admit to letting go first, either, even when Harrison hollered something about the water hose.

"Just promise me one thing," Carter said, his breath still coming fast as he laced their fingers together.

"What's that?" Avery asked.

"That we'll have at least a thousand more adventures together."

"Bet on it," Avery said, kissing him again.

"Hey, you two," Harrison called from the boat. "Break it up, will ya? I'm taking you out on the boat."

"Where are we going, Harry?" Avery hollered as she stood up, still holding Carter's hand, and grabbed her wrap.

"I thought we'd see if we could find some trouble to get into."

"Now you're talking," Carter said.

The Emperor's Palace
The Turner and Mosley Files Book 5

Unearthing a relic might be their only hope, but its location has remained a secret for centuries.

A panicked midnight phone call rips Carter and Avery from a remote research expedition in South America. Carter's young niece has disappeared from her summer camp without a trace, and her safe return home instantly becomes their sole focus.

Despite Avery's wealth and the best detectives money can buy, the days stretch on with no leads, no answers, and no sign of the child. Hope begins to fade—until a ransom demand arrives, explosive and terrifying in its simplicity. The kidnappers don't want money—they seek something far more dangerous.

Because they want the impossible: a legendary Chinese relic lost to history for centuries. And they'll stop at nothing to get it.

**Get your copy today at
severnriverbooks.com**

ACKNOWLEDGMENTS

No matter how many times we do this (and this one makes an even 20 for LynDee), it's incredible how much work it takes from our team to get a book from our computers into your hands, and this one was no different. Many thanks to our fantastic team at Severn River Publishing: Cate, Amber, Lisa, and Randall, who helped make the story, the cover, and the pages shine. Our agents, John Talbot and Paula Munier, thank you both for believing in these stories and our ability to tell them. And last but never least, we'd both like to thank our families for keeping us on track and making sure the story got told: Karen Coffin, Justin Walker, and all three littles, you are the talent behind the scenes that we'd be lost without. As always, any mistakes you find are ours.

ABOUT BRUCE ROBERT COFFIN

Bruce Robert Coffin is the award-winning author of the Detective Byron Mysteries. Former detective sergeant with more than twenty-seven years in law enforcement, he is the winner of Killer Nashville's Silver Falchion Awards for Best Procedural, and Best Investigator, and the Maine Literary Award for Best Crime Fiction Novel. Bruce was also a finalist for the Agatha Award for Best Contemporary Novel. His short fiction appears in a number of anthologies, including Best American Mystery Stories 2016.

Sign up for the Turner and Mosley Files newsletter at
severnriverbooks.com

brucerobertcoffin@severnriverbooks.com

ABOUT LYNDEE WALKER

LynDee Walker is the national bestselling author of two crime fiction series featuring strong heroines and "twisty, absorbing" mysteries. Her first Nichelle Clarke crime thriller, FRONT PAGE FATALITY, was nominated for the Agatha Award for best first novel and is an Amazon Charts Bestseller. In 2018, she introduced readers to Texas Ranger Faith McClellan in FEAR NO TRUTH. Reviews have praised her work as "well-crafted, compelling, and fast-paced," and "an edge-of-your-seat ride" with "a spider web of twists and turns that will keep you reading until the end."

Before she started writing fiction, LynDee was an award-winning journalist who covered everything from ribbon cuttings to high level police corruption, and worked closely with the various law enforcement agencies that she reported on. Her work has appeared in newspapers and magazines across the U.S.

Aside from books, LynDee loves her family, her readers, travel, and coffee. She lives in Richmond, Virginia, where she is working on her next novel when she's not juggling laundry and children's sports schedules.

Sign up for the Turner and Mosley Files newsletter at
severnriverbooks.com

lyndee@severnriverbooks.com

Printed in the United States
by Baker & Taylor Publisher Services